"Tim Lebbon takes the British dystopian horror novel and creates a modern classic set in a terrifying near future, where the only thing that stands between humankind and a savage prehistoric predator is the ability to stay silent."

Stephen Jones, Horror Writers Association Life Achievement Award, International Horror Guild, Bram Stoker and World Fantasy Award winner

"A book that I want to make a lot of noise about… in the best way possible."

Pat Cadigan, Arthur C. Clarke Award-winning author of *Synners* and *Fools*

"Horror master Tim Lebbon spins an inventive and deeply disturbing apocalyptic fable. A classic blend of horror and science fiction."

Jonathan Maberry, multiple Bram Stoker Award winner and *New York Times* bestselling author of *V-Wars*

"What I've always admired about Tim Lebbon's fiction is the delicate characterisation he creates amidst such monstrosities; the cinematic apocalypse of The Silence is no exception."

Adam Nevill, British Fantasy Award-winning author of *The Ritual* and *Last Days*

"When the end of the world comes, pray it isn't masterminded by Tim Lebbon. His apocalyptic scenarios shred the nerves and The Silence is one of his best, a chilling, edge-of-the-seat thriller packed with vivid characters and creepy situations. It will haunt you long after the final echoes have died away."

Mark Chadbourn, bestselling and British Fantasy Award-winning author of *Whisper Lane*

"Bright, vivid, horrifying and beautiful. Make sure you have some free time ahead when you start this book, because you absolutely won't want to put it down. I loved it."

Alison Littlewood, bestselling author of *A Cold Season*

"The Silence is a scary, compelling, and heart-pounding novel, not just for the terrifying creatures that get unleashed on the world, but for the reminder that even when everything goes to hell, the most dangerous threat is ourselves. Be vigilant, and don't make a sound."

Robert Swartwood, *USA Today* bestselling author of *The Calling* and *Land of the Dead*

"Tim Lebbon is the undisputed champion of end-of-the-world fiction, and in The Silence he presents us with his most intense and compelling apocalypse to date. Focusing on a single family's desperate struggle for survival in a world engulfed by deadly, voracious predators, this is heart-pounding, white-knuckle fiction of the very highest quality."

Mark Morris, British Fantasy Award winner and International Horror Guild Award nominee

"The Silence is very nearly a perfect book. From the opening page to the final sentence the prose is tight and driven as it chronicles one family's struggles with the end of the world we have all known... Lebbon displays his literary merits here, showing an intimate, and often inspiring glimpse of the apocalypse. I cannot recommend it highly enough. The Silence is golden, indeed."

James A. Moore, Bram Stoker Award nominee and author of *Seven Forges* and *The Blasted Lands*

"The Silence is Hitchcock's Birds 2016: the enemy isn't just the monsters, but modernity. It's a clever, fast-paced thriller with vivid, memorable characters. You won't put it down until it's done."

Sarah Langan, Bram Stoker Award-winning author of *The Missing* and *Audrey's Door*

"Absolutely riveting. The end of the world has never been more terrifying... One of Tim Lebbon's best."

Brian Keene, Grand Master Award-winning author of *The Rising* and *Ghoul Chased*

"Nobody ends the world quite like Tim Lebbon. He's the grand master of destruction, the lord of the literary apocalypse. The Silence might just be his best novel to date: an ingenious mix of intimate character study and epic monster mash, a story that is clever and thoughtful in terms of themes and ideas but utterly relentless in its execution. Just don't read it out loud, or the monsters will get you."

Gary McMahon, multiple British Fantasy Award nominee and author of *Rain Dogs* and *Hungry Hearts*

"Somehow both epic and intimate, Tim Lebbon's The Silence is a masterful symphony of horrors that deserves a spot on your shelf of favorites. The Silence reads like a blend of John Wyndham and Stephen King, and reminds me why I fell in love with horror in the first place. It's a must-read."

Christopher Golden, Bram Stoker Award winner and *New York Times* bestselling author of *Snowblind*

"Nobody ends the world as unflinchingly and heart-wrenchingly as Tim Lebbon. Make no mistake – The Silence will put you through the wringer. It will make you sob, and cheer. It's as gripping and jaw-dropping as many a horror film – and I mean that as high praise. Stephen King would be proud. So, actually, would John Wyndham."

Stephen Volk, BAFTA and British Fantasy Award-winning writer of *Ghostwatch* and *Afterlife*

"Utterly compelling; grim, grisly and all too real. Tim Lebbon leads you on an extraordinary journey from order to chaos at a terrifying pace and it's a stark warning to us all never to become too cosy or complacent... This is a novel that unlocks what a cataclysm would look like it if were to befall us, and where the moment you think things can't get any worse, they do. I loved this book and I have to know what happens next..."

James Barclay, David Gemmell Legend Award nominee for *Ravensoul*

THE
SILENCE

THE
SILENCE

TIM LEBBON

TITAN BOOKS

THE SILENCE
Print edition ISBN: 9781781168820
E-book edition ISBN: 9781781168837

Published by Titan Books
A division of Titan Publishing Group Ltd
144 Southwark Street, London SE1 0UP

First mass market edition: September 2016
1 2 3 4 5 6 7 8 9 10

Visit our website:
www.titanbooks.com

A CIP catalogue record for this title is available from the
British Library.

Printed and bound in the United States

Did you enjoy this book?
We love to hear from our readers. Please email us at
readerfeedback@titanemail.com or write to us at Reader Feedback
at the above address.

To receive advance information, news, competitions, and exclusive
offers online, please sign up for the Titan newsletter on our website
www.titanbooks.com

For Ellie Rose, still my little sweetie, in her big exam year.

and

For Graham Joyce, who saw beauty in everything.

PART ONE

NOISE

1

...an historical occasion, the first time an important scientific discovery like this has been broadcast live. The excitement here above ground is palpable; we can only guess how thrilling it is down at the entry point. The scientists and potholers are all at a safe distance, and the specially designed and constructed robotic systems are now ready to start dismantling the ancient cave-in. What we might find beyond, no one is certain, although a recent series of seismic surveys suggest that the hidden cave system, isolated for perhaps millions of years, is vast. Rumours abound that it might contain caverns larger than the recently discovered Son Doong Cave in Vietnam, and extensive systems as long as the legendary Mammoth Cave in Kentucky. I, for one, have never been so excited. This is a day that everyone connected with this expedition will remember for ever. And I hope you, the viewers, will remember it too.

Hidden Depths—Live!, **Discovery Channel,
Thursday, 17 November 2016**

As I watched three black-clad figures adorned with climbing gear being lowered into a cave, Jude threw an apple core at my head. It just missed, hitting the wall

13

behind me, splitting and showering me with fruit flesh and pips.

"Piss off!" I shouted. His shadow flitted from my bedroom doorway—he was obviously wary of retribution—but his left hand and head reappeared around the jamb.

"I'll tell Mum you swore," he signed.

"So tell her!" I said. My words were a vibration formed from little more than memory. I felt the regular *plod-plod* of my younger brother's footsteps as he stalked back into his own bedroom, and a moment later a thud against the wall as he jumped on his bed. He'd be back. Little turd was in that sort of mood.

Brushing moist apple from my shoulder, I turned to the television once more. I had only just turned it on. I'd been strumming my guitar for an hour or so, before succumbing to the urge to slouch down on my bed and watch some undemanding crap on TV. But the first image I'd seen had immediately caught my attention.

It wasn't a jungle, exactly. More like a heavily wooded landscape, hillsides rich in trees and shrubs, more distant peaks bare and stark and swathed in mist. Creepers hung from trees that grew far above, feeling their way into the shadows like dormant tentacles, and a stream zigzagged slowly along the base of a ravine. Several large tents were pitched there, a few smaller ones close by, and a storage compound was piled with plastic crates and khaki bags. There were people moving in the ravine, and it was their expressions that had made me watch so intently.

They were excited. Not just caught in the moment but properly thrilled by what they were doing, and whatever it was they'd found. The "Live" motif in the screen's corner gave the scene even more immediacy. Men and women clustered around the camp in the background, and the camera was focused on one small group—the three people draped in ropes and harnesses, the propped metal winch, and the dark gulf of the cave entrance set in the hillside. Two women worked the winch, and one by one the explorers were lowered out of the light and out of sight.

I was confused why there was no narration, but then I pressed a button on the remote and subtitles popped up. Jude must have been watching my TV again, messing up the settings. Annoying little shit.

"—just over a mile, so although that doesn't yet make this anywhere near the longest or the deepest cave system in Europe, that unique feature does set it aside as the most fascinating, and the potential for deeper exploration is huge. As Dr Krasnov said earlier, you're watching history in the making, live on the Discovery Channel. So as these three cavers are lowered into the vertical cave mouth, further inside the robotic systems are already…"

What unique feature? I wondered. The cave mouth looked unremarkable, a sinkhole perhaps fifteen feet across, its edges shrouded in bushes. Daylight seeped down one side, revealing a plant-covered wall that seemingly led straight down. It was a bit spooky, I supposed, and watching the last caver disappear into the darkness I wondered whether I'd stumbled onto a new drama or movie. But I checked that it really was the Discovery Channel, and then the presenter appeared in shot for the first time. I'd seen her before, reporting from all across the world. *What an amazing job*, I thought.

At fourteen, I was just starting to get a feel of what I wanted to do, and watching this reporter filled me with anticipation. Being deaf wasn't going to stop me from trying to become who I wanted to be.

"As we said earlier, there's already a team of fifteen camped out at this system's furthest extreme," the presenter continued. "They include experienced cavers, a botanist, a biologist, a geologist, and a palaeontologist, and they've been underground for almost six days taking samples and trying to catalogue the new species of plant and insects already discovered down there. But now that the entrance to the next passageway has been found, and the explorers are ready to start moving aside the rockfall that seems to hide a much deeper, vaster system beyond, it could be that this becomes one of the greatest scientific discoveries—"

I picked up my permanently open iPad and accessed the scrapbook app. I'd adapted and personalised it, and now used it whenever a news story grabbed my interest, attaching reports, video clips, and social media content. Sometimes I'd let my parents read my analyses. I knew they were pleased I wanted to be a journalist, but once Dad had said it would be hard work. He meant because of my accident, though he didn't say it. But it was hardly surprising that communication was important to me. His doubt had surprised me a little, especially as he often listened to me playing music. Jude wanted to form a band with me, him as frontman, me as songwriter, musician, and everything else that didn't involve stage-diving into the adoring audience. I'd replied to Dad, *Say that to Beethoven*. He never doubted me after that. Not to my face, at least.

I opened a new file, called it "New Worlds?" and was just about to start the introductory text when a movement caught my eye.

Jude slipped around the doorway again, crawling like a sniper, elastic band tensed between thumb and forefinger and paper pellet folded across it. I saw him and ducked, but he'd reacted faster. The pellet caught me an inch above my left eye.

I howled in pain, then roared in rage.

Jude tried to scamper away, wide-eyed and laughing.

I dropped the iPad on my bed and launched myself across the room, reaching for my annoying little brother. Years of ballet and athletics gave me the advantage, and I was across the room before he could find his feet.

My hands clamped around his ankles. He looked back over his shoulder. I grimaced, trying to put on the most evil expression I could muster. He annoyed the hell out of me, but sometimes I couldn't bear to wipe that manic, delighted grin from his face.

"And now, with vengeance close—" I began.

"No, Ally, I'm sorry!"

Something wet nudged against my side, nuzzling my hip where my tee shirt had ridden up.

"Otis!" I shouted, jumping. Jude took the opportunity to slither from my grasp and crawl away, crouching in his doorway ready to defend his turf.

The dog sat and nudged me again. "Coming!" I called, because I knew Mum had sent Otis to fetch me. He wasn't a proper hearing dog—not professionally trained, at least—but I'd spent long hours coaching the Weimaraner to let me know when people were calling for me, when the landline was ringing, and when someone was at the front door. Otis and I had a deep relationship, and it still amazed me how he seemed to differentiate between moods and tasks—serious was being my hearing dog. Play was pretty much everything else.

"Good boy!" I said, ruffling his neck and scratching his chest. Otis gave a short, sharp bark—I actually felt it, heavy in my chest—and pounded back down the stairs.

Jude and I fought down the staircase on our behinds, side by side. We laughed. I'd already forgotten about that faraway ravine, the hole in the ground, and the people disappearing into deep, deep darkness.

It was just another hotel room, in another bland hotel that Huw would forget the moment he drove away, and this one smelled of piss.

The place was presented nicely enough. The rooms were all different—his was unimaginatively called the Red Suite, with red curtains and bedclothes, and a series of abstract paintings depicting stark fleshy landscapes and bleeding sunsets—and the couple who ran the hotel seemed friendly and efficient. The wife was a little older than Huw, and she'd smiled just a little too much when he'd noticed the undone buttons on her blouse. It was only a peek, a bit of lacy brassiere. He couldn't *help* noticing things like that, but notice was all he'd ever done. He had a table booked for dinner later, and the hotel seemed to have a great reputation as an eatery as well. So it was fine. It was quirky. But his room still smelled of piss.

He'd moved slowly around the room, sniffing here and there, ducking into the en suite to see if the stink came from the most obvious place, but he couldn't pin it down. It was only a slight tang, nothing too heavy and alarming, not enough to persuade him to ask to be moved. Certainly not enough to make him complain. Huw just wasn't like that. He hated trouble, and avoided confrontation at all costs. If there'd been a huge turd in the middle of the floor, he'd probably have complained then. Probably.

He sighed, sitting back on the bed and sinking into the four pillows he'd stacked against the headboard. A book lay unread beside him. A cup of tea cooled on the bedside table, a good idea at the time but tasting of… well, piss, with the faux milk they provided in those little plastic containers.

That was another thing he'd do if he ran a place like this. A small fridge in the room with a jug of proper milk. He spoke with Kelly about it often, and once or twice they'd had serious conversations about actually buying a small B&B here on the Cornish coast. She could paint, more than the occasional dabbling she sometimes found time for now. He could surf. Jude could explore the rock pools down on the beach, and Ally could indulge whatever her latest interests might be—shell-collecting, kayaking, coasteering. Huw smiled. Ally would probably want to try them all, and more.

He glanced at the book, sighed, flicked on the TV and started surfing the channels, sound muted.

It had been two long days, working on the new house. Or mansion, more like. The client was a racehorse owner, sixty years old, rich, and readying to retire. A nice guy with lots of interesting stories, he inevitably kept Huw behind for an hour longer than each meeting really needed to be. But Huw really didn't mind. Max would sometimes pull a bottle of wine from his briefcase, and they'd had more than one boozy late afternoon on the building site that would soon become his luxury home.

Max was paying Huw's company almost a million pounds to build the house, so he guessed Max was entitled to own just a little bit of his soul.

He sighed and reached for the tea. Moving seemed to agitate the air and bring another waft of ammonia. The clock said almost six, his meal was booked for seven, and there was sod all on the box. Maybe he should go for a run. It was a long time since he'd even got as far as slipping on his trainers. There was always a reason not to run, and today that was tiredness. His limbs ached. If motivation was there it was buried deep, and not coming out to play.

Huw thought of the woman who'd registered him, her welcoming smile, and wondered whether that blouse button had been left open on purpose.

Kelly sometimes jibed him a little about his frequent spells away from the family home near the town of Usk, in Monmouthshire. They were rarely more than three nights; still, she prodded and poked, never quite serious but, he thought, never completely joking either. She'd ask whether he had his hooker booked for the night, or whether he had a regular fuck buddy in whichever town he was staying in. Huw would go along with it, never taking things too far, and then he'd hug her and say she was the only one for him. And truth was, he completely meant it. After twenty years of marriage, the two of them still loved each other, differently from before but just as deeply. He knew of other guys working away who'd had flings—a regular shag, casual visits, or just a one-off screw in their hotel room with someone they'd met that night and whose second name they'd never know. But that had never been for him. Huw was a family man, and his family always made him look forward to returning home.

He took a swig of tea and wished he hadn't.

Maybe he'd run a bath, relax with a book. Mind made up, he reached for the TV remote, but before turning it off he flipped through a few more channels, a casual habit he'd picked up from Kelly.

An image caught his eye.

Several people were gathered around an apparatus of some sort, two of them working hard to turn a handle while a third seemed to be tinkering with a control mechanism. The camera must have been handheld because it was jumpy and uneven. In the background were several tents, lights strung between them, shadowy people dashing back and forth. They were somewhere wild—trees, a starry sky, gnarly terrain.

It was the looks on their faces that grabbed his attention.

They were scared.

"New movie trailer," Huw muttered. He talked to himself quite a bit, and usually didn't even notice. But this time he did notice, because he wasn't quite sure. If this was a trailer, it was incredibly realistic. And graphic.

The people kept turning the handle, and it was only as Huw saw something glistening and red rising out of the ground that he realised the sound was still muted.

He hit the sound button and winced as a soul-shattering scream tore through the room.

"Shit!" Heart pounding, Huw chuckled at how easily he'd been scared. He leaned across the bed and grabbed his mobile phone, glancing quickly at it to check the time. Almost six-fifteen.

No way they should ever be showing anything like this before the watershed.

I loved spaghetti bolognese. Mum made it from scratch, and it came out differently every time. She enjoyed experimenting. She always said that a recipe was just a guide.

Parmesan cheese, though. That was always in it.

Jude sat across the table, and Mum was on my left. She was a graceful woman, someone who wore her middle age with dignity rather than trying to see it away with expensive make-up, hair dye, or denial. I sometimes told her that the grey at her temples—spreading now, from streaks to splashes—made her look somehow super-heroic. Mum laughed at that, and Jude had called her Superchef.

"Is that all I am to you?" she'd asked him.

"Yep," he'd replied. "Where's pudding?" Well, he was only ten.

Otis sat with his head on my leg, looking up with sad feed-me eyes. If Dad were here, he'd send Otis to his bed while we ate. He didn't like the dog begging, but I didn't mind. Otis always knew when the man of the house was away.

"Where's Nan?" I asked. My grandmother was staying for a couple of weeks, and she always ate dinner with us.

"Having a lie down," Mum said. "Do you have homework?"

She was the only person who I found it easy to lip-read. With Dad I had to really concentrate, and with most of my friends I usually only picked up one word in three. Weird.

"Well, yeah, geography. But that isn't due in till next week."

"You should still do some tonight."

"Yeah, maybe."

Jude nudged me under the table, his usual sign that he wanted to say something abusive. I glared at him.

"You smell," he mouthed. I picked that up well enough.

"Jude," our mum said, a soft warning.

We tucked into the meal. Jude snatched at the loaf of garlic bread in the middle of the table, and I was quick enough to grab some back. It tasted great. My friend Lucy hated when I'd had garlic, and I always made a point to sit closer to her on the bus to school the next day, breathing out of the corner of my mouth. Childish, but it made me laugh. Lots of stuff made me laugh. I was a happy girl, and some people—mostly ignorant, more often than not arseholes—found that difficult to understand.

A boy once took the piss out of me at school, calling me names he thought I couldn't see—mong, spazz—and pulling faces behind my back that my friends only told me about later. He was known for being a dickhead, but now he was being a dickhead to *me*. I'd confronted him and gave him an earful, concentrating hard to make sure those harsh words I used so rarely were well formed, sharp-edged, cutting. Then I'd turned away before he had a chance to respond, so he was left shouting at my back, and I flipped him the bird over my shoulder. The smiles around me had mirrored my own.

Sometimes, not hearing had its benefits.

Jude dropped some food, and Otis ducked beneath the table to lick it up. Jude shouted, making a big drama of being knocked off his chair. Mum scowled and said something to him that I didn't catch. I just carried on eating, looking down at my plate.

When we'd finished, knives and forks together, Mum dished up a small bowl of ice cream for each of us. I glanced across at Jude to find him staring at me expectantly. Grabbing my attention, he started signing in what I always thought of as the Andrews family dialect, a form of sign language expanded and adapted from what we'd all learned after the accident. My parents had been great with signing, but Jude—barely six years old at the time—had picked it up amazingly quickly, and it was the two of us who'd started coming up with our own altered version. Mum and Dad simply had to follow.

"Want to play Twenty Questions?" he asked.

I shrugged, but my brother could tell that I was keen.

"Okay, you two," Mum said. "I'll clear the table this time. Keep it clean!"

I laughed, and Otis pointed his nose to the ceiling and howled along with us. I remembered what that sounded like—not too loud, a sort of ululating song that was filled with mischief and joy—and apart from my family's voices, it was the sound I missed the most. I tickled Otis under the chin as Jude asked the first question.

I won three points to two, but agreed when Jude

asked, "Best of seven?" And of course, I let him win. He knew that, and perhaps that was why he celebrated so much more enthusiastically. We ended up rubbing knuckles into each other's scalps while Otis jumped around, nudging us with his nose and barking. Mum came in to tell us off, but I averted my eyes. I got in one more good ear-tweak before catching Mum's eye and stern gaze. I blinked, smiled, shrugged.

That might have been the last time Jude and I fought together playfully. Like many great milestones it passed without us noticing. Later, I'd reflect upon that meal as the last good time, ever.

I ran upstairs to my room and the terrible, noisy future.

I loved horror films. Dad had started showing me some of his favourites—*The Thing*, *Alien*, *Invasion of the Body Snatchers*, *The Shining*. I liked them, and liked watching them with Dad even more; he enjoyed sharing the films with me. But when he'd told me there were certain movies I wasn't quite ready to see, I had of course sought them out. *Hostel*, *Saw*, and all manner of tie-them-down-and-cut-them-up torture movies, I'd watched them with a feeling of sick interest, but little more. They didn't really scare me. Sometimes they disgusted me. I thought they were shock films rather than horror films, and had decided that it was much easier to shock than to unsettle or terrify.

When I walked back into my bedroom, I thought perhaps I'd left one of those movies running on the DVD player. But within seconds I knew that wasn't the case.

This was real.

However realistic the films I watched were supposed to be, I always knew they were made up. It formed a block in my mind, a horror-sink that I was not really aware of until I saw real pain. Some scenes on the late evening news upset me, and I didn't watch the more extreme stuff my friends watched online: beheadings, car crashes, real-life deaths and murders—I knew that they'd be too much.

Besides, buried memories of the accident often surfaced at the most unexpected of times.

It took me a few moments to really register what I was seeing. Something red and meaty hung from a rope, swinging gently as if only just touched. Beyond, a couple of spreads of tent material slumped low to the ground, and on one of them a shape thrashed and lashed out, limbs moving rapidly. It looked like a wind-up toy that had been overwound.

I blinked and sat on my bed. *That's the place I was watching earlier.* The cave was now out of sight, and the camera was still and steady, as if it had been set on a tripod. The lights slung between tent uprights were swinging, agitated, throwing frantic shadows.

I blinked again, as if to reset. Kept my eyes shut for longer than usual, thinking, *What is it that I'm seeing?*

When I looked again, somebody dashed from the cover of trees and tried to get into one of the large tents. Something—a shape in the air, a blot on the screen, perhaps even a ghosted image—followed them across the clearing. When it touched them, they went down.

My heart was racing, pounding painfully in my chest. I leaned in closer to the screen, but the person was a long way off, hidden in flickering shadows, and moving close merely made their image appear even more pixelated. They seemed to be fighting. Their face was no longer white.

It was red.

If this had been a horror film, I would have laughed at the effects. I couldn't see what was happening. Everything was confused. The thrashing shapes were merely squirming now, as if winding down. The meat continued to swing.

Something parted from the object hanging from the rope—the object that was, I now had to acknowledge, the remains of one of the cavers. It clung there for a while, a hazy image almost seeming to sprout from the sickening mass of red. Then it spread what looked like leathery wings and flitted quickly out of the picture.

"Mum," I said softly. I didn't like this at all. It was too real.

The subtitles were still switched on, but there was no one left to speak.

"Fucking hell, fucking hell," Huw muttered. He was cold. Chills tingled his skin, settling across his damp back, armpits, balls. Whatever this was, it was bloody effective. He hit the remote again and frowned. Discovery Channel. Surely they'd never agree to something like this? It was a science channel. A serious channel. It was November, and Hallowe'en was two weeks ago. "Fucking hell."

Several shapes shot up from the bottom of the picture, spiralling and veering off into the trees like large, frightened birds. He turned up the volume until the digital readout on the TV read one hundred, a loud hum

27

filling the room. Something rustled, the sound ending quickly. Something else ran, pounding steps in the distance that ended as quickly as they'd begun.

More creatures—birds, he assumed, although there was something off about that description—flickered across the screen, one of them hitting one of the upright tents and seeming to disappear inside.

It was the pauses that convinced him this was real. There were periods of frantic movement, mostly off-screen but audible, and those occasional flickers of life on screen. But it was the quieter times between these events—long moments when there was the gentle swish of leaves in a breeze, the electrical grumble of the TV on full volume, flies and insects buzzing into the camera and making random patterns in that unknown forest clearing—that gave it the true sense of reality.

That, and the thing on the rope. It reminded him of a lure, a bloody red chunk of meat slung on a rope ready to act as bait. But it wore the shredded remains of clothing.

"Gotta be a movie." He spoke aloud to break the dreadful silence, and as if to comfort himself.

Someone sobbed. The sound was so unexpected that Huw jumped, looking around the piss-stinking hotel room for whoever had sneaked in while he wasn't looking.

"I think… they came from there," the voice said. It was low and scared, but definitely a woman's voice. "I think—"

Several shapes burst into movement on the screen. It was as if they'd been hanging, sitting, or floating utterly motionless, invisible in the picture because they were as still as everything else. But when they moved, and the woman screamed, Huw had a second to truly see them.

Like birds, but pale. Leathery wings. Teeth.

The picture suddenly changed, spinning, blurring, and then more screaming, loud and piercing, filling the room, so loud that Huw wanted to turn the TV off. But he couldn't not see.

The camera fell onto its side, filling most of the picture with long grass. Then something dropped onto the camera, squirming and shuddering as the screaming grew higher, even louder.

The picture blinked to blackness. The sudden silence was shocking.

Huw, breathing heavily, snapped up the remote control, lowered the volume, and switched immediately to the news channel.

"—seeking a majority Conservative government for the next term, and he reiterated his commitment to make Britain a land of opportunity. The opposition leader launched a tirade against the Prime Minister, suggesting that his policies…"

He muted the volume and watched the news presenter delivering familiar, comfortable news. Nothing horrific, nothing filled with blood and screaming. Politicians baiting each other, business leaders casting warnings, celebrities entering rehab. He giggled. "Fucking hell." He'd really scared himself there. Stupid.

He thought once more of running a bath, but it had lost its allure.

"Mum!" I was running downstairs, still full from dinner and vaguely queasy at the thought of what I'd been watching. I'd left the TV on, the scene still playing out, but didn't want to watch it any more. Not alone. "Mum!"

Otis sauntered from the living room to the bottom of the staircase. I scratched his head as I pushed past him. Mum and Lynne—my grandmother insisted on us using her first name, and it had long-since stopped being weird—were in the living room, both looking at the doorway as I entered. They smiled, but it was strained. I wasn't sure why. The television in there was off, and it looked like they'd simply been chatting and drinking tea.

"Hi, Lynne," I said, smiling.

Lynne returned the smile. She was a tall, thin woman, what Dad called prim and proper, and her poise often revealed where Mum's natural grace had come from. But now she just looked weak and tired.

"What is it?" Mum signed.

"Something on TV. On the Discovery Channel. It was horrible, people were being killed and… I don't know, there was blood. In a cave." I shrugged, not really knowing what else to say. I couldn't stop myself from glancing at the big flatscreen TV on the living-room wall, as if its darkness would be revealed as the image of the cave's interior. *I might be looking at them right now*, I thought, immediately troubled at where that idea had come from.

"Watching another horror film?" Lynne asked. I had to frown and ask her to repeat herself, and Lynne tried to sign the words.

"No, no, this was on live, Discovery Channel. They don't show horror films. It was…" I picked up the TV remote and switched it on, scanning across channels. Nothing. "I did see it."

"Shouldn't you have been doing your geography homework?" my mum asked.

Lynne waved her hand to get my attention, then asked, "What's the capital of Norway?"

"Oslo," I said. "But geography's a lot more than just that, Nan."

Lynne mock-scowled at the use of that term, and I looked at the TV again. The Discovery Channel showed a holding screen of a mountain landscape, with a message along the bottom reading, *Sorry for the break in signal, normal service will be resumed soon.*

"Normal service," I said, thinking of the bloody, swinging thing.

"Come on," Mum signed. "You can help me—"

"Mum!" Jude shouted, rushing into the room. "I was on my iPod… messaged me… thing on now… the news…!"

I only picked up half of what he said, but he fired the last word at me again in sign language. Our Andrews family signing—teeth bared, hands clawed, eyes rolled back.

"Monsters."

2

Several deaths are reported in a caving accident in northern Moldova. The Discovery Channel was broadcasting a live transmission from the site when the accident happened. There is no indication that Discovery Channel employees are among the dead. The nature of the accident is unclear, and claims that "creatures" were seen emerging from the cave have yet to be independently verified. Dr Kyrylo Orlyk (Moldova State University, Chișinău) who saw the footage from the scene says, "It's quite evident that a scientific expedition, or perhaps the coverage of that expedition, has been hijacked by publicity hounds seeking coverage for some as-yet unnamed media event."

Reuters, Friday, 18 November 2016

I surfaced from one of those nightmares that follows the sleeper into reality. As sleep faded and my whole life rushed in—reminding me of the person I was, my mind once again rescuing itself from the endless void that dreams can become—the monsters were still there. Normally I could not identify them, nor could I really say what they looked like. They were just a presence, a background threat, a weight behind every waking

33

moment, and with them came the usual soundtrack to my nightmares: the screeching of brakes.

The screech went on and on, as it sometimes did when I was having a nightmare. It didn't matter what the bad dreams were about; they were always about the accident.

This time it was different. Trying to open my eyes, squinting against the dawn sunlight that pierced through a crack in the curtains, I saw one of those ambiguous flying shapes circling the fragmenting landscape of my dream. Its mouth was open. It emitted an endless, limitless screech of desperate car brakes, and I hauled myself up at last to escape the inevitable crash.

I sat up quickly in bed, and silence smothered the dregs of my nightmare. It was so unfair that the only times I could hear were in the grip of my worst dreams.

I looked around my bedroom. I loved that room. Beside my bed was the iPad that linked me to the world. My small desk was awash with sketches, notes, open schoolbooks, other bits and pieces. There were several posters on the walls, ranging from a stunning Canadian landscape to a cartoon version of that summer's Olympic Games in Rio. My guitar stood on its stand in the corner; clothes were strewn at the foot of the wardrobe; and in one corner lay the mixed chaos of my constantly changing sporting preferences—a hockey stick, running shoes, basketball. I sighed, breathing away the bad dreams. *Just a nightmare*, I thought. *That's all*.

Touching the tablet screen, several messages popped up from friends. One of them glowed red—I'd given one name that distinctive tint—and I felt my own cheeks flushing the same colour. Rob had messaged during the night. He might not have been my best friend, but he was my best *boy* friend. Dad took the mickey out of me about that. But that's all he was, a mate, and something of a special one. Apart from my best friend Lucy, he was the only other kid in school who could sign.

I opened Rob's message.

Don't ever ask me to go caving with you.

I frowned, and everything rushed back in. *Not a dream at all,* I thought, and I remembered all the fears and doubts of the night before. Watching the strange, confused news item had been bad enough. There was little detail, and the snippet of film they showed again and again was nowhere near as distressing as what I'd been watching live on the Discovery Channel. The people in charge of the news reports must have decided that most of the footage was too traumatic to show.

But as well as that, there had been the troubling atmosphere between Mum and Lynne. They had been sitting close together, and the tension that I'd felt between them when I'd entered the room had not dissipated. I had become very sensitive to atmosphere and emotion. Sometimes Mum said it was because of my deafness, but I didn't think that was the case at all. Maybe I did compensate in some ways, but empathy and an ability to sense the emotional load of a situation had always been with me.

Later that evening I'd asked my mother what was wrong, but she'd simply shaken her head and kissed me goodnight.

I swiped the screen and accessed the BBC News home page. The fact that the headline stretched right across the page alerted me to its seriousness, even before I started reading.

The details did little to make me feel better.

Something was happening in a region of Moldova. No one seemed to know what. There was talk of a chemical spill, a terrorist attack, even a plague of hornets. A couple of clips of mobile-phone footage showed two scenes that disturbed me more than their content alone should have: a car stuck on a bridge with a huddle of clothes beside the open driver's door; and fleeting things like large, agitated moths fluttering through the shadows beneath trees, the camera turning to reveal two frightened, silent faces. Death tolls were mentioned. Russia had closed its borders. The UN was watching. It was a news report that relayed no real news, only the fact that *something* had happened.

I scanned the report again, and it was only on second reading that I spotted a mention of the caving operation, and only as a passing mention at that. It was almost as if the two had barely been connected.

Surely anyone who'd seen the Discovery Channel footage would link the two?

A meeting of Cobra is being chaired by the Prime Minister…

No comment from the Russian President at this time…

The United Nations says…

I picked up the tablet and went to wake up Mum. The house was still, and as I opened my parents' bedroom door I looked at the time. It was earlier than I'd thought, barely 6 a.m.

"Mum?" I said. Mum opened her eye, face screwed up, hair awry, and she instantly came alert.

"What's wrong?"

She never stopped worrying, I knew. Ever since the accident she'd become someone on edge, a light sleeper; sometimes she admitted to me that she always feared the worst. Even when I told her that I'd been lucky—the crash that killed my paternal grandparents could well have killed me too—Mum found it hard finding any luck in what had happened. No good luck, at least. The accident had changed my whole family, and I constantly did my best to edge that change for the better.

"There's something—" I began, but then I saw the pulsing blue tone of the phone on the bedside table.

I grabbed the phone and looked at the name on the screen: *Huw*. I handed the phone to my mother.

"Hey, babe," Huw said. He suddenly felt foolish, calling Kelly about something happening so far away. TV news had a way of upping the ante on things, and sometimes the constant barrage of repeated information made events seem more serious and significant than they really were. *Am I being stupid here?* he wondered. Maybe he was more homesick than he'd first thought. He had one more day and night away before heading home, but he'd woken up feeling maudlin.

But he was also unsettled.

"Hi," Kelly said, groggily. "You okay?"

"I'm fine, fine, just… have you seen the news?"

"Hang on," Kelly said, and Huw heard the rustle of sheets. "Ally's just come in to show me something."

Ally! But Huw should have guessed. His daughter had always been an early riser, and she was developing a keen interest in world events. Whereas lots of kids her age would log on to Facebook the minute their eyes opened, her first call was usually one of the news sites. She was a bright kid, but sometimes he mourned her childhood.

"So what am I looking at?" she asked.

"The thing in Moldova," Huw said.

"Yeah, yeah, I've got that. But what is it?"

"No one seems to know." He was sitting on the edge of his bed, TV flickering before him. He'd muted the sound to call home, thinking, *That's how Ally sees the world.* "I saw something on TV last night. It's just scary."

"Yeah. Well, at least it's a long way away."

Huw thought of the map of Europe, but he couldn't accurately place the country. Just how far away was it? Moldova was one of those places only talked about when something bad happened there.

"It's just… it sounds serious." He heard more rustling from the other end of the line, imagined Kelly sitting up in bed and Ally propped next to her. "It's confused right now, and a bit panicked, but it's got the feel of one of those stories that'll really expand soon. Know what I mean?"

A pause. He heard Kelly sniffing. Then she said, "But it's in Moldova."

"Yeah. Yeah."

"Hang on," Kelly said. The line fell silent for a moment, then he heard Ally speaking.

"It's what I saw on the TV last night."

"Tell her I did too," Huw said. There was silence while Kelly signed to their daughter.

"It was horrible," Ally said.

"It was," Huw said. "Babe… I might come home now instead of tomorrow."

"Because of this?" Kelly asked. "Have you finished up there for the week?"

"No, plenty to do here: we've hit problems with the site drainage, might need to install a pump and Max is arguing over who's responsible."

"So shouldn't you leave things in good shape there?"

"Yeah," he said, because he knew his wife was right. "Yeah, maybe I should come home later this evening." But he watched the muted news reports, already back at the beginning of the loop because they had nothing new to show or talk about. "Several deaths reported," they'd said, and even that had a vague, remote feel, because there was no talk of how the deaths had happened, who had died, or where. *I saw at least one of them on the end of the rope,* he thought, and he wondered yet again why those images he'd watched live the night before did not form part of the news report this morning.

"Missing you," Kelly said.

"You too. All of you. Ally okay?"

"Yeah, she is. You know her, she fixates on things sometimes. And I know she was a bit upset last night at the stuff they were showing."

"It wasn't nice." He turned the TV off. He couldn't talk to his wife while watching that—the pile of rags beside a car that could be a body; the things in the trees.

"Let me know what time you'll be home," she said. "I'll cook us a nice meal. Steak."

"Sounds good to me." They exchanged goodbyes and hung up, and his room suddenly seemed quieter than ever. At his loneliest, those moments just after he'd spoken to his family on the phone were always the worst. The old analogue clock beside the bed ticked away the seconds, and from somewhere else in the small hotel he heard the muted rumble of another TV.

It was an hour until breakfast. Huw hit the shower.

"Morning," the hotel owner said. Her buttons were done up today. "Just choose your own table and help yourself to cereal. I'll come and take your breakfast order in a couple of minutes."

"Thanks," Huw said. She offered a business-like smile and turned away. He walked through into the dining room, glad to see other people already seated. There was an Indian couple with their daughter, a middle-aged woman working on a laptop, and a couple of young men wearing sports kit and consulting a map. The men chatted and laughed loudly, and the little girl made faces at them. One of them reciprocated, and the kid giggled.

Soft music played in the background, not too loud to be cloying, but loud enough to give some privacy to conversation. It was a nice atmosphere. No one seemed unsettled or disturbed. *Maybe none of them saw the news,* Huw thought. He exchanged nods with the men and smiled at the family, then took a table close to a window. It was more likely that they'd all seen the news but it had made no impact on their day. The men were probably planning an adventure—a bike ride across the moors, or perhaps a coastal trail run. The family might be here on holiday or visiting relatives in the area. And the woman was obviously on a business trip, already working at seven-thirty in the morning.

They weren't like him. They weren't doomsdayers.

Kelly was always gentle when she called him that,

and with good cause. His parents had both been killed in the car crash that had seriously injured his daughter; she'd broken several ribs, a collarbone, and fractured her skull. Most of the physical damage had been repairable. But her cochleae had suffered severe deceleration injuries, and combined with a bleed on the brain from her skull fracture, this had resulted in profound deafness, changing her life and theirs irrevocably. It was the worst day of his life. From what they'd been able to gather from police and witness reports, the crash had been caused by a fox running into the road. His father had swerved, clipped the kerb, and rolled the car into a stone wall. Ally could remember little about the crash or the several hours before. She found that loss of memory almost as traumatising as the hearing loss itself, because she was desperate to remember what she and her grandparents had been doing. She told her parents that she felt like she'd lost the last good times she and her grandparents had spent together, and Huw sometimes lay awake at night wondering what they had done and where they had been. Maybe they'd taken Ally to the cinema. Perhaps one day, when she was watching a film for what she thought was the first time, she would suddenly remember the end.

Huw was doing his best to move on, but during his worst, most pessimistic moments he had no trouble justifying his doomsdaying. He'd project the path of events to the worst conclusion imaginable. Say Jude asked for a skateboard for his birthday, they relented, and he went out on his first jaunt. Most parents would worry that he might fall and break his arm. In Huw's version, the fall would result in a broken arm, which would lead to Jude staggering home crying, and then he'd faint in the road and be crushed beneath the wheels of a passing car.

His mental gymnastics were often horrific, but he could not help himself.

The previous evening, and then while experiencing an unsettled sleep, he'd been doing the same with that disturbing news report.

"What can I get you?" The hotel owner had appeared beside him while he was daydreaming, and he jumped in his seat. "Oh, didn't mean to startle you, darling!" She touched his shoulder and squeezed, and Huw had a sudden, shameful thought—*I wonder how many guests she's fucked in their rooms*. It was offensive and probably very unfair, but it arrived as surprisingly as the woman.

"No problem," he said, smiling up at her. "I'll have the full English, please. And coffee."

"Coming right up. Help yourself to cereal." She left without waiting for a reply. He looked around the room at the other guests, all caught in their own world, their own day. The two men on the next table were poring over a map, and one of them glanced up.

"Mountain biking?" Huw asked.

"A bit," the man said. He was maybe mid-twenties, fit-looking, with a casual rugged appearance that only comes of loving the outdoors. "Bit of running, bit of hiking too."

"Coast to coast," his mate said. He was older, his hair thinner, but he looked just as fit. "Starting at Polperro this lunchtime, hitting Tintagel in two days. Hopefully our wives will still be waiting there for us!"

"So you're going across Bodmin," Huw said.

"Yeah, my favourite place on the planet," the first guy said. "Do one thing every day that scares you, right?"

Huw found himself feeling outlandishly jealous of the men. They seemed worry-free, ready to spend time purely fulfilling their own desires. He'd once spent an enjoyable year training for his first marathon, soon after Ally was born. He'd completed the challenge, run his marathon in a little over four hours, and had made plans for what to do next. But work had got in the way. Then Jude came along, and the spare hours in his life seemed to dwindle down to spare minutes. He hadn't run in over a year, though he frequently considered digging out his trainers. He took them with him every time he stayed away from home, tied in their little blue bag. They'd probably gone mouldy by now.

In truth, he knew it was motivation rather than time. Many of the days he spent travelling could have been bookended with a run. It was just that he'd rather have a pint in a hotel bar or sit in his room, watching a film and ordering room service.

Middle-age spread had crept up on him, and sometimes he thought that if he'd jumped ahead to where he was now from ten years ago he'd be shocked.

He wished he was going with these guys. Wished he had a mountain bike that wasn't rusted solid in the garage back at home.

He sighed, and then the hotel owner was placing a coffee pot on his table.

"Lovely morning out," she said. "You staying for the music festival tomorrow?"

"Actually I was thinking of checking out this evening,

after work," Huw said. "I'll still pay for the night. I'll need to come back later to shower, then I'll head off."

"Fine by me," the woman said, and he wasn't sure whether he imagined the shimmer of regret in her eyes. Probably. Maybe he was just kidding himself.

The sound of cutlery clinking, subdued conversation from the family, and the men planning their outing filled the room, and Huw sighed and poured his coffee.

It was going to be a long, hard day. Max was a decent enough sort, but like any successful businessman, he didn't like waste, nor did he entertain avoidable mistakes. The drainage problem they'd encountered on the site of his new mansion was both. Huw's difficult position was that the drainage engineer they were using had been recommended by Max himself. Max's position was that Huw had given a guaranteed price for the work, based on the designs and ground investigations carried out at the time. It was the engineer's fault, but his company was not keen on taking the hit. Softly-softly was probably the way to go with this, but Huw feared that Max would explode when cost was mentioned. Thirty grand was a conservative estimate of the additional work required in rerouting a main drain, and incorporating a pumping station to lift the site waste up into the neighbouring system.

He drank his coffee, wishing he was back at home. He ran a good, profitable business, and it had given them a decent standard of living over the years. But it had aged him.

He looked at the two men again. "Got room for one more?" he asked. They glanced up from their plates, the younger one automatically looking him up and down and seeming unimpressed with what he saw.

"Got a bike?" the older guy asked.

Huw laughed softly, took another sip of coffee. "I wish."

"Got some first-world problems, mate?" the young man said through a mouth of food. Huw decided he didn't like him very much. He carried a cockiness that his older companion did not.

"Something like that."

"Breakfast," the owner said, crossing the room and placing the plate before him. "I gave you an extra sausage."

Huw laughed aloud, and then from across the room the businesswoman said, "Oh my God!"

The dining room fell silent. A knife clanged against a plate as it was put down. The Indian woman paused with a napkin to her mouth; her daughter rocked back on her chair.

The woman was looking at her tablet computer, from which tinny, unidentifiable sounds played. For a moment she seemed unaware of the sudden stillness around her, then she looked up. But her expression did not change— no embarrassment, no shy smile as she waved away her outburst. "Have you seen this?" she asked.

Huw rose and crossed to her table instantly. She flinched back a little as he stood close beside her, shocked by his sudden proximity, but he didn't care.

Some celebrity split from her husband after nine days and a thirty-million dollar wedding, he thought. *Or the Prime Minister being arrested for squeezing an assistant's arse.* He really hoped it was something inconsequential. But then he saw the screen, and the first thing he did was reach out to tap up the volume.

"...isolated incidents in Ukraine and Russia, and unconfirmed reports of similar events in Romania. This footage was captured on a mobile phone east of Donetsk." The footage played. It was silent, and showed the view from a second- or third-floor window looking down onto a street. People were running. Several cars had crashed, and further along the street a fire raged, consuming several smaller vehicles and a bus. Some people had already fallen, and others soon followed. It was a depressing echo of recent images from the troubled Moldova. But then there were the *things*.

"We're not quite sure what we're seeing here..." the newscaster said.

They flew through the air, landing on people, bringing them down.

"They seem to be... bats? Birds of some kind? Attracted by the violence, the rioting and unrest, perhaps, but they seem to be..."

"They're the *cause* of the violence!" Huw said. Hadn't anyone seen that thing at the cave last night?

The camera moved violently left and right, blurring the picture. Then it steadied again, zooming in on a shape crawling along the road below. It was a woman in a short white and red dress. Several of the winged creatures—they were about the size of a small cat, Huw reckoned—were clasped to her back, and two more flapped their wings to reach under her. Clawing at her face. Biting.

"These images are distressing, but as yet they haven't been independently verified."

The woman rolled onto her back and slapped at the creatures attacking her face. One of them came away, and it seemed to take some of her with it. She opened her mouth to scream, and in the silence the action seemed even more terrible.

She bled.

The image flickered and then cut out, replaced by the two newscasters back in the studio. The man seemed shocked, but the woman was as professional as ever.

"More on that breaking news as and when—"

The businesswoman cut out the volume and sat back in her chair. "Horror movie," she said. "Viral marketing. Very clever, and to have it on national news is genius."

"No," Huw said. "It's not that." He and the woman swapped glances, and he knew that she knew the truth as well. She was simply in denial.

"I saw something last night," the Indian man said, standing beside his wife and daughter. "I turned it off. It was horrifying." The two men gathered around to see the tablet screen. The younger man still chewed his breakfast, and he seemed more interested than concerned.

"Thought it was something on the movie channel, or something," his older friend said. "We switched to the match. United got their arse handed to them."

Huw continued watching the tablet. The sound was muted now but the newscasters were still there. The woman was talking, but the man next to her seemed to be listening to his earpiece, fingers tapping across his laptop. His eyes went wide. He looked around, first at his companion and then off-screen. Very unprofessional.

"Look," Huw said, and the woman turned up the volume again.

"…some breaking news coming in right now," the male newscaster said. "This time from Buzau, seventy miles north-east of Bucharest in Romania. We've no footage, but there are reports of a massacre at a nursery, and further deaths at a restaurant, electrical component factory, and several other places. Erm... there's no indication of who is responsible for these attacks. Or how." The newscasters were becoming more fidgety, and the man pressed his earpiece in again, head tilted to one side.

"And another report from closer to Bucharest," the woman said. "A train has been attacked by what's described as a 'swarm of flying rats'." She frowned, staring down at her laptop screen. It was one of the first times Huw had seen a newscaster showing anything approaching emotion. Usually they were cool, calm, almost inhuman. "Oh, my God," the woman breathed.

Huw backed away, feeling suddenly crowded by the others. He caught the young girl's eyes and saw that she was scared, huddled into her mother, chairs now side by side.

"It's spreading," he said.

"What is?" the businesswoman asked.

"Last night, the thing on the Discovery Channel. It was at a place in northern Moldova, now there are attacks in Ukraine and Romania. That's hundreds of miles. And they said Russia too?"

"So what is it, terrorists?" the younger man said through a mouthful of sausage sandwich. "At least it's a long way away."

Huw just looked at him, searching for an answer but finding none that made sense. "Excuse me," he said. He left the dining room, dashed into the hotel's large hallway and ran up the wide staircase. He caught a whiff of something—it smelled like stale piss—and realised that the whole hotel smelled of it. Perhaps it was the carpet cleaner they used, or the little dishes of potpourri scattered around.

He fumbled with his room key and slammed the door behind him, but he felt no more protected. Of course not. He was on his own and his family were at home, without him. Four hours away in the car, and that's if he did the journey in one go and there were no hold-ups.

He was breathing too fast, and not just from running up the stairs. *Doomsdaying*, he thought, *that's all I'm doing*. Whatever had happened—was still happening— was more than a thousand miles away, in towns and cities whose names he'd never heard before, and countries that he rarely even considered. He was safe. His family was safe.

But it spread hundreds of miles overnight!

He stood there for some time with his back against the door, but in reality he'd already made his decision. It was unreasonable, irrational. He hadn't rushed home to Kelly on 9/11. He'd been overseas when the Japanese earthquake and tsunami hit, visiting a building firm in Brittany and circling the idea of going into partnership. He'd watched in his gîte's bedroom as Fukushima exploded, wondering whether the hazy image would change the world. That business association had never solidified, but he'd not felt the need to jump on a plane and fly back to his family.

So why now?

He didn't know. What he *did* know was that it felt right, it felt good, and he was not going to fight his feelings on this one.

Before pulling his bag from the wardrobe and starting

to pack, Huw held his breath and turned on the TV once more.

The weather forecast was on. It was going to rain.

3

Been coming for years. Mother Earth gonna eat us all
back up. Nom-nom.

@GaiaZombie, Twitter, Friday, 18 November 2016

I felt much better after leaving the house and walking
through the village to the bus stop. I met Lucy in the
usual place, and we exchanged hellos. Lucy didn't
mention anything about the news. By the time the bus
came, I'd tried to forget about it too.

But those images stuck with me.

"TFIF," Rob signed as I jumped off the bus in the
school grounds. *Thank fuck it's Friday.*

"You doing anything this weekend?" I asked.

"We're going to north Wales to visit my uncle."

"Nice," I said. "Mountains. Lakes. Cold. Grey."

"My uncle's cool, he takes me mountain biking and
hiking." Rob was cool, too, and his coolness wasn't a
pretence or a mask. Good-looking and smart, he had a
manner about him that compelled me to watch the way
he moved, the way he was. I knew I wasn't the only girl
who felt that way. In fact, I was pretty sure plenty of
boys felt that way too. Girls wanted to go out with Rob,
boys wanted to be him, and the fact that his charisma

51

was unforced and unconscious made him even more attractive. There were the Beautiful People in school, so taken with their own appearance that the outside world existed purely as a mirror for that vanity. Rob was beautiful without being a Beautiful Person.

"He does sound cool," I said, smiling. My dad would be home late that evening, Mum had said, and I was glad. I always missed him. I knew that he worried about me, but in truth I worried about him more. I hated him being away working. I'd lost my hearing, but he'd lost his parents in the crash. Sometimes he had a look of restrained panic about him, as if he was always waiting for something worse to happen. I wanted to tell him it was all right, I was fine, I was there. But I suspected that nothing would be all right for Dad ever again. The world had shrugged at him and revealed its indifference.

"What do you think about the news?" I asked.

Rob frowned briefly, then realised what I was talking about. "Oh, that! Weird, pretty sick. Bet the movie rights are sold already."

"Aren't you worried?"

"Nah. It's a long way away." He gave me a friendly punch on the arm and left for his form class.

I walked through the crowded, raucous school, surrounded by silence. I'd managed my deafness amazingly well, not letting it hinder me any more than it had to. I'd been brave and clever, determined and unrelenting in my attempts to live a normal life.

That's what I was told, anyway.

In reality, I felt just like a normal girl, and all I'd done was survive. So many people had helped, and were still helping, that I actually found the word "brave" a little offensive, as it threw a shroud over everyone else in my life. My parents, teachers, the guys at the school for the deaf where I went once a month, my friends, Lynne. Even Jude, the little shit. They were brave for adapting to accommodate the awkwardness some of them must have felt, or perhaps still felt now. As for me, I'd just got on with things. I had been the lucky one in that car crash, and living in silence was just another aspect to my new life post-accident.

Sometimes, however, I felt smothered. Walking through the corridors and hallways towards my form room I could see and sense so much laughing and banter, so much noise—I could even feel it as vibrations against the fine hairs on my skin and transmitted through my feet—that the silence was like a weight crushing me down. I felt one step removed from the world I did my best to be a part of. That's why I loved Lucy so much. My friend always stayed with me during the more chaotic school moments, and although I'd never spoken to her about it, I knew that she sensed my occasional unease.

My form tutor, Miss Hughes, was already at her desk, sitting back casually as she chatted with the pupils already there. She waved and smiled at me, then stood and told the class to calm down. Chairs scraped, desks were bumped, everyone sat.

This was the time when I settled in for the day. We read for ten minutes each morning while Miss Hughes took register, and that quiet time was comforting. I sat next to Lucy and we took out our books. Lucy was reading a Twilight novel; I read one of Ranulph Fiennes's memoirs. For girls so similar, the gulf in our reading tastes was huge.

My first lesson was geography. I always enjoyed the lesson, and liked even more that I got to sit next to Rob. But as soon as I saw him I knew that something was wrong.

"What is it?" I signed. Sometimes I liked the fact that Rob and I could have secret conversations in the midst of a crowd.

"That news," he replied. "The cave. Those weird things that came out of it. They've spread. It's all over the TV. And my cousin is in the army, based in Malta. He sent a text to his mum, she sent it to Dad, and he just forwarded it to me." He took out his phone and held it out to me. We weren't supposed to bring phones into the classrooms, but everyone did.

I read the text on the screen:

Been mobilised. Thing in Moldova bigger than they're saying.

"Bloody hell," I said.

Rob nodded. He was not his usual casual self. The frown did not suit him.

"Sir?" I asked, hand raised.

Mr Bellamy pointed to me and nodded. He was one of those who found it awkward, even uncomfortable, communicating with me. He was also a mumbler. I could barely see his lips moving, let alone read them, and he could not sign.

"Can we talk about that thing in Moldova today?"

Mr Bellamy smiled and spread his arms wide, said something, and most of the class turned to look at me. I glanced sidelong at Rob.

"He said that's exactly what he was going to do anyway."

I smiled at the teacher. He clapped his hands once and the class faced front again. He spoke to some of them, blinds were drawn, and one of the girls went to sit at the front of the class to work the computer. Mr Bellamy fussed with the remote control for the ceiling projector, then a square of flickering light appeared on the whiteboard.

I prepared myself for another incomplete lesson. The teachers were great, and if they knew I wouldn't be able to follow a lesson completely—if, for instance, they were talking about a lot of stuff instead of displaying it all on whiteboards—they'd have a printout ready at the end of the period. I'd come to terms with the fact that my schooling took up about twenty per cent more time than my fellow pupils', because I spent an hour or two after coming home every evening reading printouts. If there was anything I didn't understand, the teachers were usually available during free lessons to help. Some were better than others, and Mr Bellamy was one of the few who found dealing with me problematic.

The first image appeared on the whiteboard. It showed a cutaway section through a cave system, and I wondered if I was the first to notice what made it unique—there seemed to be no entrance.

I could see Mr Bellamy starting to talk, and Rob tapped my arm. He started signing for me.

"Let's start with a different cave to the one we saw on the news yesterday. Movile Cave in Romania was discovered by construction workers in 1986. They were drilling to assess whether the remote area was suitable for a new power station, broke through into an underground passage, and immediately sealed it up again. What scientists discovered when they ventured down was a cave system that had been cut off from the outside world for millions of years. What surprised them more was the unique ecosystem that existed down there. Apparently, it's an arachnophobe's worst nightmare." The class laughed. I focused on Rob's hands, his mouth, his facial expressions. I liked it when he signed for me; he became mine.

"There are no stalactites in the cave, so no evidence of water ingress. The atmosphere is only ten per cent oxygen. And there's no evidence of radioactive isotopes from the Chernobyl disaster. That convinced scientists that what they'd found was a genuinely isolated ecosystem, completely enclosed from the outside world. Some of what they found down there… remarkable." Rob nodded forward and I looked.

The projections changed every few seconds. Images of strange spiders, scorpion-like creatures, snails, spring-tailed insects, millipedes and worms, all of them ghostly white and eyeless. Some of them seemed almost transparent, their insides visible.

Rob touched my hand as Mr Bellamy continued.

"Only a handful of scientists have been down into the cave. It's such a difficult environment to work in, with oxygen levels so low your kidneys will fail within a couple of hours, and the heat is almost unbearable. Quite an amazing place."

A cross-section of the cave appeared on the screen and he used a light pen to point at particular features.

"It's estimated that the caverns had been cut off from

the outside world for over five million years. In that time the species within have evolved and become quite unique. It's a perfect example of Darwinian evolution, actually. There were plants and creatures that were found nowhere else on the planet. Many were familiar, but some necessitated whole new classifications."

The picture showed a milky-white spider, bloated and moist, mandibles dark-tipped and seemingly ready to snap from the screen.

"Eww," I said, and I saw other pupils laughing in equal disgust.

Mr Bellamy fell silent as the slideshow of images continued, one picture fading out as the next faded in.

A fern-like plant, the edges of its pale leaves glimmering with moisture or mineral deposits. A small beetle, its shell a soft-looking pale yellow. Several types of fungi.

"It's just one of several such sites around the world," Mr Bellamy said. "That we've discovered, at least. And the system in Moldova is the latest." He fell silent again as the screen turned to white. He seemed to be staring at the wall, lost for words. The pupils glanced around at each other, a few of them smiling, most a little worried.

"Sir?" I saw one of them say.

Mr Bellamy used the remote to turn off the projector. He turned to face us, and I'd never seen him looking so old. His face was grey, eyes dark. It was as if he'd returned from seeing something terrible without ever having left the classroom.

"I've always worried about things like this," he said. "When I was your age it was the idea of space exploration that troubled me. But as I learned more, it became obvious that there were countless places still on Earth that were yet to be discovered. Ecosystems are just that—systems. Whole, complete, sometimes in turmoil, yet usually, eventually, balanced. Introduce one unique ecosystem to another and the result is unknown. And as the world becomes smaller with advances in communication and travel, so remote dangers come closer."

One of the kids put their hand up and spoke, and Rob signed for me.

"Like with Aids?"

Mr Bellamy nodded. "Just like with Aids. Some of what are known as the hot viruses, too. Ebola, Marburg. Roads were built deep into the wilds of Africa; lifelines for many, but routes along which diseases and contagion could travel much, much faster than nature itself could spread them. Isolated valleys were explored and plundered." He stopped again, trying to smile to see away his seriousness. But the smile only made it worse. "I always worried," he said again.

"So what do you think has happened?" I asked.

Mr Bellamy looked at me, and this time he spoke clearly, for me, so that I saw the answer on his own lips. "We'll find out soon."

My second lesson was art, and Lucy and I were in the school's art department experimenting with materials. Rob had gone off to ICT. Halfway through the lesson the door opened and the teacher was called out. She left in a hurry, giving instructions for the pupils to continue cutting and preparing material for the masks we were working on.

"What was that?" I asked.

"Mr Rosen came in and said, 'Sue, you should come and see this'," Lucy said.

I looked around at the small group. Most of them were already working again; a couple sat back and looked around, vaguely disinterested.

"We should, too," I said. "Come on."

As I stood, Lucy grabbed my arm. "What are you doing?"

"Seeing what's happening." I walked to the door, not looking back because I didn't want to glimpse Lucy's disapproving look.

I opened the door and sensed Lucy behind me. I smiled. I knew that my friend could not resist a mystery.

In the corridor we moved quickly towards the central staircase, passing art displays, noticeboards, and a couple of closed classroom doors. I walked like I was meant to be there. Sneak along, crouch down, and we were sure to be seen.

At the staircase I paused and turned to Lucy, shrugging. Lucy listened, then pointed down. We descended, and several stairs up from the ground floor we saw three teachers hurrying across the vestibule and through a pair of double doors. Lucy and I froze, waiting to be caught. But the teachers either didn't see us, or didn't register our presence.

"What's going on?" I whispered.

Lucy shrugged. "Come on. I think they're all going to the staffroom."

"Well we won't be able to get in," I said.

Lucy only smiled and waved me on. We crossed the vestibule and passed through the same double doors as the teachers, entering the administration wing of the school. Pupils were not ordinarily allowed in there, but that gave us an implied authority—if we were seen, whoever saw us would more than likely assume that we had permission to be there.

Lucy led the way past the staffroom, then she glanced back and forth along the short corridor and opened a door. "Cleaning cupboard," she signed. "Come on."

"How do you know about—?" I asked, but Lucy quickly put her finger to her lips, frowning. I must have been talking louder than I'd intended.

"Izzy told me about it," she mouthed. She ushered me inside the cupboard and closed the door.

In the darkness, I felt closed in. I couldn't see my friend, couldn't sign to her. Isolation smothered us both. I hated the dark, but not for the reasons that most people disliked it.

My friend moved, then a soft light bathed the room. Lucy was standing on a fixed shelving unit, and in the wall before her a plastic air vent spilled light into the cramped cupboard. She beckoned me to climb up next to her, pressed her face close to the vent… and froze.

Lucy's mouth fell open.

What's she seeing? I wondered. And for just a few seconds, I didn't want to know.

I climbed up carefully next to her and, heads pressed together, we looked through the vent into the staffroom.

There was a big TV in there, fixed to the wall. The room itself was quite small, and it was filled with teachers. Standing room only. They were all watching the screen.

"Bucharest Burns" said the caption below the shocking, flame-filled, unbelievable image. The view was from a handheld camera somewhere high in the city, a hillside or more likely the rooftop of a tall building. The image juddered a little, but whoever held the camera knew what they were doing. They panned slowly left and right. Flames flickered all across the city. There were many smaller fires, conflagrations consuming single buildings or roofs, sending leaning columns of smoke to the sky. Two larger fires were prominent, one quite close to the observer and the other much further away. The way the flames boiled and rolled was testament to their fury, and black oily smoke billowed skyward. The closer fire was centred in a tall, blocky structure—a hotel or a shopping centre, perhaps—and every opening was a window into hell. Blazing shapes tumbled. A wall collapsed, seeming to splash flames across the street and out of sight against another building. The fire had tides and swells, pulsing away from its source and seeding itself elsewhere.

Cars screamed along streets. People ran.

The camera suddenly shifted, blurring the picture and making me dizzy. *What the hell's going on?* I thought, closing my eyes as I gathered myself. When I looked again the camera had steadied, but now it followed a haze of smoke across the Bucharest rooftops. It was a distant cloud, huge, and where it passed it seemed to steal colour and shape from the buildings and landscape around it.

Lucy's hand closed on my arm, nails digging in.

"What is it?" I asked. Lucy could hear something—a voice on the TV, newscaster or perhaps the person doing the filming.

An explosion bloomed in the distance, so slow-moving that it must have been huge, monstrous. But the camera still followed the strange cloud as it shifted left... and right... drifting *against* the breeze that drove the smoke of Bucharest's destruction at an angle to the sky.

Lucy looked panicked. Her eyes were wide, mouth open, and she didn't seem to notice how tightly she was clasping my arm.

I prised her fingers away and jumped down from the shelf. Lucy didn't move. She just kept staring at the terrible images, and listening to something worse.

I stumbled over a box as I went for the door, reaching out and clasping at shelving to prevent myself from falling. I banged my shin and groaned, then glanced back at Lucy. My friend had turned to look at me, but bathed in weak light from the air vent, her face still looked the same.

"What is it?" I asked, louder than before and more desperate, not caring whether they were heard or not.

"Ally," Lucy mouthed. I found the door and tugged it open, dashing into the corridor, running to the staffroom door and pushing it open.

It was horrible. There were at least thirty teachers in there, and only a few glanced at me. They seemed to not register my presence, quickly turning to the TV again. Miss Hughes motioned me in, held my hand, and we turned towards the screen. *She wants me to see*, I thought. *We're not teachers and pupils any more*. The disconcerting idea came from nowhere.

I could only see what I'd seen before, but in more detail. The burning buildings, the chaos in the streets. The continuing massive explosions in the distance—a fuel plant or power station, perhaps. And that vast cloud followed by the camera as it passed back and forth above the burning city, as if it had a strange, unknowable consciousness of its own.

Miss Hughes picked up the TV remote control. Another teacher seemed to argue with her, words that I could not see. Then my form teacher turned on the subtitles.

I started to understand just how terrible everything was.

4

The Central University Library is ablaze. Everything we have learnt, all the hope that building personified, up in flames. A million burning pages flutter down. Between them fly the terrible, unknowable beasts that cause this horror. They are circling. They are listening for me. Even the tapping of these keys make me fear for my life.

Cornelia, Facebook, Friday, 18 November 2016

Huw cursed his laziness. If ever he wanted a radio in the car it was now. But the aerial had been lost over a year ago, either stolen or perhaps knocked off in a car wash, and he hadn't bothered replacing it, though he'd always meant to. Just one more thing at the back of his mind that never got done.

He tried it anyway, scanning across channels in the hope that he'd find one clear enough even with only the aerial's stub to catch the signal. There was nothing but white noise and occasional haunting, distorted voices.

Settling in for a quiet drive, he nursed his phone between his legs. He supposed he could have accessed a radio through the phone, but he wasn't sure he'd get enough bandwidth on the move. His priority now was to get home. Once there with his family he could face the news again.

He'd called Kelly once more before leaving, told her that he was on his way home, and this time she hadn't tried to dissuade him. Maybe she'd realised that once his mind was made up it was very difficult to change it. Or perhaps she actually wanted him home. The kids had gone to school, but the day no longer felt like a normal day. "At least it's a long way away," she'd said again, and he hadn't even replied.

He remembered where he'd been on 9/11. It was several years before he'd started his own company, and sitting at his desk at work he'd been reading those shocking, unbelievable, almost surreal news reports on the Internet. The connection had been poor, but the breaking news had come through well enough. He'd kept glancing at the screen and then out of the office window, through which he could see the sprawl of the town sprouting generous amounts of green, no building above five storeys high, distant hills bathed in inviting sunlight. It had all felt so unreal. His boss had wandered by and watched for a while, then returned to his office, apparently unconcerned. Another colleague had viewed the image of the first plane striking the North Tower, repeated again and again, and had pronounced it a special effect. Everyone had had their own forms of disbelief that day.

Huw had felt the significance of the event. He'd called his mother, told her America was under attack. It had not felt like an exaggeration. His friends at the desks around him, already still, had fallen silent at his words. They'd carried weight, and everyone had felt them land.

Today was the same. Fifteen years later, once again

the world was gathered around TVs or computers watching the news unfold. This was another world-changing event.

He didn't understand how others could not perceive this. Upon leaving the hotel he'd bumped into the two men, preparing their bikes in the hotel's front garden, laughing and joking, efficient and experienced. He'd expressed disbelief that they were still going on their ride, and they'd looked at him as if he was out of his mind. They didn't even reply. Perhaps they didn't know what he meant.

The A30 out of Cornwall was busier than usual, but then he rarely travelled on a Friday morning. *Don't travel anywhere in Britain on a Friday,* his dad used to say, and for years Huw had been going against his father's advice. He'd come to appreciate those words when long traffic jams held him up and delayed his arrival home until midnight, or even later. But when his company was working away, it was a choice between that and returning home on Saturday morning. And he relished his precious weekends.

This weekend they'd planned to go for a long walk. Kelly liked the Skirrid, a sharp ridge of a hill sticking out of their local Monmouthshire countryside like a giant's spine. The kids loved it too, Jude running on ahead and exploring, Ally pausing now and then to take photos of the landscape and her family. Otis would go mad, pounding back and forth between them, herding his family and being just as daft as a big dog like him could be. A good couple of hours, and then they'd return home to the beef casserole left stewing all day in the slow cooker. After that they might watch a movie together. Their family life was chaotic—his work keeping him away from home, Kelly's job stressing her more than it should, Ally's monthly stopover at the school for the deaf, her netball, Jude's rugby matches and swimming lessons—and it was the simplest times with his family that pleased him most.

He hoped they could still go. He didn't see why not. After all, Moldova *was* a long way away.

He thought of those images he'd seen, and he could not shake the intense fear they'd inspired.

As he approached Exeter he considered stopping for a piss. It was still a little over two hours home from here, probably longer today with the heavier traffic. A coffee and comfort stop was probably a good idea.

And there was Max.

Huw had already heard his phone pinging as missed calls came in, and then texts. He'd glanced at the screen and seen Max's name, and although he'd sent an email, he knew that he owed his client an explanation. He did not relish the thought of that call. But at the same time it felt so insignificant that he begrudged the time it would take.

He swung off the motorway into the large Exeter services car park.

Not every missed call was from Max. Kelly had tried him at 9.20, 9.40, and 10.33. There were no texts or emails from her, and he thought if it had been urgent she'd have texted him, *demanding* that he call as soon as possible. Yet something had made her try him three times. A need to talk, even without urgency.

He called her back. She snatched up the phone after one ring.

"Have you seen?" she asked.

"What?"

"Bucharest." Her voice broke, tinged with fear.

"What about Bucharest?" he asked, and his stomach dropped; his heart seemed to thump harder as if keen to escape.

"It's horrible, Huw," she said, and now he could hear the tears in her voice. "There are thousands dead, they're saying maybe tens of thousands. The city's burning. And those things... those things from the cave, that thing last night, there are so *many* of them. They're calling them *viespi*—that means wasps, but they're not, they're... They're killing *everything*."

They talked a little more, and then Huw ran into the service station to use the toilet. A group of young men stood laughing just outside the main doors, eating Cornish pasties and drinking coffee. Inside, a family at a table in the food court squabbled, young girls poking their tongues out while their parents turned from each other and fought wordlessly. People bustled, the shops were busy, and the only signs that anything was wrong were those in corners, the quiet people looking down at their phones, either alone or in small family groups. Some of them whispered. Most watched in stricken silence.

Huw was witnessing the beginning of a changing world. He could see those who knew the change was here, and others as yet blissfully unaware. He was jealous of the latter, but glad that he was one of those who knew.

Perhaps that gave him and his family a head start.

He hadn't said anything like that to Kelly, but he knew she wasn't stupid. She'd be thinking the same as him—*What happens if they come here?*

It was unlikely that something that lived in a cave in Moldova could threaten him in a motorway service station surrounded by truckers and stag parties, holidaymakers and business people, delivery men and coach parties of grey-haired folks moving around like flocks of sheep. It was preposterous.

Crazy.

All thoughts of calling Max now forgotten, Huw went back to his car and left for home.

Maybe it was him. He thought he was driving safely, concentrating on the road and cars around him, but perhaps he was more distracted than he thought. He had to brake more heavily than usual several times. Cars seemed clumped closer together than was safe, travelling faster than normal. There was an air of anxiety on the road, and the more he analysed it, the more Huw began to think it originated in his own car. He was dwelling on things, doomsdaying, and several times he snorted an empty laugh when he imagined Kelly telling him that.

But she was panicking, he thought. *She tried to call me three times. It's not just me.*

He looked around at other drivers. He travelled a lot, and knew that the insides of cars were strange places, like islands in the midst of an ocean. So many drivers thought that their metal and glass box was impervious to outside events. There were those who excavated their noses while driving in dense traffic, texted or updated Facebook on their phones, consulted papers or maps. And in his travels he'd seen much worse than that. The woman applying eye make-up, looking at herself in her rear-view mirror while travelling at ninety along the M5. The man leaning across the front seats to search for something in his glovebox, slouched so low down that it looked like no one was driving. He'd once seen a woman sitting astride a guy driving an old Capri, trying to hunch down so that he could see over her shoulder. He'd been so amazed at the sight that he'd put on some speed to follow the classic car, just to make sure he'd really seen what he'd imagined. The woman had grinned at him through the rear window.

Now, everyone seemed to be on their phones. Some were propped on dashboards, others clamped to ears. He glanced down at his own phone, tempted. But his one aim now was to get home.

And if anything drastic happened, anything more terrible than what was already happening in Bucharest and probably elsewhere, Kelly would phone him again.

Seventeen miles out of Exeter services Huw saw the first accident. A car had slewed from the road and bounced off a bridge strut, leaving its wing and bumper behind. A man and woman were stood by the side of the road, arms wrapped around themselves as they waited for help.

Seven miles on, a more serious crash. A lorry had crossed the breakdown lane and plunged over the embankment, slamming into the deep ditch and spilling its load of beer bottles and cans across a field. Several cars had stopped, and people were milling around the stricken vehicle. Huw slowed along with the rest of the traffic, but did not stop. There were enough people there to call for help.

He drove on. Sirens blared on the opposite carriageway

and police cars, an ambulance, and three fire engines powered down the fast lane.

Thirty miles later, he actually saw the result of the next accident in his rear-view mirror. A flash caught his attention, and when he looked he saw a blooming fireball rising a few hundred metres back, rolling in on itself, scorching the air and leaving a column of billowing black smoke behind.

"Jesus Christ!" he shouted. It held his attention for just too long, and when he glanced forward again he saw cars drifting across lanes. Holding the steering wheel so tightly that his knuckles cracked, he swerved around a campervan and drifted across the slow lane. His wheels struck the breakdown lane line, rattling and vibrating up through the car. Horns blared. Huw put his foot down and powered into the clear space ahead, and when he looked in his mirror again he saw several vehicles jockeying for position, settling eventually into a steady direction again. Way behind them the smoke continued to billow.

If he'd been behind that accident, he might never have been able to get home.

He considered calling the emergency services. *Not my problem,* he thought, shocking himself, because on any other day he would have *made* it his problem. But today was not any other day.

Huw felt a moment of pure anger at those careless drivers. He needed to reach his family! He had to get home, and how dare they—

But then he realised that someone might well be dead or dying on the road behind him.

"Fucking hell," he muttered. People were so wrapped

up with their phones; they were throwing caution to the wind. An air of desperation had settled over everything, and it was *not* just him, it was *not* only inside his car.

Everyone was doomsdaying today.

It took him two hours longer than normal to reach home. He was pleased at that, happy that he'd avoided any major hold-ups or accidents. Approaching the Severn Bridge, he'd passed a terrible crash on the opposite carriageway. A coach was involved, and several cars, and a petrol tanker, and people were rushing back and forth trying to help, driven back by the voracious flames. He'd tried not to look too closely. He'd told himself that the squirming shapes had only been flickers in the fire, nothing more.

Numbed, shattered, emotionally drained, and feeling as though during the drive he'd passed through some veil separating his reality from something not quite level and true, Huw pulled into his driveway and turned off the engine.

The front door opened and Kelly dashed out. He was glad it was still only three o'clock; they'd have an hour together at least before the kids arrived home from school. He could get up to date on the news, and they could talk about what to do. There would be the official word, of course—helplines for those worried about relatives and friends, government statements, soothing press releases designed to keep the population calm in the belief that everything was under control—but he and Kelly could put that to one side and consider the facts for themselves. Twitter and Facebook would be alight with events, and somewhere in that universe of comment and chaos would be kernels of truth.

But then his children appeared behind Kelly, standing in the open doorway. Jude looked edgy and excited. Ally looked afraid.

He opened the door and got out of the car.

"Oh, Huw," Kelly said. There was such hopelessness in her voice that his heart lurched and his stomach sank.

"How bad is it?" he asked. Kelly did not reply, and Jude's excitement gave way to a look the likes of which should never be seen on his young boy's face. His family's expressions gave the only answer he required.

He sat on the sofa on his own. Kelly and the kids were in the kitchen, and his mother-in-law was upstairs in her room. He heard the kettle boiling, a spoon dropped into a cup, and Kelly's soft voice. Her words were interspersed with those quiet moments that were an integral part of his family's mode of communication, as she signed to her daughter. Jude wasn't interrupting like he sometimes did.

They were giving him time to stare.

I should have checked my phone, Huw thought. But he remembered the accidents he had seen on the way home, all of them likely caused by people doing just that. No, he'd made the right choice.

It had given him a few more hours of uncertainty, at least. He'd known that things were changing, but had held out hope that the next day would bring them all back to normality.

He could not believe that any more.

5

A woman stands alone on a hillside.

It seems to be a park, with ordered planting, trimmed lawns, a statue in the background.

In the distance behind her, a swirling cloud containing countless *viespi* is visible above the unnamed city. There are distant sounds: explosions, gunfire, car motors, sirens, screams.

The woman stares at the camera. She is terrified.

She seems to hear or see something, goes to scream.

She squeezes her eyes closed and presses her index finger against her lips. *Shhhhh*.

Vesps fly past her, just one at first, then several more. Then a cloud.

They are a sickly yellow, their wings opaque and leathery, thin legs hanging like tendrils. As big as small cats. They have no eyes.

They have teeth.

One of them hits her, tumbles, then flies on.

She grimaces, squeezes her eyes shut even tighter.

She's shaking. The vesps fly away.

The woman's finger remains pressed so hard against her lips that they bleed. *Shhhhhhh*.

Clip from VidMe social website,
Friday, 18 November 2016

I watched Dad seeing the truth.

I stood silently in the living-room doorway holding his mug of coffee. He didn't know that I was there. My parents and friends often told me that I moved silently, sometimes almost ghost-like. Perhaps I moved so quietly because, in a way, I was always hoping to hear the faintest sound.

He sat on the edge of the sofa and leaned forward, elbows on knees, remote control in one hand, looking as if he were about to launch himself at the TV at any moment. His mouth hung slightly open. The little finger of his right hand twitched with his pulse, and I wondered how long he'd been driving to reach us.

I'd seen many of the clips and images before, but I watched again as Dad experienced them for the first time. There was professionally filmed footage from news reporters across Europe. Amateur film from mobile phones, much of it shaky, some of it grainy and flickering. Aerial shots from helicopters. Talking heads—experts from across the globe discussing what, why, where, how.

It all amounted to the same terrible, unbelievable, undeniable truth.

Bucharest burned. The ancient city now consisted of islands of buildings in swirling seas of fire. I'd seen this portion of film before, knew what was to come, could not look away. *The terrible fascination of death,* I thought. The aerial view tilted as the helicopter banked over the Dâmboviţa river, showing several boats floating freely and seemingly under no control. One of them had already struck the bank and stuck fast. Across its decks lay prone shapes, bodies piled on one another and splattered red. Things crawled across the bodies, feeding.

The vesps, I thought. That's what they were calling them now. *Viespi* were wasps, and though they were nothing like wasps—I'd seen a few close up; the images had been horrible, and they would be on screen again soon in this terrible loop of destruction the news channel was showing between updates of newer tragedies—the name "vesps" seemed to have stuck. There was nothing else, no name better, because no one really knew what they were.

The film seemed to blur then, the image speckled with spots as if the lens was suddenly dotted with sand or dust. The helicopter juddered. Then the first shapes flew in crazy spirals directly at the cameraman. He must have been strapped into the open doorway, because the first vesp hit the camera lens and knocked it to one side.

A confused, uncertain view of a man's panicked face, a waving hand, the thudding rotors seemingly staggered by the film's frame speed, and then more vesps streaking across the sky, wings flapping frantically as they converged on the aircraft.

The picture broke and returned several times as the camera plummeted towards the ground.

I watched Dad put his hands to his face and pull his cheeks down, as if to hold his eyes open in light of the terror.

The newscasters returned and spoke silently, then the next clip came on again. I'd seen this one, too, and I groaned. Dad turned and saw me, and I took him his coffee. He took it gratefully and held my hand, drawing me down to sit beside him. He hugged me tight. I enjoyed his smell, his warmth, his closeness. He felt safe, because that's what dads are for.

He turned on the subtitles, but I shook my head and he turned them off. It was bad enough just seeing it.

The caption said it was the view inside a shopping mall in Belgrade. Maybe it was a security camera or a webcam; either way it was a fixed, motionless view across a wide walkway and series of staircases and escalators in front of two large department stores. It didn't seem particularly busy; the shoppers seemed calm and unworried. A mother sat on a bench nursing a baby, a toddler sat beside her eating ice cream. A man stood close by playing a guitar, the instrument's case open before him and gleaming with change. Shoppers passed back and forth carrying bags, looking at mobile phones, talking, laughing.

Something happened off-screen that caught everyone's attention. Heads snapped around as if on strings. A couple of shoppers started to back away. One fat man turned to run and stumbled, slipping down a staircase on his behind. No one went to help, because no one really saw him.

The first vesp winged into view and slammed into the guitar man's chest, knocking him back against glass balustrade. He slapped at it with a strange grin on his face, almost embarrassment. Then his mouth opened in a scream as the thing clawed, thrashed, chewed, and blood spotted the white floor at his feet.

More vesps seemed to zero in on the man's cries, and soon he was smothered in the creatures. They were pale yellow and moist-looking, their leathery wings flapping faster than most birds'. I'd never seen anything like them, and it seemed no one else had either.

The mother hugged her baby in close, wrapping her

jacket around the child and reaching for her toddler. The young child shouted. A vesp flitted in at the left of the image, skimmed the floor, and powered up into the underside of the boy's jaw.

I closed my eyes, but I had seen this before, and remembered.

I kept my eyes closed, feeling my dad's reaction to the horror. He tensed, stopped breathing, and his arm held me even tighter. *He'll be seeing the clouds of those things now*, I thought. *The feeding. The blood pooled on the white floors, the man tipping back over the balustrade and disappearing with those things flying after him. The windows breaking.*

When I judged it was safe I opened my eyes again, and the newscasters were back. They looked harried and tired, and in the newsroom beyond the glass walling behind them people dashed back and forth, computer screens flickered, and phones were picked up and thrown back down. The man's tie was loose, and a film of sweat shone on his top lip. I was fascinated by that. Newsreaders had never seemed so human before.

There was more. Scraps of footage from Hungary, Romania, Bulgaria, all showing attacks or, in fewer cases, the results of attacks. People were on the move, fleeing westward. One scene showed a road full of refugees that must have been caught by a wave of vesps, and this time only select stills were aired. When that film had first emerged a couple of hours ago they had broadcast it all, and I would never forget the things I'd seen. So many bodies so badly mutilated, open to the world, steaming and glistening red, and all of them seemed merged with the vehicles and their belongings, forming one large, long dead thing that had once moved along the road.

A man in Croatia was transmitting from his apartment high in a tower block in Zagreb. It was a webcam feed, grainy and uneven, and he kept picking up his laptop to show the scenes beyond his window. There was a small balcony with a single seat, a dead potted plant and several empty beer bottles, but he did not open the doors. Instead he would hold the laptop against the glass, integral webcam aimed through the glass to what lay beyond. Zagreb also had its fires, and though nowhere near as bad as Bucharest, still they gave the city the look of a war zone.

Vesps flitted past his window. Sometimes they seemed to veer off at a tight tangent and disappear from view. Other times they flew in rough lines, like migrating birds following a leader. In the distance, close to a wide park where a lake glimmered in the afternoon sun, a great flock of the creatures twisted and turned in patterns that should not have been beautiful, but were. It was almost hypnotic.

The view tilted and became chaotic, and then the man appeared again. He was holding up a card with hastily scrawled words. He slipped the card away and showed another, then another, and then the first card again. He went through the process several more times. His eyes were wide, his face drawn and so grey that I wondered whether he'd plastered himself in ash. Then he tilted the laptop's lid to show the view deeper in the room behind him.

A woman and two children sat on a sofa. They had thick packing tape across their mouths, but their hands were free—they were silent of their own free will. The woman nodded at the camera.

When the view switched back to the newscasters, I picked up the remote control and switched on subtitles. I had not seen the Croatian man's footage before.

"...we'll get a more accurate translation later for you, but it seems that the man's written message reads..." The newscaster checked her laptop, frowned, then continued. "Noise brings them. Stay quiet. Stay alive."

I felt the rumble of Dad saying something, and then Mum, Lynne and Jude came into the room. But I kept watching the screen as they spoke, thinking about those words.

Noise brings them.

The vesps had come from beneath the ground. How there were so many, how they'd spread so far so quickly, these were things I couldn't know and it hurt my head just thinking about them. But it made sense that if they'd lived for so long in utter darkness, they were blind and hunted by sound.

Stay quiet. Stay alive.

Something else was happening on screen. The "Breaking News" logo remained, and the two newscasters had been handed cups of coffee. The woman was saying something and the subtitles were rushing to keep up, misspelled and missing words. But the gist was there.

"...news coming in of incidents in Slovenia and northern Italy."

I turned to look at my family. Lynne was shaking her head, saying, "Oh dear, oh dear." Mum hugged Jude. He was a bright kid, and his earlier excitement at these unusual events had given way to terror. He'd been crying.

My mother made sure I was looking, and then she spoke.

"We should talk about what to do."

We sat at the small table in the kitchen. There was no TV in the room, and Dad and Mum had left their phones face down on the worktop. Jude had opened some crisps and dropped them on the table, but instead of picking them up he was moving them around with his fingertip. Neither of our parents told him off.

Lynne had made a fresh pot of coffee, and hot chocolate for me and Jude. Watching the kettle boil gave us pause to gather our thoughts.

I said nothing. I was afraid to speak, because whatever was said next would move events onwards. And I was becoming so, so terrified that onwards might mean away from home.

Home was the only place where I felt totally safe. People sometimes said that they admired me for how I'd adapted and how I was determined to do things that were made more difficult by my condition. But sometimes I was also scared. The world often seemed bigger and wider now that I could no longer hear it, as if it could creep up behind me. Heavier and more malevolent. So after I'd spent time being strong and determined, there was always home to go back to.

"We can't leave," I said at last.

"I don't want to go anywhere!" Jude said. I only just picked it up on his lips.

"No one's leaving," Lynne said, signing as she spoke. In a family conversation like this it came naturally for them to sign for me. And I'd become used to anticipating who would talk next, analysing the dynamics of conversation and understanding it to a greater degree than anyone with functional hearing. Jude sometimes called me a witch. I called him a little shit. Equal scores, I reckoned.

"Let's talk about it sensibly," Mum said.

"There's nothing sensible about this," Dad replied.

Lynne tapped the table with her knuckles until we fell silent and looked at her. "We can't panic and overreact," she said. "But we can't ignore what's going on and not react at all. We have to do what Kelly says, Huw. Talk about it sensibly."

Huw shrugged, hands held out to both sides. *So?* he seemed to be saying. *Who's going to begin?*

"Won't the Queen tell us what to do?" Jude asked.

"…in her bunker," I caught Dad muttering.

"Jude's right," Lynne said. "We've been watching the news, that's all, and we know how sensationalist journalists can be. Twenty-four-hour news, I've always hated it. They can make a crisis out of a drama just to fill the day."

"You're saying this isn't a crisis, Lynne?" Dad asked.

"Not at all. I'm just saying we should wait. Hear what the authorities have to say."

"I'm amazed the Prime Minister hasn't been on already," Mum said, and I think Dad said something about a bunker again.

Jude flicked a crisp across the tabletop at me, then grinned. I couldn't help smiling back. However scared, he was a kid, and his attention was wandering.

"We should check other channels," I said, and Lynne smiled at me. I'd always thought of her as the strong one in our house. Since losing her husband when I was just a toddler, Lynne had lived a fiercely independent life, staying in their cottage in the Brecon Beacons, driving a 4×4 so that she could get about in the harsh winters, holidaying overseas alone. She had not once let my grandfather's death stand in the way of her dreams. Now almost seventy-five, since he'd been gone she had visited Egypt, Mexico, Morocco, and Canada.

Lynne was being stronger than ever now. I thought perhaps she might even take control.

"Yes, we need to know exactly what's going on," Mum said.

"We've seen!" Dad said. "You've seen more of this than me. Hasn't there been talk of… intervention? The military? Any discussion about what those things are?"

"It's all been scattered news reports and amateur footage," Lynne said. "The government's emergency… thingy, that was meeting last night."

"Cobra," I said.

"Yes, them. But there's been no official word."

"There must be soon," Mum said. "Jude, bring my laptop, will you?" Jude jumped to her words.

Dad touched my wrist, waiting for me to look at him. Then he signed, "Can you fetch me the atlas from the living room?"

I nodded. I knew what he wanted, and why. I was already trying to work out distances and times myself. *But it's still so far away*, I thought. *And there's the Channel. They'd never cross the English Channel, they couldn't. Could they?* I dashed into the living room, and as I passed the TV that had been left on with sound on mute, I caught sight of a face I recognised.

"Mum! Dad! There's a press conference!"

The rest of my family crowded around. Even Jude, no longer bored, hugged the laptop to his chest.

Mum said something to Dad and he put his arm around her shoulders, drawing her close.

Lynne picked up the remote, turned up the sound, and switched on the subtitles as the Prime Minister approached the microphone and lectern set on the street outside Number 10 Downing Street.

He looks tired, I thought. *And I've never seen him looking so glum.*

He shuffled some papers, tapping their edges to straighten the pile. Then he looked around at the assembled cameras, attempting a smile that turned into a grimace. He coughed. Several microphones and handheld recorders poked into the picture.

"By now…" the Prime Minister said, and he coughed again, holding his hand to his mouth. Someone appeared from out of picture and handed him a water bottle. He nodded thanks, took a drink, and seemed to compose himself. "By now you will all be aware of the events in eastern and southern Europe. Rumour and conjecture is widespread, both on the TV and Internet, including social media sites and independent news outlets. Overnight I chaired a meeting of Cobra, and all through last night and into today, my government and I have been in touch with our embassies overseas, and the governments of those countries affected.

"What we are certain of at this point is this: a swarm of creatures, not yet identified and of unknown origin, has been sweeping across several countries in Europe. They have caused widespread panic and, regrettably, many deaths. It appears that they attack any living thing other than those of their own species. There's evidence that they eat some of their victims, lay eggs in their flesh, and that these eggs have an accelerated birth rate, hatching within hours. The creatures' young are able to fly upon hatching. They eat their host. They multiply at an aggressive rate. Communication with infected areas is sporadic at best. Attempts to infiltrate infected areas have been mostly unsuccessful. The creatures…"

He coughed again, took another drink.

"It appears that they are blind, and they hunt by homing in on sound. Built-up locations, areas of dense population, are therefore worst affected. Death tolls are unknown, but several sources from Moldova, Romania and Ukraine have described them as 'catastrophic'."

There must have been questions shouted from the reporters, and the Prime Minister held up his hands to calm them down.

"Please," he said. "Please. Let me finish my statement and then I'll take questions. I have spoken to as many European leaders as I can, and I assure you of this: we are doing everything in our power to ensure that Britain remains safe. All military, police and other emergency service leave has been cancelled indefinitely. All public service leave is also cancelled. All foreign travel is postponed, and we are commencing a phased shutdown of all major air and sea ports. We are offering whatever help we can to those countries affected. Scientists are striving to find out more about this swarm… this plague… and we will find a way to stop them." He paused, and was immediately deluged with more questions. They came thick and fast, too quick for the subtitle service to list and type them out. The Prime Minister looked harried, glanced left and right as voices clamoured to be heard.

Someone appeared behind him and whispered into his ear. He tilted his head, and for a second I thought he looked like a little boy, a bullied kid being offered an easy way out. But then he seemed to remember himself. He shook his head and said something to his aide, then held up his hand.

"One at a time."

A question was asked.

"No, evacuation is not an option."

Another question.

"No, my government and I will not be seeking cover in any shelter. We will remain here in office, serving the country to the best of our ability."

Another.

"Yes, I saw that, and yes, the caving expedition is a possible source of these creatures. That is being investigated. But let me say…" He suddenly looked scared. He glanced back towards Number 10, where several aides stood huddled by the door, and a dozen security men kept a good watch on their surroundings. *It looks like he's seeking permission to say something more,* I thought. *But he's the Prime Minister!*

"Let me say," he continued, "the reports we have are… serious. These things—they've been called 'vesps' by the popular media, and that's as good a name as any—they hunt by sound. I've seen footage, heard first-hand accounts, read reports. They seek out noise, in the same way as other animals hunt by smell or sight. Helicopters that fly over the infected zones have been brought down. They're reproducing and hatching at a staggering rate, and they're *voracious*!"

He's gone off-script here, I thought, and sure enough his aides suddenly seemed nervous, glancing at one another until one of them stepped forward. She whispered something to the Prime Minister, but he ignored her. It was as if he didn't even know she was there.

"Honestly, we don't know much more than you." He stopped then, blinking into the camera lights and seeming to look much further. "We're doing everything we can. I'm being completely honest and open with you, and I promise that I'll be here, on the hour from now on, to give you any updates. God help us." He paused for a moment as if to say more, then turned and walked back towards Number 10. His aides were already fluttering around him. He looked like someone under attack.

"That wasn't what I expected," I said. I stood and turned, looking at my family so I could be part of any ensuing conversation.

"What were you expecting from the spineless idiot?" Mum asked.

"Kelly!" Lynne scolded. "Didn't you see? He wasn't the Prime Minister there at the end, he was a human being, just like us. Scared and confused."

"Much as I hate it, I agree with your mother," Dad said, smiling softly. "I think he's being as honest as he can be."

"He made me frightened," Jude said. "It's like a film, except it isn't."

"No evacuation," I said. That's what had unsettled me most. Awful though it was, the idea of moving, fleeing, seemed to be the only action we could take. I'd already been thinking things through. *We have an attic, but we can't stay up there for long, too small. No cellar. Could barricade one room, maybe, and...*

Memories of the old Cold War information films I'd seen came flooding back. Take down doors, form shelters beneath your stairs, stock up on canned goods, take a bucket for a toilet, make sure you have plenty of water, and a radio and spare batteries...

As if any of that could possibly have helped against an atomic bomb. It had been guff, hollow instructions designed to make the public think they could do something useful instead of just sitting there waiting to be killed. And to stop them running.

The last thing the country needed was millions of refugees streaming out of the cities.

"Nothing's safe," I said. "Nowhere. No one."

"What do you mean?" Jude asked, and it shocked me to see him crying.

"They hunt by sound, and where's quiet? Nowhere." *Only in my head,* I thought. *That's the only quiet place.*

6

There is evidence that the spread of the creatures popularly known as "vesps" is slowing. Contact has been made with all affected governments, and policies put in place. Great Britain is as prepared as it can be, and we have one distinct advantage over our European neighbours—we are an island. There is no evidence of the infestation crossing large bodies of water. Our message to you at this time is as follows:

1. Do not leave home. Mass migration is not the answer, and may impede the ability of military or emergency personnel to travel where required.
2. Continue monitoring the BBC News channels— television, online, and radio—through which all government statements will be released.
3. Do not panic. All necessary measures are being taken to combat the threat.

BBC News Emergency Broadcast,
Friday, 18 November 2016 (repeated hourly)

What a heap of fucking shit.
BBC Newscaster, Friday, 18 November 2016
(her final broadcast)

They needed to eat. Lynne had suggested that, and as she went about preparing a meal with Ally and Jude helping—Ally sensible and efficient, Jude instantly dropping a bag of dried pasta across the kitchen floor which Otis commenced to crunch on—Huw had to admit that the old woman was worth her weight in gold.

He had a strange relationship with Lynne. She annoyed the hell out of him sometimes, but he also loved her, and knew that she'd given Kelly just about the best upbringing anyone could hope for. When her husband Philip had died of a heart attack soon after Ally was born, she had barely stumbled. She was crying on the inside, she'd always told them when they asked how she was. Kelly had crumpled, Huw had been her rock, and Ally—still so young and demanding much of their time—had been her reason to pull through. But Lynne had sailed her own sea of grief and loneliness alone, only asking for rare help when the storms became too great. There were some who would call that stubborn and proud, and once Huw might have been one of them. But he also knew Lynne was a dignified woman.

She'd need that now. It was three weeks ago that she'd been told her cancer was terminal. She'd faced the news with her familiar stoicism, insisting that Ally and Jude not be told until she was ready to tell them herself. Lynne had also spent a long time quizzing the oncologist about managing her symptoms, and how her independence would be affected. She wanted to live in her own home as long as possible. It wasn't about being a burden on anyone—she knew that Kelly and Huw would have looked after her without a qualm, and to the best of their efforts—it was about being able to look after herself. Not misplaced pride, but dignity. Lynne had always lived on her own terms, and she intended to die the same way.

Such choices might now be taken from her.

"I can't believe this," Kelly said to Huw.

"Yeah." They were in the living room together, with the hallway door closed. "He looked scared! You never see him like that. Angry, sure, a lot of the time. Even when he tries to smile he looks angry. But it was almost as if he didn't want to be there."

"Would you?" Kelly asked. "With what's going on, it's no wonder he looked like a rabbit caught in headlights."

Huw sat beside her on the sofa, shoulders and thighs touching. They weren't very physical with each other any more. She usually dismissed it if he brought it up, said they had busy lives. It upset him sometimes. Made him think there was something wrong in their marriage when, in all other respects, they were tight. Maybe it was just a part of starting to grow old together. Whatever the reason, he took comfort from that contact now.

"So what do you think?" his wife asked. She leaned in against him, also taking comfort.

I think I'm not going to be like him, Huw thought. The Prime Minister had looked like a man who didn't know what to do. Someone scared to make choices, because of the impact his choices might have on the whole country.

Huw couldn't afford to let fear distort or confuse his actions. He had always been afraid, he was smart enough to realise that. But now that Doomsday might truly be here, he could still fear the worst, but had to start thinking the best.

"Map," Huw said. He stood and went to the bookcase, scanning the reference books on the lower shelf until he found the atlas he'd asked Ally to fetch. The TV had distracted her, all of them. But now was the time to work things out.

He sat back down in the armchair, apart from Kelly but able to open the atlas on the furniture arms between them. He flipped it open to the political map of Europe, suddenly shocked at his lack of geographical knowledge.

"Here," Kelly said, touching Moldova.

"Sure it was northern Moldova? Shit, I hardly knew it existed before today, and it's as big as Wales."

"Yep, somewhere close to a place called Edinet. Pretty certain I heard that."

"Right, so that was about six last night." He delved down into the magazine rack between the seats and fished out a pen, writing the place and time on the edge of the map.

"By six this morning there were incidents in Ukraine and Romania."

"And Hungary," Kelly said.

"Right." Huw tore a strip of paper from a magazine, placed it on the map's scale and marked some distances. Then he placed the paper spanning the northern tip of Moldova. "So that's... maybe four hundred miles."

"Twelve hours," Kelly said. "About thirty miles an hour."

"Look at you, Miss Maths," Huw said, but he was examining the map. It was chilling to think what might now be happening in these countries he was looking at, and which he knew so little about. Moldova. What the hell was Moldova known for? Had he ever seen anything about it on TV, read anything? It was a blue country on his map, roughly the size of Wales, and yet he knew nothing about it. Not its capital city, its currency, even its language.

"There can't have been that many of them down in the cave," he said.

"They say they breed quickly, grow fast."

"Like *Alien*."

"Huh?"

"Nothing." He'd said it as a joke but it didn't feel remotely funny.

"First mention of Bucharest was about ten this morning," Kelly said.

"Earlier. I was having breakfast at the hotel." Huw measured the distance. "Almost four hundred miles."

"Thirty, maybe forty miles an hour."

"Then this afternoon, 3 p.m., Austria and the Czech Republic." He measured. "Maybe eight hundred miles, twenty hours."

"So how far is Moldova from here?" Kelly asked softly. He looked up. She was scared, and beautiful. He wanted to protect her. He wanted to protect his whole family, though the weight was heavy, the pressure crushing. All the badness he'd spent much of his life fearing seemed to be settling around them now.

He measured. "Maybe thirteen hundred miles to the Channel, as the crow flies."

"The crow," Kelly said, and he knew that she was thinking of those pale, flying things. Perhaps the size of crows, but so much more deadly and terrifying. No one seemed to know what they were, but for Huw's purposes that did not matter.

"Couple of days' travel, if they keep up the same

speed of spread," he said. "So tomorrow evening they might hit the French coast."

"If nothing's done to stop them," Kelly said. "If the military don't have something. Gas, chemicals, or something. If no one finds a way to kill them, or if they don't die of natural causes. Sunlight, perhaps. If they've been in the dark for so long..."

"Too many ifs," Huw said. He sat back and stared at the atlas. He felt sick, the same way he felt when he watched people on TV free-climbing or illegally scaling tall towers.

"Fight or flight," Kelly whispered.

He reached for her hand, clasped it tight. They often jokingly said that they were parents now instead of husband and wife, but for Huw that joke had a sharp, sad edge. Romance was rare. They made love, they were a good, solid family unit, but though they loved each other he wasn't sure they were still *in* love with each other. It was never something that he'd say to Kelly, but he guessed she thought the same way. They were still together when many of their friends were not. They were still secure and comfortable. But so often he wished for more.

"I was thinking the same," he said. "If what they say is true—"

"About them using noise to hunt?"

"Yeah. Usk's a small town, but it's still noisy. We're surrounded by countryside, but... we're not remote. Where can you go where you don't hear traffic noise, or see signs of civilisation?"

Kelly frowned, looking at the wall. "Mid Wales. We go to Snowdonia."

"No," he said. "Not far enough. Not remote enough." *We're talking about running*, he thought. Actually vocalising it was making it real, and that was scary. This house, this home, had always been their castle, the place they retreated to during good times and bad. He'd tried to make sense of his parents' deaths here, and Ally's terrible injuries following the crash that had killed them. Kelly had mourned her own father within these four walls. This house was more than a home, it was part of the family. It held their history like layers of paint. The structure had heard the raised voices of arguments and the sighs of lovemaking, Jude's baby language changing and growing, Ally's words remaining even though she could no longer hear them herself. They could not leave it behind.

But inaction would be too tempting for too many people. *Let's wait to see what we're told to do… the Prime Minister says not to flee or clog the roads… they're saying it might end soon…*

Everything had changed too quickly for anyone to truly grasp what was really happening, or how to react.

"We have to make our own luck," Huw said. "You think that?"

"I think I don't want to leave my home."

"Neither do I. I really don't. But I'm afraid that if we stay here too long, we might regret it when the time comes to leave. We might get caught up in the rush, instead of having a head start."

Kelly looked around their living room. Evidence of their life decorated it—photographs of their children, a painting they'd bought together in Newquay, a plant that they'd been given before Ally was born, books they had read and talked about. They had made love on the sofa and drunk wine watching TV and painted the walls together. The room was warm with them.

"So where?" she said, voice barely a whisper.

"Red Rock."

"Your parents' old place? We sold it."

"Doesn't matter. It's huge, and the people who bought it were rich London types. Holiday home. I doubt they'll be there, and even if they are…" He waved it away. It didn't matter. Red Rock was in Scotland, a place called Galloway Forest Park. It was a location his parents had valued for its peace and remoteness.

It was perfect.

It was also almost four hundred miles away by road.

Kelly was nodding slowly.

"We'll be fine," Huw said. "A quick jaunt up there, and it'll be over before we arrive."

"You said you never wanted to go there again."

"Yeah, well." He remembered the place and everything that had happened there, and felt sick to his stomach. But such things no longer mattered. They felt petty. Family squabbles, that was all.

"We'll need food, supplies," Kelly said, ever the organiser.

"That's it? You agree?"

"I think so, yes," she said. "I think we have to go." She leaned across the chair arms and held his head, pulling him closer and kissing him. "We'll be fine. We'll look after them together."

Huw's eyes burned. He nodded, stood, slammed the atlas closed.

"I'll go into town, get some stuff together."

"Mum's cancer..." Kelly said, and she really started to cry then. Huw leaned over and held her, and she buried her face against his shoulder. Three deep sobs, and then she pulled back again.

"No time for this," she said, wiping her eyes.

No time, Huw thought. When he pictured Red Rock's intimidating facade, and thought of the distance they had to cover, he felt sick all over again.

They lived a ten-minute walk from the centre of town. Usk was really more of a large village than a town, though its main road was lined with shops and a couple of pubs, a hotel, several takeaways, a bank, and a square surrounded with more shops and pubs. There were several hundred houses surrounding these central areas, lining roads leading out from the village and with one large estate huddled against the hills to the south. It had a strong community spirit; it was a good place to live, to raise a family. It was safe.

Today it felt strange. Huw took his car and went on his own, refusing Ally's help, telling her she needed to stay at home and keep Jude occupied and calm. Jude was bright, and soon after watching the Prime Minister give his unsettled, jittery statement, Huw's son had started misbehaving. He was growing scared and confused. Huw could relate to that.

He and Kelly had yet to have an open discussion with their family about their intentions, but they all seemed to know a decision had been made.

It was usually a two-minute drive to the main street, but for a Friday afternoon, it was incredibly busy. It took

Huw several minutes to pull out of their small estate onto the main road, and then he was almost instantly in a line of traffic queuing to edge out onto Usk's main street. The other drivers seemed edgy—cars inching forward when there was no movement ahead, horns blaring, a small shunt which caused a brief delay. Huw saw several people he knew driving away from town. He raised a hand in greeting. Some waved back, a couple of others did not. They seemed intent on the road.

Should have walked, he thought. It felt so strange. Busy as Christmas except with very little good cheer.

It was almost dark, and streetlights complemented the many vehicle headlights to cast dancing shadows along the road's edges. When people walking into town began to overtake him, he pulled into the doctor's surgery car park and left the car. He glanced back at the surgery several times as he walked away, expecting someone to open the doors and tell him he couldn't park there, this was for patients only, he'd have to move on. But the building seemed deserted, and he chuckled at his concern.

"Mad," he muttered. "This is all fucking mad. I must have eaten something dodgy at dinner last night. Wake up, it'll be a dream." But he walked, did not wake up, crossed a side street, looked down it and saw some kids playing football and a guy carrying in shopping from his parked car. He turned to look at Huw. He knew the man enough to nod hello—saw him at the school gates sometimes, if he was ever home to take Jude or pick him up from school—and he nodded now. After a pause, the man returned the gesture. From this far away Huw could not make out his expression.

He walked on. To his right the line of traffic continued. Engines revved, fingers tapped steering wheels. Most cars had only one person inside, but a couple contained whole families, boots packed to the ceiling and some with roof pods attached. One had an old couple in the front and their three beagles in the back. He knew some of the drivers, but he kept his head down and walked quickly, concentrating on his feet, trying not to step on the cracks in the pavement.

"Huw!" He knew that voice immediately. It was Glenn, one of their closest friends. Huw paused and turned, and Glenn ran along the pavement to catch him up. He was what Kelly called a "proper bloke"—lived on his own, had a succession of girlfriends and fuck buddies, was fit and athletic, a rugby player, a karate black-belt. Good-looking. Charismatic, funny, kind. Huw joked that he loved to hate him.

"Hi, mate," Huw said.

"What the fuck?" Glenn asked. He looked at the traffic, the darkening sky, and held out his hands as if expecting rain.

"Yeah, what the fuck."

"I was just finishing off a job out at old woman Florrie's place, needed to get home sharpish, got a hot dinner date with Maxine from The Swan tonight. And now… this? What, butcher Ben got a sale on or something?"

Huw knew that he was joking, and could see that his friend was troubled. He owned a small but thriving plumbing firm, was gruff and sometimes crude, but he was also sensitive and intelligent, and a loyal mate. Had been for many years. Huw had always considered himself rich in friends, and right now he felt like hugging Glenn.

"Seen the news?"

"Yeah, of course."

Huw started walking again, and Glenn walked with him.

"Where you parked?"

"Left the van back by the river."

"We're going north."

"Huh?"

Huw glanced across at his friend. "How much have you seen?"

"What, about those things in Moldova?" He shrugged.

Mind the crack, mind the crack, Huw thought, looking down at his feet. He hadn't done this since he was a kid. *Step on a crack, break your mother's back.* It was stupid, but he also knew it was a form of avoidance.

"Thought you weren't home till tomorrow?"

"I saw people dying today, mate."

"Yeah. Rough."

"I mean in real life," Huw said. "Accidents on the motorway. A coach, a petrol tanker. People checking their mobiles. It's serious. I mean… it's *really* serious. People are scared. Those accidents haven't even appeared on the news. Everything's in turmoil, and if those things keep moving at the same speed, they'll hit the Channel tomorrow evening."

They walked in silence for a while. As they passed the vehicles Huw heard the rumbles of radios inside, words never quite clear but the tone of the presenters' voices sombre, serious. He glanced to his right once or twice and saw drivers and passengers facing ahead, their expressions the same. Even the few kids he saw in the backs of cars were still and silent. It was spooky.

"You serious?" Glenn asked. "You're going?"

Huw paused and grabbed his friend's arm. They were standing outside the Plump Duck, a pub they'd been drinking in since they were teenaged friends. Glenn had punched Huw in the back bar when they were seventeen, a drunken fight over a lost game of pool. Huw had had his first blowjob in an empty upstairs function room late one Saturday night. All through their twenties and thirties the Plump had been a fixture, even though its owners had changed a dozen times in the past twenty-five years. It was a place rich in memories, and Huw couldn't figure out why it now seemed so sad.

Perhaps because he might be seeing it for the last time.

"We're going north," he said again. "Scotland. My folks' old place."

Glenn half-smiled as if it were a joke.

"I mean it," Huw said. "Come with us."

"You're really serious," Glenn said.

"I'm getting food and supplies. Kelly's getting the kids packed and ready. Lynne's been staying with us, so she's coming too. You've heard how these things hunt? They home in on sound?"

"Yeah, Florrie was muttering on about that."

"So we're going somewhere quiet."

Glenn looked around at the traffic queue crawling slowly into town. Then over Huw's shoulder at the pub, perhaps sharing the same memories. "I just came in to get some steaks, spuds, few bottles of wine. Maxine's hot after wine. And I need a shower."

"Glenn!" Huw said. "Really. Think about it, okay? Please?" He started walking, feeling vaguely ridiculous, then stopped again. "You still got those shotguns?"

Glenn laughed. "What, you want to borrow them? Protect yourself against the mad masses?"

"You could bring them with you," Huw said. He went on ahead of Glenn, waiting for his friend to catch up. They walked the rest of the way in silence, and by the time they reached the main road, Huw was starting to think this might be a wasted journey.

The street was rammed with traffic. A truck and a car had collided outside the post office, blocking the road in both directions. The drivers were arguing about whose fault it was.

"I've got to go the grocer's," Glenn said. "Huw... walk back to the cars together? Meet you here in twenty minutes? Be good to talk it through."

"Yeah," Huw said. "Got your phone, just in case?"

Glenn nodded. He didn't ask "Just in case what?" and Huw didn't elaborate.

Glenn headed along Usk's main street, weaving through people on the pavements and dodging into the road now and then. Huw watched him go. *The traffic's this bad because of the accident,* he thought, and there was something comforting in that. Not because of panic buying. Not because hundreds of people were having the same idea as him and Kelly.

He passed between waiting lines of vehicles and crossed the road, turning the corner by the bank and entering the village square. It was bustling, and there was something strange about the movements of people, the atmosphere, that took him a while to perceive. Then he saw it, and really it shouldn't have troubled him so much. Shouldn't have been a surprise.

Everyone was moving. There were lots of people in the square, but unlike on a normal late Friday afternoon when groups of people might mill around chatting, sit outside the little arts cafe drinking coffee under the patio heaters, stand by the small car park waiting for lifts or simply passing the time, none of these people stood still. Many walked on their own, a few moved in pairs or small groups. Heads down. Bags clasped in their hands.

He and a teacher from Jude's school exchanged glances. Huw smiled and half-raised a hand, but by then she had already turned away and skipped across the opposite pavement, disappearing behind the corner cafe and along the road beyond.

One old woman sat outside the cafe, hands resting on the walking stick propped before her, a bemused expression on her face.

Huw crossed the square and approached the butcher's shop that stood two doors along from the cafe. He caught the old woman's eye—he'd never known her name, but saw her sometimes tending the flowers in the local churchyard—and smiled. She smiled back and raised one clawed hand in greeting. He was afraid that she was going to wave him over, but she only watched as he neared the butcher's.

It was closed. He didn't waste time wondering why, diverting instead back across the square to the grocer's on the opposite corner. It was an old shop, owned by the same family for over forty years, and Huw used to buy sweets from the current owner's father. Matt stood in the doorway now, arms crossed and a slightly dazed look on his face.

"Huw," he said, nodding.

"Afternoon, Matt." The older man did not step aside to allow Huw access. "So… you open?"

"Not any more," Matt said. "Not unless you want washing powder, greeting cards, toilet rolls, that sort of stuff. Food's gone. Even the pet food's gone."

Huw raised an eyebrow.

"Sold out!" Matt said, standing aside at last. "Best day's business I can remember. I'm closing up early, off to the Plump for a swift one before Margaret realises. You be there this evening?"

"What?" Huw asked. He looked inside at the bare shelves. The shop was almost unrecognisable.

"Pub," Matt said.

"No. No, I won't be there tonight. Thanks, Matt." He turned to leave.

"Don't bother with Jim's place down the road, either. Last I heard they were as empty as me."

"Right," Huw said. *This is mad*, he thought. *Insane. Crazy.* But of course, it was not. This was Britain. If the Met Office forecast three inches of snow, people stormed the shops to buy up all the bread and milk they could lay their hands on. Over Christmas when shops were shut for a day—sometimes even two—the bulk-buying madness beforehand was laughable.

He shouldn't have been surprised. He and Kelly couldn't have been the only ones who had decided to take positive action.

Huw walked back across the square and passed the old woman outside the coffee shop.

"Busy today," she said. "Nobody's got time to sit and chat with me. Have you got time?"

Huw looked into the cafe and saw a young girl behind

the counter, leaning back against the worktop and using her phone. She had headphones in. She frowned, pouted.

"I'm sorry," he said to the old woman.

He had to get home. They'd pack what they needed, leave, and pick up some food on the way. He felt bad turning his back on the woman. He called Kelly as he went, pleased to hear her voice, and told her what was happening in the town.

"It's still spreading," she said. It was all he needed to hear.

"Pack whatever you can," he said. "I'm going to try to get some cash out, then I'm coming home. I saw Glenn, asked him to come with us."

"Good idea," she said, and she sounded pleased. He was relieved. He'd worried about what she might say. "Be home soon."

"I will. Love you."

The bank's cash machine was empty, and it had closed for the day.

Even though Huw was back at their meeting place early, Glenn was already there. He looked pale, scared.

"Mark Francis and a guy I didn't know were fighting in Jim's," Glenn said. "I think it was over food."

"Fighting?"

"Fists, feet. Blood on the floor."

"Fucking crazy," Huw said.

"Maxine called me," Glenn continued. "Said there's been plane crashes. A few. She sounded confused."

Huw only nodded. He'd lived in Usk most of his life, but it was starting to feel like a strange place.

On the way back to where they'd parked their vehicles, they walked against the flow of traffic, looking into every car and van and seeing the people sitting there, impatient, scared. Huw was already worrying about what state the roads north would be in.

"Can we meet at your place?" Huw asked. Glenn lived in a nice house in the country. He'd built half of it himself. "Maybe you should bring Maxine."

Glenn looked dazed. "When we spoke, she said she was getting the basement ready with her folks. She's staying."

Huw nodded. "So you'll come? Your place, an hour?"

"Yeah," Glenn said. "Right. I'll dig out the shotguns."

1

The man is in tears. Distraught. Bereft. I have never seen such human misery. It sends a chill through me. He's in a small room lined with photographs, clothes piled on one chair, a blank TV in the corner. It's a family room, but he is without family. The scrolling text across the bottom of the screen, beside the BBC News 24 logo, reads, "Daniel Thornson, Austrian correspondent, live from Vienna".

The man stands and turns to the double doors. He opens them. (There are no subtitles, but I do not believe that what he says, what he screams, could ever be translated.)

It takes fewer than ten seconds for the first of the vesps to hit him.

The transmission is broken.

Eyewitness Online, Friday, 18 November 2016

"I'm not leaving without Otis." That was it. I would not have it any other way, and I turned my back on Dad. It was unfair, even cruel, to use the fact of my deafness against him, and I felt wretched doing so. But there really was nothing to discuss.

If we *had* to leave home, Otis was going with us. He

was one of the family. I whistled softly and the dog, who'd been sleeping in his bed in the kitchen, sauntered in, completely unaware of the tension.

I looked out at the garden. It was dark and there wasn't much to see, just the weak glow of solar lights around the patio area and silvery moonlight reflected from the greenhouse. I also saw my parents reflected in the window. I could just make out that they were talking—Mum reached out and touched Dad's arm, and he stepped in close and hugged her. That brief, unexpected sharing of comfort was a surprise, because I wasn't used to seeing them so affectionate. I turned around, but for a few seconds my parents still seemed to be on their own.

Mum looked at me. "Dad's right," she said. "The car's not big enough."

"So leave Jude behind!"

"Ally, don't be—"

"I'm lost without Otis," I said. "You know that, Mum. Dad."

I saw the moment when Dad relented. His expression didn't change noticeably, but the tension in his shoulders lessened, and his left arm around Mum relaxed a little.

"He'll be in the boot," Dad signed. "Lynne will be in the back with you and Jude."

I nodded.

"We'll need the pod for the roof," Mum said. She wasn't signing, but I picked up most of the words by lip-reading. "I've got clothes ready for all of us, and Mum and Jude are in the kitchen getting some food together. So… what was it like?"

"Busy," Dad said. He looked at me and smiled. Clicked

his fingers, scratched Otis's head when the dog went to him. "People are panicking. It's scary. We need to take all the food we have; the shops are already sold out."

"All of them?" I asked, shocked.

"The ones I checked. Glenn's coming with us, too." Dad turned away and said something that made Mum open her eyes wide. I looked from the window again. It had been a deliberate exclusion, and I tried to not mind.

My favourite time of year was upon us. Several days earlier there had been a windy, stormy night, and the following morning a carpet of leaves had fluttered across the garden, gathering in piles against the garage and fence. I loved the colours of autumn, the textures, the smell of bonfires and fireworks in the air, the feel of leaves crumpling beneath my feet when we walked Otis.

But now there was something different about the garden. It was no longer a safe place.

Otis nuzzled my hand, and I turned around to find my parents looking at me.

"Go and grab anything else you want to take," Mum said. I had to ask her to repeat herself, because my eyes were watering. I only noticed when I couldn't lip-read properly.

"When are we leaving?" I asked.

"As soon as we can," Dad said. "Meeting at Glenn's. Come on, Ally. Hustle." He tried to smile, but there was no humour in it.

I scratched Otis behind the ear, then stood and hurried through to the hallway. Jude was there, sitting on a suitcase. He was concentrating on his iPod Touch and I didn't disturb him. Next to him was my own suitcase, packed with clothes Mum had plucked from drawers and wardrobes without really thinking. We'd need shoes, coats. And I'd need books and toiletries.

I started to shake. It was a strange feeling, but I could do nothing to shrug it off. My jaw rattled, scalp crawled, limbs shook, and I had to grab hold of the staircase to prevent myself from slipping to my knees.

Jude looked up and smiled at me. "We'll be okay, Ally," he said. "We're going on an adventure!"

I nodded and waited for the shaking to subside before going upstairs. I was afraid that this adventure had already begun.

In my room I turned on the TV while I was grabbing stuff Mum had left behind. But I didn't even pick up one item before becoming transfixed by what I saw. And I didn't need to read the streaming subtitles to know that I was witnessing something terrible and world-changing.

It was a piece of film perhaps two minutes long. I turned on just in time to catch the shocking finale, and then the BBC News channel repeated it. Across the bottom of the screen a banner read, "Vienna, Austria".

Did I just see that?

The city appeared in a view from above. The camera was moving slowly, so I assumed it was on board a helicopter. Directly below I could see roads jammed with traffic, and the camera zoomed in and down so that people could just be made out, filing out of the city like ants following scent trails to safety.

Did I really see that?

The view changed again, and in the distance was a

skyline I would not have expected of Vienna—skyscrapers, modern glass and metal buildings, and a wide, ship-like structure that might have been a sports stadium. Beyond, smoke rose from fires that were mostly out of sight.

Because if I did see that, how can this scene change so quickly into—

A cloud swept across the city. It originated behind the skyscrapers, manifesting from the drifting clouds of smoke beyond, and seemed to swell around and over the buildings like a slow-motion tidal wave. Pale white, smeared yellow in places, it was opaque, spreading across the city and blurring the view, as if a special filter had been used. But I knew otherwise, because I had seen this before.

It was them, but in numbers so vast that my brain couldn't comprehend.

The view shimmered for a few seconds, then, when it levelled again, the helicopter the cameraman was filming from had tilted sharply to escape the approaching storm. Two dark objects streaked across the sky below, shades across the city, and they unleashed streaks of smoke that blossomed into expanding splashes of fire, exploding high above the ground and searing gaps in the swarm of vesps. Two more aircraft arced across the upper part of the picture, unleashing their own ordnance before disappearing from the screen. Their bombs seemed to explode lower down, and I caught a glimpse of fire boiling between buildings, queues of traffic consumed.

I know what's to come, I thought, but I could not turn away.

Even as the jets disappeared from view the gaps they had blasted in the clouds of vesps were all but gone. The creatures came on, sheets of them dipping down across the city, others spreading quickly in from the distance. Far below, another explosion bloomed briefly, soon lost amidst the blurring effect of the tide of creatures.

The helicopter shuddered, the image shook.

Close now, I thought. *It can't be long until—*

And then I saw the end of the footage, the several-second clip I'd walked in on two minutes before. The clouds closed on the helicopter. The cameraman fell back, dropping the camera, closing the door, his pale face screaming silently as the camera rolled to the rear of the cabin and jammed there, showing the window in the aircraft's side door darkening as yellow, fleshy bodies and leathery wings slammed against it.

The window broke. A tumble of vesps poured in.

The view stirred sickeningly, and then the picture snapped to black.

Two news presenters stared from the screen, seemingly speechless. One of them touched her ear, the other kept glancing at a small laptop screen in front of him.

I turned the TV off. *They're bombing them now. Even above the cities they're trying to bomb them, and there are so many. How can you kill so many?*

I looked around my bedroom and felt a sudden, shattering sense of sadness. This was the place where I felt most at home and protected, my place of safety. It reminded me of those bedrooms I sometimes saw on TV or read about in books, kept by parents exactly as they had been when their child disappeared or was killed years before. It was an old room filled with things that suddenly didn't seem important. My CDs, books, make-up, posters, trophies.

None of it mattered any more.

I'd just seen people dying on TV. Why would I need make-up? How could I even be considering taking a book with me?

I left my bedroom without a backward glance. Otis was waiting at the top of the stairs, head down and ears drooping.

"It's okay, boy," I said, but his ears barely lifted. Maybe he knew the truth.

We left the house an hour later. Dad had fitted the car's roof pod, and Mum stood on the door sill and filled it as we passed things up to her. Mostly food and bottles of water. Dad shoved one big suitcase into the boot and I almost objected. Otis usually went in the boot of the estate car, and because he was such a big dog we rarely put anything in there with him. But this was no normal trip. And I had insisted that the dog come along.

Sitting in the car on the driveway—Mum and Dad in the front, Jude sandwiched between me and Lynne in the back, Otis standing and alert in the boot—I had to wonder whether we would ever see our house again. I saw that our parents were talking, and I felt the rumble of Jude's voice where our arms touched. Mum turned around to answer him.

"Everything's going to be fine," she said.

As we left the street, I looked down at my mobile phone. I'd sent Lucy a text telling her what was happening, but she had yet to reply. She went swimming with her family every Friday evening, but I couldn't believe that they had done so today.

Driving along the short street, however, I realised how differently everyone was handling the unfolding tragedy. The Pritchards three doors down already seemed to have left, both cars absent from the driveway and curtains closed, no lights on inside. The Coopers were still at home—I could see their father in the living room, and two bedroom lights were on upstairs. I liked Mr Cooper; he'd given me sweets when I was a kid and did the same for Jude now.

I started to cry.

"I don't want to go," I said. I caught Dad's eye in the rear-view mirror but couldn't see what he said. My grandmother reached over Jude and tapped my knee, trying to offer comfort. But my little brother was crying too, probably because I was, and I could feel Otis's breath on my neck where he rested his head sadly on the seat.

I didn't say any more, and neither did anyone else. None of us wanted to go, but there was nothing to debate. Our course of action was set, and all I could do now was wonder whether it was even worthwhile.

I leaned against the window and watched everything I knew pass by.

As we reached Glenn's big country house—Dad sometimes said he must rattle around in there, but Mum said there were always women to soften the blow—the phone vibrated in my lap. I snatched it up and saw a text from Lucy.

You're really going to Scotland?

Yep. All of us. Mum and Dad think it's for
the best.

Didn't tell me you were going on hols this
week. What about school?

I blinked at the message. Lucy's apparent ignorance
and lack of concern washed a wave of doubt over me.
But now that we'd taken action, left home, everything
I'd seen weighed heavy and real on my mind, and that
wave soon receded.

My family had left the car. Mum and Dad spoke with
Glenn, while Jude kicked a ball around the large floodlit
patio area. Lynne leaned against the car, looking out
over the fields.

Not a holiday. We're getting somewhere safe.
You seen what's happening?

I hit send, and there was no immediate response.
I checked the message had been sent. Sat there. Otis
nuzzled my ear and I reached back to stroke his head.
I felt him whining, and I whispered kind words to
settle him.

Glenn and Dad seemed to be arguing, but I couldn't
see what was being said.

My phone vibrated, and Lucy had sent,

Yeah.

So we're getting away from it. They might

reach England tomorrow evening, Mum and
Dad reckon.

There's nothing to worry about.

That what your folks are telling you?

Lucy didn't answer. I waited for a minute or two, but
there was no response. Maybe I was scaring my friend.
Or maybe Lucy was drying her hair, dancing around her
room, oblivious and ignorant to what might come.

The door opened, startling me, and Mum appeared
beside me.

"We're waiting here for a bit," she said.

"Why?"

"Glenn's decided he doesn't want to leave."
Mum shrugged. I guessed that if I could hear, I'd sense
a quake in her voice. I hated seeing Mum scared, and
I climbed from the car to stand beside her.

It was hardly surprising that Glenn didn't want to go.
His house was beautiful, and most of his three acres of
land was given over to a smallholding. He had a dozen
lambs approaching slaughter age, geese, chickens,
rabbits, and three big bounding dogs, probably now
locked away in their large kennel. A year ago I had spent
a few weeks over the summer helping with Glenn's
animals, and he'd paid me to come over every day to
feed and tend them. But one day the largest goose had
gone for me. I'd been searching for eggs—a goose-egg
omelette was a real treat—and I hadn't heard the
trumpeted warning, the pattering feet. The monster
pecked and prodded at me even as I ran and leaped the

fence, and I'd been left with several dark bruises and one bleeding wound on my behind. A trip to the doctor and a tetanus injection had followed, and while I saw the funny side, I'd decided that my time with geese was over. Jude had laughed for a whole evening.

If Glenn came with us, who would tend the animals?

Dad and Glenn were walking slowly across the large gravelled driveway towards the house, talking animatedly.

"The vesps will kill the animals anyway," I said.

Mum only squeezed my hand.

"Glenn!" I called. Dad and Glenn paused and turned around. "The vesps will kill all the animals! You can't keep them quiet. And they'll kill anyone still here with them."

Dad said something, but he was too far away for me to read. I turned to Mum.

"Glenn's brother Rudy and his family live in Switzerland," Mum said. "He's watching on TV."

Sad, I walked off to join Jude kicking the ball around the big patio. When I glanced back at Lynne, she was leaning against the car and looking out across the fields, a pained expression on her face. She seemed to be breathing heavily.

"Lynne?"

"Go and play," Lynne said, then she looked away. She seemed to be struggling to control her expression, standing tense and straight as if defying whatever tried to twist her up. She was in pain. Something was wrong, I had suspected it for a while, and now it was just another shard of fear piercing my heart.

Everything was changing, everything was going bad.

8

Oh no, that's not correct at all. We've had plenty of contact with people inside the infested areas. I myself have spoken to our embassy staff in Chişinău. They're barricaded inside. They're surviving. The idea that all those areas exposed to the infestation have been swept clean of any living thing is rumour. These things, these so-called vesps, are dangerous animals, not... not monsters. Deadly, yes, but blind. Stay hidden, stay quiet, and they will pass you by.

(Non-subtitled question)

Er... no, we've not yet heard of any military response that has had significant results.

(Non-subtitled question)

You'll understand that because of security reasons, no, I can't outline any military response that the UK is preparing.

(Non-subtitled question)

That is ridiculous scaremongering, and at a time like this, people who spread rumours of apocalypse, people who start shouting about the end of the world... they should be arrested. They *will* be arrested.

(Non-subtitled question)

Under the Terrorism Act. Or something else. I'll pass an emergency Act, if needs must. Listen, we're facing—

(Non-subtitled interruption)

No, not martial law. We're facing something shattering, but it's something we have to face together. All of us. Britain has survived worse than this.

Prime Minister's statement, 6 p.m.,
Friday, 18 November 2016

In the end, Glenn turned off the TV himself. He'd tried to contact his brother and family in Switzerland by phone, but there was no connection. He called the helpline for the service provider, but the tone was constantly engaged. He buzzed his family over the Internet, but the Skype and FaceTime calls went unanswered.

Saying nothing, he walked through the large kitchen and went down into the cellar to collect his shotguns. Huw had seen the tears in his eyes but said nothing. He had a complex relationship with Glenn, although he guessed most of the complexity was on his own side. Though they were good friends, he saw the man as many things he would never be. Glenn was fit and excelled at sports, handy with his hands, effortlessly confident around women, and the sort of character who lit up a room. Huw had an element of all those aspects, but was superior in none. Glenn probably didn't even recognise that fact, and that was just one more thing about him that made Huw feel insecure—his complete confidence. He was at ease with himself and with life, and though irrationally jealous of that, Huw couldn't help loving the guy.

Huw continued stacking bags of food by the open back door.

"Maybe they're dead," Glenn said from behind him. He stood at the open cellar door, two shotguns in cases slung over his shoulder. They suited him. Of course they did.

"There's nothing about Switzerland on the news," Huw said, realising how lame that sounded.

"Yeah," Glenn said. He blinked a few times, then shrugged the guns higher on his shoulder. "Yeah, okay. Sorry. I'm fine now. Come on. Let's get the fuck out of here." He snatched up a couple of heavy holdalls and edged sideways through the back door.

"You're sure about this?" Huw asked.

Glenn sighed. "Maxine. Jesus, if you saw the things she could do with…" He laughed. "Yeah. I am sure, now. It's the sensible thing to do and I can try Rudy again when we're on the road."

"The animals—"

"Are animals. And Ally was right." Huw could never get used to the idea that Glenn's livestock was reared for slaughter, but Glenn called him a hypocrite and suggested he become vegetarian. Huw knew that his friend had a farmer's outlook, but he was a product of the consumer age. Meat was prepared food in sealed packets, not animals with characters, gambolling and eating and sleeping.

"We'll be back soon," Huw said.

"You think so?"

They packed Glenn's Land Rover in silence. Kelly and Lynne stood chatting, and Ally and Jude were kicking a football around the garden, laughing. That almost broke Huw's heart. They were just kids, even Ally, and seeing them playing made him want to scoop them up and hold them tight, protect them in any way he could.

But that's what he *was* doing. Protecting them, in the only way he knew how. And he realised then just how glad he was that Glenn was coming with them.

They left the big house at almost 6 p.m., Huw leading the way in their Mazda. On any normal day he would have reckoned on a relaxed ten-hour drive with a couple of stops for toilet breaks and food.

But this was not a normal day.

"Twenty-four hours," Kelly said, and Huw glanced across at her in the passenger seat. She was examining her phone, the light from the screen revealing how drawn she looked and giving her face a terrible grey tinge. "Maybe less," she muttered.

"Huh?"

"Seems to be spreading faster." She didn't look up from the phone. Huw resisted the temptation to glance at the screen and looked ahead instead.

Once they were away from Usk, the roads seemed only slightly busier than normal. Huw had already started to wonder whether the gridlock in the town had been more due to the accident in the main street than any sense of panic or mass migration. There were the empty shops, true, but it was more likely that people were huddled in their own homes than pouring out onto the roads. That's what the authorities had been telling people—*Stay at home, stay safe*. And at times like this, most people would do as they were told.

To begin with, at least.

So why was Huw running?

He'd played this question over and over in his mind in the hour since they'd left Glenn's house. Glenn's big, secure house, where they could have stored enough food and water to last for weeks, which was large enough for all of them to exist together reasonably comfortably. And although safety was the priority for all of them, his thought processes were rarely straight and defined, and he realised that this decision boiled down to one factor: Ally. He'd almost lost her once before and he was not prepared to risk that again. He knew that Kelly felt the same way. Their protectiveness of their children had manifested in very different ways since the accident. Kelly wanted to wrap Ally and Jude in cotton wool, keep them in sight at all times, not let them do anything risky, and generally be there to protect them, standing between them and any potential danger like a royal food-taster ready to take the poisoned bite.

With Huw it was different. He still felt an aching, almost agonising need to make sure no harm came to the children, but he also understood the concept of freedom. He wanted them to live good, great lives, have whatever opportunities he and Kelly could give them. He wanted them to live, not simply exist, and Ally's near-death and subsequent disability only amplified that.

For Huw and Kelly, fleeing their house, friends and home town amounted to the same thing, though for different reasons. She wanted to put as many obstacles as she could between the vesps and her children, distance being the one she could partly control. And Huw wanted to preserve their futures for wild, wonderful things.

Jude sat in the back playing on his little iPod Touch, tapping the screen frantically as he tried to vanquish zombie hordes. Lynne seemed to be sleeping. Ally was working on her iPad. Huw loved reading her analyses of current events, and he wondered what she had to say about all this. Maybe soon, when they were safe, he could start reading what she had written.

"You called Mags and Nathan?" Kelly asked. The names landed heavy, and Huw felt a stab of guilt.

"Not yet. I'll text them when we stop."

"Maybe they'd want to join us up there."

"God, I hope not." Huw's relationships with his sister and brother were troubled. Mags and Nathan did not talk to each other at all, and his contact with both of them consisted of a few awkward phone calls each year, and an occasional visit. The visits rarely lasted more than a day, and the calls several minutes, filled with hollow platitudes and promises to be in touch more frequently in the future. It was strange. He loved them as siblings, and there were no overt problems between them. But the three of them were all so unalike that contact felt like an imposition rather than a pleasure. His own life—work, family, friends—was busy enough. The guilt he felt upset him at times, but not enough to do anything about it.

I'll call them soon, he thought. Mags lived with her girlfriend in London. Nathan and his wife lived on Anglesey. *Soon enough*.

"Just saying, you might want to let them know." Kelly was an only child. She sometimes told him he was lucky having a brother and sister, and he had never been able to make her understand why they weren't closer. Probably because he didn't really understand himself.

Close to Ross-on-Wye, the traffic suddenly became

heavier. Both lanes were slow-moving, and in the distance Huw caught sight of a warm glow in the dark sky. Something was on fire.

"What's happening?" Ally asked from the back. Huw glanced at Kelly, and she turned around and started signing. He kept his eyes on the road.

Behind them, Glenn started flashing his lights and indicating that they should pull over. The hard shoulder was clear—even with the horrors of what was happening far away, drivers still obeyed the Highway Code—and Huw cruised to a standstill.

"Wait here, I'll see what's up." He jumped out, stretched, and looked back at the lines of headlights behind them. The road was already jammed as far back as he could see. Engines rumbled and muttered, and looking ahead he tilted his head to see if he could hear anything. But whatever was burning was too far away.

Sirens sang in the distance, but Huw couldn't see any flashing blue lights.

Glenn jumped from the Land Rover and jogged along to him. "Big smash ahead," he said.

"Looks like it."

"Seems a lot of people have the same idea as us." Glenn ran his hand through his long hair, scratching at his scalp. He might be confident, and sometimes brash, but Huw could tell that he was worried. "You keeping your eye on the news?"

"Something new?" Huw asked. In truth, he'd wanted to avoid it while he was driving. Kelly had been checking her phone, but he figured she'd have told him anything important.

"Heard on the radio, something big's happening

around Moscow. Military stuff. They're saying chemical weapons of some kind. Really confused, but they're saying there's no contact between Moscow and the West any more."

"Who's 'they'?" Huw asked.

"Well, you know." Glenn waved his hand. "They. The press, the news, the pundits."

"I can't fucking believe this," Huw said. A flush of unreality washed over him, a coolness tinged with shards of icy fear. They were out in the middle of nowhere in the dark, running from everything they owned and knew, the people he loved most in the world in the car beside him. Events seemed too large and cruel, so indifferent to his own fears and concerns, and all he wanted was to dig a hole and hide with his family for ever.

"Hey, we'll be fine," Glenn said. "Really."

Huw looked ahead along the vehicle-clogged road. It disappeared up a gentle slope and around a forested hillside, and the glow of flames came from beyond. "They're not fine," Huw said. "Poor bastards."

Glenn grabbed his arm. "They're not us. Now listen, we've got to get off the road. Nearest junction is couple of miles ahead, past whatever's happened up there. But I've got another idea."

"Which is?"

Glenn smiled. "Time for you to follow me."

"There's no way!" Kelly said. "This car won't handle it!"

"We have to try," Huw said. "Can't stay here all night." He squeezed Kelly's leg and she blew through pursed lips. She could see the sense. From the back seat, zombies groaned and growled as Jude cleaved them in two.

Ally tapped Huw on the shoulder. He turned around and waited until she turned on the overhead light. Then he spoke slowly and clearly, knowing that she had trouble reading his lips.

"We're getting away from the road," he said. "Strap yourselves in."

"Is there a turn-off ahead?" Lynne asked. She seemed a little dazed, and Huw wondered how deeply she'd been sleeping. He knew that the painkillers she'd been taking could knock her out sometimes, and he was amazed that the kids hadn't noticed. But of course, Ally probably *had* noticed. She just hadn't said anything yet.

Ally checked her brother's seatbelt. He glanced up with screen-dazed eyes. "There's more to life than your bloody gadgets!" Huw would sometimes say to both of them, but right now he wished they could play on their devices for ever.

"No turn-off," Huw said. "We're making our own."

Glenn's Land Rover passed by on the right, squeezing between the Mazda and the queue of traffic, and Huw could already see what would happen. Once Glenn did what he planned, others would start to follow. That didn't matter, so long as no one tried to race ahead or do something stupid.

"What's Glenn doing?" asked Jude.

"Watch," Huw said. He followed Glenn for a bit, then the Land Rover turned sharply to the left and nudged bumper-first against a bolted metal gate in the low hedge. It pushed forward, the gate eased back against its fixings, then the hinges both blew with audible cracks and the vehicle pushed the gate aside as it entered the field.

"He'll scratch his car!" Jude shouted, and as he followed through the gate, Huw realised just what this moment signified. It was the first time they had done something out of the ordinary. Packing the car, leaving home early on a Friday evening, going on an adventure, all these had been acceptable in Jude's mind. He was a bright kid, and fully aware that something bad was happening far away in Europe. But he was also still young enough to believe that the whole world was everything he knew and loved, and anything more remote barely mattered. And now this—driving across a field in the darkness—was the first real out-of-the-ordinary move that they'd made.

"His is a big car, mate," Huw said. "Did you see it crumple that gate?"

The Mazda hit the rough ruts in the field and rocked left, right, left again. Otis barked from the boot. Huw saw Ally turning in her seat to pet the dog, and the barking reduced to a gentle whine.

"Dad!" Jude protested. "He's four-wheel drive! We'll get stuck or broken, or something."

"I'm following in his tracks," Huw said. "Don't worry."

"Don't worry?" Kelly whispered beside him, just loud enough for him to hear. Huw gripped the wheel with both hands. It fought against him, jarring left and right as he followed Glenn's tail lights across the stubble-field. The chassis struck the ground with a thud. Jude cried out, startled, his shout turning into an excited giggle.

"Thank God it hasn't rained for a few days," Lynne said. Huw nodded. But the ground was still damp, the soil heavy, and in the glare of his headlamps he could see heavy clots sticking to Glenn's wheels. If the Mazda picked up enough dirt and it compacted beneath the wheel arches, the wheels might seize and they'd be stuck here. There was room in the Land Rover for all six of them, Otis, and the supplies and luggage they'd brought, but it would be an uncomfortable squeeze.

Glenn slowed a little, changed direction, then moved off quickly. Huw pressed on the gas. If he slowed too much or stopped, they might never move again.

It struck him just how much of a risk they'd taken, and glancing in the rear-view mirror only reinforced that. Past the kids' and Lynne's shadowy heads, past Otis where he swayed back and forth in the boot, he could see the brightly lit line of traffic a few hundred metres away. No one had followed them. Maybe everyone else knew what a bad idea this was.

Kelly's phone rang. "Glenn," she said as she answered. She held the phone to her ear, nodded, said, "Okay," and hung up.

"What?" Huw asked.

"Gate, maybe onto a lane, but it's uphill. Glenn said he'll move quickly, but for you to take it a bit slower in a low gear."

Huw nodded. "All okay back there?"

"Affirmative!" Jude said. Ally caught his eye in the mirror but didn't smile. Her face was ghosted by the iPad light. He couldn't see Lynne and she did not reply.

The Land Rover lurched away ahead of them, throwing up clots of mud that pattered across the Mazda's windscreen and bonnet, sticking. Heavy, wet mud. *Fuck it,* Huw thought, and as the ground sloped upwards he pressed gently on the gas. The car seemed to drag itself up the slope, back end slewing and spinning, and Jude giggled again. *Come on, come on,* Huw thought. The Land Rover had nudged the gate aside and was now parked behind a hedge a little uphill, and he saw Glenn standing behind the vehicle at the open gateway, waving them on, then gesturing slowly up and down with his flat hand: *Slow down, take it easy.*

They made it. The car lurched from the muddy field into the lane beyond, and Huw almost wasted the whole effort by driving into the ditch. But he parked up, handbrake on, and released a held breath. He melted into his seat.

"That was fun!" Jude said. "Let's do it again!" Otis barked in agreement.

"Let's not," Kelly said. But she smiled at Huw, and he could see that her own tension had been partially released.

He got out of the car and stood with Glenn close to the broken gate. Looking back downhill towards the gridlocked road, the hill looked even steeper than it had seemed before.

"Japanese engineering," Glenn said.

"Hey, it was all down to the driver. So which way?"

"You got a satnav?"

"On one of the gadgets, I'm sure," Huw said.

"Got an in-car charger?"

Huw's stomach dropped. He hadn't even thought of that. Why would he?

Glenn grinned. "Fucking Luddite. Hang on, I've got a spare one. Jude want to ride with me for a bit?"

"Sure, I'll ask," Huw said. But even as he bent to Kelly's open passenger window he was already wishing he'd made up a reason to keep his son with him. He trusted Glenn implicitly, but right then he wanted his family together.

Too late. Jude had opened his window, heard Glenn, and he was already slipping his trainers back on.

"Okay with this?" Kelly asked softly.

Huw shrugged, thinking, *No, not at all*.

"You know how he loves Glenn," his wife said, and as always she spoke sense. "And it'll give Ally and Mum room to get comfortable. Might be a long drive."

"What's the time?"

"Almost eight."

Twenty-two hours, he thought, although what they'd worked out had been distinctly unscientific. He nodded at Kelly's phone.

"All bad," she whispered. "Come on. Let's get moving."

I didn't like travelling in cars. The reasons were complex, and not all so obvious.

The last thing I remember before the crash is sitting at the table in my grandparents' kitchen, the smell of toast just a little too burnt, the taste of thick strawberry jam and rich butter, the sight of Granddad sitting at the far end of the kitchen smoking and laughing at his own jokes, Gran moving around on unsteady legs as she cooked breakfast. Granddad stood and brushed crumbs and ash from his trousers. Gran admonished him, but gently, because little Ally Mally was with them. Granddad clapped his hands, Gran jumped, I laughed. And then I was in the hospital bed, and I would never hear again.

Later, asleep in the hospital and then when I was finally back at home, fragments of the crash intruded into my dreams. They were fleeting and painful, and at first they'd been frighteningly real, so grim that even as a little girl I'd understood that I was reliving exactly what I had witnessed. My grandfather driving, cigarette hanging from the corner of his mouth, grizzled, yellowed hands resting lightly on the wheel, one finger tapping in rhythm to the music that whispered through the car's speaker. Gran in the passenger seat, turning to her husband and laughing as she said something that I would never hear. The sudden sense of something wrong, jarring movement. The impact.

But then those unreliable dream memories started to become even more nightmarish. I couldn't stop them coming, and soon could not discern truth from terror. Granddad grasped the wheel and turned to me, his head almost all the way around on his head, cigarette scorched against his lips and mouth pulled open in a wide-toothed grin. Each tooth looked like a slab of burnt toast. His hands were the claws of a giant parrot gripping the wheel, nails curved into talons. Gran was still turned to speak to him, and her mouth was too wide as she said, "Isn't it time to kill Ally Mally?" The blur, the impact, and I always woke as the windscreen hazed into a million pieces.

A nine-year-old girl who had been through a terrible ordeal, I could never shake the idea that those were the last words I ever heard. *Isn't it time to kill Ally Mally?* Even though I knew they had never been spoken, the memory of them stung.

My world had gone quiet, and my mind became frantic in its efforts to fill the void left behind. I'd suffered a serious head trauma and damage to the brain, broken collarbone, several cracked ribs, and lacerations that had required over fifty stitches. Bad dreams were the least of my doctors' or parents' worries.

My parents told me that was my way of dealing with things. At the time we could still only communicate in writing, and I'd kept that slip of paper with my mother's graceful handwriting that said, *This is how you cope*. I'd stuck it in a frame above my bed, and sometimes when things seemed too tough I looked at it, and it could have meant anything.

My ways of coping had become many, and as time went on the truly nightmarish dreams became much less frequent and intense, confined mainly to times when I was ill.

Now I was fourteen, my memory of my dead grandparents remained a complex thing.

The other reason I hated travelling in confined vehicles was that, ironically, they made me feel cut off from those around me. During the daytime I could tell when Mum and Dad were chatting in the front, but I could rarely read their lips. Whoever was in the passenger seat might turn around and try to sign to me, but it was difficult to do twisted half around, with the seat and headrest between us. If Jude was in the back with me we could sometimes hold conversations, but he was more likely to be engrossed in a game on his iPod.

In the darkness it was so much worse. With Jude now travelling in Glenn's Land Rover, Lynne and I had more room to stretch out in the back. But it was Otis who brought me most comfort. I sat with one arm over the back seat, stroking him where he was lying beside the suitcase and hastily piled bags. He didn't have much room and he'd curled into a ball, nose to tail. I could feel an occasional rumbled sigh as I stroked him.

Lynne was asleep. She looked dead. I thought perhaps she would be soon, and that the secret whispers and grim looks I'd been noticing over the past couple of weeks were something to do with an illness. The suspicions burned at me, a pressure that gave me a headache, but I didn't know how to ask. And now there was so much more.

I rested the iPad on my thighs, left hand scanning the various sites I frequently used. Facebook, Twitter, BBC News, others, they were all filled with the vesps. Consumed by them, as the vesps themselves consumed. I had my scrapbook open, and the file name made me ache for the calmness of a day ago. "New Worlds?"

I thought not.

9

Here's what we think we know about the creatures popularly known as vesps:

Origins: It's believed that they originate from an isolated underground environment, exposed by a scientific expedition in Moldova. Footage of the expedition was broadcast live. The initial wave of vesps was seen emerging from the entrance to the apparently extensive cave system before communications were lost. Dr Vladimir Krasnov led the team, and it's known that he spent a large portion of his life searching for contained ecosystems. The Moldovan cave was suspected to be not only the largest yet found, but, of those, the system cut off from the rest of the world for the longest. Some estimates suggest that the caves had been isolated for upwards of ten million years.

Biology: Few specimens have been gathered, but some are under analysis. Initial results are not yet officially published, but it seems that the creatures are cold-blooded, flying reptiles. Adults are around twenty-five centimetres long and weigh less than half a kilogramme. Their skin is segmented, pale, soft, and protected with a moist secretion. The wings resemble those of a bat, similarly tipped with a spiked digit. They are eyeless and hunt by sound. Sound receptors cover the forward half of their bodies, both traditional ears and more sensitive vibration detectors on the skin's surface. Their mouths are wide and contain over a hundred sharp teeth.

Reproduction and life cycle: The vesps are able to reproduce at any time, laying eggs in their partially eaten prey. The eggs hatch quickly; the young consume their host and grow with great rapidity. They are vicious, voracious eaters. They will feed upon any living creature, large or small. We have seen evidence of them eating flies and beetles, as well as attacking fully grown cows and dogs. The young can fly from birth, and within just a single day they are two-thirds the size of an adult and able to reproduce. Females appear to outnumber males ten-to-one. Each vesp can lay up to forty eggs at one time.

Projection and conjecture: Proliferation is staggering. Upon being exposed to the environment beyond the cave, it appears that something was triggered in these beasts, a dormant instinct or ability, enabling them to reproduce at a stunning rate. Although the caves have not been explored, it is unlikely that the population below ground would have multiplied so quickly, due to the lack of space and sustenance. If only a thousand escaped from the cave and started laying eggs immediately, within a day their offspring could number half a million, and a day later tens of millions. Beyond that the numbers become shocking. Some believe the oxygen-rich atmosphere boosted their metabolism, strength and speed. It's also suggested that the sudden availability of vast amounts of food has disrupted the delicate balance of their previous existence.

Nothing like them is known to science, other than at a microscopic level.

Nothing else like them exists in nature.

They are an anomaly.

We don't know how to stop them.

**Statement from a government scientist
(identity withheld by request), London,
Friday, 18 November 2016**

They're fucking monsters! No one knows what they are or where they come from or why they reproduce so quickly, and you know why? Because they're fucking MONSTERS! Don't try to make sense of this. Don't try to see a pattern, or blame God or the government, just—
**BBC Radio Midlands News presenter (since removed),
7 p.m., Friday, 18 November 2016**

I was missing my little brother. That was pretty rare—we had a real love/hate relationship, and time away from each other was usually appreciated—but I wished he was with us now. It had only been a couple of hours, but I felt his absence. At times like this a family should stay together.

I couldn't even contact him. My iPad was 3G enabled, but his iPod wasn't. He was likely still killing zombies while I was watching...

What *was* I watching? The end of the world? It had all happened so quickly, seemed so unbelievable and surreal; the full impact had yet to hit. But the news was inescapable. Everything I read through official channels was backed up by countless images and messages on social media.

I wished I could stop looking.

Lynne had stirred a couple of times, clutching at her stomach and drawing her legs up, barely rising from sleep. I guessed she was groaning too, because Mum glanced back at her. I caught her eye. Mum smiled, but it barely changed her face.

We moved along B roads, through the darkness, the lights of the cars passing in the opposite direction illuminating the car's interior. I watched Dad, his profile grim and set, hands clasping the wheel firmly. He usually drove with one hand, laid back and casual. But now he had purpose. I watched Lynne, nodding beside me in the back seat. I checked the charge on the iPad and saw that it was down to less than twenty per cent. Glenn had lent us an in-car charger, and I'd ask Mum to plug it in soon.

Two hours after leaving the jammed main road we pulled to a halt.

"What's wrong?" I asked. Dad said something but forgot to turn around, so my mum leaned around the front seat and signed.

"Toilet break."

"Here?" We'd pulled into an unlit lay-by. It was almost 9 p.m., and now we were sitting stationary I saw just how much traffic was on the road heading north.

"Come on," Mum said.

We left the car. I stretched my legs and opened the boot, slipping Otis's lead on and guiding him to the side of the road. He sniffed around and did his business.

Glenn and Jude left their car and came to chat to us. *Making plans,* I thought. *Talking about where's safe and where isn't.* Jude stood beneath the overhanging heavy trees and peed into the darkness, giggling and looking back at me as he did so. It was good to be out of the cars. Cold, a drizzle in the air, but nice to be able to stretch our legs.

I sensed something wrong to my left. Lights leaping, shimmering back and forth across the wet trees and bushes before me instead of drifting by. I turned and felt Otis pressing against my leg.

A car bucked into the lay-by behind us, jerking forward, lights nodding up and down. It jarred once more and came to a stop fifty metres away with its front nudged against a tree.

Vesps! I thought, backing away. *They're here already, moved so quickly, and now we're living everything I've seen!* Otis barked and I tugged on his lead, hurting him, feeling bad. "Otis, quiet!" I said. I turned around and looked for my parents, but they'd already seen. The three adults stood in a group beside the Mazda. I held out my left hand then pressed my finger to my lips. *Quiet, it's the vesps!* But they weren't looking at me.

Then I saw their faces drop as one, and Otis started barking again.

What will I see when I turn around? I wondered, I *dreaded*, and in my silent world it was a familiar thought.

A man was walking quickly towards us. The road was quiet for now, and with his car lights on full beam he was splashed in silhouette. But I could see the long shape in his right hand, and as he closed on me he brought the shotgun up and pressed it against his shoulder.

Otis tugged at the lead. He sensed the threat and wanted to protect me. The man shouted something and shifted his aim to the dog, and I pulled him back, crouching down and hugging Otis to me. He continued barking and I felt each one through his chest.

The man paused a few steps away. Behind me, beside the Mazda, my parents and Glenn must have reacted, because the man shifted his aim only slightly to me. He was shouting a lot more now, and as a car flitted by the light shifted across his face. He looked weird. I'd never seen anyone look like that before.

I shook my head. Maybe he was telling me to move, or to let go of the dog, or to lie down, but I didn't know.

I looked back. My parents were both standing with hands held out placatingly, both speaking. Mum saw me watching and made sure she spoke very slowly.

"Shout all you want, my daughter's deaf." She pointed. "Ally, baby, just stay there, he doesn't want you to move."

I didn't want to turn back to the man. I wanted to keep my parents in sight. Glenn was behind them, and I could see Jude huddled against the side of the Land Rover ten metres in front of the Mazda. He was crying.

Glenn was taking small, rapid backward steps towards his vehicle. *He's got those guns in there,* I thought. But then his eyes suddenly went wide and he held his hands out, saying something I couldn't see.

My parents seemed to freeze.

I turned around and was looking into the twin barrels of the shotgun. The man had moved much closer and was aiming right at me, though he looked at the adults.

Otis was growling now, a deep vibration that I felt through my bones as if he and I were one. I'd wrapped his lead around my hand and the tension was constant, hard. *If I let him go…* I thought, but there was that gun, and my fear was a physical pain.

"Shhh, Otis," I said, pressing my head against his. "Shhh."

The man looked directly at me then. And although the gun never wavered I saw something that took away some of the fear. I saw his terror, his shame. It didn't make it any less likely that he'd shoot me—I thought perhaps it was *more* likely. But I did understand that he was driven to this. Like us he was trying to get away. Probably had family in the car. Ran out of petrol, so now what?

Now what?

The man looked up, raised his gun and backed away, aiming over my shoulder. He shouted again, words lost to the darkness.

I glanced back and saw Dad walking towards me.

"Dad, no!"

He didn't look at me. He was focused on the man, lips pressed tight together. Furious. And I knew then that he would never, ever let anything bad happen to me again.

"Dad, please, no, he'll shoot you and—"

A flash. I felt the blast in my ear and skull, a compression of air as the shockwave hit. Dad's eyes went wide and he stopped walking, hands held out from his sides. I looked frantically from him, to Mum, to Glenn and Jude standing further away by the Land Rover. They all jumped and grew instantly still again. No one fell. No one clasped a wound or span around with blood spilling. He'd fired into the air, but in doing so emphasised his seriousness.

Dad was only a couple of metres away and he rushed to me, gathering me in his arms and standing.

I looked back at the man. The shotgun barrel was smoking, and he was more agitated than ever. He shouted again and this time I saw the words on his lips. "Keys! Now!"

"Don't hurt my family," I said. "We're just like you."

He looked directly at me. "Shut up, bitch!" That struck me harder than the shotgun blast, harder than the sight of my parents' fear for me. Perhaps he *wasn't* like us at all. Maybe he *would* murder, just for a car.

"Give them to him, Dad," I said, never taking my eyes from the gunman. He seemed to have gathered himself now, looking more determined than ever. He was no longer shaking. He was determined, and he turned his aim once again to Otis and me.

"Dad," I said again. Dad moved in front, pushing me behind. Otis started struggling against my hold, eager to get free and attack the man threatening his family, his pack. I squatted beside him, grasping the lead with both hands.

I looked back at the others. Mum had ushered Glenn back towards the Land Rover, and now Glenn was urging Jude inside the vehicle. I could see my little brother's tears and I hated the man for that, fucking *hated* him!

If I let Otis go—

Dad stood before me, protecting me with his shadow, and I saw him throw something at the man. He caught the keys, examined them briefly, pocketed them. Then he called back over his shoulder without taking his eyes from me, my dog, and my dad.

Behind him the car doors opened. A woman and two young children scrambled out, the woman carrying a baby in a blanket hugged to her chest.

More cars passed them by. *Won't anyone help?* I thought. *Doesn't anyone care?* Maybe someone would see what was happening, edge their car to the left and run the man down. But I had no wish to see anyone killed. Not someone I loved, and not even this man who thought he was protecting his own loved ones.

As the man's family passed him and approached the Mazda, he lowered the gun and seemed to slump a little. I relaxed, too.

Otis's lead slipped from my grasp.

"No!" I tried to shout, but I was breathless with fear.

The dog streaked past Dad and leaped at the man. He brought the gun up again but was too late, the barrel too long; the dog was inside its reach and leaping for him, claws scrabbling, teeth gnashing, all fur and fury. The man tried to stagger back but tripped over his own feet.

As he fell, the shotgun fired.

Dad dropped to the ground and I screamed, crawling for him and draping myself across his body, trying to drag him back towards me. He looked up at me, then sat up and hugged me tight. He pulled back just a little to show me his finger and thumb in a circle—*I'm okay*. Then his face fell.

Otis was on top of the man, teeth clamped around his arm.

"Otis!" I called. "Leave! Leave, Otis. Otis!" The dog backed away, circling the man and trotting back to me with his tail raised.

Dad moved me gently aside and stood, and I stood with him, turning to see what terrible thing he had seen.

The woman was on the ground close to the Mazda's rear end. Her two kids were huddled by her side, and my mum had already reached her. I hated the flush of relief that washed through me when I saw it was not one of my family on the ground. But at the same time I thought, *Not our fault.*

The man was struggling to stand, eyes locked on his wife and children. He went to pick up his gun.

"Dad!" I said. But Dad had gone to the Mazda too, moving the kids gently back so that Mum could kneel by the injured woman and take the baby from her grasp. "Dad!" I called again.

By the time he turned around again, the man had broken the shotgun and plucked two new shells from his pocket.

I saw Dad shouting something at him. I grabbed Otis by the lead and wrapped it around my hand again, tighter. This was going from terrible to nightmarish.

Lynne climbed from the back of the Mazda, looked down at the woman splayed on the tarmac, and went to her knees.

The woman's leg looked out of shape, and I stared with sick fascination at the ruin of her ankle and foot. Blood flowed black in the headlights. Cars passed by. *We need to call the police and an ambulance,* I thought, but the man had other ideas.

He aimed the shotgun as he approached his family. His kids backed away from him but he shouted at them, and they scurried into the back of our Mazda. Lynne tried talking to the man but he edged around her, clasping his wife beneath the arm and pulling her upright. She screamed. The look on her face was terrible, and now I could smell blood. It was like the air after a thunderstorm.

He dumped her into the passenger seat and held out

his hand for his infant. Mum handed the baby over, and the man placed it gently in his wife's arms.

"But all our stuff's in the car," I said, and Dad turned and shook his head.

Otis growled again.

The man moved around the car, closing doors, still aiming his gun in our general direction. A truck came along the road. Its horn blared and its lights revealed the man's pale, sweaty face. He looked lost.

The truck did not stop.

"Get your wife to a hospital!" I said. The man didn't even look at me.

As we watched our car pull away, my parents drew me and Lynne close to them. Otis nudged their hands with his nose, demanding to be part of the group hug. I felt like crying.

But I didn't. Something inside pushed the tears down. A realisation, perhaps, that things were changing more rapidly than I could ever have appreciated.

The vesps had touched us now, though indirectly, and I knew there was plenty more to come.

"It was horrible," I said, sobbing into Dad's chest. "I didn't know what was happening, I couldn't see everything, not in the dark and not with everyone spread out. I didn't know what he was saying or… or what you were… saying back at him…" I cried some more, shaking, needing the feel of his arms around me and his familiar, safe smell. I'd never known exactly what that smell was—his aftershave, sweat, or a combination of everything that was him—and I didn't want to know.

It was comfort and security, and right then that was all that mattered.

He stepped right in front of me.

"And I was scared he was going to shoot you, Dad."

Right between me and the gun. And if he'd been there years ago when we crashed, he'd have thrown himself between me and whatever cracked my skull open.

"He looked ashamed and shocked, but really mad too. Do you think he'll kill other people? Do you think he's done it already?"

Because he's my dad, and that's what he has to do. Protect me from danger.

Dad's chest vibrated gently as he spoke, but I had him too tight in my grasp to look up.

"It was just so scary. I was there, but not. In the dark. I didn't know what was happening."

He stroked my hair.

"It was horrible."

He tapped my shoulder. I pulled back at last and looked up into his face. He was crying.

"I know," he said.

10

The trouble is, this isn't like anything we've fought before. These things aren't like an enemy. They're not marching in waves, following known strategies, nor are they discouraged by any level of loss. We know so far that other countries have tried machine guns, gunships, fuel air bombs, surface-to-air missiles, flamethrowers, and anti-aircraft guns. There are rumours of some limited effect in Bosnia where a chemical agent was employed, but there's no accurate reports of just how effective it was, and nothing concerning the effects on civilian populations. Russia appears to have released a biological weapon in several partly evacuated towns in Kazakhstan, and there are large military engagements around Moscow. Again, no accurate reports or feedback are available. While analysis of foreign efforts will hopefully be beneficial if and when the vesps cross the English Channel and hit the UK mainland, one aspect troubles me more than any other: weapons are loud. And, more and more, it seems that the only way to avoid detection by these things is to maintain complete, utter silence.

General Michael Holgate,
Friday, 18 November 2016

Glenn drove. Huw and Kelly squeezed into the passenger seat, enjoying the close contact. In the back, Lynne sat against one door with Ally and Jude beside her, and a couple of Glenn's food bags stowed against the other door. Jude stared straight ahead, letting Ally rest her arm around his shoulder. It wasn't often he'd allow that. She was his yucky big sister.

Otis was in the boot, curled in the small space they'd made for him. It seemed that he'd resigned himself to having little room.

Huw called the police. It took three attempts to get through, and then he relayed information about the man who'd stolen their car at gunpoint. He gave them the location, time, and a few details of the incident. It was only after he'd hung up that he realised they hadn't even taken his name.

"They just didn't sound that interested," he said. "I might as well have been ordering a burger."

"More going on," Glenn said, and then they sat quietly for a while, thinking of what that more might be.

An hour and almost forty miles from the lay-by, they agreed that they couldn't go far like this. The Land Rover was roomy, but with the food and other supplies Glenn had piled in, along with the guns and bags of clothing, that room was rapidly feeling more cramped. They also had plans to pick up more provisions along the way, either from a motorway service station or an all-night supermarket. So another vehicle was their priority. How to find one was proving more of a problem.

"It's not as if it's a normal situation," Glenn said. "Really, we find a local garage with an owner's house attached, knock them up."

"And pay how?" Huw asked. "We've got perhaps two grand credit left on our card. And what about registration, tax, insurance?"

Glenn glanced across at him. "Really?"

"That's how the garage owner will think," Huw said quietly. "Not me."

"I've got ten grand on my card, at least," Glenn said.

"I can't ask you—"

"Mate, for fuck's sake," he muttered. "We just saw a nutter almost blow his wife in half over a car. He was aiming at you. He was aiming at *Ally*, Huw. It's not a normal situation."

"He's right," Kelly said.

"Yeah. I know." Huw was trying to forget the sight of the gun aimed directly at Ally's face, but it was all he could remember. He'd experienced a surge of fury and a haze of hopelessness. He still couldn't work out how he hadn't got himself shot.

He liked being squeezed up on the seat with Kelly, and took comfort from her warmth, her closeness. He knew she did too.

Huw unplugged Jude's iPod from the charger and strained around to look into the back seat. Lynne was sleeping again. Ally caught his eye and they exchanged smiles, and he felt a rush of love for her. She seemed fine. She'd been through so much, and he was constantly amazed at her resilience. Jude was nodding, falling asleep at last.

Huw handed the charging lead back and Ally plugged it into her iPad.

He'd left his phone in the Mazda, as had Kelly. The bastard had also taken their food and clothes, Otis's food, and Kelly's handbag. He was only relieved that Lynne had carried her pain medication in a bag in her jacket pocket. And that was something else they would have to confront soon.

There was too much to think about. Already, before the vesps had even hit the British coast, they were screwed.

"Let's do it sooner rather than later, then," Huw said. It was almost eleven o'clock. The A roads they travelled on were still busy, but so far they'd been lucky not to hit another accident or traffic jam. They'd seen a few police cars, but they'd simply been parked beside the road. Waiting for something to happen.

They'd decided to aim for the motorway again north of Birmingham. Kelly was trying to check traffic conditions on Glenn's phone, and while some sites seemed to be updating, she wasn't actually sure that the information was changing. The motorways should be the fastest route north, but they might also be the easiest way to get trapped in an accident-induced gridlock.

Maybe travelling by night would be easier.

There were so many maybes, and Huw had confidence in none of them.

They didn't even know the name of the town. But when they saw a converted petrol station up ahead, now signposted as '4WD Salesroom', it seemed perfect.

Glenn pulled off the main road and parked beneath the wide station's canopy. Vehicles ranked both sides of the plot, several were parked across the grass verge between road and forecourt, and others were lined around towards the back of the building. The main building was a two-storey redbrick; modern, functional and ugly, with curtained windows upstairs. No lights were on, but it looked like living accommodation.

Kelly and Huw jumped out and closed the door quietly. Jude and Lynne were still asleep, and they wanted to keep it that way if they could.

Vehicles passed them by, none slowing down, lights splashing from car windows and throwing slanted shadows across the forecourt. Glenn had turned his headlights off. Unless anyone looked closely, his would look like just another car for sale.

"Let's check for a bell, or something," Kelly said. She took Huw's hand and they approached the wide glass window fronting onto the forecourt. She'd surprised him holding his hand. He guessed she was as afraid as him.

"No lights on," he said, shading his face against the window with his free hand. He couldn't see much. There was no bell by the locked front door.

"Check around the back?" Kelly suggested.

"Yeah."

They walked around the side of the building. Lights from the road didn't reach this far and there were no security or safety lights, so they moved slowly to avoid tripping over anything in the blackness. Clouds had obscured the moon now, and the gentle breeze brought occasional hints of rain.

"How much trouble are we in?" Kelly asked softly. Something in her voice made him stop and hug her in the dark, kiss her cheek, hold her close.

"You know as much as me," he said. "We're doing our best."

"But people with guns are doing more."

"Hey, that was just bad luck. All the cars on the road and he had to choose ours."

"And what if we run out of petrol, or we can't get another car and Glenn's breaks down? What then? Do we use his guns to steal a car?"

"That won't happen," he said.

"How do you know?"

"Look, babe. Every problem as it presents itself, okay? I'm out of my depth here, totally. But Glenn's... you know, he's adaptable. Handy. He's strong and tough, and I'm glad he's with us. He'll see us through this."

"You weren't out of your depth back there," she whispered.

"That bastard threatened our baby. Now come on. Door, bell, whatever. Let's wake someone up."

But they couldn't wake anyone. They found a rear access but no bell, and two minutes spent pummelling on the door brought no reaction from inside. Huw tried the door handle, Kelly hissed at him to stop it. He banged on the door again.

"Maybe they're scared."

"I don't think there's anyone inside at all," he said. "Come on. Back to the gang."

"We're going?"

"No." Maybe the darkness made it easier to say what came next. Kelly couldn't see him, and more importantly he could not see her reaction. "We'll break in, find the keys. Take a car. Leave our names and address, an IOU."

"Huw, you can't be—"

"Of course I'm serious. *This* is serious! Come on, let's talk to Glenn."

Their friend was standing beside the Land Rover

shielded from the road. Huw noticed with a shiver that he had one of the shotguns resting against his leg, close so that it was difficult to see. Glenn nodded up at the windows as they approached.

"No sign of anyone there. Been watching the curtain; I reckon they'd have twitched by now if there was anyone inside."

"We're taking a car," Huw said. "Me and Kelly will stay and do it; maybe you should drive down the road a bit, find somewhere to pull off and wait for us."

Huw wasn't surprised when Glenn took only a moment to think about it. He nodded, glanced from Huw to Kelly, handed her his phone.

"Your mum's got hers, I've programmed her number. Ring if there's a problem."

"Kids all right?" Huw asked.

"Jude's sleeping. I'll tell Ally."

"No. I will."

Five minutes after watching Glenn drive away with their family, Huw held a folded tarpaulin against a glazed door, and Kelly hit it with a chunk of wood. The shattering glass seemed incredibly loud, and they both crouched down in the darkness, listening for any reaction. Huw's heart was jigging. He felt stupidly excited, like a kid doing something wrong. He and his cousin had enjoyed some trouble in their early teens— smashing windows, stealing bikes, scrumping apples; not big and clever but part of what had made him who he was now. He felt that same sense of delicious danger now, and though he knew this was serious, he relished the sensation. It lit his senses and made him feel alive.

This is all for my family, he thought, trying to justify their actions. The guy with the shotgun must have thought the same. But there were lines to cross, and lines to stand behind. Knowing where those lines were made him strong.

He felt around inside and found the handle, flicked the night latch, shoved the door open. Inside it was pitch black. Kelly had already switched on the torch app on Glenn's phone, and it revealed a messy hallway piled with boxes of files and loose papers. Huw paused and waited for any response. He imagined a dog darting from the shadows and running at them, all slavering jaws and deadly intent.

"Hello?" he whispered. Nothing.

"Hello!" Kelly shouted. "Anyone there?" She made Huw jump, but he listened carefully. There was no sign of occupation.

Kelly led the way, heading along the hallway. She opened another door onto a small room. It looked like a workshop, scattered with bits of electrical equipment, packets of screws and fixings, other oily parts. She swept the light around and paused on a wall calendar showing a naked woman sitting on a sports car's bonnet, legs akimbo.

"Haven't seen one of those in a while," Huw said. He had thought such calendars long consigned to history.

"Not that hairy, anyway," Kelly said. She giggled, he chuckled, a brief but welcome moment of humour.

She moved through the room and opened another door. Huw followed, staying close, keeping his wits about him. He couldn't hold back the strange blend of excitement and disbelief that they were actually doing this. Kelly paused in the doorway, and he looked past her at the room beyond.

It was a large office with two desks piled with papers, and a seating area with a low coffee table and espresso machine. Messy but well-used, the room had pleasant pictures on the walls and smelled of fresh paint.

Kelly remained motionless, phone light aimed ahead and down.

"Look, above the desk," Huw whispered. There was a square metal locker there, and he was pretty sure it was a key safe. He'd seen them in the site cabins he sometimes hired for larger jobs. "Kel?"

"Other wall," she said. He looked.

Three red lights blinked on and off. There was no sound.

"Alarm?" he asked.

"I think we've already triggered it. Remote feed to the local police station, I bet." She turned and blinded him with the light. "Huw, let's go. If we're caught what happens to the kids?"

"We won't be caught. We already know they're worried about more important things than this tonight."

"You're sure?"

No, he wasn't sure, not completely. But he pushed past Kelly and reached for the key safe. It was open, and at least thirty sets of keys were hanging there, most of them heavy with key-fob remotes. He grabbed a handful and stuffed them in his pocket.

"Okay."

Kelly ran back through the workshop and corridor to the smashed door and outside, switching off the torch.

Huw followed, tripping on the sill and almost going down. They paused, listening. Out of sight, several cars passed along the road in front of the building, lights splashing the trees skirting the garage's compound. None of them slowed down.

"We were going to leave—" he began, thinking of names, addresses, phone numbers and apologetic explanations.

"Fuck that!" Kelly said. "We've done it, and now—"

"Get out!" someone screamed. It came from behind them and inside the building, location uncertain, and the voice was so loud and screeching that it was androgynous. "Get out get out get out!"

Huw shivered, and a chill ran down his spine. He wasn't sure he'd ever actually felt that before, thought it was a clichéd saying that meant little. His balls tingled, the back of his neck felt suddenly cool and exposed, and he grabbed Kelly's hand and ran.

"Get out get out!" The shouting followed them. Huw wondered which room the person had been hiding in, and whether they'd walked right past him or her, crouched beneath a desk or in a cupboard. He tried to shake the idea.

"Get out!"

He took out the keys as they ran and started pressing remote buttons one by one. The first was a hatchback. Its lights flashed, but thankfully there was no accompanying beeping from its alarm. A nice car, but nowhere near big enough for Otis in the back.

The second was a five-year-old Jeep Cherokee.

They both ran at it at the same time, no words necessary. It was perfect. Kelly snatched the keys from his hand and jumped inside, and even as he opened the passenger door, the engine growled into life. She was breathing heavily, but she moved out through the narrow gaps between other vehicles without incident, keeping the headlamps off.

"Fucking hell!" she said. "What the hell was that?"

"Someone scared," he replied.

"I think I need clean knickers."

"I think I pissed myself."

Their laughter was nervous and high, and she flipped on the lights and pulled out onto the road. They were both panting, but Huw also felt buzzed. They'd achieved something together. Over the years, their frantic lives so busy that their drifting apart was as unnoticeable as the movement of a clock's hour hand, he'd come to realise that they rarely did anything meaningful together. But right then everything between them was fresh and young again. Daring. Dangerous. It was a feeling he'd never expected to love so much.

"Not much fuel," Kelly said.

"One thing at a time. Let's get the kids."

"So I suppose we're criminals now," she said.

"Britain's most wanted." Huw reached for the radio. "Do you want me to…?"

Kelly sighed, nodded. Maybe she also felt like this was a moment that shouldn't be broken. But they could not hide from the truth.

He turned on the radio.

"—Black Forest regions of Germany, and there are already unconfirmed reports of incidents in Switzerland and southern France. As noted before, none of these contacts have been officially confirmed, but in a rapidly developing situation it is social media that is becoming the go-to source for up-to-date information. The Prime Minister is expected to make his next hourly statement in around twelve minutes, but in the meantime—"

Huw clicked it off. They sat in silence, heartbeats settling, breathing becoming normal once again. A couple of minutes later they saw Glenn's Land Rover parked in a cafe's car park ahead, close to the exit and with its lights on. The cafe was closed, the car park deserted. Kelly parked beside them. Before she lowered the window she looked across at Huw.

"It's spreading faster," he said.

"We won't make it," she whispered. "Not that far. Not Scotland."

"We'll go as far as we can." He glanced past her at Glenn leaning out and waiting to talk.

Kelly sighed and lowered her window.

"How'd it go?" he asked.

"Not a problem," Huw said. Maybe he'd tell his friend later. But he thought it more likely that they'd keep their brief adventure to themselves.

They drove hard. After queuing for twenty minutes to top up with fuel, and buying a bag full of sweets, crisps and drinks, they hit the M5 motorway and headed north. No one complained that the petrol station had doubled the price of fuel and quadrupled the cost of snacks. Glenn paid with cash, and the station owner's eyes were alight with profit.

Huw couldn't understand how the man did not see the truth.

Kelly drove for the next couple of hours, but Huw

didn't sleep a wink. He kept checking on the kids and Lynne in the back seat. Jude seemed warm and content, huddled so deep in blankets they'd borrowed from Glenn that only the tip of his nose and mouth were visible. Ally had the iPad on her lap, but she was doing the nodding dog. He knew that his daughter didn't like travelling in cars, and whenever he caught her eye he smiled and shared a few words. Her eyes were haunted. When she whispered about what she saw on the Internet, he knew why.

Lynne remained sleeping, leaning against the door, groaning occasionally. He was glad that Ally couldn't hear those sounds. He wasn't even sure just how much she knew about her grandmother, but now wasn't the time to talk about it with Kelly. Lynne had her medicines, though there was no telling how long they would last. It was a problem for later.

Huw tried to imagine the future but it was a hazy, troubled place. He could not quite believe that everything was going to change so much. Try as he might, he could not doomsday them into a broken, bleeding land, and that inability surprised him. It went against his usual pessimistic self. But surely the vesps would stop, die out, be defeated by some simple, effective method? If they'd been cut off from the world for millions of years they would have no immunity to any number of common bugs or viruses. Could they really fly across twenty miles of ocean? Would they even bother? Perhaps his natural pessimism was not broad or deep enough to encompass what was happening, and in such dire times he found himself, ironically, thinking the best.

But stark realities pointed otherwise. Maps displayed

on the news, statistics, film clips, interviews. The desperation in the eyes of the Prime Minister. The shocking imagery flooding the net, none of it censored, too much to control. While officials spoke of calm, the truth was chaos.

He tried calling Mags, but her phone was diverted to voicemail. He left a message, thought of trying again later, but decided that she would call him back. He wasn't even sure what he'd called to say. He also called Nathan, who answered the phone and then dismissed him angrily. He'd been asleep, and he sounded drunk. Huw ended the call feeling cold and indignant.

I tried, he thought. *I called, told them where we're going. What they do is their choice.* His troubled calls to his siblings made what he had closer by even more precious. His family was everything to him, and anything beyond was simply added stress. In this changing world, you had to keep close what was most precious.

By midnight they were north of Stoke-on-Trent on the M6 and approaching Manchester. Traffic was heavy, but no more so than on a normal busy day. They saw the results of several accidents, only one of them attended by the emergency services. They passed a van and car burning in a ditch, one man pacing back and forth on the hard shoulder, hands entangled in his hair. A few people had stopped to help. None of them could.

Several times they saw three or four police cars parked together by the side of the motorway. Sometimes lights flashed, more often the officers stood together on the grass verge, smoking, drinking coffee from flasks, watching thousands of people fleeing north. Though the authorities had advised people to remain at home, they could do little to stem the flow of traffic. A single roadblock with no facility to redirect vehicles would soon cause a reaction all along the motorway, and gridlock would follow.

The southbound carriageway was quiet. A few cars and lorries drifted past, and now and then they saw military convoys heading south, trucks and other vehicles camouflaged by night. Huw wondered what those soldiers were thinking. They'd been trained to fight wars, not monsters.

Around 1 a.m., a car drifted across the carriageway several hundred metres ahead of them, clipped the central reservation, flipped into the air, and rolled back across the motorway. Brake lights flared, and two other vehicles collided after the rolling car struck them. It ended up on its roof on the hard shoulder. A few cars stopped, but most moved into the outside lane to pass.

Glenn indicated left to pull over. Kelly flashed her lights at him repeatedly, glancing across at Huw as she did so. "We can't stop for everyone," she said softly.

Huw looked over his shoulder. The kids and Lynne were asleep.

"Let's move on," he said. He called Glenn on Lynne's phone, and after a brief exchange his friend agreed.

By the time they crawled past the wreck a few others had stopped to help. Huw tried not to look at the wrecks as they passed, but he couldn't help it. People were being dragged from the two cars, and they seemed miraculously unhurt. But the car that had rolled was a ruin, and within its shattered interior he saw the ruin of people. They glimmered wet in the collective headlights.

"Checking their phones," Kelly said.

"Or maybe they fell asleep."

They drove on in shamed silence.

The roads became clogged around Manchester and they ground to a halt. They left the motorway via a police lay-by and went off-road again. They crossed a muddy field, skidding and sliding eventually onto a farm lane that led to a B road. Others followed them, quickly becoming mired in the wheel-churned mud.

Both vehicles had built-in satnavs. They programmed them to set a course for Lancaster, avoiding motorways, and most of the time the satnavs agreed with each other. When they didn't, they followed Glenn's because it was newer.

By three in the morning they'd passed Manchester, and they stopped at a service station to switch drivers and take a toilet break. This time, no one carjacked them. Glenn stood between the parked vehicles with a shotgun resting over his left arm, while Huw and Kelly took turns taking the children and Lynne into the building to the toilets.

There was a strange atmosphere inside. Huw took Jude, the boy tired and dazed from sleep, and it was an odd experience. Usually such a busy service station would be noisy with chatter, but even though there were plenty of people inside they were all but silent. One coffee stall was open and doing a thriving trade. A food counter had been smashed and the food taken, and the shop at the building's entrance seemed to have been looted. Magazines, CDs and DVDs lay scattered in front of the forced metal grille, and a trail of trampled chocolate bars led across the lobby area.

The toilets were a mess. No one had cleaned them for some time, and Jude complained that there was no toilet roll. Huw searched his pockets for a few tissues and handed them around the cubicle door, standing in front of it so that no one could enter.

But surreal though the atmosphere was, it was not threatening. Everyone was here for a reason, and that reason was survival. These were the people who were *doing* something instead of sitting passively at home, waiting for the threat to reach them. Huw had no idea how many people were on the move across Britain, but he didn't think it was the majority. The roads were still flowing, no busier than on a public holiday.

He exchanged a few nods, and a couple of men made conversation with him. But they were half-hearted exchanges at best. Like him, they all had their own people they wanted to look after. When he caught someone's eye he saw himself staring back—haunted, tired, confused and scared about what was to come. A sense of urgency made the silence loaded.

Back at the cars they stood for a while listening to the heavy sound of military helicopters. Lights flashed to the east, accompanied by the *whukka-whukka* of rotors. Chinooks.

They started out again. Huw took the lead. He tried to find music on the radio but there was none. So he switched it off, because he couldn't drive while listening to so much bad news. Kelly dozed beside him, curled up in the passenger seat. He felt a fierce, uncompromising love for her, a depth of emotion he hadn't felt for some time. They were looking after their family together, because no one else seemed able.

Ally was awake. Huw heard her tapping her iPad intermittently, and several times she tapped him on the shoulder to relay some more information.

"Some of them are dying in Switzerland. They don't like cold. People are fleeing to the Alps."

"There's been an explosion in Russia."

"Someone's transmitting from inside an underground shopping centre in Milan. They've cut themselves off, the vesps are passing them by."

"They've reached the Channel…"

That was at five in the morning. This late in the year it was still dark, and as they approached the junction that would take them back onto the M6 south of Lancaster, Huw indicated and pulled off into a highways maintenance area. There should have been a barrier preventing access, but it had been forced open. Giant yellow machines sat in shadows like sleeping dinosaurs. They parked amongst piles of gravel, stacked cones, and safety barriers.

Huw wound down his window. Glenn parked beside him and lowered his window.

"You heard?" Glenn asked.

"The Channel. We won't make it much further."

"We should try to make it to the Lakes," Glenn said. "Wide open country, plenty of places to get lost in there."

"And everyone else will be thinking the same," Kelly said.

"Think of anything better?" Glenn snapped. He closed his eyes, shook his head. "Sorry. Sorry."

"It's a good idea," Huw said. "How far, thirty miles?"

"Give or take," Glenn said.

"So let's go!" Kelly said.

"Mummy, I want to go home," Jude said from the back seat. Huw heard Lynne trying to comfort him, swapping seats with Ally so that she sat in the middle.

"What if we get split up?" Lynne asked from the back seat.

Won't matter, Huw thought. *Once they're all around us, what the fuck does anything matter?* His stomach rolled. He'd never felt so scared, not even after the accident and seeing Ally in hospital. Then there had still been some level of control, a system of procedures and protocols to grasp onto—hospital, rehabilitation, physiotherapy, operations. Now, there was only an unknown future ushering in dreadful danger.

"We've got the phones," Kelly said.

Huw nodded. "But make sure they're on silent." He powered up his window and circled the compound, leaving the same way they'd entered.

"They're attacking ferries in the Channel," Ally said. She'd been sitting in the back, unaware of the conversation and probably feeling terribly cut off. She was their source of information. "They were evacuating people from France. Now they're stuck on the ships, locked in their cabins while the vesps…" She drifted off, leaving the rest to the imagination.

Huw tried not to imagine too hard.

11

We're locked in down here, sightless, deaf, fifteen of us. All lost someone. Wish we'd run. Maybe we'd still be ahead. #fucked

@JennyFall, Twitter,
Friday, 18 November 2016

…in an old minibus… have to whisper because… still see them. Like ghosts in the night. Pale. They… against the windows. Maybe… listening, or feeling for… vibrations. We drove as fast as we could, then had a puncture. Trapped now and… seen what happens to those who make a noise. My daughter. (Silent tears.) My little girl…

BamKrauss, YouTube, Friday,
18 November 2016

We stopped and hid when we knew they were getting close. Isa says she thinks we should have gone on until the last moment. But we're here now, trapped, in a field with a hundred other cars. Five of us in a Volvo. No food, no water, the stench of sweat and piss and fear. The vesps circle. They roost. And if anyone opens a door, they swoop. There are bodies. They have become birthing grounds. I wish we'd driven faster. Wish we'd run further.

But they'd have probably still caught us. Sometime soon we'll have to open the door.

David Mendoza, CNN Correspondent, France,
Friday, 18 November 2016

There had been much to fear since the accident and losing my hearing. Travelling in cars upset and sometimes scared me. I didn't like being alone in the house, even with Otis keeping me company. I sometimes found myself turning around and around, as if to catch sight of someone always just behind me. Dense crowds— public transport, sports venues, busy shops—could sometimes send me into a nervous, escalating panic. But it was a deep irony that one of my most traumatic memories was from before the crash.

I was maybe five or six years old, and it had all been a nightmare...

Jude was only a baby, and Mum wore him in a sling across her chest. Dad came in from the sunny, bee-buzzed garden one peaceful afternoon, while I was drinking orange juice and eating biscuits and listening to my favourite CD of Disney songs, and gestured Mum towards him. I thought they were going for a hug. I liked seeing my parents hug; even at that age I didn't think they did it enough. Sometimes they even kissed, and they laughed when I told them it was gross because we all knew it really wasn't. It was love, and whether awake or asleep I loved seeing that. But this time Dad only spoke to Mum in lowered, serious tones.

The sunlight immediately faded, replaced by a heavy, almost tactile shadow that fell over the garden and stole all colour.

Next thing I knew we were running, all of us, sprinting across our garden as if it were the size of a field, not the tiny lawn-and-flower-bed plot it really was. My dad grasped one of my hands, Mum the other, my little brother bouncing against her chest with every panicked step she took. I saw the swing pass by on the left, my sandpit on the right with its cover ripped off and strange, clawed prints shadowed in the damp sand, and with almost every step I kicked away an array of coloured balls of all sizes.

The thing that chased us was unseen but so obviously there. Its presence was a heavy, dense thing, a gravity behind drawing us back. The faster and harder we ran, the slower our escape seemed to be. It was a vast weight, and every time I tried to turn to look, to see what dreadful thing had invaded our happy, perfect world, my parents squeezed my hands and dragged me along.

The worst thing—the *very* worst, more fearful than the sudden darkness, the endless garden of discarded and progressively more broken toys, and the sense of that monstrous thing bearing down on us—was the expression on my parents' faces. Terror for themselves. Dread for their children. The very real sense in their eyes that every step, every breath was hopeless and they were merely delaying the inevitable.

I'd screamed myself awake from each and every iteration of this nightmare. Over time their frequency had decreased, and at some point the nightmare stopped without me even noticing. Childhood was like that, I'd come to realise. A series of milestones, large and small, that were never really acknowledged until they had passed.

Sitting in the car, in the darkness, I remembered that

nightmare. It bore down on me with suffocating weight, compressing my chest and making each breath laborious. We were being chased.

I saw Dad's face in profile, and it reminded me so much of those dreams. Lynne held my hand and squeezed, and that reminded me as well. Each time I blinked, my vision was blurred with a pulsing, spotted image of countless discarded balls, and I thought they might deflate and spot that lawn for ever. The child that had played with them was long since gone.

I could see that none of them was talking. Even Jude had picked up on the tense atmosphere, snuggling into Lynne's side. I wished that my brother was still beside me. It was a big sister's job to look after her little brother in times like these—not that there ever had been times like these before. We might fight, but the fights didn't mean we didn't love each other. Mum often said, *Just you wait until Ally grows up and leaves home, Jude, then you'll miss her like crazy.*

I leaned forward and looked across at him, catching his eye, smiling and making a circle with my thumb and forefinger. But he didn't smile back. He knew that things were bad.

I checked the iPad again. I was following Twitter, a new trend labelled #vespsUK. When it had started trending I'd been shocked, because in truth, I hadn't really expected it. Plugged in though I was to the information superhighway, until recently this had been something happening elsewhere in the world. *We're safe. We're an island. This is all happening to someone else.*

Not any more.

There were too many new tweets to read them all, but a few random ones I picked out said everything.

@DoverDoll
I see explosions out to sea.

@PottyBonkkers
The horizon is on fire, what R they doing?

@UKPM
Our forces are engaged with the vesp plague above the English Channel.

I rolled the folding cover down over the screen. I didn't want to see. My scrapbook app was open, filling, scattered with folders and links, but right then I only wanted to be alone with my family, wishing I was ignorant of all that was happening. I turned in my seat and reached for Otis, splayed out now in the stolen Jeep's empty boot. I scratched his stomach and he rolled onto his back, legs in the air. I felt him grumble with innocent contentment and wished it could be so simple for all of us.

We were back on the motorway. Glenn was behind us in his Land Rover, keeping close on our tail. There were lots of cars, moving fast. I leaned forward and clocked the speedometer reading sixty, and in the dark, with so many vehicles surrounding us, knew that was dangerous. *There'll be accidents. One little bump and everyone grinds to a halt.*

But a few minutes later I saw why accidents were no longer holding us up.

Mum and Dad swapped a comment, then Mum spoke

briefly into her phone. The lines of traffic slowed. Ahead, past the flaring of brake lights, I saw the glow of a fire. Vehicles in the inside lane slowed to a crawl, and Dad nosed across into the outside lane. I looked back to check that Glenn was still with us. He was so close that the Land Rover's headlights were shielded by the back of the Jeep, and I could see Glenn plainly through the windscreen. I turned around again without waving.

We were still doing almost thirty miles per hour when we passed the wreck. Several cars had crashed, two of them entangled and burning, and there were stark scrape marks across the carriageway where they had been shoved aside and dumped on the hard shoulder. The fire still raged. A few people stood along the grass verge, one of them on her knees puking, some of them hugging, all of them confused and lost. *We should pick them up*, I thought, but then we were past and accelerating away again.

No one spoke.

There had been people in those burning cars, I was almost certain.

"Are you okay, Dad?" I asked, and he nodded without glancing back. His expression didn't change. That fear, that tense concentration pressed in and moulded the way his lips were set, his eyes wide and filled with reflected light.

Mum turned and nodded at the closed iPad in my lap, then spoke very carefully. "Ally, see if you can find any traffic updates. We don't want to be stuck in a jam."

I nodded. *Damn right we don't*, I thought. *Not now. Not when they get here, in however many hours they'll take*. The idea of being trapped in a line of thousands of vehicles with grumbling engines, blaring horns, crying children and screaming people…

I searched. There was little to see. No one seemed interested in road conditions when there was much more to worry about elsewhere. I tried the recovery services— AA, RAC—to see if they were updating reports, but their websites seemed to be static, frozen several hours ago. It was strange. I was already looking at something as it *had* been. History looked so calm.

"Nothing," I said, but when I looked up no one seemed to react. "Nothing on traffic," I said again, louder, and Dad raised one hand to indicate he'd heard.

Lynne put her arm around me. *I'm all right,* I thought, but then I saw my grandmother's face and realised that maybe the comfort was meant to go both ways. She was crying softly. Maybe it was pain from whatever was wrong with her, or sadness at what was happening. Frustration at not being able to help.

Traffic slowed again, and then the Jeep skidded to a sudden halt. I glanced back and saw the Land Rover, nose down, braking hard behind us.

Dad slammed his hands on the wheel, then opened the door and stood on the sill, only his lower body visible.

"Dad?" I asked. But Mum touched her finger to her lips.

Dad climbed onto the Jeep's roof, one foot on the open door's armrest, the other in the junction of door and frame. He disappeared altogether. I looked back and saw Glenn watching him. Around us people were leaving their cars, standing to look ahead. They threw jumping shadows in the sea of headlights.

I couldn't see anything obvious causing the hold-up,

but perhaps it was miles away.

I glanced at the Twitter feed.

@PottyBonkkers
Reached the coast. We're locked in. Hear shouts, screams.

@UKPM
Our forces continue to combat the infestation.

@ReggieBeNold
An aircraft crashed close by, military, massive explosion, and we can hear those things crawling on our roof.

@ReggieBeNold
Saw old Mrs Rogers from next door chased down and killed.

@ReggieBeNold
Can't stop our fucking dog from barking!

I looked back at Otis. He was on his feet now, tongue out and panting softly at the sudden change in circumstances. *Will I be able to stop* him *from barking?* I thought, and he looked at me with dark, loving eyes.

Dad clambered back into the car, looked across at Mum, and the fear burned in his eyes. He spoke briefly, then looked back, signing for me. "There's a big fire on the road ahead, out of sight. Maybe it was a petrol tanker, or something else. We'll not get past that way."

Jude asked something, I missed it.

"Off-road," I saw Dad say. He took the phone from Mum and called Glenn.

A minute later, seatbelts secured, we were driving

along the grass verge. The hard shoulder was blocked with parked cars, and there were others doing the same as us. Glenn was still directly behind, and now that we'd moved out of the static line of vehicles, I could see the glow in the sky ahead.

To our left was a steep bank leading down into a ditch. There was no way we could drive down there; we'd either roll or get the car's nose stuck. I closed my eyes, worried that the Jeep would slip and roll, trying to banish memories of the accident from my head. Lynne squeezed my hand again, and a flash of nightmare hit home once more—running across our garden, my swing seat swaying in an absent breeze, shadows solidifying and crushing us down, down, into the ground.

The Jeep bounced over the kerb and then turned left, tilting, light splaying across the interior and showing my parents leaning to the right and bracing themselves. Dad grasped the wheel in both hands and I could see him fighting it, knuckles white and muscles knotted. The Jeep flattened out, then there was an impact and broken wood and wire bounced across the bonnet against the windscreen. I felt a vibration as something scraped across the sides of the car, and Lynne tensed at the noise.

The Land Rover followed us through a broken fence, scraps of wood and barbed wire trailing behind for a moment. Then we were bumping across an open field.

Others were doing the same. We hadn't been the first to make this choice, and the further we moved from the road, the more I could see of the raised motorway and the slope and ditch beside it. I counted at least six vehicles on their sides or roofs in the ditch along the stretch, and several others seemed to be trapped against the heavy wooden fence. A few more were crossing the field behind and around us, mostly four-wheel drives and at least one motorbike. And now that others had seen what was happening, I saw a dozen more cars attempting the same manoeuvre.

As one of them slid down the slope and thudded side-on into the ditch, I turned away.

We bounced and jolted across the field. Otis was barking, his breath warm and stale. I reached back and he licked my hand, then let me tickle his chest. He was standing, swaying and stumbling left to right, and I wanted to shout at Dad to slow down, take care, the dog was getting scared.

But we were *all* scared. Unlike Otis, we knew why.

Glenn pulled alongside and lowered his passenger window. He shouted as he drove and Mum shouted back. I tried to imagine the noise, remember what it must be like—the roar of engines, the slam of bodywork on the uneven field, the creak and groan of the vehicles' movements, raised voices, and Otis barking once again behind me. In silence, all I had was vibration and memory.

Glenn took the lead, and my parents swapped a few quick words. Lynne said something. Dad shook his head.

"What?" I asked, but no one told me anything. I looked down at my covered iPad, not wanting to open it but feeling even more shut off from my family. I stroked the blue case and wondered what new horrors it might reveal.

Jude tapped my hand, leaning across Lynne's lap. When I looked up he sat up again and started signing.

"Glenn says we need to stay away from the roads for a bit," he said. "And he wants to lead the way."

"Why?" I asked.

Jude glanced forward, obviously hearing something Dad muttered. Then he signed, "He thinks he knows best."

I smiled at Jude. He smiled back, weakly, then huddled into Lynne again. He'd been so young when the accident happened, he didn't know me any other way. Sometimes he knew instinctively what I wanted, and right then he'd sensed my anxiety at being cut out. Our parents didn't mean to ignore me, I knew that. But sometimes including me in everything was hard work. I knew that too.

Ahead, several cars converged on a gap in the hedge and started passing through. Four of them made it, then the fifth got stuck in the mud churned up at the gate. Its wheels spun, splashing mud onto those cars waiting behind it. But it didn't move. Another car edged forward behind it and shoved, but there was no movement.

People jumped from vehicles, panicked, shouting in mute anger.

Glenn led us away from the blocked gateway, heading for the field's corner. We kept a couple of car lengths behind, and I noticed that Dad also kept a little to one side, trying not to follow in the Land Rover's tracks. He wanted to give the Jeep's wheels something to grab hold of. The field was ploughed and light glimmered from standing puddles. We could get stuck at any moment.

We reached a thick hedge of bushes and trees and Glenn angled along it, zigzagging slightly to shine his headlamps at the obstruction.

I was getting more and more frustrated. We were heading back towards the motorway, where the traffic was still static. More cars had poured down the steep bank, and there were now scores stuck in the ditch at the bottom. Shadows spidered back and forth along the roadway, silhouetted by the glare of headlights. Some of them seemed aimless, but small groups of people were now clambering down the embankment. They were already abandoning their cars.

I couldn't imagine the traffic jam moving again. It already stretched as far as the road was visible to the south, and was probably growing longer by the minute.

I found myself wishing the people away. *They'll be scared. They'll be noisy.* The idea surprised and shocked me, and I felt ashamed. I wished I could close my eyes and imagine us all up to Scotland and into Red Rock, the place I'd last visited when I was too young to even remember.

I flipped the iPad cover off and opened the BBC News page. The live update feed streamed as it caught up, then I read the latest postings.

06:04—Several ships burning in the English Channel. Many more adrift. It's thought that engines have been turned off to cut down on noise.
06:11—Vesps sighted along south coast from Ramsgate to Eastbourne.
06:23—Many reports of attacks now coming in from across South East England.
06:28—Military assaults taking place.

Military assaults taking place. I was old enough to be chilled by how non-specific that was. Anything military was noisy, wasn't it? Guns, explosions, aircraft, helicopters, bombs... The only stuff that was quiet might be chemical weapons, gas, stuff like that. But this was Britain. They never would.

"They've crossed the Channel," I said.

The Jeep hit a dip and bounced, startling me. When I looked up I saw that we were following the Land Rover through a gap in the hedge, and a heavy vibration travelled up from beneath as the wheels struggled for purchase. Plants scraped and scored along the Jeep's sides, and then we were through, lurching into the next field and accelerating after Glenn.

I saw Dad actually puff out his cheeks in relief.

Lynne reached over and closed the iPad cover. I frowned, glancing at my grandmother and leaning towards the door to see her face properly. I raised an eyebrow in an unspoken question.

"We know what's going to happen," Lynne said very carefully, then she drew me to her side.

I let myself be hugged. When I blinked I glimpsed that nightmare, running from shadows, the weight of dread.

12

I've never seen such a mass of humanity on the move. Hundreds of thousands have already left London, but those who never really believed it could happen here are now re-evaluating, and millions are trying to flee. The streets are gridlocked. These are biblical scenes, with millions attempting to work their way out of the city on foot. Many are carrying bags or belongings; many more have only the clothes on their back. In places the flow has been interrupted with what looks from up here like riots, but there's no indication of the cause.

Blue lights flash, but they are swamped.

The Tube has been deluged, and there are reports of tragedies at several Underground stations as people panic. Hundreds of helicopters are picking people up from private helipads and ferrying them north and west. The military no-fly zone is being ignored, and although scores of Royal Air Force choppers and jets are buzzing above London, they're not trying to stop anyone. We're one of over a dozen press helicopters currently reporting from above London. Air Traffic Control is offline, and our pilot is taking great care to watch out for other aircraft in our vicinity.

Every school is closed. Emergency services are helpless in the jammed streets, and reports are coming in of untended fires in several parts of the city. In scenes that have not been witnessed since the Dunkirk evacuation during the Second World War, the Thames is clogged with ships and boats of every size, all of them sailing downstream for the open sea. I've seen several collisions, and one large tourist boat that appears to have capsized.

It's horrible. I can't believe this is happening. London, our capital, the world's greatest city, is in utter turmoil, and there's no one or nothing that can help. If you're a praying person, pray for the people of London.

This is Jane Lane, Sky News, reporting from the skies above London. I'll stay here as long as I can, but I'm not sure… Yes. Just as long as I can.

Sky News audio-only broadcast, 6.55 a.m.,
Saturday, 19 November 2016

Part of Huw didn't want to know. He felt the pressure of the countdown, the ticking clock, the doom closing in on them, unstoppable. The thought of that final moment before the vesps overtook them was sickening. It gave him the same sense of deep dread as a dream he often had. He was edging out across a cliff face, no ropes or climbing equipment, sitting on a ledge just a foot wide and looking at the vista before him. Woods and valleys, hills and ravines, as far as the eye could see. Below him was a thousand-foot sheer drop.

Moving, he was fine. It was when he stopped that the terror flooded in. He knew then that he could sit there and eventually die, or start moving again and perhaps reach the other end of the ledge, and safety. But in his dream he could do neither.

He always fell. He never hit bottom. When he jerked awake and told Kelly about the dream she'd laugh softly, and tell him that if he hit bottom in his dream, he'd die in real life. *It's not the falling that kills you,* she'd say.

Now he was still moving. Still driving north, however slowly, however messed up their route had become. But soon, when the vesps drew close, they would have to stop. And he did not want to fall.

Glenn had always been one to take control: confident, brash, cocky. Huw found it even more annoying because he really *was* as good at things as he claimed.

After taking the lead, Glenn had found a route through the hedge into the next field, and a few minutes later they were on a country lane. As dawn lit the cloudless horizon, they wound their way north and west towards the Lake District. The urgency was terrible. The silence in the car almost deafened Huw. His heartbeat was fast and he was uncomfortably aware of it. He tried to breathe slowly, calm himself.

"You okay?" Kelly asked quietly.

"No," he said.

"We'll be fine. We're together."

He didn't know how to reply to that. What did she mean? They were together and that was all that mattered, in the end?

Glenn flashed his hazard lights and pulled over into a gateway. The lane they were following was narrow, and if anything came from the opposite direction it would be a tight squeeze.

He jumped from the Land Rover and waved. He looked tired, strained, and Huw felt a burst of affection for his friend.

"Toilet stop," Huw said. The cool air hit him as he jogged around to the front of the Land Rover and stood beside Glenn. They pissed into the hedge, comfortable in their silence. The view was opening up as dawn came, and Huw remembered what a beautiful part of the world the Lake District was. He and Kelly had been here on holiday before they had kids, and they'd spent a long, passionate weekend in a hotel close to Windermere. Lots of walking, lots of great food and fantastic sex; the memories made him realise just how much they'd changed.

The others were out of the Jeep, the women climbing the gate and disappearing behind the hedge. Jude was on the other side of the road, giggling as he pissed into the hedge.

"Few hours," Glenn said. "You think?"

"Maybe less," Huw said. "We need to find somewhere suitable. I don't want to drive until the last minute and get trapped in the cars."

"So what are you thinking?"

They zipped up and walked along the lane a little. It was amazingly quiet. *Good,* Huw thought. *This is what we need.*

"Farmhouse alone in a valley, maybe a holiday rental up on a hillside. Somewhere away from towns and villages. Private, can't be seen from the road."

"Sounds good," Glenn said. His voice shook. His eyes were wide, but he looked exhausted.

"You okay?"

"Knackered."

"We'll manage," Huw said. "Really. People are hiding, staying quiet."

"We'll need food," Glenn said. "Supplies. I have some, but you were cleaned out by that bastard."

"If we pass somewhere we can buy some stuff, but shelter's the priority. I don't want to get stuck in a supermarket."

Glenn shrugged. "Might not be a bad idea."

"Until people start looting."

"You think it'll get that bad?" his friend asked. But Huw didn't even need to reply. They both knew it already was that bad.

"Jude, you ride with Uncle Glenn," Huw said, catching his wife's eye, loving her when she smiled and nodded. "He's tired. Tell him some of your jokes, yeah?"

"Yay!" Jude said.

"Come on then!" Glenn shouted, clapping his hands. "Back in the cars!"

"Shhh!" Kelly said. "Quiet! We've got to be quiet."

"They're not—" Huw said.

"But they will be soon," Kelly cut in. "And we've got to get used to it. Don't you think? We've got to get used to not making a noise." Otis trotted up to her, nuzzling her hand and grumbling for some attention. She caught Huw's eyes and he saw how hopeless she felt.

He wished he could say or do something to make her feel better.

They met the roadblock less than twenty minutes later. Two big garbage trucks were parked across the road at a point where it curved uphill, their noses driven into hedges and tyres slashed so that it would take a heavy tow truck to shift them. There was definitely no way through, and no way around, either.

They backtracked to the nearest turning and continued up towards the low ridge to the west.

The next roadblock was manned. Several cars were queued there already, and a small group were arguing with several people sitting atop a supermarket's delivery van. It was parked across the road, and behind it two tractors had been driven into the ditches on either side.

"What the hell?" Kelly asked.

"Let's find out." Huw glanced back at Lynne and Ally. "Wait here. We won't be long."

"Dad!" Ally said. "They're in London now."

Huw didn't know how to reply to that, so he said nothing.

Glenn was already approaching the other drivers. Huw and Kelly jogged to catch up. He waved to his son in the Land Rover as he passed. Jude pulled a funny face.

He could already hear how heated the discussion was. A tall man stood on the van, nursing a shotgun menacingly.

"Selfish bastard!" a woman shouted.

"I'm protecting my own," the tall man said, voice calm and measured. He sounded very much in control.

"So you'll just leave us out here to—"

"What's up?" Glenn asked. His voice was one that always commanded attention, and even the tall man paused to look down at him.

One of the drivers pointed. "Him and his mates won't let us through. Says the Lake District is theirs, and the more people flood in, the more chance those things will spread through it."

"They'll spread anyway," Huw said.

"But we'll keep quiet," the tall man said. "A million

people like you come here because they think it's wild and safe, and you make it unsafe."

"That's so selfish!" another driver shouted. "I've got kids!"

Huw touched Glenn's arm and pulled him to one side. "We need to turn around and get away from here, now. There are a hundred roads in, not worth getting stuck on this one."

Glenn nodded. There were already three more cars pulling to a stop behind theirs, and it wouldn't take much for the road to become blocked.

Back in the cars, Huw performed a tight three-point turn and led the way back down the lane. At the junction he turned left, following a curving, tree-lined road that led along the foot of the hillside. The sun was up now, casting its glow across the countryside. It was beautiful, desolate, deserted. He could understand why the man had wanted to maintain that.

The next road wound up the hillside, passing a couple of houses, farmsteads, and several camping and caravan sites. It grew steeper and more remote, and after twenty minutes Huw could see ahead to where it passed over the ridge and into the landscape beyond. He was starting to hope they'd found a way in when they hit the next roadblock. Whoever had made it had done a thorough job. There was no way around.

"Where are they, Ally?" Huw asked. Lynne was sleeping. Ally looked exhausted, but she was still checking in on her iPad.

"London," she said softly. "The army is fighting them, but there's no effect. Everyone was trying to leave." She looked stunned. She had seen things no one should ever see, and Huw found himself selfishly glad that he was driving. He didn't want to look, didn't want to know.

"How long until—"

"The city was so noisy," Ally said. She was looking through the windscreen at the roadblock, hadn't seen him speak. "They said... they said that everyone started screaming. They called it a feeding frenzy. Now it's a birthing ground." Her voice was curiously flat, not textured with the pleasing musical lilt it had picked up soon after the crash. Kelly had said that her daughter always seemed to be singing, and Huw liked that idea. But she was not singing now.

"Not long," Huw said. "We don't have long." He was starting to panic. There were those houses back down the hillside, but they were too close to the road, too close to this roadblock that others would find. They could abandon their vehicles and cross the hills on foot, but there was a good chance they'd never reach shelter in time. Lynne would be slow, and though he knew that Jude was capable of long walks, he didn't know if he'd last for hours, even days. They'd be caught in the open. Night would fall. The thought of that was like getting stuck on the cliff ledge in his nightmare.

Glenn tooted behind him and started reversing back down the hill. When he reached a gateway he paused, then drove straight through. The metal bent, buckled, broke, and then he was into the field.

Huw reversed and followed.

They drove quickly, aiming uphill when they could, edging sideways along the hillside to avoid rocky outcroppings or copses. Sometimes the slope was so steep that Huw feared they would roll, and he found himself holding his breath. Kelly grasped the door handle beside her, staring across at him but not saying a word. Lynne muttered to herself. Otis whined.

The hill grew even steeper. Glenn aimed directly upwards, crawling up the rough terrain, and Huw was careful not to follow too close behind.

"Too steep," Lynne said from the back, but Huw didn't bother answering. What was there to say? If it *was* too steep they'd soon know.

The ground eventually plateaued below a sheer rise, a small, flattish area just large enough to park the two vehicles side by side. The small cliff was only twenty feet high, but more than enough to halt onward progress. To one side a rocky outcropping prevented movement, and to the other side, a farmer's drystone wall blocked the way.

"Now what?" Lynne said.

"How about now we be a bit positive!" Huw said. It should have been ridiculous, because there was very little to be positive about. But Lynne sighed and said no more, and Kelly reached over and touched his hand. They must have touched more in the last two days than in the two months previous.

They all jumped out to survey the scene. Downhill, in the direction they had come from, a line of traffic clogged one road in the distance. Horns blared. When the wind was right, it even brought the whisper of outraged, scared voices. They could not see its beginning or end, and Huw wasn't even sure whether it was a road they had travelled. But it proved that they had done the right thing. If they became trapped up here, they'd be better off than most.

He tried to imagine what it would look like—clouds of vesps swarming in, sweeping across the landscape, attacking any living thing that made a sound and planting eggs in the still-warm flesh.

Jude ran past him and sat on a rock, staring down into the valley. "Wow, that was steep!"

"Sure was," Huw said.

"Sorry," Glenn said.

"What for?"

"Getting us up here."

"We haven't stopped yet," Huw said. "Come on."

Ally went with them. They climbed the small, sheer slope and continued uphill, frustrated to find that the ground beyond was actually much more gentle. They weren't too far from the top of the hill, either. There was a public footpath heading that way, but they didn't go that far because time was short. Huw hoped that beyond would be a gentle descent into the next valley, and they would be beyond the roadblocks.

It would be much quieter down there.

"We've got to try," Huw said. "Come on. Let's see what we can do."

"But we're trapped!" Glenn said.

"It's not over till the fat lady sings. Come on." Huw jogged back downhill, the others following. Kelly was silent, and Huw wished he could stop and speak with her, find out what she thought, what frightened her. But just being together felt good enough.

Scrambling down the steep drop to the vehicles, Huw took a good look around. And maybe there *was* a way. If they could dismantle a portion of the wall they might be able to squeeze through, and then perhaps they'd skirt around the steepest portion, over a few dangerously rocky bits, and then up towards the hill's summit. It was risky and dangerous, but other than going back down the way they'd come, it was their only option.

Kelly was already standing at the wall looking that way. Glenn joined her, nodded, and turned to Huw.

"So let's get cracking," Huw said.

They all helped. To start with, all six of them went at the wall, but they got in each other's way. So they formed a chain, Jude and Glenn hauling stones from the wall, Lynne and Kelly passing them on, Ally and Huw tumbling the stones over the edge of the small plateau. Some of them came to a quick stop on the hillside, but a few of the bigger chunks found some momentum and skipped downhill, smashing into other rocks or being caught by spreads of dying, browning ferns.

Glenn tried singing, but no one took up the song. It faded into an uncomfortable silence, and Huw immediately wished that he'd joined in with his friend. But it would not have felt the same to start it up again. The impulsiveness had gone, it would have felt forced, and forced good cheer never worked.

But the physical work felt good. Huw even caught Lynne smiling, though she looked tired, and that got him thinking. She had prescription painkillers, but radiotherapy sessions had been scheduled, beginning in just ten days' time. That would not happen now. She was an intelligent woman, and she'd know what that meant. But she was not complaining.

"Working up a sweat there, Jude the Dude," Huw

said. He hadn't used that nickname for a while, and Jude burst into a fit of giggles. Ally looked from Jude to her dad, and he mouthed, "Jude the Dude." She laughed as well.

"Jude the Dude," she said as she and Huw hefted another rock down the hillside, "liked his food, got in a mood, and pooed."

Jude laughed some more and it was good to hear.

"Look at those biceps!" Glenn said. "Gonna be as strong as me!"

They carried on working, bantering, enjoying the feel of the sun on their skin and the clear sky, despite it being November. The Lake District was renowned for its heavy annual rainfall. When he and Kelly had holidayed there it had been the height of summer, and for four days it had rained every afternoon and on into the evenings. But today looked like it was going to be clear and beautiful.

Half an hour in and the wall looked barely touched. The stones had been so well stacked that each one took heavy tugs to pull it free. Glenn's hands were bleeding, and he'd already told Jude to stand back a little while he worked. He stripped off his jacket and grunted with the effort, wiping his bloodied hands on his trousers. Huw thought he looked like a movie star. He chuckled, swept sweat from his forehead. If they had any hope of survival—if there was even the smallest chance that they'd find somewhere safe to ride out this storm—having Glenn with them would boost their chances hugely.

He was a proven survivor. He'd had meningitis as a child, and when he and Huw were sixteen they'd been in a serious fight, a random attack. A bunch of drunk men had stumbled from a pub just when Huw, Glenn and their mates were walking by. The men hurled abuse. Glenn alone returned it with gusto, and so it was him that they chose to beat to a pulp.

Huw and his mates waded in and were punched and kicked to the ground. But Glenn remained defiant, standing as long as he could stand, fighting back, and he'd ended up with a fractured skull and a bleed on the brain. Three weeks in hospital had followed, and by the time he came home Huw's own bruises and cuts were all but gone.

Glenn had recovered, surprising the doctors and his parents with his resilience. It had taken several months of physiotherapy to regain ninety-five per cent usage of his left arm and leg. None of the attackers were caught. Not by the police, at least.

But Glenn had a memory for faces.

Out of the five men who'd been involved in the attack, there were only two who he'd never faced down. The first was only a couple of months later. Huw hadn't been with him, and Glenn had only told him one night when they were drunk on scrumpy cider, listening to the newest metal albums and talking about fingering Donna Francis.

"I found that fat fucker," he'd said. "The one who liked using his feet on my head. I was on my bike and I saw him putting petrol in his car. Had his two little kids in the back. I could've called the police but…" He'd shaken his head and finished his pint. "Only hit him once, from the side. I think I broke his jaw. He fell against the petrol pump and I saw a tooth come out." He hadn't smiled, or laughed. But Huw had sensed the deep satisfaction in his friend's act of personal vengeance.

Glenn had told him about the others over the next couple of years, casual comments slipped into other conversations when none of their other friends were listening.

Hey, remember that one with the camo-shorts? Found him. Broke his arm... and... Oh yeah, bastard who punched me first, he won't be playing football again. There was never any more than that, and there were no more repercussions.

And although Huw could not help but admire his friend's sense of personal justice, all he could see when he thought about the attack was that fat guy's kids sitting in the back of his car, watching their father have his jaw broken by a total stranger. Maybe the action was justified. Maybe. But the fact that Glenn hadn't considered the effect it would have on those kids always bothered Huw. It scared him a little, too. It made him glad that he was Glenn's friend, because he could be dangerous.

He was never more glad than right then.

It was almost ten in the morning before Huw stood upright and told them all to stop.

"So?" he asked.

"Looks good to me," Kelly said. "Let's give it a go?"

"Yeah," Glenn nodded. He clapped Jude's shoulder. "Come on, dude, let's scout the route." They climbed over the remaining wall foundation and trotted along the hillside. Huw watched his son go, heart aching, loving him so much and so desperate to protect him, protect all of them. Ally was sitting on a rock wiping sweat from the back of her neck, and she smiled up at him.

"You think we can get past now?" she asked.

"It's worth a try," he said. "Yeah, I think so. Glenn's

a good driver, we'll follow in his tracks." He turned to Kelly. "You want to drive?"

"I'm okay on the roads, but I haven't driven off-road since I was twenty," she said. "I'll be ballast."

"Lynne?" he asked, offering her the keys. His mother-in-law drove a small Vauxhall, and he knew the thought of driving a beast like the Jeep would give her the jitters. She chuckled softly and shook her head, but he could see the pain she was holding back. From the corner of his eye he saw Ally's face drop. He looked at Kelly, raised an eyebrow. *We'll have to have this conversation soon.*

Lynne seemed to sense the tension. She stood and heaved a few smaller rocks aside, lobbing them far enough to be away from the gap they'd opened up in the wall. But she wasn't proving anything.

Jude came back first, sprinting downhill and leaping from a pile of rocks onto the more level plateau. He was wide-eyed and eager, and he started talking even before he'd caught his breath.

"We can get up there, it's okay, and we saw down into the valley and there's this big lake and some houses, maybe a village, but there's something on fire in the road!"

"Which road?" Kelly asked.

Glenn appeared, trotting across the hillside and over the wall. He looked troubled.

"What?" Huw asked.

"What Jude said," he said. He was barely panting. "We can get over and into the valley, I reckon, though it'll be a tricky drive. But there's something going on along the valley, maybe a mile or two to the east. Something burning, and maybe gunfire."

"'Maybe' gunfire?" Lynne asked.

"Not shotguns," Glenn said.

"Military?" Huw asked.

"What, the army?" Jude blurted.

Glenn shrugged. "They do a lot of training up here."

"It's insane!" Lynne said. "Who do these people think they are? They can't just close off the Lake District, there are hundreds of roads leading in, tracks across fields. And anyway, it's a National Park, it belongs to everyone!"

"Not so many roads," Glenn said. "Seriously, for people who know the area it'd be pretty easy to close off sections of it."

"Especially with guns," Kelly said. "Jesus."

Ally had gone back to the Jeep and was now leaning against the front grille, iPad open in her hands. The dread on her face did not need explaining, and Huw wanted to hug her safe. *My little girl,* he still called her, annoying her and making her embarrassed. But he meant it.

"Come on," Glenn said. "We'll get past the roadblocks this way, down into the valley. Find a house. It'll be much quieter down there." He ruffled Jude's hair. "Ride shotgun for me, dude?"

Jude grinned and looked to his parents for approval.

"Look after my little boy," Huw said.

Glenn grinned back. "He's looking after me!"

Glenn went first in the Land Rover, tilting alarmingly to the left as he passed over the remains of the wall they'd all sweated to dismantle. Huw followed in the Jeep. Kelly sat beside him, Ally and Lynne in the back, with Otis whining in the boot as the vehicle rocked left and right and bumped over rocks and humps in the ground. The wall scraped the left wing and doors, then they were through.

Glenn followed the slope for fifty metres, then turned right. Huw tried to keep in his tracks, figuring that a safe route for the Land Rover would also be safe for them. He could just see Jude in the front seat, arms waving as he talked to Glenn, probably advising him on where to go and how to drive.

Heading uphill, seeing the summit lit by the sun and the clear blue sky beyond, Huw began to think that they'd make it. But the idea of what they might find down in the next valley was daunting. If Glenn really had heard gunfire, and it really was the military, who knew what orders they had received? There was no saying what was happening elsewhere in the country. Perhaps the unit had even gone rogue, securing their own safety by any means necessary.

They wouldn't be shooting at people, surely. Not at civilians.

"Huw!" Kelly shouted. He jumped, twitched the wheel to the left, and narrowly avoided a rocky projection. It would have shredded a tyre at best, maybe even smashed the whole wheel. He breathed deeply, then concentrated on the route uphill.

They came to a steeper slope again, and Glenn slowed almost to a standstill, letting the four-wheel drive crawl them uphill at a snail's pace. Huw followed quite close behind, not wanting to stop and wait in case he found it hard to start again. The Jeep was digging in, but he was not used to driving something like this off-road. It was all new to him.

At last the ground started to flatten and they reached

the summit, bouncing over several deep ruts that tortured the suspension and set Otis barking as he was flung around the boot. Glenn did not stop. Jude turned and waved to them, grinning from ear to ear, as Glenn headed across the hilltop and then down towards the valley on the other side.

"We should stop and look ahead, find the best route," Kelly said.

"Look over there." Huw pointed. "No time." It was a mile away, maybe more, but the winding road leading down into the valley was obvious from the static traffic glimmering in the morning sun. At the head of the line of motionless vehicles, several cars and vans burned. Beyond them were more vehicles, all of them a bland colour that almost faded into the landscape. Military. Huw didn't want to stop, didn't want to hear any gunfire. It chilled him to the core, and he only wanted to get away.

Glenn must have been looking as well. Talking to Jude, maybe, trying to comfort him and persuade him that the fires should not concern them, his attention snatched for just a moment too long. That was the only explanation for what happened next.

The Land Rover thudded into a series of dips in the hillside, depressions where loose earth had fallen away. Glenn must have revved the engine because the bonnet rose, the tail end slammed down again, and then the front offside wheel struck a rock.

Lynne cried out behind Huw, her hand reaching past his face as if she could grab the Land Rover, hold on, prevent it from tipping.

It fell onto its right side. Huw slammed on the brakes, stood on the pedal as he tensed forward, disbelief and terror combining to steal his breath.

The Land Rover rolled. Inside, shadows danced. It flipped onto its roof and momentum kept it going, bouncing off a pile of rocks, glass exploding and flowering around it as the rear window shattered.

"No, no, no!" Kelly screamed, Lynne and Ally shouted, but Huw could only watch in stunned disbelief.

It rolled twice more, the final roll flipping it almost completely off the ground, before it slammed down on its roof against a tree-topped pile of boulders. Its wheels spun lazily. Steam burst from the front grille, and Huw thought of a hundred action films he'd seen where crashed cars immediately burst into flames and then exploded.

Kelly was out of the Jeep first, sprinting downhill, and Huw followed quickly, slipping in mud and going sprawling, grasping at Ally as she reached for him and pulled him upright, crying out when the truth of what he'd seen slammed in and the reality of what he might find clasped a cold hand around his heart.

Lynne dashed past him, then he was on his feet, he and Ally sprinting over the crushed vegetation and torn ground that marked the Land Rover's descent.

Kelly reached the vehicle first and fell to her knees. She screamed.

13

Remain inside. Keep quiet. Stay safe. This can't last forever.

Metropolitan Police website,
Saturday, 19 November 2016

As I ran downhill beside Dad, the world kept spinning. I might have been in the rolling car myself, limbs thrashing, hair swaying, stomach lurching with every step I took. I was terrified of what I would find, but desperate to get there.

This is too real! I thought. I'd had a gun pointed at my face, but seeing the crash and knowing that Jude might be hurt had brought home the shattering, sickening reality.

I could see Mum kneeling on the ground, and though I heard nothing, I could tell by the way her shoulders and chest moved that she was screaming. She had her hands to her face as she looked into the upturned Land Rover, and whatever she saw must have been terrible.

We reached the vehicle at the same time as Lynne. She went to Mum and knelt at her side, while Dad and I skidded against the Land Rover's dented metal wing. I could smell petrol, heat, oil, exhaust fumes. I dropped to my knees.

TIM LEBBON

Blood. Someone was hanging from their seatbelt, bleeding across the airbag that had deployed at the first impact. It was stark and wet and there was so much. *That's not Jude*, I thought, and then Dad reached past and grasped at Glenn's arm where it was lashing at the car's smashed window. He held his friend's hand.

I slipped around the front of the Land Rover and found its other side pressed tight against a pile of rocks. Above the car's exposed underside, several trees grew out from the rocky facade, one of their trunks now splintered and pale. I crouched down but could barely see inside; the Land Rover's nose was dipped into a hollow in the ground. I lay down flat, crawling forward, feeling hot water from the ruptured radiator dripping onto the back of my scalp and neck as I pulled myself beneath the bonnet.

The windscreen had smashed and I tugged it aside, cutting my hands and spilling diamonds of glass to the ground. Then I dug my fingers into the soil and pulled myself further in.

"Jude!" I shouted. The passenger airbag was slowly deflating, drooping like a landed balloon. And though I dreaded what it might reveal, I grasped the bent windscreen frame and pulled myself closer. To my right I saw Glenn's airbag deflating, blood running as it revealed the man still hanging upside down in his seat, held fast by the seatbelt. His face was a mess. I didn't look for long.

Dad was trying to lift Glenn, struggling to get past him to find his son. The red maw of Glenn's shattered mouth opened in a silent scream. Dad was spattered with blood.

"I'll get to him!" I said. I reached out and clawed my hand into the airbag, pulling it towards me so that I could see behind.

Jude hung in his seat. He was looking around, confused, blinking rapidly, and when he saw me he burst into nervous laughter. His nose was bloodied, blood dripping up over his eyes and forehead.

"Can you reach the seatbelt clip?" I asked. "Jude, unclip yourself. But you'll fall, so try to turn so you don't bang your head." He said something, but he was upside down and I couldn't read his lips. "Just do it!"

To my right, Mum was trying to crawl into the narrow gap between the bonnet and the ground. I waved her back. "He's okay, Mum, he just needs to unclip himself." Mum was frantic, barely hearing, clawing at the ground and kicking with her feet to get closer to her son. "Mum!" She looked directly at me. "He's okay."

I turned back to Jude. Seeing Mum's tears wouldn't help right now, and it would only bring on tears of my own. I needed my vision clear. Needed *all* my available senses clear, because I could still smell petrol.

"Jude, I can't see what you're saying, but do your best to undo your seatbelt. I'll help you out. There's lots of glass, but if you crawl carefully you'll be fine. Okay?"

He stuck up both thumbs, then started feeling for the seatbelt release. I stretched my right hand through the smashed window for him, glancing again at Glenn. Dad was trying to help him but his bloody face was stretched in a terrible upside-down scream. The deflated airbag hung before him, and Dad tried to tuck it out of the way into the steering wheel.

Movement, a thud, and Jude was free of the seatbelt.

He'd landed on the Land Rover's ceiling, still tangled in the belt but no longer restrained by it. He started to thrash and struggle, one foot kicking against Glenn's shoulder.

"Jude!" I said. "Take it easy, be calm! Come on now, squirt, calm down." He calmed, looking at me with startlingly white eyes. His nose was still bleeding, and I was amazed at how much blood could come from one person.

Mum started reaching for him too, and Jude worked his way free of the seatbelt.

"Through the smashed window," I said, and I felt my brother's hand in mine. It was a good feeling, and I squeezed and pulled, helping him crawl through the narrow space and out. I winced as glass cut into my hands. I could feel Jude's frantic breath on my face, and I smiled to try and calm him down. He was free, out, and he would be fine.

We stood together and hugged. I couldn't remember the last time we'd held each other like that, but it felt good.

Then Mum was there holding us both, and Lynne, and a cool breath of November air chilled the sweat that had popped up across my back and neck.

"Glenn?" I asked, pulling away so I could see. Mum grimaced. I ruffled my brother's hair, then slipped around the side of the stricken vehicle and ducked down beside Dad.

He was still holding Glenn's hand. The man was motionless now, no longer writhing in pain.

"What's happened?" I asked. Half in the shattered side window, Dad turned so that I could see his face.

"Can't reach the seatbelt," he said.

"I'll get in and—"

He grabbed my arm with his free hand. "There's petrol leaking."

"There's nothing to light it." I wriggled free of his grasp and turned away before he could respond. But I could not be sure at all. Had Glenn actually switched the ignition off? Could that do something to ignite leaked fuel? Would contact against hot metal parts be enough?

I crawled back beneath the bonnet and through the broken windscreen, and it brought vague, shadowy memories of my own crash. The feel of glass beneath my hands, the smells, the sight of Glenn and his blood, all seemed terribly familiar.

Inside, I searched for Glenn's seatbelt release. Finger on the red button, I looked past the hanging man at Dad.

"Ready?"

He nodded. I pressed. Glenn stiffened, shifted slightly, then stuck fast.

"That's it," I said, "seatbelt's out. He must be…" I looked up at his legs and saw why he had hardly moved. The whole steering column had shifted, dropping onto his thighs and pinning him to his seat. It was difficult to see past the mess of deflated airbag, but his jeans were crushed and dark with blood. The steering wheel was buckled.

I put my hand on Glenn's shoulder and felt him breathing shallow and fast. He turned to look at me, his upside-down, blood-covered face so close to mine that I could smell his breath.

"We'll get you out," I said, but when he answered I had no idea what he was saying. I felt useless. "Dad?" I couldn't see my father, either. I backed out through the windscreen, cutting my hands some more. *We're flailing,* I thought. *It's all starting to go wrong and the vesps aren't even here yet!*

Lynne and Mum were fussing around Jude, cleaning blood from his face with tissues and checking him over. He was standing, shaking with shock, but he seemed fine. He smiled at me. One of his last remaining milk teeth had been knocked out and his lip was swollen. His nose bled. He'd have two black eyes. But he was still standing and conscious. He hadn't suffered in his crash like I had in mine.

"How's Glenn?" Jude asked. I had to get him to repeat it past his swollen lip and the distracting blood on his face.

"Trapped," I replied.

"How long do we have?" Mum signed.

I shrugged, then realised the urgency. I blinked. At first I thought my family were staring at me, but really they were looking past me at the rolled, ruined vehicle. It could have been worse, I knew. If it hadn't come to a halt against this pile of rocks it might have rolled some more. Two more tumbles and Glenn might have had his stomach crushed by the steering column. Three more and Jude might have had his skull caved in by the warped doorpost. A spark, a ruptured engine block, an explosion…

I jogged uphill, scrambled into the back of the Jeep and snatched up my iPad. Otis was barking, I realised, and I tried to shush him. But he was beyond comforting, and I turned my back on the dog instead. Letting him out now might only make the situation worse; he might try to get into the upturned vehicle, slice his paws on the glass. There were enough injuries already.

I accessed my scrapbook app. It had a direct link to

the *Live: Breaking News* feed on the BBC site, and I only had to check a few of the postings with times and locations to see just how fucked we were.

How truly fucked.

I closed my eyes and dropped the tablet back on the seat. Otis was trying to scrabble through the cargo net that separated him from the back seat, and I stretched my arm around so that I could pet his head, scratch beneath his jaw. His eyes were wide and dark with excitement.

"Good boy, Otis," I said. "Shhh. Good boy."

Then I went to tell them the news.

"Maybe two hours," Huw said. He was crouched beside Glenn on the upturned ceiling of the Land Rover. His friend was still trapped in the driver's seat, legs stuck beneath the displaced steering column and wheel. He'd tried adjusting the seat's height settings, lowering its back, and when he'd attempted to shift it back Glenn had screamed loud enough to hurt his ears. He'd had to stop after that. Glenn spent a few minutes in and out of consciousness, and when he came to again his breathing was faster, lighter. "Maybe a little less."

"How long can someone hang upside down without passing out?" Glenn asked.

"I think that's a myth."

"Doesn't feel like it." His voice was distorted by the damage done to his face and lips. There were bones broken there, Huw was sure, but it seemed minor compared to his legs. Maybe his stomach, too, and his spine. Glenn was already saying that he could no longer feel his feet.

"I'm going to try to open the door again," Huw said. "Maybe get you out that way."

"Not yet, not yet." Glenn reached for him, grabbed his arm and squeezed tight. "Just sit here for a bit, yeah? Let me gather myself. Think things through."

Huw almost laughed. He was hanging upside down in a wrecked car, possibly bleeding to death, trapped with no emergency services about to come to the rescue and a plague of monsters bearing down on them, and still he thought he was in charge. But that was Glenn all over. It was why Huw had been pleased to have his friend with them.

But he wasn't with them any more. Huw could see that already, and Glenn wasn't stupid. Even if they did manage to get him out, his injuries meant he'd be prone in the back of the Jeep, in the short term at least. Maybe his legs weren't broken or his spine cracked, but it would be a while until they knew for sure. And they no longer had a while.

"Okay," Glenn said, voice slurred. "We don't have long. So one try to get me out through the door, then if that doesn't work you'll have to leave me."

"What? No!"

"Yes," Glenn said. "And keep your voice down. Don't want to upset..." He trailed off, tensing as a wave of pain swept through him. He gasped, panted, and held onto the wheel crushed against his thighs. Huw pushed his friend upwards a little, easing some of the pressure. Close like that, tight in the confines of the overturned Land Rover, they could feel each other's warmth, smell each other's fear. Glenn's blood was damp and warm against Huw's shoulder.

"Sorry, mate," Glenn said.

"Hey, I'll get you out, don't start—"

"I mean I'm sorry about Jude. He's okay, yeah?"

"Yeah."

"I'm sorry. He was my responsibility. I should have been more careful, less gung-ho. After everything you've been through… I should have looked after him more."

"Glenn, he's fine."

"Might not have been," Glenn said. "Look at Ally. See how she turned out."

"She's fine too!" Huw said, automatically defending his daughter. He'd done so a dozen times through the years when people expressed pity for her deafness, as if it made her a lesser person. But he knew Glenn hadn't really meant it that way.

"You're such a good dad," he said.

"Fucking hell, mate, you're making this sound like a goodbye. This isn't a movie, you know. Now shut the hell up. I'm getting out to go around to the door. I'll get it open, and you'll scream your head off when I pull you out, I'm sure. Then we'll be away. Nice cottage, open fire, wine cellar." Huw relaxed, letting his friend take his own weight again, ignoring the loud groans.

He scrambled from the vehicle and stood, looking around. Across the hillside, further down in the valley, smoke rose thicker and wider. There was no more gunfire, but none of the vehicles seemed to have moved. The military vehicles were still there. He wondered if those guarding the roadblock would see them, and if they did, whether they'd come to investigate. But he was powerless to change that.

He had to concentrate on things he *could* change.

"Huw, we need to get him out," Kelly said. Lynne and the kids were back uphill with the Jeep. Ally had taken Otis out and was throwing a stick for him, the dog blissfully unaware of the drama. Jude was talking to Lynne, his face cleaned up but his clothes stained with blood.

"I'm doing my best."

"How bad?"

He shrugged. He didn't want Glenn to hear them discussing his situation. "I'll get him out now," he said, louder, and he turned his back on his wife.

But they knew each other so well, and he saw the doubt and fear in Kelly's eyes.

The door was warped in its frame. He tried the handle again, tugged. It wouldn't budge. He knocked out the rest of the shattered glass, careful not to flick it inwards at Glenn, then grabbed the window's sill and braced his feet against the door column. He pulled, increasing the force until he heard a gentle creak. But there was no movement.

"Okay?" he asked.

"Hanging in there," Glenn said, his muffled voice turning into a wet cough.

Huw went to the back of the vehicle. One side was rammed against the pile of rocks, and petrol still trickled from the crack the impact must have put in the fuel tank. But he was able to open the lower portion of the rear door. It was a mess in there, with bags of food, clothing and other supplies tossed around and burst open, much of it soaked in petrol. Even if they did have time to rescue any of it, most would be unusable.

He'd always liked the smell of petrol. Kelly called

him weird. He didn't like it any more.

Huw pulled aside one tumble of bags, trying to orientate himself. The little tool hatch in the boot's side popped open when he touched it and a jumble of tools clanged out, falling into the mess of opened bags. He winced.

Sparks! he thought. Would he even feel the *whoof* of fire if a spark ignited the fuel? He guessed so. And he guessed his family would be far enough back to escape the conflagration and see him staggering around as he burned to death, and hear Glenn's screams.

Heart still jumping, he rooted around for the tools and found a tyre iron, jack, and other bits and pieces.

Back at the door he wedged the sharp end of the tyre iron in beside the handle and leaned on it. He swayed back and forth, exerting more and more pressure with each forward swing, but succeeded only in bending the metal framing. The door catch and lock remained solid.

"Shit. Shit!"

"Try the jack," Glenn said. He sounded different. Woozy, weaker. Maybe there really was something about being hung upside down for too long. Blood rushing to the head? Unconsciousness? Huw thought it was a myth, but he didn't know for sure.

Kelly was beside him, touching his arm.

"The jack," she said. "I'll help." Together they tried to figure out some way to wedge the jack into the space between door and frame. It wouldn't go. It was too thick, even in its lowest profile. And even if they could, Huw feared it would rupture the metal around the framing before popping the lock.

"Okay, back inside," he said. "I'm going to try and

jack the column up from his legs."

"Huw," Kelly said softly.

"No!" he said. He wouldn't talk about leaving Glenn here. Didn't even want to think about it. But with that on his mind, it was all he *could* think about.

"She's right," Glenn said.

"Shut the fuck up," he muttered. He dropped down, slid back in through the windscreen and scooted himself into a sitting position next to his friend.

"Really," Glenn said. "You need cutting gear. Fire brigade. And I don't think they'll send a rescue helicopter today, do you?"

"Shut up," Huw said again. "Don't try to be in control. You're not in control of this."

"No, you are," Glenn whispered. "Your family depend on that, mate. Kelly's strong. Right now she's stronger than you because she's right. Think about it."

"I can't." He moved the jack up beneath the wheel, trying to figure out where he could place it without it crushing Glenn's legs. If he propped it on the seat between his legs, wouldn't it just compress and break the seat? He needed somewhere solid to hold it against, something stronger than the ruptured steering column he wanted to move.

He tried not to look too closely at Glenn's wounds. His legs were broken and compressed, but his stomach had been injured as well.

"I don't want you and your family here when they come," he said.

"We won't be. Neither will you."

"I fucking mean it!" Glenn said, hissing as pain scorched through his body. "Now you made me raise my voice. But I mean it, Huw. Leave me, go find somewhere to hide and ride it out. A cottage. Nice fire, wine cellar."

"You'll die."

He'd said it. They were all thinking it, but he'd said it, and now it was out there it couldn't be unsaid.

"Maybe, but only me," Glenn said. "Lots of people are dying. But not your kids. You want to see Jude torn apart by those things?"

Huw propped the jack, but there was not enough room to turn the handle.

"Fuck!"

"Huw," Kelly said. She was crouched next to the door, looking in past Glenn's trapped legs.

"Tell him, Kelly," Glenn said.

"Huw, we have to get the kids away. We'll come back. Glenn can keep quiet, stay safe, and we'll come back when—"

"When it's safer?" Huw asked, feeling hysteria pressing in on him.

"Maybe," she said. "But we don't know what's going to happen when they come."

"She's right," Glenn said. "What if I pass out, shout, scream? Because honestly, it hurts like fuckery, mate."

Huw threw the jack down. It clattered against metal, sparking, and he held his breath. Beside him, utter silence.

"Well that could have been bad," Glenn said, and Huw couldn't help laughing. It was manic and felt dangerous, but even Glenn managed a chuckle before he hissed and held his breath again.

"I'll come back," Huw said. "Couple of hours…" But he trailed off. He couldn't promise anything. "I don't want to leave you to die." He was crying now.

"Pussy," Glenn said. "Go on, I'll be fine, I've survived worse than this."

This time Huw couldn't find it in himself to laugh. He crawled from the Land Rover without another word and marched uphill, head down, not meeting his family's eyes. Kelly went with him and tried to hold his hand, but he shook her off. Glenn might be watching. He might see the hope between them, and Huw didn't want that.

"Dad?" Jude asked. "Where's Glenn?"

"We'll be coming back for him," Kelly said. "As soon as it's safe."

"Safe?" Ally asked, and whether it was a question, or she'd simply picked up on Kelly's final word, Huw could not tell.

He jumped into the Jeep and started the engine, slamming his door and waiting for the others to get in. Jude was speaking, pleading, and Kelly tried to quieten him down. Lynne said something in that deep, quiet voice he so fucking despised, self-righteous and know-it-all. He hated himself for hating her right then. Hated himself for everything.

Ally urged Otis into the boot and she was the first to climb in behind Huw.

"He told you to go, didn't he?" she asked.

Huw didn't turn around to reply, nor did he nod. He simply gripped the wheel and stared downhill at the stricken Land Rover.

The smell of petrol hung heavy in the vehicle. It was on their clothes. The scent of blood was more subtle.

When everyone was inside he slipped into gear. Kelly

was beside him. He waited, ready to let off the handbrake, drive away, edge down past Glenn and into the valley beyond. He saw all this in his mind's eye, and actually experienced the sickness that he'd feel with every minute he put between himself and his dying friend.

He closed his eyes and turned off the ignition.

"No way," he said. "There's no way."

14

Even while the enemy advances, people are writing history texts about the Day of the Vesps. They're recording events that happened in Eastern Europe, the rapid spread across the continent, the vesps' limited incursions into Asia and North Africa, the efforts made and battles lost. They are charting world reaction to the tragedy, including the USA shutting all sea and land borders, Australasia isolating itself from the world stage, and the military skirmishes in the Far East between Japan, China, and North and South Korea. Interviews are being collated, opinions sought, and books written, even while vesps occupy airspace above the writers' retreats, and danger still stalks the streets. And I find this encouraging. Looking ahead in this manner is testament to the human spirit. It speaks of a belief in survival, and on this dark day, such belief is vital. So I say to these historians… keep writing. You are already creating our brave new world.

Prime Minister's Address to the Nation (audio only), 11 a.m., Saturday, 19 November 2016

"I can prepare you to live in silence," I said. "Listen." We were all there, sitting on the ground close to the overturned Land Rover so that Glenn could hear too. We'd made a renewed effort to free him, but to no avail. He groaned and hissed in pain whenever we touched the steering wheel, and trying to push him out sideways had made him scream in agony. I had seen my family's reaction, and it made me glad I couldn't hear.

I'd suggested going across the hillside towards the distant roadblock and seeking help. But Mum told me that there was still intermittent gunfire coming from that direction, and several new fires had sprung up further along the line of stationary traffic. She and Dad feared that if we made ourselves known it would bring trouble, not help.

"It doesn't feel right," I said. "To see you, know you're with me, but to not hear your voices. It's unnatural. It's wrong. But you can get used to it." Lynne sat on a small rock with Jude standing beside her, arm around her shoulder and leaning in. Mum and Dad knelt close to the Land Rover. Dad was squatting down holding Glenn's hand. I couldn't see if Glenn was even aware, didn't know if he could hear. Mum had told me that he was drifting in and out of consciousness.

Otis was sitting by my side, panting softly, pupils dilated with excitement. I wished he could understand my words as well because I worried about him. His zest for life, his excitability. His barking.

"You feel cut off from the world. Like a wall has gone up, and things are moving on without you. It was like that for me to begin with. But we all have an advantage that most people won't have—we can sign. Lynne, you're not as good as the rest of us, but you've got to know a lot of our sign language, haven't you?"

"Yes, I—" she began, but I cut her off.

"Sign it," I signed.

Lynne smiled, nodded, and very carefully and purposefully started signing. "It takes me a little time to understand. But I get there in the end."

"So we won't be cut off from each other," I said. "Perhaps in the Jeep we'll be able to whisper. But even that might be dangerous. So to begin with, when they get here, I think we should stay silent. Completely. Until we know more about them."

Mum waved to get my attention and then spoke. "We'll all face each other," she said. "So that none of us feels alone."

I smiled. Mum knew me so well, and understood why I hated travelling in the car. The rest of my family would be feeling like that soon. Seeing each other's faces would give us all strength, the means to communicate, and the confidence to do so in silence.

Dad leaned forward, low down, and looked in at Glenn. He said something to him, then looked up and repeated what he'd said for my benefit. "I told him we'll be very close."

I nodded. Otis whined and I ruffled his neck. Dad looked at the dog.

"What if we need to go toilet?" Jude asked.

"We'll go now," I said. "And if we need to go in the Jeep, it'll have to be in the boot."

"It'll stink!" Jude said, with the familiar fascinated disgust that only young boys can muster.

"Then you'll be used to it," I said, grinning at him. He signed something rude that nobody else saw.

"We'll have one of the shotguns," Mum said. "Glenn

221

will keep the other one with him."

"But we can't use them," I said. The whole idea of guns was shocking to me, and when I blinked the twin, dark barrels of the shotgun I'd faced seemed to float before my eyes. The concussion of the blast, the man's shocked expression, the sight of his wife's shattered ankle and dragging, blood-smeared foot was horrifying.

"For later," Mum said. "After it's safe to leave the Jeep. Just for protection."

There was so much we didn't know about *after*, and I felt eyes and attention on me. They wanted me to say more—I'd been following the news, taking accounts, building my own picture of what was happening, including rumours and speculation about the nature of the vesps. But I knew little more than anyone else.

"People are surviving," I said. "Shut away in basements or sealed buildings. Keeping quiet and still. But I don't think all the vesps move on. Infants hatch and swarm, but the ones who lay eggs hang around."

"Where do they lay their eggs?" Jude asked.

"In their prey," I said.

"What, in people?"

I didn't reply. No one else spoke.

"In their eyes and their mouths?"

Lynne muttered something, and Jude's eyes went wide as he glanced past Dad at Glenn.

We all fell silent.

A cool breeze drifted across the hillside carrying the stench of smoke. I saw my family glance up and past me as one, and guessed there had been more gunfire. I had no desire to turn around and look. *I'm going to be seeing enough as it is,* I thought, and a chill went through me, deeper and colder than the wind breathing across the barren hills.

Mum stood. "We should get ready," she signed. "Let's make sure we've thought of everything."

How can we think of everything when we don't know anything? I thought. But I took a deep breath and tried to steady my nerves. Now was not the time to start panicking.

Now was the time to be silent.

Dad went to move the Jeep close beside the upturned Land Rover, but I saw him and Glenn talking heatedly. I couldn't make out anything Dad said, but it resolved with him leaving the Jeep where it was and stalking to the back of the ruined vehicle.

In case he makes a noise, I thought. *Glenn doesn't want to put us in danger if he starts shouting in pain.* I wanted to kneel down and talk to him, but knew how awkward it would be. He could only sign a few basic phrases, and with his bloodied face and swollen lips, I'd have great difficulty reading him. It would be a one-way conversation, and I knew how awkward those were.

So I busied myself getting the Jeep ready instead. We sorted through the bags in the rear of the Land Rover and pulled out the supplies that hadn't been spoiled by the leaking fuel: tinned food, a few packets of dried pasta, and some cans of lemonade and bottled water. Most of the clothing was stinking and unusable, but Mum scattered a couple of boxes of shotgun shells on a flat rock to dry. She checked over both weapons thoroughly, then loaded one and knelt close beside

Glenn. She was there for some time, and when she stood and walked away she left the weapon behind.

It disappeared through the smashed window as Glenn pulled it inside.

I raised an eyebrow at Mum, and she signed, "My grandfather took me shooting a few times when I was your age. You've got an action-mum."

Lynne wiped the outside of the Jeep's windows so that we had a clear view. Dad walked across the slope a little, scouting the way ahead and down for when the time came to leave.

If the time ever comes when we can risk starting the engine, I thought. The future was a stark, dark place, shaded by unknowns and tainted by fear.

At two o'clock that afternoon the fear came home to roost.

"Vesps," I whispered. "Mum, Dad… vesps!" I pointed across the hillside in the direction of the distant, traffic-clogged road. Smoke still rose from several burning vehicles, and the military roadblock remained in place. I squinted, wondering if I was wrong and had simply imagined the worst when I saw a cloud of specks in the sky. But then I saw movement on the ground, starting at the top of the slope where the road appeared over the hillside, and panic settled over the land.

People were running. They flowed downhill past parked vehicles and the hedges lining the road, every colour of clothing, heads bobbing, individual shapes falling and rising again to continue their flight. *Maybe they're screaming,* I thought, hoping against hope that they were not.

In the air above and around them the pale shapes flew. They flitted and swirled, spiralling above the road, dropping and rising again. People tripped and were immediately smothered in vesps. Some fled into the fields, leaving their cars and loved ones behind. The creatures darted after them, swerving back and forth before closing in and landing on their targets.

The flicker of gunfire—muzzle flashes, coughing smoke—erupted from among the military vehicles, and a cloud of creatures quickly converged on the roadblock.

I'm seeing people die, I thought, and horror gripped me, crippling, paralysing, shattering.

I sensed movement beside me and instinctively ducked, glancing that way with a hand held up to ward off danger. Dad was reaching for me. He held my hand and pulled me gently towards the Jeep.

Mum, Jude and Lynne were already inside. As Dad climbed in behind them, I checked for Otis.

He was standing halfway between the Jeep and the rolled Land Rover, staring uphill past the Jeep with his hackles bristling, teeth bared.

"Otis," I whispered, tapping my leg gently as I always did when I wanted him to come to me. He ignored me. I turned to see what he was growling at.

Pale shapes had appeared above the hilltop and were drifting down towards us, veering back and forth across the landscape.

"Otis!" I whispered, harsher, and the dog leaped past me into the Jeep. I followed into the back seat, pulling the door almost closed behind me, both hands on the handle, unsure whether or not to tug it. Lynne reached across and hauled the door closed. I felt the impact and my whole family froze.

Then we turned as one and looked back at the Land Rover.

It was difficult to see Glenn from this angle. I could just see his head and arm, the stark, dark shape of the shotgun lying beside him, and the puddle of blood beneath him on the upturned ceiling. He was motionless. I hoped because he knew what was happening.

Still looking outside, I reached over and grabbed someone's hand. I wasn't sure whose it was. Mum and Dad were in the front seats; me, Jude and Lynne were in the back, and Otis had jumped over into the boot, already used to travelling there.

The vesps came. There were not as many as I had expected. Several flew by on the left a couple of metres above the ground, circling the Jeep and Land Rover and then moving on.

They must have echolocation, like bats, I thought, and it had never occurred to me before. If they were blind and hunted by sound, they must also have a means to navigate, feel where they were going.

And they were horrible. The size of large kittens, leathery wings perhaps twice as long as their bodies, skins or hides a pale, sickly, slick yellow, flowing tails like several split tentacles, the nubs of legs on their lower bodies, and teeth. I saw the teeth even as they flew by, because they were bared. Small but glinting, their lips were drawn back like folds of skin, mouths exposed and ready to attack, eat. And what was worst about them was their unnaturalness. They simply were not meant to be. They were like a child's drawing of a monster given life, all whimsy stripped away, only horror and ugliness left behind. They reminded me of deep-sea fish, blind and ugly. I had always appreciated nature for what it really was; if we were watching a natural history programme where lions caught a zebra and Mum made some comment about the poor creature, I would say that the lions had to live. But these things…

They had shattered the natural balance. A mutation. A plague.

A vesp whispered along the side of the Jeep, larger than the others. Perhaps the first few I'd seen had been infants, but this was clearly an adult. Its trailing wing left a moist smear across the windows, and Otis bared his teeth.

I touched his head and whispered, very softly, "Otis, no." I could feel the rumble of a growl beneath my hand, and I glanced around at the others.

They stared, wide-eyed and terrified. Jude was crying, pushed into the gap between front seats so that Mum could sling an arm around him. My parents had kept their promise and they were turned in their seats, looking back so that we could all see each other. Lynne sat upright against the opposite door, jaw clenching and unclenching. She looked strong. I'd always thought of her that way, and now her eyes were cool, expression determined.

Mum held the shotgun pointing upwards.

Dad was looking past me at the dog, and when he caught my eye he mouthed, "Keep him quiet!"

I reached over into the boot and gently, slowly, hugged Otis to me. He resisted at first, then leaned into my embrace. I felt the growl rumbling deep within him, but his teeth were no longer bared.

Something hit the Jeep. I felt the impact and glanced

up in time to see the slick smears on the back window. Three or four more vesps landed there, those strange tentacles on their abdomens squirming for purchase against the glass. Then they fell and flew away.

It was like the beginning of a snowstorm. Across the hillside the vesps drifted down from uphill, gliding back and forth, dodging rocky outcroppings and trees, circling in some places if they found something interesting and then moving on again. I saw some catching birds in flight, suddenly mimicking the singing birds' flight patterns before plucking them from the air. Another dropped down onto something just out of sight, and several other vesps zeroed in on the struggle.

There were only scattered groups at first, then over the space of a couple of minutes more and more came.

One of them drifted close and gently struck the window close to Otis's nose.

The dog started barking. "Otis, no, Otis, no!" I whispered, but it was too late, and it was as if Otis had become senseless to everything but the vesps. He nudged forward between barks, butting the glass and the creature that clung to the other side. Its wings flapped rapidly, tentacles slicking down the window before finding some purchase below. Then its body seemed to tighten and flex as muscles held it taut, and the animal's teeth scratched at the glass, scoring it deeply. Other vesps came.

Dad grabbed my shoulder and pulled me around. "Make him stop!" he said, and I saw how scared everyone was. Jude had crawled into Mum's front seat, and Lynne sat back with her hands to her mouth. Behind her, three vesps struck her window and started scraping.

I pulled Otis towards me and leaned into the back seat, pressing my mouth to his ear and saying, "Otis, *no!*" I injected as much command as I could into my voice.

The dog pulled away and jumped at the rear window where several vesps were now attached. He bounced from the glass and sprawled on the floor, shaking his head and spraying slobber. Then he crouched and started barking again, jumping in circles.

I could just see past the creatures assaulting the Jeep, and across the hillside others were streaking towards us. *They must release a signal, like bees,* I thought.

Someone started hitting me. I twisted awkwardly in my seat to see Jude reaching over to strike at me, tears streaking his face, and he said, "Make him stop!" He must have shouted because Dad pulled him back, hand across his mouth and calming words ready.

"Otis, please!" I said. But the dog was both excited and terrified. His hackles were raised, his eyes dilated, and he leaped at the windows where vesps were attached. They scraped and scored with their ugly teeth, and in several places the glass was obscured by deep scratches. I could not imagine anything chewing their way into a car. It was impossible, wasn't it? But in time, I guessed anything was possible.

It depended on how long they stayed. And how long they would remember the noise, when and if I eventually made Otis stop.

I tried to catch his collar and drag him to me. He was a big dog, strong, and it was only when Lynne leaned over and helped that we managed to hold him against the rear of the back seat. I tried closing his mouth with my right hand, but he twisted his head away and barked again. I reached again and he snapped at me. He missed. But I sat back on my heels, shocked, saddened. Otis had never, ever gone for me before.

More vesps landed, thudding against the bodywork and windows. There were so many now that the interior of the Jeep had grown darker, sunlight jittering and dancing between bodies as they moved across the glass. I felt like screaming. Jude did too, I could see it in his eyes. It must have been even worse with the sound of the beasts hitting the vehicle, the screech of teeth on glass, and Otis barking us towards doom.

Something happened. I felt the tension in the Jeep shift. Everyone turned their heads as one to look downhill at the Land Rover, and several vesps dropped from the windows and darted that way. The glass was smeared with their secretions and clouded where they'd been scratching with their teeth, but it was clear that the Land Rover had now become a newer, more attractive target.

"What happened?" I whispered. There were only a few vesps left on the Jeep now, and Otis stood panting, no longer barking.

"Glenn," Lynne mouthed to me, and then I knew.

"Oh, no," I whispered. Mum and Dad were pressed to the windscreen, breath held so that they didn't mist the glass. Past them, I could see vesps converging on the Land Rover from all directions. Many of them landed on the upturned chassis and crawled across it, their movements awkward. It seemed they only had grace in the air. Others dropped to the ground close by and hobbled forwards, while some flew straight into the vehicle's interior through the smashed windows.

The shattered driver's window faced uphill, and in

moments it was a squirming, pale yellow mass of vesps, seemingly struggling against each other to reach what lay inside.

A mess of bloodied parts and smoke blasted outward, smoking flesh pattering across the grass. But the gap made in the crowd of vesps soon filled again.

"What did he do?" I whispered.

"Shotgun," Mum signed. "Now he's shouting."

"Still?" But no one answered that. We all watched. Lynne attempted to reach forward and cover Jude's eyes, but he shook her off and she did not try again.

I was shivering. The more I tried not to imagine what was happening to Glenn, the more I saw.

Dad turned away but I did not catch his eye, could not. I looked past my family at what was happening to our friend. I didn't doubt for a minute that he had done it for us. He'd seen and heard what was happening, and although he perhaps already believed himself doomed, it didn't make the decision he had made any less awful.

"He killed himself for us." Tears blurred my vision but I wiped them angrily away.

"What?" Jude said, nudging me and saying it again so that I saw. But no one said anything else. We were all equally shocked and horrified.

Dad climbed between the front seats and I edged sideways, pressing against the door, because I didn't want him to hug me. It felt wrong taking comfort while Glenn was still suffering. *He's dying right now,* I thought, and I watched because I felt a duty to witness his death. Even though I could not see through the chaos of vesps, I was seeing his final moments. He'd been there ever since I could remember, my Uncle Glenn, and now he was dying.

But Dad did not remain in the back seat. He reached out and took the shotgun from Mum. I caught her eye as she passed it over the seat, and then I knew.

I didn't shout. To do so would have betrayed Glenn's sacrifice. I struggled instead, throwing myself against Dad, trying to stop him climbing over the seats into the boot area. But I was too late, he was gone, and Otis jumped around delighted, licking Dad's face and raising his head to howl in that way that always brought tears to my eyes, even though I only actually heard it in memory. It was a sign of pure joy.

The howl did not come.

"No," I whispered, allowing myself that. Mum drew me back, putting her hands across my eyes from behind, but I shrugged her off, tearing her hands away from my face. I was not a fucking kid.

I watched Dad choking my dog to death with the shotgun. He kept his back to us, at least, trying to shield us from the worst. I could see Otis's kicking legs, and the muscles on Dad's neck standing out.

Afterwards he knelt there breathing hard, and I allowed my tears at last.

As vesps continued flying past the Jeep, no longer landing, I realised that Dad was not panting at all, but crying.

PART TWO

SILENCE

15

Consider what you have in your life that might produce noise:

—All electronic devices should be muted or switched to silent: TVs, phones, tablets, personal music devices, satnavs, GPS, digital watches, etc.

—All medical warning devices should be deactivated: medication reminders, hearing aids, etc.

—Babies should be comforted at all times. Do your best to prevent your child from crying. If you cannot prevent it, try to remove yourself from other people, somewhere as secure and safe as possible.

—Do not attempt to start any vehicle engines, generators, or other mechanical equipment.

—Pets should be silenced.

Cobra Emergency Text Transmission #14,
Saturday, 19 November 2016

When he was fourteen, waiting for his music teacher to arrive at the start of a lesson, Huw and his friends had been larking around, not causing chaos but generally acting in the manner of teenage boys. Some mild abuse, amusing banter, and all of them cognisant of the girls watching their every move.

A fly had been buzzing around him, and several times Huw snapped out his hand in an attempt to catch the insect. He wanted to look cool, especially in front of Ashley Hughes, who was watching him with a calm, appraising expression. She was his first real crush, and much of what he did was to impress her.

He couldn't catch the fly. It was too fast for him, or he was too slow, and Ashley had eventually leaned back in her chair and started talking with her friend, pointedly ignoring him.

The fly had landed on the window, and Huw snatched up a sheet of music and jumped forward, placing it flat on the glass and trapping the fly. He'd pressed gently around the insect, feeling soft vibrations as it buzzed between glass and paper, doing its best to escape. Light shone through the paper and he could see the dark, manic button of the fly twisting back and forth.

Then he'd placed his thumb over the fly and gently pushed. He felt the tickling buzz of wings transmitted through the paper and against his skin, then a soft pop as the body burst, then the splash of blood and insides.

"You enjoyed that, didn't you?" their music teacher said with evident disgust. He'd been standing directly behind Huw when he'd crushed the fly to death.

"Yes, sir!" he'd said, keen at the time to impress his friends. Maybe he had, maybe he hadn't. He could never remember anyone's reaction—his friends', Ashley's, even his own. It was only many years later that the incident came back to him, in the way that seemingly random events from years before so often do.

As he grew older, Huw had started to relate more and more to his teacher. Not at all religious, he had developed a respect for life that prevented him from killing any living thing. If Jude found a spider in his room Huw would catch it in a glass and take it all the way downstairs to let it loose in the garden. If a mosquito buzzed at night, he'd stalk the bedroom naked, a pint glass ready to catch it, and then release it from a window.

Kelly sometimes took the piss. "It's only a fly," she'd say. Mostly Huw would just shrug, not bothering to reply because she was the one still in bed and he was the one doing the saving. It shouldn't matter to her whether he killed the thing or let it go.

When he saw roadkill he felt pity for the creatures. He'd wonder whether their deaths had left any defenceless young behind, now destined to starve to death or be picked off by predators. He didn't like watching hunting on television. Images of cruelty, to animals or humans, disturbed him.

Kelly found it difficult to understand. He ate meat, and didn't seem to mind the fact that he was eating dead animal flesh. But he took time selecting where he bought his meat and whether it was free-range, ethically sourced. He reasoned to her that if he ate a creature that had been treated well and had a comfortable life, then that animal would not have lived at all if it were not for him wanting to eat it.

It troubled him. It amused Kelly.

Once, after she'd killed a wasp and he'd berated her, she'd lost her temper with him. And he'd told her why. "That wasp was alive. It was more amazing than anything humans have ever made. It was incredible, and because it annoyed you, you crushed it to death."

She'd called him a knob.

As an adult he often thought back to that fly he'd killed, and what his music teacher had said. And he was glad that the man was no longer the boy. Yes, he'd enjoyed it then. No, he would not enjoy it now.

Huw didn't kill things, because life was a gift.

Otis had pissed himself while Huw was choking him to death.

The dog lay across his outstretched legs, still warm. His right jeans leg was soaked with dog urine, his left ankle badly scratched where Otis's panicked, lashing claws had caught him. His shoulders and arms ached from the force he'd had to apply, pulling the shotgun up beneath the animal's head and crushing it back against his neck, as hard as he could, desperate to kill the dog as quickly as possible. And not because of any noise he might make, but because he didn't want to hurt him.

He didn't want Otis to suffer.

Now he was dead, and Huw could not hold back the tears. He felt eyes boring into him. Maybe his children would never forgive him, but he hoped that they would at least understand. You couldn't tell a dog to be quiet. You couldn't explain mortal danger. He remained kneeling down facing the rear window, shoulders shuddering with each silent sob. It seemed unfair that Otis was dead and they hadn't killed one single vesp, but the beasts were gone now, drifting by like giant snowflakes, leaving behind slick smears and scratches on the windows.

Then he thought of Glenn, and shock dried his tears.

That amazing thing, life, was gone from Otis and Glenn, and now they were just sacks of dead meat. Between one moment and the next they had ceased to live, their histories venting to nothing, memories disappearing, everything they had been existing now only in the memories of others and what they had left behind. But they'd both fought hard.

The bleeding scratches on Huw's ankle were testament to that.

And he believed that Glenn had fought for them.

He let out a slow breath and bowed his head. He closed his eyes so that he did not have to look down at Otis, then opened them again. He tried to take stock of their situation, because after what he had done, and what had happened to Glenn, they had to make the most of things. They had to honour the dead by surviving.

They're all going to hate me, he thought, and he could not bear to turn around.

Vesps still flew by, weaving down the hillside and parting around trees, rocks and the Jeep like water around obstructions in a river. Though blind, they could still see, and Huw guessed they had some form of sonar. If that was the case, perhaps sound of a certain frequency could confuse or hurt them. But that was not for him to test or speculate on. A thousand scientists in a hundred bunkers around the world would be doing their best to find these creatures' weak spot.

Across the hillside, in the distance, he could just make out the line of vehicles twisting up towards the ridge. A couple of them still burned, but there was no longer any movement. If anyone had survived, they were also trapped in their vehicles. But it had been so much louder over there—gunfire, burning, more people panicking and running. He wondered whether the vesps would have given up so easily in their efforts to break into the cars.

Leaning closer to the rear window, he could see the tracework of scratches etched into the glass by their teeth; sharp, curved patterns among the smears of saliva and other fluids. Some of the scratches looked superficial, but there were a couple that seemed to have scored deep. That would have necessitated retracing the scratches again and again, which would have meant a sense of purpose. The vesps had known what they were doing. They weren't just blindly gnashing and thrashing, they were consciously using their teeth to carve their way inside.

He shivered. They were so lucky that Glenn had drawn them away.

Huw slumped down against the side of the boot's interior, gently lifting Otis's head from his leg and resting it on the floor. Then he turned around to accept his family's hostile glare.

Jude had his face buried in Kelly's neck. Good. Huw hoped he'd been like that for some time. Kelly looked sad, teary, but she nodded at him to show that she didn't blame him, and that he'd done what he had to. Lynne retained her usual cool stare, but he could see no resentment in her eyes.

Ally would not meet his gaze. Wide-eyed, pale, she stared past him at her dead dog, or as much of him as she could see over the back seat. Maybe she was remembering all the good times she'd had with Otis, and how much he had helped her. She called him her hearing dog, and although she'd trained him herself he had been surprisingly adept at helping her with certain tasks. He let her know when the phone was ringing, when someone was at the front door, and he'd also been trained to warn her about the presence of fire. They'd had to practise that every three months, just to ensure that he hadn't forgotten. Kelly hadn't liked doing that, as she said it was tempting fate, but Huw had scoffed. There was no such thing as fate, he said, and not training Otis about fire would be putting Ally's life needlessly at risk. If she was alone in the house and a blaze started downstairs... it didn't bear thinking about.

Now her hearing dog could hear no more, and there were dangers greater than flames.

Huw leaned into the Jeep's rear seat, reaching for Ally. She turned her head away from him, eyes closed. He held her shoulders and felt her stiffen. They had to remain silent. By turning aside she was denying him the chance to say sorry.

He looked at Kelly instead and she beckoned him to her.

It was awkward climbing over the back seat, squeezing past Ally—still stiff, still looking away from him—and into the driver's seat again. He moved slowly and cautiously, careful not to kick a window. They didn't know how much noise the vesps needed to home in on, how loud or persistent it had to be. They knew nothing.

Jude slid over and crouched beside him on the seat. He hugged his father and Huw took so much from that. It could have been forgiveness, but he thought it was more a sense of need. Whatever he'd done to the dog, Jude needed him to be there.

Huw hugged his son back and looked through the

smeared windscreen.

Twenty metres downhill, there were still vesps crawling across the overturned Land Rover. Others smothered the rocks and the sparse trees sprouting from them. They slipped in and out of the vehicle, emerging with blood smeared across their sickly yellow skin. Their mouths were wet, dark, red holes. He could not see much inside, other than a bloodied, tattered arm and hand slumped from the window. Glenn was dead in there, and perhaps now home to vesp eggs that would hatch very soon. They'd killed and eaten of him, but left enough for their young to consume.

Huw was determined that would not happen. It was too much. Glenn had distracted them from the Jeep, and Huw believed that he'd known very well what he was doing. He could not bear for him to become a birthing ground for more of those monsters.

Soon, he would perform one last favour for his friend.

A strange calm had settled over his family. They had been waiting for this moment for days, and now it was here some of the pressure had been relieved. Fear sat in its place. It was a heavy, tactile fear, fed by what they could see all around them rather than by nebulous news reports from afar. They sat still and silent, watching vesps flying past, sometimes slow, often much faster. The sense of being surrounded was very real, and Huw knew that was the immediate danger—becoming too scared to leave the Jeep.

And they would *have* to leave. They could not remain here indefinitely, with very little food and hardly anything to drink. Five of them could not live and sleep in such confined quarters. And there was Otis.

He'd soon begin to smell.

Huw caught Kelly's attention and started to sign.

"We'll have to get away from here soon."

She nodded.

"We'll leave it a couple of hours, see how many of them there are."

"Maybe they'll thin out," she replied.

"Or maybe there'll be flocks of them."

Kelly shrugged. None of them knew.

He looked in the rear-view mirror. Ally was huddled with her back against the side door, legs drawn up, arms hugging her knees to her chest, staring from the rear window. Huw didn't think she could see Otis from there—the back seat was in the way—but he wished he could reach out instead of her having to comfort herself.

Lynne tapped him on the shoulder and started signing. She was clumsy, and had never really perfected the Andrews family's personalised signing language. But she had gone to classes to learn, made a big effort, and he could only love her for that.

"Don't be angry at yourself. There was no other way."

Huw nodded his thanks. Lynne smiled and touched his shoulder again, leaving her hand there this time.

"I'll need one of your secret cigarettes later," he said.

She raised her eyebrows.

"Not to smoke."

She nodded, confused. He'd explain when the time came.

Jude squirmed beside him and looked from the windscreen. He was staring at the Land Rover.

Huw pressed his mouth to his son's ear and whispered, "He did it for us."

243

No vesps came. None hit the windows at the folly of a father's whisper. Good. They could talk, at least, though it had to be muted.

Jude nodded slowly, but he was only a little kid. What a terrible thing to see. What an awful thing to accept, that a family friend had sacrificed himself for them.

We're all learning again from scratch, Huw thought. And perhaps everyone might soon be in that position. It was a new world now, and they were all children.

Kelly was the first one who needed to urinate. She signalled this to Huw, pointed into the boot, shrugged.

Otis was back there. Bad enough that he'd killed the family dog, no one was going to piss on the poor mutt's corpse.

Huw nodded, then gestured outside. He'd been keeping track of the time, and it was now mid-afternoon. If they didn't move soon, they'd have to face spending the night in the Jeep.

Cuddling Jude, becoming warm and sweaty with the boy curled on his lap, Huw had been weighing up their options. Maybe they could stay in the Jeep and open the door whenever one of them needed a comfort break. Would the door opening and closing again be noise enough to attract a vesp? Would the sound of piss hitting the ground? There was no room to move around, and he could already feel his legs stiffening, the dog urine drying into his jeans. They had a few tins of food. They'd already drunk most of the bottled water. He'd risked turning on the ignition and lowering his window an inch, so at least they had fresh air, though it had a strange odour. Perhaps they were safe for now, but he was afraid that the longer they stayed put, the more difficult it would be to start moving again.

He favoured walking. It meant going outside and being among them, but over the past hour the number of vesps passing by had diminished. They were always in sight, but now only ten or so passed by each minute, rather than dozens. He could see some of them resting or roosting, usually in elevated positions—on rocks, in the branches of trees, and several remained on the Land Rover's underside—and a few seemed to settle comfortably on the ground. If they moved cautiously, slowly, and quietly, he was confident that they could pass the creatures by.

A house would be a far better place in which to hold out. If they were lucky they'd find one with a supply of food and water. But any solid building would be better than this.

He had briefly considered driving the Jeep downhill, but that was a non-starter. The vesps would swarm to the noise, and in moments the windscreen would be covered and they'd be blind. This time, with nothing to lure them away, the creatures might persist in their glass-scratching.

He had ideas of a distraction to set them on their way.

Ally still hadn't looked at him. He thought perhaps she'd fallen asleep with her head resting on her knees. The more time passed, the more nervous he was about the moment when they would have to communicate with each other again. He didn't want her to hate him. He didn't think he could handle that, not now.

Huw signalled to Kelly that they should get ready to move. She nodded slowly. Her mother had seen the exchange and she also agreed.

"You all move along the hillside that way," he signed, pointing north away from the traffic-clogged road in the opposite direction.

"You?" Kelly asked.

"I'm going to see to Glenn and set a distraction."

Kelly held out her hands in a *What?* gesture.

Huw went to answer, but that was when Ally turned around and looked right at him. He stared back, more scared right then of his daughter hating him than the creatures outside. He felt utterly wretched about what he'd done, but also as certain as he could be that it had been necessary. But if Ally did not believe that, there was nothing he could do to persuade her otherwise.

"We're leaving?" she signed.

Huw nodded.

"Okay. But I want to say goodbye to Otis." She offered a sad smile, and Huw could not hold back the tears that burned his eyes. He watched his daughter lean over into the back seat, ruffle her dog's fur, scratch him behind the ear. She stayed there for some time.

Jude stirred and saw what was happening. He scooted across to his mother, rubbing his eyes, watching Ally then turning to look through the windscreen.

Lynne touched Huw's shoulder and signed, "We should all leave through the same door."

Huw nodded. "I'll need that cigarette now."

He was surprised to see how shamefaced she looked as she pulled the packet from her pocket and handed him a couple. She gave him a lighter too, and he tucked them all into his jacket's breast pocket.

Kelly had one eyebrow arched at her mother, then she fired a questioning look at Huw. He glanced downhill at the overturned Land Rover. And that was enough. She knew, and seemed to accept what needed to be done.

Ally sat back into her seat and rubbed at her teary eyes. Then she checked the iPad charge and disconnected it from the charger. Packing her small rucksack, she looked like a different girl.

Huw leaned between the seats and touched her knee, ready to sign to her, tell her how much he loved her and how he could see no other way. But she made all of that unnecessary.

"It's okay, Dad," she whispered. Hearing her voice was a welcome surprise. He nodded, thinking that perhaps it would be some time until it was completely okay. But at least she seemed to understand why he'd done what he had done. He hoped that time would give them the opportunity to talk about it properly.

They all took a few minutes to prepare. Kelly packed the tins of food they'd rescued from the Land Rover, Lynne massaged her legs where they'd gone to sleep, Jude fidgeted nervously. When the time came, Huw felt a stab of doubt.

Were they doing the right thing? Couldn't they at least try to stay here until help came? But he shook those thoughts aside. Help was not coming. If they stayed here they would die. He made sure everyone was watching before he signed, "I'll go first."

16

My dad just killed my dog. We saw our friend die.
Suddenly it's a different world.

Twitter, @SilentAllyA, Saturday, 19 November 2016

The first thing that hit me was the smell.

It was rich, harsh, sour, acidic, a sickly and overtly
biological stench that nevertheless bit in like industrial
chemicals. It did not belong up here on the wild hillsides,
and even the breeze did nothing to disperse it.

The vesps stank. That was one more thing to note
about them. Perhaps that knowledge might help us in
the future. The creatures drifted by, coming from uphill
and flying a couple of metres above ground as they flew
down into the valley. To our left lay the ruin of the
Land Rover, and a dozen vesps still roosted on the
upturned vehicle, rocks, and the trees sprouting above
them. Some were smeared with Glenn's blood. I hated
them, felt a rage burning, but knew that there was
nothing I could do.

Through the smashed side window I could see Glenn's
shredded arm and hand, but little else. I was glad. At
least this way I could remember him as he had been,
not as the vesps had made him.

We stood motionless for a while after getting out of the car, huddled in a group and staring around, trying not to move. I caught Jude's eye, and though petrified he was also fascinated. "They're totally silent," he signed. "Can't even hear their wings."

I was worried about the vesps' echolocation. I'd watched them swerve around static obstructions, and they had to know where the ground was, which direction they were heading—and there was no saying whether or not they also used it to hunt. Once we started moving, perhaps the vesps would see us as prey.

But I thought not. From everything I'd seen and gathered in my digital scrapbook, it appeared that they hunted exclusively by following the sound of their prey.

A vesp flitted past my head, close enough for me to feel the breath of its leathery wings. I froze, shock driving through me, but managed to not cry out. I pressed my finger to my lips and looked around at my family.

They were good. Scared but alert to the dangers. But none of them were moving. They stood in a huddle by the Jeep, door still open behind them. The vehicle suddenly felt like safety, but I knew that there was no going back.

I was the first to start walking. I took slow, gentle steps, looking where I placed my feet so that I didn't stumble or disturb a stone, focusing ahead, holding my rucksack tight over one shoulder. I felt the pressure of my family's gaze, and I was afraid that if I turned around they'd be beckoning me back. *We can't go back,* I thought. *Not after what's happened. Not after Glenn and Otis. The only way left is forward.*

I reached a small tumble of rocks and skirted around

them, concentrating so hard on my footsteps that I didn't see what was coming.

They flew past so quickly that one snagged my hair and tugged my head sideways. I winced and held my breath, holding in the scream. I glanced uphill in time to see several more vesps sweeping down towards me, but at the last moment they swerved, none of them colliding. They flew in close formation but did not touch. For the first time I found myself admiring their grace.

Once past the rocks I signalled the others to follow. Again I planted my finger to my lips, signing that they should remain silent. But they did not need telling.

Lynne came first, then Jude and Mum. My mother still carried the shotgun. It was so unnatural in her hand, made her look almost like someone I didn't know. I didn't like it one bit. The shotgun would offer scant protection against a swarm of vesps, but I knew it was more to defend against other people than the creatures. That was the way the world was going, and why I didn't like it.

Dad stayed behind at the Jeep, and he had a cigarette in his mouth. I'd seen him smoking when I was a kid, but as far as I was aware he hadn't smoked for ten years or more. I knew that Lynne still stole an occasional puff. I could smell it on my grandmother's clothes, and was surprised when no one else seemed to notice.

When the others reached me, I raised an eyebrow at Dad, and he signalled that we should move on. Mum nodded to me and started leading the way.

Jude grabbed my hand. I liked that, though I didn't like the look on his face. It was a very adult fear. Witnessing Glenn and Otis's deaths had made my little brother grow up quickly. Another change forced upon us all.

Mum veered slightly downhill, past a clump of trees and onto a narrow sheep trail that wound through bracken and across a small stream. Several vesps flew by from right to left as we walked, and once or twice a creature passed between us, shedding a trail of stench behind it. How something alive could smell so rank I did not know. Perhaps it was to do with how they communicated. Maybe it was a sign of their excitement at being on the hunt.

A couple of minutes later we paused and looked back the way we'd come.

Dad waved, then leaned into the Jeep. *What's he doing?* I wondered. Then the vehicle juddered and began to roll downhill. He leaped away and crouched down, watching the Jeep pick up speed and just skim past the rolled Land Rover. It struck the clump of rocks, jumped slightly, then rolled on, gathering momentum and bouncing across the rough, uneven ground.

Where it had struck the rocks, several vesps quickly converged, hovering, darting down and up again, finding nothing of worth. They continued on, seemingly agitated and dancing in the air, sweeping left and right as if searching for whatever had made the noise.

When the Jeep struck another large boulder and rolled, they found it. It tumbled onto its roof, rolled one more time, then slid to a stop on its side further down the hill, nose thudding into a hollow in the ground. As its back end tilted up at the sky, dozens of vesps streaked in toward it.

They passed by my crouching father, veering around

him and downhill towards the Jeep. Others flew quickly past where we waited, trailing their strange tentacles and rancid smells behind them. Striking the Jeep, they crawled across its surface and disappeared inside, and I suddenly realised a terrible truth—they would find Otis in there, and perhaps they would eat him.

Maybe they would even lay eggs.

I sank down to the damp ground, wanting to cry in rage and grief but knowing that these must now become restrained emotions. Whatever enraged me in the future, I could not scream. Whatever grief was visited upon me, I must cry in silence.

Part of me hated Dad for what he'd done, but I knew it had been the only way. I'd already been worrying about Otis, but my blind love for him had come in the way of any solution. There *was* no solution to him making a noise, so I'd blocked it out. A problem for later. As it turned out, somebody else's problem.

I knew that Dad was feeling terrible, and that my haze of hate was already melting to a deep sadness for us all. It was selfish to think that only I had loved him.

Dad edged downhill to the Land Rover, lighting the cigarette as he went. He took what looked like a long, deep drag, and then lobbed the cigarette in through the open portion of the boot door. He hurried towards us across the hillside, watching his footing, and then the fuel ignited with a blue flash. He didn't look back. By the time he reached us, face grim, the Land Rover was fully aflame. Vesps flew from it and circled the heat before drifting away downhill towards the Jeep.

I found the sight strangely hypnotic. The fire was somehow comforting, because it gave warmth to the desolate scene, and it took Glenn away from us at last. I hoped some of the monsters had been trapped inside. I hoped whatever eggs they'd laid in our friend were bubbling and boiling.

Other vesps flew quickly around, zeroing in on the now silent Jeep. They must have been answering whatever strange call their cousins put out when they were hunting. It was another aspect to them that I would note down, if and when we ever reached somewhere safe.

My parents hugged briefly, then we set off downhill, heading away from the burning vehicle and the Jeep that had brought us this far. Sometimes, when I caught them from the corner of my eye, I thought that distant vesps were snowflakes.

That idea stirred a thought that I could not quite grasp. Confused and troubled, we went in search of safety.

The cities had fallen first. Loud and chaotic as they were, finding a quiet, safe place in built-up areas must have been next to impossible. Hide your family in one house, and if someone in the next house screamed and attracted a flood of vesps, a chain reaction of terror would doom even those struggling to maintain silence. There was mounting anecdotal evidence of the vesps letting out some sort of signal when they found prey— the strange stench, perhaps, or maybe a sound out of a human's range of hearing. They acted very much like ants or wasps in that regard, and it made them even more deadly.

People attempting to flee in cars and aircraft would have quickly been taken down. I'd seen the terrible evidence of that, and was pleased to be out in the open, however much it stank, however terrible it was feeling a vesp's wing snag my hair or brush past my arm.

So far, none of us had cried out in fright. Not even Jude, bless him. But then kids always do adapt quickly.

Right then, the future was barely an hour long. Find safety, somewhere we could hole up and rest, sleep, wait for whatever was to come. A place with food and power if possible, so I could monitor world events without worrying about the iPad running out of charge. After that we'd have to think about our future in the long term. Days ahead, we might have to consider how long our food supplies were going to last. Weeks, and if the power and water failed, we would have to adapt even more.

Months? Would help come, would anything change? Could it really last that long?

But it was the immediate future where the greatest danger lay. So I thought less than an hour ahead, less than ten minutes, and tried to concentrate on putting one foot in front of the other, treading carefully and lightly, so as not to bring down a cloud of vesps.

One wrong move from any of us would put us all in danger. It was a heavy burden, but sharing it brought us closer together.

At one point we all stopped and turned back the way we'd come. I saw a cloud of smoke boiling up into the sky. We could no longer see the burning vehicle or the upended Jeep downhill from it, but I guessed that something in the Land Rover had exploded. Vesps darted rapidly towards the noise, and I could just make them out, so many of them circling the smoke that they formed their own patterns in the sky.

Mum waved us on. Lynne smiled, kissed her fingertips and touched my cheek. I smiled back. Such communication had become precious.

I saw them taking lots of birds. Mostly they plucked them from the sky, eating them on the wing, but sometimes the vesps dropped down into the undergrowth or glided into leafless trees. The birds didn't know to keep quiet. The beasts were stripping their songs from the countryside, and I remembered it clearer than ever.

Mum had to stop and pee. She squatted down and we turned our backs, giving her some small privacy. Dad remained alert, glancing all around to see if even the sound of pee hitting the grass would attract the beasts. But we were safe.

We came to a well-used path that veered along the side of the hill, and after a brief pause Dad turned right. He was still taking us roughly north, away from where we'd left the vehicles and the blocked road we'd seen further to the south. I could see far across the countryside here, but it was a surreal sight.

It should have been beautiful. This must have been a rare November day in the Lakes, because the sky was mostly cloudless, the air clear, and the breeze breathing across the landscape was cool but not cold. A few sheep still speckled the hills and fields, though when we came closer we saw that most of them were dead. In the distance sprawled a small town.

But familiar though the scene should have been, I could not see it without also seeing the vesps. Close by they drifted north and west, sometimes crossing paths, flying in groups here, individually there. Further away they were pale, slow specks dusting the view. Here and there I could see denser concentrations of the creatures, like wafting mist. In one place a couple of miles to the south-west a spiralling mass circled something out of sight. And above the small town there was a swarm.

Smoke rose from a couple of places between the buildings, too thick to be from chimneys or garden bonfires.

As we walked, I turned to Lynne and signed, "Can you hear anything?"

My grandmother glanced at the town and shook her head. "Too far away."

I wondered if there were screams, and how far they travelled before fading to nothing.

The path wound down behind an old stone wall, and we had to work our way around an area of waterlogged ground and through a couple of wooden gates. We all walked slowly, worried that splashes might alert a passing vesp, or even the squelch of shoes in mud. I moved close to the wall, reaching out now and then for balance as I concentrated on my footing.

A stone moved beneath my hand. I fell to the left, shifting my hand quickly and stopping my fall before I struck the wall, but the stone tumbled away.

I held my breath and winced, glancing quickly around at the others. They all stared at me wide-eyed. *It made a noise!* I thought, and I crouched down and looked for vesps coming for me.

A few metres along the path, a vesp flew quickly past, sweeping over the wall and just missing it. The creature didn't seem to notice us.

I let out my held breath slowly, carefully. Dad waved us on.

The muddy path continued, and a few minutes later

the wall disappeared and the path swung down towards a road, and a wider parking area beside it. There were several picnic benches and a few litter bins, and an information board with cracked glass and a fading map of the area. It might have been a nice place to stop in the summer, with a spectacular view out across the wide valley and the walk up into the hills. But now it was a quagmire.

And there were the dead.

They were about a hundred metres along the road, down a gentle slope and just before a bend cut behind stark, leafless trees. Three cars had come to a halt on the other side of the road, one of them tilted precariously over a steep drop. The people had left the vehicles. Maybe they'd all been one group or even one family, but most of them had died alone. There was a huddle of bodies close to the rear vehicle, and six more were scattered along the road.

Several vesps roosted on and around each car, and a crowd of them bickered over the body that seemed to have made it furthest along the road, a couple of hundred metres away. *The one that nearly got away,* I thought.

We stopped when we saw the dead and grouped close together. I felt sick. At first I thought a couple of the people were still moving. Crawling away, perhaps. But then I saw the reality, and I almost cried out in disgust.

On each body, nestled amongst the bloody remains opened to the world, several vesps pulsed and squirmed. They were laying eggs, I guessed, and each grotesque flex of their sickly-pale bodies might have been another expulsion. I wanted to run at them and knock them aside. I imagined my mother shooting them away, disintegrating their disgusting bodies with shotgun blasts. But neither course of action could save those already dead.

Dad turned and signed to us all, "Across the road and down the hill."

Lynne pointed in the other direction, along the road and away from the nesting vesps. But I shook my head.

"That's back towards the roadblock, around the side of the hill."

Lynne nodded, but looking across the road she frowned. Trees grew close to the road there, and the land dripped sharply away into woodland.

I could understand my grandmother's misgivings. I'd have much preferred to stay on the road or the path we'd been following. Into the trees meant into the wild, and with the vesps abroad, that felt like a more dangerous place. But truth was, it was probably safer. Where there were people there would be vesps. The wild was the safest place to be.

Mum leaned close to Dad and pressed her mouth to his ear. I held my breath, but saw Dad listening, and there were no signs that the vesps along the road heard anything.

As he started to nod, I saw movement from the corner of my eye.

A vesp squatted atop one of the litter bins less than ten steps away. Its small feet were clawed into the heavy rubber lid. Its strange tendrils were splayed behind it, like a featherless peacock's tail. Its head, level with its body, seemed to be turned to one side. It was all teeth.

Mum, Dad, no! I thought, but even in panic I did not speak. I waved instead, and as Mum whispered something else to Dad he saw, his eyes went wide, and he pushed her to the ground.

The vesp flew at him and he fell, bringing his arm up in front of his face so that its mouth closed on the thick sleeve of his jacket.

I froze. But it was Mum who did not let terror slow her down. Even as she stood she was swinging the shotgun, and the metal barrel connected squarely with the vesp's head. It flipped from his arm, tearing the jacket, sharp teeth trailing threads of material, and bounced across the gravel.

Lynne took three steps and brought her foot down on the stunned creature's head. It burst apart in a spray of dark red blood, tendrils stiffening and then slumping to the ground.

I scanned around for other vesps, afraid that more might have heard, terrified that the dead creature had transmitted a scent signature or a call of some kind. But though some of them flew higher up, and those creatures still roosted on the cars and bodies along the road, none approached.

Lynne stepped away from the bloody mess. When she reached the grass she wiped her foot slowly.

Jude, little boy that he was, walked towards the dead creature to see. I grabbed his arm and shook my head. There was no telling how dangerous they were, even dead—that blood looked thick, and darker than it should. My brother pulled a face.

Dad checked his arm. Even though the vesp had been at him for mere seconds the jacket was shredded, but his skin was intact. The thick material had saved him from any serious injury.

I wondered what would have happened if he had been hurt. We had a few basic first-aid items like plasters and bandages, but nothing more heavy-duty. No needle and thread, no antibiotics. There was no saying what diseases those things might carry. *Unknown*, I thought. *Whatever bacteria or viruses they carry will be unknown to medicine, so even if we did have antibiotics they'd probably be useless.* The creatures were as good as alien. The idea depressed me. We were less than an hour out of the vehicles, and already we'd had a close call.

I tried to bring the future in close once again, not projecting ahead. But I couldn't help imagining Dad fevered, diseased, and dying of some terrible blood poisoning.

"Clean your arm," I signed.

"There's no wound," Mum signed back.

"The teeth might still have touched him."

Dad nodded, but signalled across the road. I understood. He wanted to get away from the dead creature as quickly as possible, just in case any others somehow sensed it and came to investigate.

Slowly, careful not to scuff our shoes on gravel or trip over in a shallow pothole, we crossed the road and entered the woodland.

17

We were expecting another statement from the Prime Minister over an hour ago now, but so far there's only silence.

BBC Radio 4 News, 3 p.m., Saturday, 19 November 2016

Please remember—listen through headphones.

BBC Radio 4 News, 3 p.m., Saturday, 19 November 2016

Huw was shaking. *Holy fucking shit, she barely whispered and that thing heard!* The shocked realisation as the pale shape on the bin resolved into one of them, its wings unfurling, shoving Kelly away and down, and then the sudden movement as it flew at where it had heard her voice, a blur of wings, the gaping mouth… it all rebounded back at him again and again, and other possible outcomes played out with equal, horrendous clarity. Kelly with the thing burrowing at her face. Jude, the vesp clawing and biting at his throat.

He'd taken a moment to examine the dead vesp. The teeth were incredibly sharp, reminding him of the mouth of a piranha. It had long, slender claws on its stumpy legs, and the tips of its bat-like wings were also tipped with a vicious-looking claw. A clear fluid dripped from them. Poison, perhaps. For such a small animal it was comprehensively armed.

He glanced back to make sure his family were following and saw similar shocked expressions on their faces. *It's only just begun,* he thought. Looking far uphill he could still see a spreading haze of smoke from the burning Land Rover, and in that smoke would be the stench of his dead friend. *It's only just begun, and already it's too much.*

As they crossed the potholed road he looked at the bodies. Three vesps were walking around one of them, as clumsy on the ground as they were graceful in the air. They reminded him of penguins, so awkward on ice, yet quick and adaptable under water. These creatures seemed to be guarding the corpse, the odd tentacle-like appendages at their rears waving at the air like sea anemones. Guarding the eggs they had just laid.

A stone scraped beneath his foot and he stopped. Nothing happened.

Moving again, he heard a pebble kicked across the road. He froze, seeing the pebble from the corner of his eye, looking around for the flash of yellow that might be a vesp homing in on the sound. Still nothing.

When they reached the grass verge and ditch that gave way to the wooded area beyond, he was grateful to be walking on a soft surface once again. He smiled at Kelly and the kids, nodded at Lynne. His mother-in-law was suffering in silence as she always had. He'd always been frustrated at that, because although she believed she was perhaps too proud to accept help, in reality he thought she was just stupid. They were family, and if they couldn't support her in her illness, who could? But now he was pleased. He could see the discomfort in her eyes, but he knew that to deal with that right now might upset Ally and Jude. He didn't want to see them crying again.

It was Jude who worried him most. Poor kid, he was only ten years old and he had seen too much already. Huw found it amazing how quickly his attitude to his son had changed. Days ago he'd have been angry if he found Ally showing the boy a horror movie, but now they were living in one. He'd done nothing to prevent Jude from seeing the corpses along the road. Maybe in his own panic Huw was beginning to realise that to survive in the new world, his son would have to understand it.

He glanced at his watch. It was almost three-thirty, and in another hour it would be growing dark. He didn't want them spending the night outside. Shelter was a basic human need, and one which he'd never had to worry about before. It felt strange not knowing where they were going to sleep, how they were going to survive the night. It would be very cold, perhaps windy, and they might even wake up to a frost. Could they sleep under the stars in such conditions? He didn't even know. All the programmes he'd seen on surviving in the wild had been presented as entertainment. Now he wished he'd taken more notice.

Would one cold night be enough to kill them?

Was it safe to sleep in the cold, or should they keep moving?

He was starting to panic. By deliberately heading into

a region that was sparsely populated, they'd driven themselves into a different kind of danger. It was ridiculous, it was almost unbelievable, yet it was a sign of how quickly things had changed.

Huw headed down into the woods. He crossed the ditch beside the road first, checking his footing before moving forward. The ground sloped down, gentler than he'd feared, and for a while the way amongst the trees wasn't too difficult. The fallen leaves underfoot had been mulched down by frequent rainfalls; only a few weeks before this path would have been deadly, the leaves crisp and noisy. He deliberately took the lead and stepped slowly, checking every step for twigs or loose stones hidden in the undergrowth, and looking around to spot any vesps roosting nearby. Several of them veered through the trees, dodging trunks, but he saw more passing above the bare outstretched limbs.

The slope grew steeper. The woodland was not large, and he could see down the slope to where it appeared to end. There was more open ground down there, swathed in ferns turning brown as they died back and spotted with rocky outcroppings. Beyond that he could not tell. But he was already beginning to doubt this course of action.

He'd wanted to stay away from the road because the road meant people.

But coming this way drastically cut down their chances of finding somewhere sheltered. Along the road there would be homes, farms and pubs, any one of which might provide somewhere suitable for the night, or even longer term. Cutting across country meant that they would only find a building by luck.

Huw held up his hand and turned to face his family.

Being unable to talk was so unnatural. He wanted to share his ideas with them, discuss. Though they might well be luckier than most—they could communicate silently—this craving for conversation, for noise, was something he had never experienced before. He liked peace and quiet, but he was coming to realise that he liked the voices of his family more.

"Maybe we should go back?" he signed.

"Not up there!" Jude said.

Ally shook her head. Lynne raised an eyebrow.

"I'm afraid of not finding somewhere before it's dark," he said.

Kelly frowned, and he knew she'd been thinking the same as him.

"We're ill-equipped to spend the night out in the open," she said.

What if we talk in our sleep? he thought. Ally was a deep sleeper, but Jude often chatted his way through dreams, and he had been known to sleepwalk. Inside they could handle that, but not out in the open. Not with vesps drifting past a few metres above them, huddled down in undergrowth or in the elbows of tree branches.

And they couldn't move in the dark. They would be blind, while day and night held no distinction for the vesps.

"It's too dangerous back there," Kelly said. "We've got to balance the dangers. Do what's best."

Lynne started signing but then waved her hands, nodded, and pointed downhill.

Huw looked at his daughter. She also nodded.

Balance the dangers, he thought. *Bad or terrible. Great. Maybe a lot of our decisions will be like that from now on.*

***

Fifteen minutes later, he was convinced that they'd made the wrong choice. They had emerged from the wooded area and were still heading downhill. The undergrowth around them consisted of drying, dying ferns, tough heathers, and clumps of bramble bushes which were similarly dying down. Winter was coming, and the dried rustling of dead plants sounded like a last breath.

Every step brought another gentle crunch, and it was not long before Huw held up his hand and called a halt. He scanned around them for vesps; he could see a few pale shapes on distant mounds that might have been gatherings of fallen leaves, or might have been something else. More creatures continued to fly past. Some of them curved across the hillside and circled back again, describing seemingly random patterns solo or in small groups. He'd seen a few taking birds from the sky, zeroing in on birdsong and seemingly ripping them apart in mid-air, a brief meal to fuel their onward journey. Others seemed determined to reach another destination. These flew faster, generally erring between north and west, and he wondered how they knew to keep going in that direction. Their spreading towards areas as yet untouched seemed intentional, and that could only happen if they communicated in some way.

But understanding them, musing upon their physiologies and habits and instincts, could come later. Now his priority was survival.

"We're making too much noise," he signed. *We're also walking too close together,* he thought. But there was no way he could suggest putting distance between them.

Closeness brought comfort, and that was a feeling in scant supply.

"We can't go back," Ally insisted. "We'll just have to move slowly."

Dusk was settling. The sun had already dipped into the westward hills, settling its deep winter colours across the landscape and allowing shadows their space. Darkness grew and smothered the sky, and the air was becoming heavier by the moment. Very soon he knew that they'd have to face the prospect of spending the night out here. In the open, the dark, the cold, when movement in any direction could give them away. Nothing to keep them warm. Very little to eat or drink. Even the tins of food might make a noise if they tried to open them.

Panic circled, and Huw felt the situation running away from him. Since letting the Jeep roll downhill and torching Glenn's car, he'd been trying to place himself in control. In truth, that had never happened. He'd been floundering since the moment Glenn died, and now he was close to drowning.

"Look!" Jude whispered. It was too loud, too sudden, and Huw caught his breath and crouched, looking around for a pale flash. But there was nothing. And after a few panicked heartbeats, he looked in the direction Jude was pointing.

His son had his other hand pressed over his mouth, eyes wide. But he might just have saved them.

Beyond a low ridge to the north-west, where the hillside sloped down towards the wide valley, rose a faint haze of smoke. The breeze caught it above the hill and smeared it across the sky, but lower down it was a slightly leaning, pale tower.

That looks normal, Huw thought, and he was convinced it was from a chimney as opposed to a vehicle or building fire. Intentional, not disastrous. He wasn't sure *how* he knew—perhaps it was simply that he needed it to be so—but he stuck with that feeling.

He waved so that everyone was looking at him, then signed, "Let's go."

They skirted a mound of boulders tumbled from the hillside aeons ago, doing their best to step carefully. As they passed the rocks Huw saw several vesps sitting on top of the largest, mouths pointing upwards and those strange tentacles splayed in the air behind them. Perhaps they were ears, or similar organs used to detect the slightest sound. The mad idea came to test that theory— he could lob a stone as far as possible and see how the things reacted. But stirring up prone vesps did not feel like a good idea.

Maybe soon, once they had settled into this silent new existence, he could start gathering more information. Because he was certain that the time would come to fight back.

They climbed a small hump on the lower hillside. At one point Ally froze, looking down at the ground just in front of her. Huw moved quickly, but whatever danger had been there was gone. A bloodied animal lay curled atop a fall of dead ferns, its black-and-white fur speckled red and torn. It still wore a collar, but Huw had no wish to know the cat's name.

Ally blinked at him a few times, her face blank. She was remembering Otis.

When they reached the summit they looked down into the gentle valley beyond. There was a house down there, at the foot of the hill and surprisingly close. It was an attractive, large redbrick building with a double-vaulted roof and bay-fronted windows at front and back. The expansive garden was surrounded by a stone wall, with a parking area and outbuildings, a couple of them attractively dilapidated. One vehicle was parked there, a small car. A rutted lane disappeared around a spread of trees towards an unseen road nearby. Lights shone in several windows, doors were closed, and a curl of smoke rose from one of the two tall chimneys. Whoever was inside was doing nothing to conceal their presence.

"Let me go first," Huw signed.

"I'm coming with you!" Kelly replied.

Huw shook his head.

"Huw's right," Lynne signed, and she stepped forward and repeated it so that they could all see. "Huw's right. He has to see how things are before we all go down there. We don't know who is in the house, or how they might react."

Huw nodded, both pleased that she'd stuck up for him, and also suddenly afraid of going on his own. It made total sense but he also felt vulnerable.

Kelly held the shotgun out for him. At first he took it, surprised at the weight she'd been carrying for the last hour. But then he gave it back to her. He wanted to appear unthreatening to the house's occupants, and if there *was* cause to fire a shotgun, he'd likely already be doomed.

He put his left arm around Kelly's waist and brought her in close, not quite whispering in her ear but breathing there, and hearing her breath in turn. He smelled her familiar smell and took comfort from it. Then he softly

271

kissed her neck and moved away.

"Wait here," he signed. "Stay low and quiet, and if something bad happens, don't move. Don't come to help."

Jude shook his head and turned away. Ally grabbed her brother's arm and pulled him close, giving him a glare that said, *Listen to Dad!*

"I'll be fine," Huw said. "I'm only saying those things just… in case of an emergency. Like the emergency procedures when we flew to France last year. Remember?"

Jude nodded, still sulky but accepting.

Huw waved his arms left and right like an air steward, pleased when Jude smiled. He held up his hand, fingers splayed. Five minutes. Then he turned and started down the hillside.

He could smell the smoke from the house's chimney and it was so inviting. He imagined sitting in front of that fire, warming his cold extremities, a mug of hot coffee in his hands, and the house's owner bustling in the kitchen to prepare a meal for these sad visitors. The warmth of the interior lights was similarly calming, and as he drew closer he looked for signs of movement.

Yet the sight troubled him. Whoever lived there was making no effort to hide their presence. No one really knew whether the things would be drawn by smell, like the musky scent of wood smoke; or whether in darkness they might flock like moths to the subtle heat of any obvious light source. He could not believe that anyone didn't know that the vesps were here. So as he walked carefully down a well-trodden path towards a gate in the garden wall, he had to consider the possibilities.

The owner was ignorant of the threat and might make a noise upon Huw's arrival.

They might know what was happening but doubt the veracity of some of the reports. A stubborn streak could have kept the fire going and the lights on, defiance in the face of obscure dangers. That would also present particular dangers once Huw drew close enough for them to see him or, worse, call out to him.

Or perhaps they were already dead. Maybe a door or window hung open, and inside a body or bodies lay host to newly laid eggs. In that case he would find only vesps guarding the corpses, and he and his family would be forced to make a decision—attempt to clear the house of the creatures, or move on.

Huw reached the garden wall and paused. Closer, the house looked equally inviting yet even more out of place. He'd seen terrible things, and such normality had no place in this new world.

He glanced back up the hillside. His family were crouched down watching him, just visible in the fading light. Kelly waved. They gave no sign that they'd seen anything dangerous.

Several vesps flew across the garden and swerved around the house, one of them even curving over the roof and flying through the column of smoke rising from the chimney. Its path seemed to flitter slightly, then it continued on its course. He hoped that answered the question about smell.

He assessed the gate, saw the heavy metal catch and how the wooden gate fitted tightly against the uprights, and decided that it would be quieter and safer to climb the wall. It was only four feet high and he was soon over, standing on the well-tended lawn. Light washed out from two of the downstairs windows and illuminated some of the garden closer to the house, but the further extremes of the garden were already in shadow. He had to act quickly if they were to be inside before true darkness fell.

Taking in a breath, a sudden shrill cry made him crouch down in terror. He looked around, trying to see where the noise came from. Then he looked up.

Almost directly above the house, a buzzard was in combat with several vesps. It seemed to have one clasped in its deadly claws, but as it flew several others attacked it. The bird called again, folding its wings and dropping, flapping and rising once more. A pale shape closed on it and a flurry of violence erupted, both shapes plummeting quickly. The vesp continued to fall and thumped down on the other side of the garden. The bird of prey rose, issuing several long, triumphant calls. They sealed its doom. More vesps quickly closed on it, and the bird was smothered in pale bodies.

Huw rooted for the buzzard. It was a huge animal, easily five times the size of the vesps. But it was outnumbered, and perhaps even outmatched. The vesps parted and the bird fell, and almost before it struck the ground beyond the garden's far wall they were on it again.

Huw sighed and turned back to the house. He took three steps across the garden before the woman started shouting.

"You're trespassing! Get the hell out of my garden!" She was standing at the left corner of the house and behind her, set in a lean-to portion that might be a kitchen, a door stood open. She was old, frail, but he could see the anger born of fear in her eyes. For a crazy moment he almost replied—it was a natural reaction, and something that anyone would have done—but as he took a breath to shout back...

They were flying across the garden, low and fast.

He waved at the woman, trying to signal to her to move back, get inside, slam the door—

"I said get the hell out of my bloody—"

The first vesp hit her from above, swerving over the lean-to's roof and slamming down onto the top of her head. She swiped her hand and sliced the thing almost in two, and it was only then that he noticed the carving knives she carried. She staggered, leaned against the wall, and slashed out at the other vesps as they closed in.

Huw hunched down, hands held to his face. He wanted to go and help; every instinct told him to run towards her and tackle the beasts. But he also felt the weight of his family behind and above him. They'd be watching this, biting their lips to prevent themselves shouting at him, demanding that he back away and protect himself. He couldn't help his family by dying for this poor old woman.

He stood, meaning to back away but actually taking a step forward, and then two vesps flew so close to him that he felt a wingtip slap his hip.

The woman fell as the creatures smothered her, biting, raging, frantic in whatever blood- or food-lust took them when they found new prey. She battled hard. Both hands waved and slashed, and several more vesps fell, flapping across the gravelled yard like landed fish as they bled out. She screamed in defiance and pain, swearing, and Huw heard no fear in her voice. But her valiant struggles did not last for long.

The feeding frenzy did. Something prickled at Huw's ears, a sound so high pitched that he was not certain he heard it at all. But when more vesps flocked to the dead woman, he realised it must have been a call of some kind. They had found food and were signalling their brethren to come and feed.

They did not want to save this corpse for eggs. They ate, and he crouched low against the garden wall and watched. He was too terrified to move, too shocked to do anything other than witness her end.

Night had fallen, but not quickly enough to hide the sight. A cruel light spilled from the house.

A couple of minutes later, Huw realised that he'd dropped down behind the wall and that his family would no longer be able to see him. *They'll know that I'm here hiding, keeping safe,* he thought, but a glimmer of panic bit in as he stood and looked back up the hillside.

There was just enough moonlight to silver the scene. Ally was almost at the foot of the hill and less than twenty metres away, and behind her he could see Lynne, then Kelly and Jude following. Ally saw him, froze, and brought her hands to her mouth, face crumpling with relief.

Huw held up both hands then pressed them slowly down. And separated from each other, yet still just close enough to see, they waited while the vesps' feeding frenzy drew to a close.

It was at least fifteen minutes before the first vesp took off from the body and flew away. Others soon followed. Illuminated by the splash of light from the open doorway, the woman was a ruin, a tangle of torn clothes and bloody bones no longer even remotely identifiable as a human body. If he hadn't seen her fall, he would never have known what he was looking at.

His family had slowly moved closer, and now they stood on the other side of the wall, close enough for him to touch. They held hands. In their silence they spoke volumes.

Huw pointed at the house. "It's empty now."

"What about them?" Ally signed. "Some might have gone inside."

"That's why you have to wait here again," he said.

"Cold," Lynne said.

"It'll be warm in there. The fire's still burning. Give me a while, I'll wave from the door when it's safe."

"You're going in that door?" Jude asked. He was staring at the thing that lay in the splay of light from the open doorway. Huw had no wish to go that way and see what remained. He would have to walk *through* her. But the door stood open, and the others might be locked. It was the quickest, easiest way inside.

"I'll wave," he said again. "We'll be inside soon. Safe." The last word he signed hung hollow in the air between them all, unanswered. Kelly smiled tiredly at him, then nodded towards the house.

This time, Huw took the gun.

He crossed the shadowy garden, and as he neared the house he felt more and more at risk. The light made it easier to see where he was stepping, and everything pointed to the vesps being completely blind, but he still felt naked and exposed.

He paused and took a deep breath, preparing himself for what he had to see.

Clothing soaked in blood lay scattered across the crazy-paved patio area. Her bones had been exposed: an arc of ribcage, the gleam of skull peering from a grey, clotted mass of hair. One hand lay clawed around a knife handle, many of the fingers chewed to the bone, several nails still visible. They were painted pink. Huw breathed deeply to hold back the nausea.

There were several dead vesps too, their blood thicker and darker than the woman's. He approached slowly, stepping lightly, but he still could not bring himself to touch one of the dead creatures with his foot. Though they were opened up and their guts spilled, he was too afraid that they would fly at him.

He stepped past the remains and approached the open door. It led directly into a huge kitchen. There was a big farmhouse table in the centre and cupboards and worktops around three walls. Two doors led off from the room, but he was pleased to see that both were tightly closed. Standing in the doorway, gun half-raised, he held his breath and listened. All was silent.

Ingredients for a meal were scattered on a chopping block on the table—onions, mushrooms, a carton of eggs, a mixing bowl. His stomach rumbled, and he tried to remember when he'd last eaten anything substantial. He couldn't. Time seemed to have distorted, and this new life had been for ever.

Huw entered the kitchen, walking slowly, checking the floor in case he kicked or stepped on something, moving steadily around the island table and scanning the room for vesps. There was a big dresser against one wall with plates, cups and jugs displayed. Nothing else sat on the shelves. A rack hung above the table with pots and pans clipped on. No vesps. He ducked and checked beneath the table, and as he reached the two doors leading into the main house he gently shoved against them. Their catches were engaged.

There might have been other people in the house. There was no way of knowing without opening the doors, but he didn't want to do that until his family was safely inside and the outside door was closed.

He stood in the doorway, trying to think about anything else he should have done. The dead woman's remains glistened before him. His stomach lurched.

They'll all have to see this, he thought, and he waved to his family, urging them towards him.

A couple of minutes later they were there. Kelly held Jude tight against her side so that he didn't have to see what was left of the old woman, but he still stole a glance. His face looked so pale in the artificial light.

Inside at last, the door gently closed and locked, Huw turned to his family and whispered, "I think we might be safe here, for a while."

Ally leaned over the table, pressed her face into her arms, and started to cry.

18

The cataclysm has brought about such a radical change in the way we live, communicate, and rely on each other that it's almost as if we are killing ourselves. Society is built upon interdependence, and has been for thousands of years. We congregate in great communities of millions of people, creating complex webs of contact that cannot easily be unspun, and in times of chaos and need—times like now—it is human nature to draw that web in closer. To be with each other even more than we have before. We have come to rely on others for well-being—doctors, pastors, soldiers. Relying on oneself is too much of an alien concept for so many. That is why millions have died. If this had happened ten thousand years ago the vesps would have been called devils, but those small communities affected by them might well have been better equipped for survival. We need to return to that time. Flee the cities, don't run to them. Find solitude, not solace in others. And remember, you are never alone. God is still with us; I believe that with every part of my terrified body and every shade of my battered soul. But now we can only pray to Him in silence.

Reverend Michael Morris, personal blog,
Tuesday, 22 November 2016

We're calling them sound ships. Holds filled with high explosives and fuel drums, superstructures mounted with speakers, cattle tied to the decks, floating far out to sea on remote control, blaring music and deafening horns, luring vesps out to them in their tens of thousands. Then the ships are detonated. I've been involved with seventeen so far in the English Channel, and hundreds more have been used elsewhere. But even this is just a drop in the ocean.

Anonymous, Royal Navy, Thursday, 24 November 2016

It's like trying to cure the common cold with a machine gun. We need something that they will spread among themselves—a disease, an infection, a virus. Experiments are ongoing, and the sharing of resources, knowledge and data across the globe is unprecedented. But it all takes time.

Anonymous, MoD, Saturday, 26 November 2016

"So what have we found out today?"

With the others—his wife, son, mother-in-law—Huw had taken to communicating in soft, gentle whispers, each utterance separated by a long pause while they made sure nothing else had heard. Being able to talk again was welcome, but it was also accompanied by a terrible sense of dread. Each time he spoke he remembered that vesp flying at him and Kelly, its wide open mouth, its trailing tendrils, its teeth. It was the time in his life when he'd come closest to dying.

But it was these moments with Ally that he treasured

the most. Each evening since arriving at the house they had spent half an hour or more together in the dining room, her iPad open on the table and plugged into a wall socket, two mugs of hot tea and a plate of food between them. They'd started on that first night, and nine days later they were still compiling information, signing to each other and existing in complete, comfortable silence. In all those years since the accident, Huw thought this was the closest he had come to understanding what it must be like for Ally. He even drank his tea quietly.

Her computer scrapbook was expanding rapidly, its front page a pinboard from which she could link through from several main headings: *Timeline, Rumours, Facts, The Vesps, Us*. She had constructed a complex file of information and cross-references, and even now Huw only had a vague inkling of just how it worked. But that was Ally all over. Once started on something like this she put everything she had into it.

He worried about what would happen if and when the power went out. He had not mentioned that to Ally, though he knew she thought about it. She'd left the in-car charger in the Jeep, so all they had was a standard issue charger that had to be connected to the mains.

Ally had changed the title of her scrapbook to *The Silence*. The *New Worlds?* moniker was still on the front page, but lined through with a heavy red line.

He leaned forward and watched as she started to type.

Monday, 28 November 2016

The usual messages from the Prime Minister's

office: "Stay inside, don't travel, the struggle against the vesps is moving forward apace." Then the lists of dos and don'ts that we've seen a hundred times before. It's like things are on hold, and there's been no new official information for days. Like during World War Two when lots of bad news was withheld and newsreels just had good news. Except there's no good news, so instead they tell us nothing.

But there are still rumours.

@CallingMeIshmael says that large areas of London are on fire. Lots of other posts deny this, and plenty poke fun—"world's-end-porn" one Tweet calls it—but there are other independent sources that appear to confirm at least some sort of major fire in London. It's strange that there's no consistency. Maybe people are scared, or don't believe what they see.

Another tweet from @maddogfucker says that the army are starting huge fires to clear the vesps. His joke name made me doubt his comments at first, but other posts make me think there's something in it. And it seems to make sense. The army knows that using guns will only draw more vesps, so perhaps now they're using fire instead of lead. Like the sound ships we heard about. Make noise to draw them in, then burn them.

I hope it's working.

There's also talk about three nuclear explosions in central Europe. Some of the news channels mention this too, but only the independents. Nothing on the BBC. Censorship? Awful if it's true (also awful if that kind of news is being censored). There are photos of mushroom clouds but also comments that they're stock images.

Some people say that vesps are the work of God. Others say Satan. Different beliefs seem to be causing friction, even violence. A man was found crucified in Birmingham. Some people say he tried to kill himself by jumping off a building, but others say he was murdered by a religious gang. On Flickr there are photos showing burning mosques, churches and synagogues. There are reports of military skirmishes in the Middle East. Even when things are this bad, religion leads to violence.

How depressing.

In Bolton, there's a webcam focused on a pile of bodies at one end of a platform at the railway station. It refreshes every five seconds, giving an almost-real-time view of the vesps waiting there. A sick rumour is going around that all the dead people are black, and that gangs of white supremacists used the vesp attack as cover to launch their own horrible crusade. But I think that's just rumour designed for... I don't know what. Hate? Why hate anyone in a world like this? What's the point?

The image from the webcam is too unclear to see.

America is clear.

America is infested.

Australia has closed its borders and shut itself off from the world.

Australia is now home to more refugees than Australians.

The vesps have a very short, very rapid life cycle.

The vesps live for ever.

There's so much out there on the news channels, social media, and blogosphere that it's becoming difficult to see the truth. And that's something else I've noticed. Something really disturbing.

Things are breaking down.

Social media has become a very weird place to be, and not only because of the content. But I'll talk more about that later.

I shoved the iPad away and sat back in the chair. I wasn't yet ready to write about what I was seeing and sensing across the Internet, because I couldn't quite place exactly what it was. Perhaps a break from the net would be good. Time spent in the real world, however dangerous and terrifying that world had become, might allow me to see clearer.

Dad also leaned back from where he'd been watching my words appear on the screen. He rested his hand on mine and edged in slightly so that our shoulders were also touching. We could take these moments, now that we were inside and mostly safe. *Mostly,* I thought, because I could never allow myself to believe that we were completely safe. Not with what could be seen outside, when we took time to look. Not with what had happened and was still happening. Mostly safe was as good as it could ever be.

We'd been in the house for nine days. After first checking that the woman had been alone, and then doing a much more thorough search for any vesps that might have got in, Dad had locked the doors and settled us in the kitchen. There was food chopped on the table and a saucepan of water still hot on the stove. For a while we left it, while we discussed—in hushed tones, barely whispers—what had happened and what the future held. But it had taken only a few minutes for us all to agree that we had to stay where we were, at least for that night.

Lynne had cooked us an omelette, and we'd eaten hungrily and carefully. One spoon clinking against a bowl might be loud enough.

A cough. A sneeze. Laughter, crying, my despairing gasp when I thought about Otis again, Jude's sobs when he huddled into Mum's lap and pressed his face to her neck. All of these might have been loud enough to bring vesps, had we not been more than aware of the dangers. My gasp had been all but silent, and it had seemed so unnatural seeing Jude crying dry tears.

Since then we had gone day by day.

On day two we took stock of supplies. The woman had kept a pantry of staples—rice, dried pasta, potatoes, tinned vegetables—and Dad said it was probably in case of snow. There had been enough to last us for a week if rationed conservatively, and maybe longer if we let ourselves go hungry.

On day three I tried again to get in touch with Lucy

and Rob. Lucy's social media pages were static, no activity. Nothing. I almost tried FaceTiming her, but imagined her phone ringing while she was crawling along a street, hiding in a garden. Rob did answer a message, told me he was in a place in North Wales and that he thought they were safe. It was good to hear from him. Even the way he typed messages felt familiar. I missed him, and we promised to keep in touch.

On day four Lynne discovered a bag of flour in the bottom of the pantry and set about making bread. This had washed the smell of despair from the house for a while, and also given us a much-needed food boost.

Day five was when I lost touch with Rob. He didn't answer any messages, and his pages were frozen. I tried again and again, trying not to cry or imagine what he might be doing, what he might look like. I promised myself that I'd try again the next day, but I went to bed that night wondering. I feared that I'd never know what had happened to him. Alive or dead, perhaps Rob was out of my life for ever.

It made the world seem very big and dark.

I knew that Dad had also been trying Uncle Nathan and Aunty Mags, with no success. He and his siblings had a weird relationship, and even talking about them always used to stress him out. I watched him when he tried to call them both and received no answer. His face looked soft and expressionless, his eyes empty. It would have been better if he'd cried.

On day six we saw a group of people walking along the ridge to the north. They remained in sight for ten minutes, seven small stick figures moving cautiously between trees and hedges, silhouetted against the darkening sky. I hoped that the people would see the house and come to investigate. But I noticed my parents' relief when the shapes passed by. Even though we didn't discuss it, that troubled me for a while. But when I really thought about what the group's arrival might have meant, I understood it a lot more.

The vesps were always there. Sometimes, and some days, there were more in the sky than others, but we always saw them roosting nearby. The garden was quite big and they'd settle in plants and on walls for a while, and beyond the garden there was a spread of woodland beside the rough lane. Their pale shapes spotted the bare trees like misshapen fruits.

Lynne found an old pair of binoculars in a wardrobe, and Jude spent a long time scanning our surroundings. He spotted what he thought were several sheep up on the hillside. On day three the last of them stopped moving, and the next day several of the sheep gave birth to clouds of small vesps like exploding fungi. The creatures spiralled and spun for a minute or two, then the clouds dispersed and they disappeared across the landscape.

I think it was day five or six when we saw the dog approaching the cottage. Jude saw it through his binoculars and came to get me, telling me about the wolf out on the hills. I told him there were no wolves here, but went to see anyway. It was an Alsatian. Big, brown and black, it was slinking through the undergrowth as if stalking something, but its eyes were fixed on us. I went to fetch Mum and Dad, and I wanted Lynne to come too, but she was asleep in the old woman's bedroom. She'd taken to sleeping a lot more during the day.

We watched the dog draw closer. I tried not to see

Mum and Dad's expressions, because I knew what they were thinking. We couldn't have a dog staying with us. But for a while I suppose I did entertain the fantasy.

He came close to the house and then lay down beyond the wall, out of sight. We didn't see him for some time. I wondered how he'd come to be out there on his own, where his owners were, how he had survived this long, and I realised that everyone and everything out there had a story, and that most stories would never be told. It made me sad. And for some reason that one lonely dog's plight helped me understand the magnitude of what was happening, more so than any reports of London burning or sound ships blasting ten thousand vesps at a time to pieces. It was the idea of that animal's own story that brought reality home.

When the dog jumped up onto the wall and stared at the house, it was Mum who moved one of the curtains at the window. I think she did it on purpose. I think she knew what she was doing. And I felt so sorry for the dog, because I couldn't help thinking that he barked with sheer canine delight at seeing people again.

He ran back along the lane when they came, but they made short work of him.

Less than a day later the eggs laid in him hatched.

Now we were on day nine, and what had been a place to stay for the night seemed to be developing into something more permanent.

I moved and sat down again at the table, turning the iPad to face me. I liked these moments in the early evening that Dad and I spent sharing what we had discovered that day, filling in my scrapbook, and just being alone together. There was a selfish stab every time

I thought like that, but also a sense of calm, even peace. I was still his little girl, and what little girl didn't believe her father could look after her?

But those moments were also troubling. And the things we'd talk about—what he had seen, what I had read—would often haunt me into the night.

"So tell me what you found," I signed. Dad had been out on a search for food, and since returning he'd been quiet and withdrawn. He and Mum had gone to the room they'd taken for themselves for a while, and I thought perhaps they'd had sex. Not that I liked to think about it, but I understood. They were like one person, even if sometimes they seemed to forget that. But the atmosphere was more tense than usual, and Lynne had been pacing the downstairs rooms ever since.

Even though Dad hadn't told us what he'd found, he'd still brought it home with him.

"Okay," he signed. "But you're not going to like it."

I shrugged. "What's left to like?" I opened a new document in my scrapbook and prepared to type.

Huw didn't really think he'd have to stay out until the next morning. He took some of the warm clothing they'd found in the old woman's wardrobe—her dead husband's, he guessed, though it seemed that he'd been gone for a while—and part of that was a precaution, just in case he *did* have to spend the night elsewhere. But he wasn't really prepared mentally. He didn't want to be away from his kids and Kelly for any longer than was necessary, certainly not through the night.

He missed home. He wondered whether they had

made a terrible mistake in running, exposing themselves to wider danger by coming somewhere they didn't know. They could have stayed in Usk, perhaps in Glenn's house. If they had maybe Glenn would still be alive. Or maybe they'd all be dead. Agonising over things did nothing, and he tried to drive it from his mind. *No doomsdaying now, Huw!* he kept thinking. *Focus on now, not the past or future.*

The spear didn't make him feel much safer. A broom handle with a carving knife taped to both ends, it was hardly high tech, though they had all seen what the old woman had done with just one knife. She'd fought hard, bless her.

He went north-west, further into the valley and down towards the lake in the distance. He intended to move cross-country or along country lanes where he could. His plan was to walk until he saw some buildings, then assess the situation, see if it was safe to approach. He took Jude's precious binoculars, promising to bring them back. He intended to sit and watch any settlement for some time before closing in.

He was hoping to find a pub or a hotel. There were hundreds in the Lake District, and a pub's larder would see them well fed for weeks. And he was also hoping to bring back some wine.

It was his first time away from the house since arriving eight days previously, and leaving was very difficult. Everything he loved was there. At the garden's edge he paused for a while, feeling them all watching him. He almost turned back to wave, but feared that if he did he might never go. So he climbed over the wall and started down the narrow lane leading into the valley.

Passing the rotting remains of the Alsatian and seeing the glimmer of its name tag gave him a stab of remorse.

There were vesps all around. Plenty were still flying, but now he got the impression that they were patrolling more than advancing. There didn't seem to be a specific direction to their movements any more. He couldn't help thinking of them as an army—they had an advancing front, taking possession of territory, driving forward; and behind was the occupation force. They cruised, looking for prey, but many of them also remained motionless. It was these that worried him most, because sometimes they remained unseen. He'd seen them roosting in trees, as still as the trees themselves. They often seemed to take the higher ground, perhaps because it gave them a better field of hearing. But sometimes they were low down too. Once Huw almost stepped on one, and he was amazed it didn't hear his gasp of shock. It didn't move. Maybe it was dead. He didn't wait to find out.

By midday Huw had travelled maybe two miles, following public paths where he could. He was much closer to the lake, and using the binoculars he could see that there was a small village at its southern extreme. Several boats seemed to be abandoned on the water. He was still a long way off, but could see no movement in the village, no signs of life.

He didn't want to go there.

Finally he took to a proper surfaced road. It was a country lane, really, but there were scraps of litter by the roadside and no weeds growing through the tarmac, and it seemed well travelled. He made a decision to follow it for a while—it seemed the best way to find a building. If he heard engines he'd get off the road and hide. If he heard voices, he'd do the same.

Approaching a gate in the stone walling, he saw a pile of dead cattle. There must have been a dozen cows there, crushed against the gate and the wall on either side, corpses bloated with gas, legs stiff, mouths frozen open and eyes wide. Some of the eyes had been pecked away by birds, but several dead crows were also scattered amongst the bodies.

Wounds pouted open, bubbled with eggs. Silent vesps nestled in the spaces between bodies. The stink was horrendous, and he breathed through his mouth as he eased cautiously by.

The stench followed him along the road. The cows must have panicked, herded together and pressed against the gate as the vesps came at them. How many had it taken to kill them all? It hardly bore thinking about, and Huw did his best to shrug it from his mind.

The road veered down. It curved around a hillock and swept across the wider hillside.

About ten minutes later he saw more bodies. These were human. They were lying in a ditch beside the road, so he paused and checked them out through the binoculars. It took him a while to work out what was so troubling, then he realised that there were no vesps guarding them. He was already so used to seeing vesps around bodies that these looked unusual without them.

Huw weighed up the option of leaving the road and skirting around the dead, but he'd effectively trapped himself—a steep wooded slope down on one side, an even steeper hillside heading up on the other. Go either way and he might make a noise.

He made sure the rucksack was on tight and held

the spear in both hands, then started downhill again.

It was a man and a woman. They were lying beside the road and it looked like they'd been dragged there, arms up above their heads, legs straight out. Still no vesps. He paused several times as he walked closer, looking around, and it all felt wrong, unnatural. He was more worried about there being no vesps than if he'd seen them.

They were in their twenties, fit-looking, both kitted out in cycling gear. Their bikes were nowhere in sight. The man had his wrists tied together with a sock and his throat was cut. Huw thought the woman had been stabbed. He didn't get any closer. The smell was bad, there were insects, and he didn't want to see any more.

From that moment on everything changed, and Huw carried that change with him. It had been bad enough seeing that bastard pointing a gun at his daughter, but seeing those two bodies brought home to him that they now existed in a very different world. They were living *after*. Before was order and society, structure and support systems, and even when the vesps came and attacked there were plans, advice was being broadcast, and they were waiting for the authorities to come and help. They had been waiting for others to put things right, and now he was unsure whether that was ever going to happen. They couldn't live in the before any more. Someone had killed that couple, because it was after. If they were going to survive, they had to embrace the change. Go with it.

Huw realised that they also had to keep doing what Ally was best at—gathering information and knowing as much as possible about the world they faced. The murdered cyclists were as much a part of that as the vesps.

He moved on quickly, upset at what he'd seen and more scared than he'd ever been. Part of him wanted to rush back and be with his family, just in case whoever had done it found the house. But the bikes had gone, and he guessed that the bodies were at least a couple of days old. Whoever had murdered them was far away. Or dead themselves. His family needed food, and if they started going truly hungry it would affect their judgement. They had to keep their wits about them.

An hour later he sensed a change in the air around him. It started feeling heavy, and it even smelled different. He worried that perhaps a new, huge wave of vesps was incoming, spreading that weird, sour smell they seemed to exude. But then he looked west and saw the heavy clouds rolling over the ridge line, and knew that a storm was building.

He didn't for a moment think about what that might mean.

He knew he had to turn around and get back. There were maybe three hours of daylight left, and it would have been dangerous to travel by night, even though he had the torch. He knew that there were more dangers out there now than just the vesps.

But he was much closer to the lake by then, heading north parallel to it so that he didn't get too close to the town, and he wanted to reach the top of the rise just ahead. *Just one more look,* he thought. And when he reached the top he looked down and saw the pub. It was maybe three hundred metres along the road, an old, attractive building with a car park, large garden, and a couple of smaller outbuildings which were probably holiday homes.

Half of the pub had burnt down. The other half was blackened, windows smashed, roof stoved in, but he could still see how nice it had once been. Lots of the ash had fallen across the road, and as he drew closer he could see only a few tracks through the ash fields. Some sets of footprints, and a few bike trails. Some of the footprints led back and forth to the pub, but it seemed quiet and still, deserted.

He approached cautiously, the spear in one hand and binoculars in the other. He paused every few steps to check out the buildings and car park. There were a few cars there, and a couple of vans with bike and canoe racks. He worried about those vehicles. There was no movement, but they all had windows covered with ash from the fire, those closer to the building scarred with bubbled paint from the flames. He couldn't see whether any of them were occupied.

Everything told him to get away. Time was passing and he had a several-mile hike back to the house before dusk fell. But he was desperate not to return empty-handed.

He moved closer. Stayed alert. Watched for movement, listened for noise. There were a few vesps flying around, though no more than usual. He noticed some birds, too. Siskins, thrushes, some blackbirds, and none of them were singing. That was amazing, and he logged that for a later discussion with Ally. Could birds really learn that quickly? He didn't know, but it buoyed him, and gave him a glimmer of hope that he'd been sorely lacking for the past few days.

He passed through an open gate into the beer garden, and it was... strange. Most of the ash seemed to have been blown out across the car park and road, and the garden was surprisingly tidy. There were still a few glasses on the tables. One was full of wasps. He thought it was too late in the season, but they'd come from somewhere, drawn by whatever had been left in the glass, and drowned. Cider, probably. He wondered why their buzzing hadn't brought the vesps. Perhaps it had, and the solidity of the glass had made them lose interest.

It was the back end of the pub that had been burned, and his spirits sank when he realised that the kitchens and stores were probably housed there. But there would still be crisps and nuts behind the bar, and drinks. That close, he started to *really* want a drink.

He needed to be careful, to take things slowly, but there was also a pressure to move fast. Time was running out. Daylight had been replaced by a heavy greyness. A breeze picked up ash from the burned buildings and bare tree branches waved. A couple of crisp packets skittered across the garden path and Huw froze, looking around for roosting vesps.

After a few moments he approached a smashed window towards the front of the pub. That was when he caught the first whiff of decay. There was something dead close by, and that meant there was a good chance there were vesps guarding it.

Unless the eggs had already hatched. He didn't know, didn't understand enough about them to guess at what stage these eggs might be. He should have turned around and left, but he'd cast aside good sense. It was partly the lure of food and drink, also pure curiosity. He wanted to be able to return home, sit with his sweet daughter, and tell her something new.

So he went to the window, trying to breathe softly

through his mouth in an attempt to avoid the awful stench of rot. He could smell the fire, too, and tried to concentrate on that. When he reached the window and looked inside, he smelled more. They say that aromas inspire the strongest memories, and...

Spilled beer, sticky carpet, and Huw was back in his twenties, him and Kelly courting and spending most Tuesday evenings out at a country pub. They'd sit in the beer garden. Usually just the two of them, but sometimes friends would go too, and some of those evenings were special times for Huw. Those moments that don't seem so spectacular when you're living them simply because you expect them to be good, but when you look back they're some of the best moments of your life, so clear in your memory that they might as well be happening on a loop. He felt that, and other things too, recognising less pleasant smells like the odour of vesp, the dampness of old burnt wood. Rotting meat. He'd never quite known the smell of human remains in decay, until then. Good old memories clashed with horrible new ones, and he leaned over and vomited in an old sand bucket sprouting cigarette ends. He tried his best to be quiet. He was terrified. After each heave he looked around, broom-handle spear raised. But nothing came at him, not from the trees and darkening sky, and not from the ruined pub's interior.

After Huw finished vomiting he moved forward and shone the torch inside.

The bar was a ruin, scorched black from smoke, bottles and optics smashed from the heat. It was a mystery how the fire had not consumed the whole building. Perhaps it had rained heavily soon after the fire began, so it didn't really get a good hold.

There were ten, maybe twelve dead people inside, all huddled around or on top of the bar. He guessed there were more behind the bar, too. They'd died after the fire. There was no sign of scorched clothing or melted shoes, no burns on the bodies. But he guessed that they had been dead for a week or more, and they stank.

They were guarded by vesps. He could see maybe eight of them. Most were motionless, roosting, but a couple walked slowly across the carpet around the corpses.

He wanted to leave. He knew then that he should have never gone so close, shouldn't have let curiosity get the better of him, nor his desire for a bottle of wine. How stupid. How *selfish*! He backed away, very slowly, and a gust of wind hushed through the trees and bushes around the damaged pub.

The vesps around the bodies shifted as one, their tendrils rising, splaying out and feeling at the air, as if they could feel the sound rather than hear it. He saw a shimmer pass through a couple of them, a shudder as their glistening skin stretched and contracted again. He brought the spear around, readying to swing it across in front of him and cut them from the air if they launched themselves from the window.

But none came. And as Huw started moving again the torchlight shifted, and through the window he saw something else. In the opened stomach of one of the bodies on the bar there were handfuls of eggs. They glistened like ice cubes, a wet glimmer reflecting the torchlight. There must have been twenty eggs, each of them the size of an apple, and he couldn't help wondering how long they had been there.

Those corpses they had seen on the road soon after leaving the Jeep were new, the eggs in them recently laid. But the ones he was looking at there were days old, maybe a week. The bodies were bloated with gas, the rot was sickening, and he saw other signs of how long they had been there. Slickness. Leakages.

He started wondering why the eggs hadn't hatched. So much of what they had seen, and even more of what Ally had read out from the Internet, indicated that the vesps had a very rapid life cycle. The eggs hatched, the young were instantly able to fly; they grew quickly and were soon able to reproduce. It all contributed to how they had come so far so quickly, and how the vesps that emerged from the cave had rapidly become the millions, or billions, that had swept across Europe. They were a virus.

But these seemed to be waiting.

Curiosity bit Huw again. He backed away across the garden until he reached the gate, then went out onto the road. The car park was on the other side of the pub, in the opposite direction to the one he needed to take. It seemed safe.

Before he could think about it for too long he picked up a stone from beside the road and threw it.

Huw thought he would never be able to make that throw again, not if he tried a hundred times. The stone arced over the road and into the car park, struck the bonnet of a car parked there, bounced, and smashed the side window of another.

It was more noise than he'd heard in over a week.

He crouched down with breath held. Then he heard it. His kids had always loved bubble-wrap, popping the little bubbles one by one. The sound he heard was a little like that except louder, and wetter. The sound of many bubbles popping, machine-gun quick. A high-pitched keening hurt his ears. Almost too high to hear, still it seemed loud.

Infant vesps. They came quickly, fluttering from the smashed window he'd been staring through so recently, more exiting through other openings, and they descended on the car park. They were clumsy at first, flitting back and forth, colliding with each other, and Huw was sure he saw some of them fighting. Several fell and twitched on the ground. But most of them swarmed across the two cars where the stone had hit, crawling wetly over the ashy bonnets and windscreens.

The bigger vesps that had been guarding them circled, never quite settling. Perhaps they could already sense that there was no prey.

He wanted to run. It was disgusting. Once when he was a kid, Huw had found a spider's nest in his parents' back garden. He didn't know what it was so he prodded it with a stick, knocking it back and forth until it fell from the fencing panel and burst on the ground. Countless little spiders spilled from it and starting crawling, everywhere, in every direction. He dreamed about it that night, and his mother told him it was the only time she'd ever heard him shouting in his sleep.

As he retreated from the pub as quickly as he safely could, his only thought was to reach the cottage. He wanted to be with Kelly that night in case he dreamed and started to scream. He looked back a few times, and the last time he saw the swarm of baby vesps dispersing in all directions, some settling on the pub's roof, most disappearing into the distance. Having found no prey at the source of the sound that had wakened them, they were going hunting.

He started running. He did so as silently as possible, remembering what he had read about effective, soft running—land on your mid-foot, roll forward, push the ground behind you. He didn't go too fast because he didn't want to pant too loudly.

By the time he passed the two dead cyclists, the storm was setting in, but it was only when the rain began that he really noticed it. The fury. The *noise*. And he stopped in the road and looked around at the rain coming down in sheets, the sudden darkening of the skies, the leafless trees waving in the wind, the plants in turmoil, and those greyish-yellowish shapes flying back and forth, confused and panicked and insane.

He spoke aloud then for the first time in six or seven hours. Without even thinking about it he said, "Oh shit," but his voice was lost to the wind. The storm had fallen quickly and heavily, and he was stuck in the middle of it. The rain and wind didn't bother him so much, nor the cold. It was them.

There was sound everywhere, and so were they.

He headed for a wall at the side of the road, thinking he might find cover. Over the wall, huddled against the other side where it was sheltered slightly from the storm, he shrugged on another fleece from his rucksack and settled down to wait.

The storm had brought an early dusk. Dark clouds surged above, and the downpour had become even heavier. Wind roared against the hillside, shaking trees and whistling between rocks. Lightning flashed and thunder smashed. And the vesps were everywhere.

He could see them flying in confused patterns, crawling across the ground, leaping from rock to tree and back again. Some of them seemed to attack wherever they landed, others simply flew or crawled. Most were alone, and he thought perhaps they could not hear each other's calls in the chaos.

A few minutes after he took shelter, a vesp dropped down beside him. It was less than a metre away, and for an instant he was frozen, staring at it. The thing's mouth was wide open but not facing directly at him. So many teeth. Its little legs were straight and stiff, holding it up from the wet ground, and those tail tendril things were splayed behind it, squirming as they tried to make sense of the storm. It jittered left to right and back again, and the tentacles became tangled as they switched direction.

He picked up the broom handle and stabbed it at an angle through the mouth. It struggled a bit, but Huw pushed hard, then lifted it against the wall and pressed it there. The knife sliced out through its side and the thing dropped dead.

Huw so wanted to run right then, but it took only one glance over the wall to make him realise he was safer where he was. It was strange how he was thinking of that old woman's cottage as home, surprising how a dangerous place could seem so idyllic when he was somewhere far more dangerous. But he guessed home was where his family was.

He remained behind the wall, and it was one of the worst nights of his life. Not since the crash had he felt so alone. While the storm raged he weathered some rough times—terror over what might be happening back at the cottage, sorrow that his family might lose him and never know what happened, even jealousy that they were all together and he was alone.

There was more thunder and lightning, and that seemed to rile the vesps even more. He saw them attacking each other.

Three more times through the night he killed a vesp with the spear. He used the torch as much as possible. He was concerned that the batteries would fade, but even more worried about being in complete darkness. He didn't know what might be out there in the night. He had not been afraid of the dark since he was ten years old.

The storm raged until the early hours, then slowly began to fade. Huw was soaked through. Shivering. Trying to stop his teeth from chattering, because as the wind faded he saw vesps roosting in trees and across the top of the wall once again.

He returned home through the dawn, shaking so much from the cold that he could hardly breathe, empty-handed, bringing only the story of his expedition for Ally's expanding notes.

He felt like a failure, but sitting at the dining table and telling his tale, Ally put him right.

"You came home to us," she whispered. "That's a success."

I sat back from the keyboard, fingers aching from the rapid typing. I hated the idea that Dad had been out there alone all night, scared and in danger. But I remembered my own delight when I'd seen him crossing the garden early that morning, cold and wet but coming back to us. Coming home.

None of us minded that he had returned without food.

"So now we know more," I said. "The eggs sometimes rest until noise wakes them. The vesps don't seem able to differentiate one noise from another. They're unpredictable in a storm."

Dad nodded and signed, "And don't forget the cyclists. People are killing, too."

I hadn't forgotten the cyclists.

"The more we know, the better."

19

I saw him open the car door and get out. It took him a while to stand, because he'd been stuck in the car for more than seven days. I don't know what it's like out in the countryside, but here in the city the vesps are everywhere—lining roof ridges and window sills, fences and hedgerows, sitting on car bonnets, just waiting. It's as if they can smell or sense all the people still hiding from them. And I think they can wait longer than us. And there are the eggs, too, I've seen them laid in bodies, big swollen things ready to burst at the slightest noise. I've *seen* them born. Seen them swarm, attack, eating victims like eager young suckling at their mother's breast.

I knew what he was doing and hated it.

He got out of the car, slowly, careful not to hit the door on the car parked next to him. He stood straight and seemed to take pleasure in stretching. Looked across the bonnets of four cars and right at me where I watched from inside the minibus, and his expression was so alien to me, so strange, that even now I still can't...

He sat down out of view and started singing his favourite song. He used to sing it to me when I woke up with nightmares. Weird, but I honestly don't think I'd heard it since.

Maria Roach, viral Facebook post,
Saturday, 3 December 2016

Five days after he returned from that terrible stormy night Dad went out again, and this time he took me with him.

Mum objected, but only for a while. Lynne argued more, telling Dad that he was a selfish man taking his daughter into danger. Even when I stepped into the argument and signed that I was happy, that Dad and I would keep each other safe and I thought it was a good idea, Lynne did not relent.

I could see how awkward my family found it having an almost silent argument.

Jude backed me up. He'd changed a lot during our fortnight in the house, becoming less afraid and more mature. He was much quieter—we all were, of course— but more silent in his manner, too, as if he was thinking about things a lot more. In normal times I might have thought this a bad thing. A *sad* thing. I'd had some of my childhood robbed by the accident and the years of recuperation and adjustment that followed, and I'd wanted Jude to make the most of being a kid. But things had changed, and were still changing.

The fact that we were running very low on food helped settle the argument.

Dad and I went west, heading across the valley towards the white specks of houses visible on the distant slopes. It was noticeably colder than when we had arrived at the house, and north and west I could see snow dusting the highest hilltops. I was glad for some of the clothes that we'd found in the house, though the jackets were too big for me, the trousers too short.

We followed the lane leading from the house for a while, then cut across country until we met a B road. A mile later we saw the first bodies. Some were torn to shreds by vesps and whatever had snacked on them afterwards, others were swollen and home to glistening patches of vesp eggs. Some didn't even look like people any more. We crept around them and continued on our way without incident.

I saw a cat. It slinked across the hillside above the road, keeping its distance but following us for a while. It paused when we paused. I thought of luring it down, but then remembered Otis. The cat disappeared a couple of minutes later. I never saw it again, but hoped that it was wise enough to stay alive. It had survived this long.

The first houses we came across were down on the valley floor. It was a small hamlet of half a dozen homes and a tiny, very old church. I felt a chill as we approached, because I could only think about what Dad had seen at the pub, and I dreaded what we might find.

There were no signs of habitation. Several cars were abandoned in the road, some parked normally, a couple askew and with open doors. I crept towards the first one and peered inside. Nothing. I looked up and Dad signalled that the second vehicle was also empty.

"Let's try the one with the open door," he signed, nodding across the street. Beyond the little church with its old graveyard and ivy-clad walls, a picture-perfect cottage stood with a gaping shadow where its front door should be.

I frowned, but Dad waved me forward.

We found no bodies in that hamlet, and no signs of life. We went into three out of the six houses, and by then our rucksacks were filled with tinned food, rice, and soup sachets. I suggested that we make our way back across the valley. I could sense that Dad wanted to explore further, but the place was starting to spook me. In the last house we'd found a table set for dinner, with glasses of orange juice furred around the edges and something dark congealed in a saucepan on the hob.

"I want to get back," I signed. "We can come here again when we need more food. If we take more than we can easily carry we might drop something on the way back, and then…" I shrugged. *And then we'll be heard*. But I didn't even have to say that.

Dad nodded and gave me a careful hug. Even though I could not see his face I liked those hugs. It was a closer form of communication.

We left the houses behind, and the church seemed to watch us go. It was a strange feeling. I glanced back several times, and the spire was the last we saw of the small hamlet, visible for at least twenty minutes as we walked as if it were stretching, straining to keep us in view for as long as possible. I was spooking myself, that was all. Lynne would have said it was God watching over me. *Yeah, right*, I'd say, *he's done a great job up to now*.

Ten minutes after the church spire finally sank from view behind a fold in the land, we saw the man.

I spotted him first. I stopped so quickly that Dad walked into me, and I felt the cool kiss of the make-do spear's blade against my ankle. He stepped quickly to the side until we were shoulder to shoulder, and I knew he was remembering those dead cyclists. We'd discussed that back at the house—who might have done it, why, and how far away they probably were now. But it was Lynne whose comment had been most chilling. *We're going back to the animal.*

The man stood in the road a hundred metres ahead of us. He was short and thin, dressed almost entirely in black, and he seemed to err to his left side, like a scarecrow with a broken stand. It took me a few seconds to recognise the collar. He was a vicar. But there was something wrong with his face.

I raised my hand in greeting, and the vicar waved back. Then he started walking towards us.

Dad caught my attention and signed, "Be careful, stay alert."

"Really?" I replied. But he'd already turned back to face the advancing man.

The vicar wore round frameless glasses with one cracked lens, and he walked with a very pronounced limp. As he walked his gaze did not shift from us. He reminded me of Otis when he saw something interesting or something that might have been prey, his head hardly moving while the rest of his body drove him forward. It was nature's way of maintaining the hunter's focus and keeping his quarry in sight. The vicar held out a notebook as he came closer, and I stepped forward to take it. His lower lip and jaw were darkened with bruising.

I am the Reverend, the note said in a spidery scrawl. *Would you like to join my flock of the Hushed?* I held it up to show Dad, then handed the notebook back.

The Reverend's eyes flickered between us, always settling back on me. *He's scared,* I thought, but then as

I examined him I realised I was wrong. He actually appeared quite calm, one hand in his pocket, his stance casual. Only his eyes moved with any haste.

"I don't like him," I signed to Dad, and he nodded in response.

The Reverend seemed fascinated with the sign language. He waved at me, nodded, perhaps urging me to use it again. But I did not. He seemed too eager, too forward. Inviting us to join his flock without even asking who we were, where we had come from? There was something presumptuous in that.

And what were the Hushed? The capital 'H' worried me. I couldn't tell why.

Dad looked around, then gestured for the notebook. The vicar handed it over along with a small pencil.

I assessed our position while Dad scribbled. We were in open countryside, the road bounded by hedges on both sides, and a few vesps drifted by a dozen feet above. I could see several more roosting on the hedge top, and there were likely others in the fields beyond. Exposed and vulnerable, I wished we could keep walking.

I looked back at the Reverend to see him reading what Dad had written. He frowned. Seemed angry. Then he opened his mouth into a smile, and I was terrified that he was going to speak.

But he could not. He winced as he opened his mouth wider and lowered his face slightly, giving us a perfect view of the bloody, ragged root of his mutilated tongue.

I gasped and pressed a hand to my face, taking a couple of steps back. Dad stood firm. I could see the whites of his knuckles where they grabbed the double-bladed broom handle. *That's it,* I thought, looking at the still grinning Reverend, *that's what I was trying to see. He's mad.*

Dad waved me on and we walked past the Reverend. He touched my shoulder as we went, not quite grabbing, and I jumped aside. He stared at me so piteously that I paused and held out my hand. But instead of reaching for me, he opened his mouth again to show me the ruin where his tongue had been cut or torn out, and I could smell something rank and rotten on his breath.

Dad took my hand and we walked on. He hadn't held my hand in years—my choice, not his—and I felt tears burning at everything he'd done, all he had given up and sacrificed to help me survive and move on after the crash. All he had lost. For an instant I felt totally, completely safe with him, a childish sensation that I had not felt for a long time. Since before the accident. The innocent, blind belief that young children have that their parents can protect them against anything. I tried to grab onto that belief now, because it drove away everything else. I wondered if my grip was as painful, as comforting, as his.

The road led across the valley floor, twisting and turning and yet visible for several hundred metres ahead. That was our way, I knew. Back to our family and relative safety, and back where something of the old world could still be touched via my iPad. For now I set aside my worries and fears at what the online world had become—

—*that's not for now, that's for later, that's for when I'm safe again*—

—and embraced the existence we still had. Whether or not the Reverend really did have a flock, removing his tongue was a sign of madness. He could still groan and screech, I was certain. He could still bring them down if he was not careful.

He was keeping pace with us. I saw Dad's expression, stern and grim, and glanced back at the man now walking confidently behind us. Gone was the limp, the sign of weakness or injury that he'd perhaps used to garner our pity, and now the Reverend looked like a new man. Even more confident, taller, more imposing than before. Stronger. He strolled while we seemed to hurry. And while there was nothing overtly threatening in his gait or his expression, he terrified me. His madness hung about him like a visible aura. What he'd done was a stain on his face.

Dad tugged at my hand and we walked faster. I concentrated on the ground, terrified that we'd trip or kick a stone, anything that might alert a nearby vesp to our presence.

A shadow closed around us then passed by, and the Reverend was walking backwards ahead of us, mouth open as he displayed the root of his new belief. He'd run to catch up. He scribbled on the pad, tore the page and let it flutter before him.

I grabbed it from the air.

With me and the Hushed you might survive. Teach me your silent speaking.

I dropped the paper and let it float away. *He's going to trip*, I thought. *Fall, and while that might not make a noise loud enough, a cry of pain will. He's going to—*

Dad let go of my hand and brought up the broom handle with the blades at either end. He aimed it threateningly at the Reverend, and the man stopped so suddenly that Dad almost speared him there and then, the carving knife's point pressing against the tight white collar around his throat. There was no blood on the collar at all. *Must have stripped before having his tongue ripped out,* I thought. *Or cutting it out himself.*

The Reverend blinked quickly behind his frameless glasses, one hand clasping the pencil, the other his pad. Slowly, he went to write something else.

Dad barged forward and pushed the man aside, and I quickly followed. As we walked down a slight slope I looked back several times to see the Reverend standing there in the road, still with his back to us, apparently looking down as he wrote something on his pad. His stance looked dismissive, but I knew that it was anything but.

The last time I glanced back he was gone.

I looked at Dad but he was focused on walking quickly, silently away from the madman. I reached for his hand again but he only squeezed once before letting go.

We reached the house an hour later without further incident. The haul of food should have made us happy, but we both stayed on edge. I didn't know whether Dad told anyone about the encounter.

I kept it to myself.

I went to the small room I'd taken and checked the iPad. Still plugged in, still fully charged. I opened the scrapbook and entered "The Silence".

Maybe it's because no one's policing it any more. Maybe it's because all the filters are down, both electronic and moral. Maybe it's because I'm looking more, delving deeper into the places I never used to go. But I don't think so. I don't think it's any of that. I think it's because everything is changing, and just as Dad sees things he'd never have believed possible in the world outside—those two cyclists murdered for their bikes—so I'm seeing and sensing things in here that weren't here before.

I sat back on the bed and ate some of the food I'd brought up with me. A bowl of tinned fruit mixed with custard. I'd loved it as a kid, but now it tasted desperate. Maybe because there wasn't much choice. I continued typing.

Social media feels changed. Weird. Stale or… no, not stale. Strange. Less reliable, more prone to hysteria. Maybe the Internet is going mad.

Before, if I'd found something disturbing there was always somewhere to retreat, a sea of relative normality because most people prefer to float in that place. There's curiosity in anyone, and sometimes that might drive people to look at stuff they usually avoid. But mostly people are pretty normal. That normality has gone.

No one really knows what's normal any more.

There's lots of talk of suicide, for a start. Whole sections of YouTube, links from Twitter, announcements and photos on Facebook and other sites, all about people finding their own way out. I stopped looking after seeing three or four "goodbye" films, because they depressed me so much. But they're everywhere, and sometimes I just can't avoid the pictures or comments.

News is still coming in from Europe and beyond, so much of it so quickly that I can't keep up, and I'm just dipping in. It's like picking out single sentences from a five-hundred-page book; there's no way I can understand the whole story from that, only isolated incidents. I'm doing my best but... it's like distances are growing larger. The walk there and back today, maybe five or six miles, felt like for ever. France suddenly seems like another world.

There are the shouts and screams, written and literal, by people wanting, craving order. Official announcements are still being put out by the government, police, army, media, local authorities. But it's becoming more and more difficult to tell real announcements from fake ones. Contradictory advice is issued and spreads across the net. Stay at home... move north. Don't touch the vesps... dead vesps are not a danger. They are dying out... their spread is continuing.

And then there are the haters. The net has always been filled with them, but they're now the ones making the most noise (sometimes I wish they would, literally, because we're in enough trouble without them). Extremists from all the big religions are saying that this is their

317

own particular end of days, apocalypse, whatever. Anti-religious people are out in force too, shouting back at them with just as much nut-job fervour. People blaming the government. Environmentalists saying it's because of centuries spent raping the planet. The French blaming the British, the British blaming Russia, Russia blaming everyone. A whole network of hatred across the web, and I wonder what sits in the middle, sensing the vibrations and waiting to pounce.

It's as if the moment society started to break down, people lost their handle on right and wrong. Did they ever really have it? Dad tells me that he's always scared of bad things happening to good people, but I'm starting to wonder if there were ever good people at all. The world's getting bigger, the groups we live in are getting smaller, and we're going back to the way things used to be. Back to the animal, Lynne said. Thousands of years ago we lived in villages. Tens of thousands of years ago, small nomadic bands.

What next?

Perhaps we're all destined to face the future alone.

"Fucking hell, that's depressing," I whispered. Speaking to myself was a strange habit, and I only did it when I was really upset or depressed or so wound up about something that I felt the need to shout. But right then, the whisper was enough.

I flipped the iPad lid closed and sat back. When I blinked I saw the Reverend and his horribly mutilated mouth, felt his eyes on me when I signed, like a hungry man seeing roast meat.

I went downstairs to be with my family.

They were all in the big kitchen. It was where we spent the most time together, doors closed and the old range cooker alight. Going into other parts of the house felt strange because it was not ours, and even though Lynne had cleared up the remains of the old woman, her presence was still felt. I often wondered about who she was, whether she had family, how long she had been alone. A few pictures around the place told part of the story, but snooping through her belongings to find out more didn't appeal to me.

When I joined them, all but Lynne were sitting at the table. Mum and Dad leaned in close whispering, foreheads almost touching, holding hands. Jude was kneeling on a chair with a plate of food in front of him, and somewhere he'd found a small box of old plastic toy soldiers. He'd lined up a few and was flicking bread crusts at them, glancing around furtively as if expecting to be told off at any moment. But Lynne was too busy stirring a pot of baked beans, and our parents were too busy with each other to notice. If they had noticed, maybe they just liked the fact that he was being a little boy.

I paused in the doorway and watched Jude for a while, and when he saw me he grinned. I smiled back. He flicked a piece of bread and it took out his army's forward defences, ricocheting onto the floor and skimming beneath a cupboard. He was already involved in his battle again, tongue protruding from the corner of his mouth in concentration. He seemed happy and I was glad.

I entered the kitchen and Lynne nodded to me, pointing at bowls piled on the worktop. They had tea towels placed between them to stop them clinking together, although we were slowly learning that low levels of sound were no risk. The vesps did not seem to be able to hear small noises through windows or walls. Still, better safe than sorry.

When we were sat down and Jude's army were placed in a defensive ring around his bowl, Lynne held up her hand. Speaking softly she said, "Before we start to eat, I have something to say."

I saw Mum and Dad exchange a nervous glance.

"Mum—" my mother began, but Lynne whispered over the top of her.

"I'm not very well." She looked back and forth between me and Jude, and I thought, *Here it comes. I've suspected it for some time but part of me, the part that's still a kid, just wanted it to go away.*

"I have cancer," Lynne continued. "It's in my stomach and has spread to my spine and hips, and it's not going to go away. In fact, it'll only get worse. It doesn't hurt that much; I have tablets to take and…" She glanced away. I wondered just how many tablets she had left. "And I'm really quite comfortable. But Jude, Ally, I wanted you to know. I don't think this is a time for secrets."

"Are you going to die?" Jude asked, eyes wide and wet.

Lynne didn't answer for a while. She stared at Jude but saw something else, something further away. Her fingers tapped the table either side of her bowl of beans and freshly baked bread.

"I wanted you to know," she whispered, very slowly so that I could read every word. "You're not children any more. Not like you were before all this."

Jude did not cry. He seemed unsure of who to go to, if anyone, so he stayed where he was. But he didn't look away.

"And not yet, Jude," she said. "Perhaps not for a long time."

Dad said something that I didn't catch, but I saw the flash of coolness in Lynne's eyes. "I know I promised, but that was before. I'm sorry, Huw, Kelly. But I think they need to know."

Mum nodded. She agreed.

I wasn't sure how I felt. Not shocked. I'd known that something was wrong, suspected what it was even though I'd tried to ignore it, shove it deep down where other secrets were kept. But now that it was out in the open I felt sad for my grandmother. It was as if by admitting the cancer to us, her grandchildren, she had finally surrendered to it.

We ate silently for a while. Jude went to sit next to Lynne. He wasn't really affectionate with anyone other than our parents, but right then he wanted to hold her hand. She let him, though to me she seemed uncomfortable. She ate, but every mouthful seemed to hurt. *She's only eating for us,* I thought.

No one completely finished their meal, despite how hungry we were. Mum scraped the leftovers into one bowl. She'd put it in the fridge and perhaps someone would eat it later.

Then she waved to get my attention and started talking, signing as she went.

"There are only two TV channels still broadcasting. One of them is the BBC News channel. It's on most of the time, though it drops out now and then. The people on there say they're broadcasting from a bunker somewhere under London, and I haven't seen either of them before. They're scruffy. That seems odd, seeing newscasters scruffy."

"Another sign of the end of the world," Dad said, smiling.

"What's the other channel?" I asked.

"Weird," Mum said. "It's one episode of *Friends* on a loop, repeating again and again."

"They've all been on eighteen million times anyway!" I said, pleased that it raised a smile.

"The One Where Ravenous Monsters Eat the World," Dad said. Even Jude smiled, though I wasn't certain he got the joke.

"They're still saying that the vesps don't like intense cold," Mum went on. "People are apparently surviving high in the Alps, Pyrenees, and in other high, cold places. There's some footage of piles of dead vesps in snowdrifts, all sort of pale blue instead of their normal sick yellow. It might be a good thing."

"I've read that too, in a lot of places," I said. "But it's getting difficult to see the truth in the lies."

Lynne said something and my parents laughed. I asked her to say it again.

"I said, 'I always trust what they say on the BBC.'"

"I'm not even sure it's the BBC any more," Mum said. "Just people using their equipment and an underground studio. I don't know. Maybe..." But she left the word hanging and it described adequately what any of us knew. Maybes. Possibles. Don't knows.

"There's always snow in the Lakes, isn't there?" Lynne asked.

"Not always," Dad said. He was frowning, distracted. "And there's that other thing."

"The Reverend," I said.

"Do you really think he's dangerous?" Mum asked, but no one answered, because no one really knew.

"And there's something else," I said. "We've talked about it already, we've been expecting it. I only saw it mentioned last night for the first time, though, and today it's all over the net. Called the Grey. It's places where the electricity's gone off, and people are getting cut off as their phone and computer batteries run out. It was only Cornwall to begin with, but now people are making lists of lots of other areas turned Grey. Lots of foreign places, but lots in Britain too. Cornwall and most of Devon, parts of south-west Wales, a few areas in London, other places. When people talk about the Grey online it's like... like places have been wiped off the map."

"Dark Ages," I caught on Lynne's lips, but I wasn't certain she actually spoke the words. No one else seemed to react.

"I don't think we should get too comfortable here," Dad said.

My mother nodded in agreement. "We can't just wait for help when none is coming. We can't sit here and hope everything gets better when..." She trailed off.

"It's getting worse," I said. I looked at my ailing grandmother, thought of the Reverend gathering his flock of the Hushed, and vast swathes of the countryside turning Grey when the power went off.

My own iPad, everything I had found out, everything I had written and recorded about the vesps, turning into nothing but useless junk.

But right then no one said anything more. Knowing that this place was not permanent was enough to set us all on edge. We'd talk about the future soon.

20

Bronnitsy, south-east of Moscow, has ceased to exist. The town was largely evacuated before the first waves of the vesp plague reached it; when it did, dozens of fuel tankers that had been parked around the outskirts the day before were ignited. The resulting conflagration consumed much of the town, and local forces then started shelling. A constant barrage of the town is underway day and night. Launch sites are fully automated, only manned when missile reloading is required. And while military losses are described as "acceptable" (which quite likely means large, but sustainable), the Bronnitsy incident is proving enlightening. The vesps keep attacking. Although the fires have been burning for almost two weeks and there is little left of any buildings, the noise of conflict still draws vesps in their tens of thousands, each new wave obliterated and burnt to ash by the next ordnance barrage. Estimates of vesp dead range widely from a hundred thousand to three million, but it reveals a lack of reasoning in the creatures. They are driven by instinct. Perhaps such instinct will be their downfall.

What Now? blog, Sunday, 4 December 2016

Silence and stillness, these will save us. Acceptance and embracement, these will be our saving graces. The tongue is danger, the root of the tongue is unholy, and removal will take us closer to God. There is a knife, and the knife-wielder will be your salvation.

The Hushed Manifesto

They make good soup.

How To Eat Vesps **blog, Monday, 5 December 2016**

It was two days later. Lynne's revelation about her condition had prompted many questions from Jude, and now the boy rarely left her side. Huw didn't view that as a bad thing. Lynne baked bread and Jude helped, kneading the dough, trying to do any work he called "heavy". He was even lifting pots and pans for his grandmother.

Ally continued to monitor the web, recording anything noteworthy but by her own admission becoming more and more sceptical about much of the information posted there.

Intermittent communications from supposed government sources promised that all measures were being taken, and announcements of advances against the vesps were made into thin air. No evidence was produced to back them up. No progress made. The Prime Minister had not been heard from in several days, and online rumour suggested that he and much of his Cabinet were dead. But again, that was all it was—rumour.

The countryside around their temporary refuge remained silent. It had started raining a lot, and Huw thought it was still unseasonably warm for early December. More than anything, he wished for snow.

He spent at least an hour each day observing the vesps. The more he knew, the better he could fight them; at least that's what he believed. That afternoon was moving on, and soon he and Ally would spend their regular hour discussing anything new and recording what they had discovered. Each day he did his best to have something new to tell her.

When he was a child he'd been a member of the Young Ornithologist's Club, and he had taken part in several national surveys of common garden birds. He could remember many Saturday mornings spent sitting at the living-room window, looking out over the garden and conscientiously recording each species he saw and how many times. It was not a boring endeavour. His mother had loved birds, and she spent plenty of time and money ensuring that their garden was full of them. She hung feeders from brackets above windows and all around the garden, as well as allowing for several areas between his dad's organised flowerbeds and vegetable patches that she left untended, letting them grow wild. This brought insects, and they attracted birds.

He'd see siskins, sparrows, finches, robins, thrushes, and occasionally a sparrowhawk hovering over the holly bush at the bottom of the garden, hungry for the sparrows that busied themselves plucking berries.

Sometimes his mother would sit with him, usually after placing a plate of biscuits and a glass of milk on the small table beside him. She'd rarely talk, other than to point out a bird or ask about how many he'd seen that day. It was a comfortable, intimate silence that he had relished. It had never been boring. It had involved the sort of calm concentration he'd never been able to achieve as an adult.

He had chosen to watch the vesps from outside. He could see more of them that way, note greater details about their behaviour. And there was something about being out in the open, in danger, that gave him a sense of thrilling isolation, and made him believe he was doing his best for his family.

He had to believe that. There was nothing else.

He'd been watching one particular vesp for the last five days. It had been roosting in the branches of a young oak tree by the side of the long lane leading up to the house, thirty metres beyond the wall. At first he'd thought it was dead, huddled close to the trunk. But over those five days he had seen no change in its posture, colour or position. If it was dead, surely it would have slumped down, fallen, begun to rot? He checked it every day, and every day it remained the same.

He watched others, too. The creatures continued to fly past, and he was trying to make sense of direction, and whether it was in any way connected to the weather or time of day. When the initial wave was advancing the vesps had all been moving in the same direction—away from areas they had infected and into areas they had not, perhaps attracted by new prey, or maybe acting with the conquering conscience of a hive mentality. Now he saw only randomness. That had frustrated him to begin with, but now that randomness itself was forming something of a pattern.

There were the vesps that guarded the eggs that were laid in dead bodies.

There were those that roosted, waiting for something to stir them.

And there were those that hunted.

He could still not make out any physical features that differentiated one from another. From what he had seen it was always adults that guarded eggs, but other than that there seemed to be no real pattern. Some of those that flew were small, perhaps recently hatched, while others seemed to be fully grown. He could not differentiate sex. Those that chose to rest and wait were of all sizes. It could have been that their life cycles were so accelerated that they had little time to learn and adapt, so the habits of those guarding an egg batch were handed down to the hatchlings. He didn't know. There was so much he didn't know that it scared him.

Everything he thought he'd understood about nature seemed to have been turned on its head by these beasts. Animals generally existed in a balanced ecosystem, but there was little about the vesps that spoke of balance. They ate everything made of meat, from the smallest bird to the largest cattle. Humans just happened to be their most common form of food. Their rapid spread and massive proliferation did not bode well for their survival as a species, because their expanding population would soon starve beneath a shrivelling food source.

Maybe down in that cavern there had been a balance, but emerging into daylight had upset it.

And even if the vesps eventually died out—starved, caught a disease, were wiped out by an engineered virus of some kind—what would happen to the ecosystem they had left behind? Nature had surely been damaged irreparably. Whole populations of wild animals had been driven close to extinction, and domesticated livestock reserves might well have suffered even more, gathered as they often were in confined spaces. No livestock would mean no food for the survivors. Hugely diminished bird numbers would lead to a massive growth in insect populations. The balance of nature had already been upset, perhaps cataclysmically. If and when the vesps died out, a very different world would grow out of what they left behind.

Huw lifted his binoculars and focused on the roosting vesp again. It had not shifted. Its tendrils were splayed across the bark of the tree trunk behind it, body laid along the branch, small legs clasping tight, claws buried in bark. Maybe it was sleeping, or perhaps this was a form of hibernation, a dormancy that would only be disturbed by the sound of food.

There was one way to find out. He'd already seen the reaction of the egg nest when he'd thrown stones against the cars at the pub. They, too, were waiting for fresh prey to draw close and make a clumsy noise. He had held back from antagonising any vesps close to the house, afraid that whatever silent signal they sent would attract more to the area. But he had to balance that against the need to learn more. Perhaps now it was time to see just how dormant this beast was.

He selected a decent-sized pebble from the old woman's garden, walked to the boundary wall, and lobbed the stone as far as he could along the lane. It struck the ground and bounced into the shadows beneath the trees lining the road.

The vesp did not move. Frowning, Huw found another stone and threw it.

This one ricocheted from the tree trunk just above the ground.

The vesp spread its wings, dropped down, and clamped its mouth against the tree almost before Huw could blink. Even though it was more than thirty metres away the animal's movement had made him jump, and his heart hammered in surprise. It hadn't moved for days, and one loud noise had galvanised it into vicious action.

Huw backed towards the house, suddenly needing to be closer to shelter. He had spotted over twenty vesps resting in various places in the countryside around the cottage, and there were four within the garden boundary. Two of those were in a tree, two more up on the roof. They'd all been there for at least a day. He suddenly felt watched. Or if not watched, then in danger of imminent discovery.

Three more vesps homed in on the tree-biting creature, answering a high-pitched call that he could not *quite* hear.

With his back against the wall beside the door, Huw raised the binoculars again and looked left to right, passing across the trees, the road, and onto the more open landscape that led up into the hills to the right.

And he saw a face.

He froze, shifted the binoculars back, expecting to see a bush's stark limbs or a rock, or some other optical illusion that he'd at first mistaken for a person.

But as Huw focused on him again, the Reverend stood out from a dip in the land.

Behind him, the Hushed.

"There's no reason to be afraid," he whispered. But he could see that Ally was unsettled. She had already met this man, witnessed what he had done to himself, been urged to join his flock. That he was here meant that he must have come looking for them. And this time he had others.

"What are we going to do?" Kelly asked. She'd grabbed the shotgun that they left leaning by the back door, and now she cradled it across her arms. It looked so clumsy and out of place.

"I'll go out to see him," Huw said.

"I should come with you," Lynne said. Jude said nothing, huddled to her side, protective and protected.

"No," Huw said, but he immediately saw that look on his mother-in-law's face, the stern expression, head tilted to one side, that meant there was no way he could win this argument.

"I know you think my being a Christian is submitting to mumbo-jumbo, but it's important to me, and the fact that he's a vicar means we'll have common ground."

"I've told you what he's done to himself," Huw said.

"And who's to say he's wrong?" Lynne said. "We've succeeded in talking in whispers, but I bet you feel like shouting at me sometimes." She offered a faint smile which he returned.

"Stay in the kitchen, all of you," he said to his wife and children. They nodded. He glanced at the shotgun, reached for it, hesitated. He looked to Lynne, automatically deferring to her judgement. *And just how did that happen?* he thought. But she had faith and the man was a vicar, so perhaps this really was her territory.

"Maybe leave it for now," was all she said.

Huw opened the door and Lynne walked out. He followed and pulled the door closed behind him, not quite engaging the catch. They all knew about the vesps within the garden boundary, and now he saw her glancing at them as she walked. For someone so ill she appeared alert and confident. That was good. Huw had no wish to display any weakness.

As they walked across the lawn to the closed vehicle gate leading out onto the lane, the Reverend and the others with him approached across the scrubland beyond. They avoided the lane, where loose stones might be kicked, or holes might trip.

We should be helping each other, Huw thought. *Pooling our resources, making sure we're all taken care of. Not this. Not mutilation and fear.*

There were six people with the Reverend, four adults and two children. They wore a variety of clothes, all of them wrapped against the rain. Most of them showed bruising around the lips and mouths.

With every step Huw took, his heart sank a little further.

Lynne reached the gate first. On the other side, the Reverend came within touching distance while his flock hung back a few paces, spread out. This close Huw could see that the two children were both girls, very young, perhaps sisters. One of them seemed to be sobbing silently, the other holding her hand. Both had bloodied chins. The adults were two men and two women. They seemed very thin, almost gaunt, and he could barely imagine the pain they must experience while eating. They all stared, and it took a few seconds for Huw to pin down why their stares seemed so strange. They were looking past him and Lynne at the house.

The Reverend nodded at Huw and smiled at Lynne,

opening his mouth to display his ruined tongue. He held out a single sheet of paper over the top of the timber gate.

Lynne took it, glanced briefly, then handed it to Huw.

The girl has to teach us, it said.

Huw shook his head.

The Reverend glared at him. He wrote nothing else, even though he carried a pad and pencil in his left hand. He did not smile or frown.

Lynne took a single step back, but Huw remained steadfast. He glanced away from the Reverend again, looking at those poor, tortured people he'd somehow persuaded to follow him, and they continued to stare expectantly towards the house.

There's only a wall and a gate.

He must have told the Hushed about the girl who signed, speaking with her face and hands and arms, silent yet filled with expression.

If they rush us, we can only run back to the house and lock ourselves in.

The crying girl shifted from foot to foot. One of the men raised a hand, opened his mouth, and almost touched the pustulant, red-raw stump of his tongue. The agony repulsed his touch. His eyes were wide and he shook with fever. His wound must be infected.

We've got to be strong.

Huw took a pen from his coat pocket, folded the note and leaned against the wall beside the gate. He wrote quickly, glancing up at the Reverend and his followers between words. The vicar still stared at him, almost expressionless behind those rimless glasses yet exuding danger. Mad, furious danger.

Huw handed him the note.

We're surviving well on our own. Please leave us.

The Reverend barely seemed to glance at the note before dropping it aside. He pointed at the house.

Huw shook his head.

The Reverend took a final step forward, pressing against the wide gate, forcing it against hinges and catch. It creaked, groaned.

Huw wished that he'd brought the shotgun.

"Go," Lynne said, her whisper seeming incredibly loud in the silence. The little girls took a frightened step back, and two of the adults raised hands to their mutilated mouths in shock. Huw wondered what they had all seen to inspire such terror, and whether the Reverend himself had provided examples to teach them the way to survive, *his* way.

For a moment he thought the leader of the Hushed would climb the gate and urge his people on, forcing confrontation that could really only end one way. The Reverend pushed against the gate so that his upper body leaned over, a small silver cross on a chain slipping from beneath his white collar and swinging slowly back and forth. Then he eased back. His face fell, suddenly sad, and a dribble of blood appeared at the corner of his mouth. Maybe he was trying to speak.

The Reverend turned to his flock and raised his hands. They lowered their heads and looked at their feet, hands clasped against their chests. Their prayer was silent. After only a few moments he led them away without once looking back. They walked on the grass verge beside the road, passing the vesp that Huw had stirred, now back in its familiar roosting place.

Lynne came close and held Huw's arm, and they

335

stood together watching until the Hushed passed out of sight behind the trees. Then Lynne tugged gently and they went back to the house.

Kelly was waiting at the back door, eyebrows raised. Huw gestured for her to go inside. Once he and Lynne had followed, he closed the door and slid the bolt across.

"He's mad," Lynne whispered.

"Yeah."

"I mean it. Did you see his eyes? It came off him in waves."

"Dad, what's happening?" Jude asked.

"We were watching from the window," Kelly said.

"Not much, mate," Huw said, answering Jude. "Some people came by and wanted us to go with them, but I said we were happy here."

"Is that the one you and Ally saw? The one who'd cut out his own tongue?"

"That was the one." He ruffled his son's hair. "But don't worry, he's got friends with him, and they'll help each other out."

"That's what I'm afraid of," Kelly said.

Huw saw his own fears reflected in his family's eyes. They'd already decided that this place could not become their home, and that soon they would have to head out for somewhere safer. Somewhere *colder*. In those quiet moments in bed, sharing warmth, he and Kelly had agreed between them that their original destination, Scotland, would be their best bet. But now perhaps their hand would be forced.

There was no telling what the Reverend might do next.

***

Huw and Ally insisted on having their regular time alone that evening, her iPad open on the table before them. They shared a bowl of peach slices in syrup, passing the fork back and forth as Ally scrolled through websites and articles she thought her dad should see.

None of it was good news. And to Huw it all felt very far away. Over the past couple of weeks their world had narrowed down to this house, this valley, where they could go for food, how long the power would stay on, when the phone reception might become problematic. He was frankly amazed that the electricity supply remained functional, but 3G reception was becoming intermittent. The Internet frequently dropped out while Ally was online. So a family being chased down by a flock of vesps in France... a man in York who paraded naked through the streets wearing the slaughtered creatures' tendrils from a thong around his neck... the American President promising aid, while several sources claimed he was not the President at all... these were all stories from another world. He cared, but nothing he read helped him and his family confront their own immediate problems. The President could not talk sense to the Reverend. The vesp-killer in York had a long way to come to help them.

After a few minutes of this, Huw placed his hand over Ally's and lifted it away from the screen.

"We're in danger," he signed.

Ally nodded.

"There's no saying what he'll do."

She nodded again. "Are you and Mum still talking about Scotland?"

Huw smiled. She was a clever girl.

"Can you tell me exactly how far it is?" he asked, nodding at the iPad.

She brought up an app and entered the details of where they were, then slid it across so that Huw could tap in the postcode of his parents' old place, Red Rock. A route map appeared with a summation of distances and times, had they been driving a car.

One hundred and thirty miles. Almost three hours by car.

"That's a long way on foot," Ally whispered. "And Lynne…"

Huw sat back and sighed. He wished Glenn were still with them. He wished they hadn't had this extra horror thrown at them, on top of what had already happened. But they had to deal with the situation rather than try to wish it away. Wishing, praying, placing fate in ephemeral hands, that was the Reverend's domain. And look where that had got him.

"We have tonight to sleep on it. I'll chat to your mum. I want you sleeping in with Jude tonight."

Ally did not argue and he loved her for that. If something happened—if the Reverend returned—they both knew that Ally would not hear.

He stood and kissed his daughter's forehead, and thought, *I'm so lucky to have her*. She really was a remarkable kid. Loving, intelligent, possessing a great sense of humour, she hadn't morphed into anything approaching the monster teen he'd once feared. She was beautiful too, in an unconscious way that sometimes made his heart ache. He'd always told her that she would be a good catch for some young lad one day, and she'd blush and tell him to get lost, *Aww, Dad, don't talk about stuff like that*. But he'd meant it.

Now, he wasn't so sure. The future was an unknown land, growing even more uncertain as days went on. The vesps were one thing, but now there was the Reverend, the Hushed, and what was happening here might well be happening all over.

Leaving the room, going to look for his wife, he wished for one more night of peace.

Huw walked the house as he had every night, checking that doors and windows were closed and locked, looking outside into the darkness, fearing what was out there. Tonight he feared a little more.

Everything looked quiet. It was raining again and almost completely dark, with very little star- or moonlight making its way through the clouds. When he shone the torch out through the window it illuminated a splay of falling rain, the splashing ground, and very little else. There was no sign of movement, no indication that the Reverend and his people were anywhere near. And why should they be? They had turned him and the Hushed away, and now he would be back wherever he came from, ready to invite other travellers into his flock. There was no reason for him to come here again. None.

Yet Huw couldn't shake the idea that the Reverend was not finished with them.

He pulled the curtain aside from the window beside the front door and shone the torch outside. Wet, puddled paving, driving rain, nothing else. He sighed. Perhaps the morning would shed more light on what their course of action should be.

Upstairs he looked in on Ally and Jude. Jude was asleep and Ally was looking at the iPad beneath her covers in the other bed, power lead snaking across the floor. He smiled and blew her a silent kiss she did not see.

In the room he and Kelly had taken for themselves, his wife was sitting up in bed. Her washed clothing hung on a rack she'd found in the bathroom.

"Kids asleep?" she asked.

He nodded, pushing the door half-closed behind him. As he stripped he realised how much his own clothes were starting to stink. They washed them as well as they could, but they'd left the vehicles up on the hillside carrying almost nothing. The dead woman's wardrobes had given them a few items they could use, but he dreamed of finding another abandoned house with fresh clothes for them all.

He crawled into bed beside his wife and she snuggled down next to him, resting her head on his chest. He put his arm around her. She was smooth, comforting, familiar and warm.

"We'll have to leave tomorrow," he whispered.

"Yeah. He's made us so on edge, we can't live like this."

"Not only the Reverend. The weather. Ally's seen more and more about them being affected by the cold and…"

Kelly rested her hand between his legs, gently kneading.

"And we need snow. And…"

She raised her face to his and kissed him.

"What was that for?"

"Because I love you."

"Love you too."

She grabbed him and started to stroke, slow and

rhythmic. Huw could not remember the last time they'd made love. Not since the vesps, and a while before that, too. They loved each other but life was busy, tiring, filled with things to think about and do; places to go for Ally and Jude, hospital visits for Lynne, work and chores and a thousand other reasons to be too tired, too bored.

They kissed again, deep and long, and she slid on top of him, her hand still working, breasts pressed against his chest. He ran his fingertips down her back, squeezing her behind, delving between her legs.

"We'll have to be quiet," he whispered, thinking of Lynne and Jude. But Kelly started laughing silently, and he felt a giggle rising, emerging as a series of heavy breaths.

"I'll scream when I come," she breathed into his mouth. "What a way to go."

They took their time making love, and for a while everything else went away.

Lying there afterwards, Kelly's fast breathing slowing into sleep, trying to make out the shape of the room around him in the darkness, Huw heard a noise. A rustle, then a soft knock.

He sat up in bed. Kelly murmured beside him but lay still, saying no more.

He breathed gently from his mouth, head to one side as he tried to listen again. One of the kids or Lynne rolling in their bed? A vesp slithering across the roof, perhaps to get out of the rain? The sound did not come again but he heard it over and over, trying to analyse what it might have been.

Maybe it was even his own heartbeat settling down.

He'd been lying down, head buried in the pillow, and perhaps he'd heard a rush of blood through his ear, or—

Another sound, and this one was from outside.

He jumped from the bed and dashed to the window, pulling the curtain aside. Very little was visible out there, other than the faintest tone difference between land and sky. He hefted the torch, pressed it against the glass to reduce reflection, then flicked it on. For just a moment he saw movement out by the garden wall, but when he blinked it was gone. He wasn't sure what it had been, or even whether it was anything other than rain and shadows dancing in the torch beam.

"What is it?" Kelly whispered.

"Don't know," he said. "Nothing." But he switched off the torch, pulled on his trousers, and went to check that it really was nothing.

The landing was silent. He could hear Lynne's gentle snoring and one of the kids shifting in their sleep. Rain hushed across the rooftop above his head. Somewhere, water dripped. There was nothing else.

He moved to the head of the staircase and paused, head tilted as he listened.

"Huw!" Kelly whispered from their room. "There's someone leaving the house!"

Ally? Jude?

He thought of that sound again, the rustle and soft bump. He turned on the torch and aimed it down, illuminating the stairwell and hallway beyond. Something dangled on a string inside the front door, hanging from the letter flap. Several other similar shapes were scattered across the entrance mat, trailing the strings that had been used to lower them quietly inside.

"Huw—" Kelly began, standing naked at their bedroom door.

And then the phones began to ring.

21

Twitter, Monday, 5 December 2016

Someone was shaking me. I'd barely been asleep anyway, or at least I didn't think so, but when I sprang upright I was groggy and confused, and the remnants of my dream held on. I was one of a group of horses running across the hills, fire leaping from my feet, the beautiful song of my brethren the theme to our escape. Whatever chased us did not stand a chance. Whichever beast pursued us into the mountains was long lost.

And then Jude was trying to talk to me; I could see that he was shouting, and in his panic he was forgetting that silence meant safety.

I held his hand and squeezed sharply, and in the light spilling in from the landing he began to sign. "There are phones!"

"What?" I asked.

"Phones ringing, some downstairs and I can hear them outside too, like they're—"

Our mother appeared in the bedroom door, a blanket about her. "Out here, now!"

Jude pulled me from the bed. I grabbed my jeans

and pullover, slipping them on as I hobbled from the bedroom and followed them onto the landing. Lynne was there, looking old and confused and so vulnerable it made my heart break. I always saw my grandmother as strong.

"Down!" Mum said. "Help your dad!" She dashed back into the bedroom, dropping the blanket and scooping her clothes from the drying rack.

Jude went first and I followed. Dad was down by the front door. He'd switched on all the lights and the first thing I noticed was the shotgun propped against his hip. The second thing was the phones. He was stamping on them, grinding them into glass and plastic and metal beneath his feet, and he wasn't even wearing shoes.

"Dad, the gun!" I said.

He looked up at us, eyes wide and panicked. Then he snatched up the gun and used the stock to smash the last couple of phones.

He paused, shotgun resting in his hands.

"There are more outside," he said. He seemed confused, moving back and forth behind the front door.

"Are there any—?" I began, but then my family's reaction was answer enough. Dad staggered back from the door and Jude clasped my arm. He looked terrified.

"Banging on the door," he signed.

"Is it him?" I asked.

Dad looked up and back, nodding. Then he looked past me to where Mum appeared at the head of the stairs, standing beside Lynne and now fully dressed.

"They've put them on the windowsills," she said, slowly and carefully so I could read the words.

"The vesps will smash the windows," I said. "But if

they get in, if we're quiet, maybe we'll be okay?"

"He's trying to kill us," Mum said. "The Reverend and his flock are trying to kill us, so we've got to prepare for that. All of us. Jude, you stay with Ally. Huw?"

I turned back to Dad. He was facing the front door, and I missed whatever he said.

Jude squeezed my arm. "Kitchen."

We went down the last few stairs and turned right, heading along the hallway and through into the large kitchen. It felt more familiar, safer, because this was where we spent most of our time. *I left my iPad!* I thought. It was tucked under the bed, plugged in to ensure the charge remained full. I knew there would come a time when the battery was all I had. Rumour across the net was that London was already Grey.

I turned, ready to dash back upstairs to retrieve it, but Lynne was already behind me, and Dad came in and closed the door.

Everyone looked panicked. I wished I could hear.

Fucking bastard! Huw thought. He clasped the shotgun tight, not even sure he knew how to fire the fucking thing. But its weight was a comfort.

He'd stamped out the ringing phones—electronic warbles, old-fashioned ringtones, and Motörhead's "Ace of Spades"—only to hear the more distant, spread out ringing from outside. And then Kelly, telling him they'd put them on the windowsills.

The thudding of small bodies continued against the front door. They'd do nothing there, not unless they chewed and ate and scraped through the wood. But as he hustled his family into the kitchen he heard the first smashing of glass upstairs. At first he thought it was a vesp making its way inside, and he watched the staircase for the first fleeting shape. But then another phone began to chime.

Louder. Closer. They were throwing them through the windows.

Which meant that they were close to the house.

He slammed the kitchen door and pressed his back against it. "Turn out the light," he said. Lynne flicked the switch. It was scary standing there in the dark, but not as frightening as seeing the looks on his family's faces. Kelly's was pure concern for their children, Ally's and Jude's were outright fear.

That fucking bastard!

Light filtered in beneath the door from the hallway, and after a few seconds his eyes grew accustomed to it. Kelly drew close.

"If we stay in here," she whispered, "keep still, keep quiet, then even if they do get in upstairs—"

Something banged on one of the kitchen windows. There were two, a large window in the end wall and another beside the back door. This lean-to building was an add-on, and Huw was pretty certain that the windows were double glazed, unlike those throughout the rest of the house. That's why those upstairs were smashing so easily.

Another *clonk* against the glass; heavier, more solid. They were throwing rocks.

"There's no phone ringing outside this door," he said. "You open it, I'll shoot."

"What?" she asked, shocked.

"What, you're against me shooting these fuckers?" He saw Jude's eyes open wider at his language. It would have been amusing if it wasn't so distressing. He was scaring his son even more. "There's going to be a gunshot," he said to Lynne and his children. "Just to let them know we're serious. So get ready."

He moved to the door and glanced back at Kelly. She seemed ready to argue but he raised his eyebrows, lifted the gun, readied the stock against his shoulder.

He had never fired a shotgun before. When they were kids Glenn had owned an air rifle, and sometimes they'd gone into the local woods with tin cans and paper targets, fired off a couple of hundred shots before getting bored and hunting squirrels. Glenn had always been a good shot, of course. The one time Huw had fired at a squirrel he'd only injured it, and it had jumped through the tree canopy screaming, disappearing, only its cries of pain left behind. He stopped shooting at live things after that.

Just to let them know we're serious, he thought. *Just so they can hear the shot and realise we're armed.*

Kelly unlocked the door, pressed the handle, and pulled it open.

Several vesps flew by from right to left, zeroing in on the mobile phones the Hushed had put on the window sills. *When I fire they'll hear they'll come they'll try to—*

A shape appeared from the darkness in the lessening rain, arm held back ready to lob something at the house, and Huw was filled with a burning rage at this bastard, this fucker who considered it acceptable to put his family at risk, to bring the vesps down upon them just because they refused to hack out their own tongues.

He didn't know whether or not it was the Reverend, but he fired anyway.

The blast was the loudest noise he had heard in

weeks. The gun punched his shoulder, smoke filled his vision, and just before Kelly slammed the door he saw the shape stagger back towards the garden wall, one arm flailing, and he heard a loud, pain-filled scream.

Kelly locked the door and glanced at Huw, eyes wide.

He went to the window and pulled the curtain aside. With the door closed there was not so much light spilling out, but he could still see the vesps streaking in from around and over the house, converging on the dark, thrashing shape on the lawn.

He scanned around quickly, saw no other obvious movement, then turned around and faced his family.

Kelly's expression had changed. She wore a tight, confident smile as she came and hugged him, kissing his ear and whispering, "We'll do anything."

Anything to protect their family. In safer, quieter times they had vowed this together, and now was the time to act on that promise. He might have shot someone. He'd almost certainly condemned someone to a horrible, vesp-bitten death. But right then he felt only satisfaction.

More vesps thudded against the door, wall and window, brought by the gunshot and now chewing and clawing at where they had heard the blast. They wouldn't be able to open this door again, but he was certain that the creatures would not gain access here.

"Locked?" he asked Kelly.

"Locked and bolted."

"Come with me." Louder he said, "Ally, Lynne, Jude, stay here. Grab knives or other weapons, stay down under the table, keep quiet."

"Where are you going?" Jude said, voice high and plaintive.

"Just to make them go away," Huw said. He grabbed the spear he'd left leaning against the kitchen dresser, handed it to Kelly, then went through the door into the hallway first. The light still glared. Thuds sounded from upstairs, and another window smashed. He could hear the ringing of several distant phones, and closer the sound of the theme from *Thunderbirds*. He almost laughed at the surreality of the moment.

Kelly closed the kitchen door behind them.

A vesp drifted down from the first floor, swerving across the hallway and missing Huw by less than a metre. It trailed that stink behind it, sour and rich, and its tendrils stroked the air for noise.

Kelly touched his arm and they stood there silent, weapons raised.

The vesp disappeared into the dark living room and did not reappear. Huw heard the nerve-shredding sound of teeth on glass as it tried to chew its way outside, to the phone ringing on the exterior sill.

Kelly drifted forward and closed the living-room door with a barely perceptible click. Then she nodded upstairs.

Huw went first, gun held ahead of him. One shot left, and the rest of the shells were in their bedroom in the holdall he kept packed in there. *Maybe we can reason with them,* he thought. *Maybe we can wait until dawn. Meet them. Talk. Parley.* More rocks struck the house and another window went, and then from downstairs they heard more smashing from the rear of the property. There was a small study and boot room back there that they'd rarely used, and now the rooms burst alive with the sound of angry ringing.

Instead of going back down Huw ran up, bursting

into Lynne's room, pausing, checking that the window was still whole. He left the light off and sensed Kelly behind him, her back to him as she prepared to ward off any vesps that might come investigating. They were being as silent as they could, but the air was suddenly filled with noise—the impacts of rocks and stones against wall and windows, shattering glass, ringing tones, and several bursts of conflicting music. Huw had a moment to wonder where they'd got so many phones.

They were above the downstairs study, and looking out he could see two shadows in the garden, still throwing things at the study and boot room windows. They hunched down intermittently, crouched and motionless as vesps darted past them towards the noise, then stood and threw again.

Huw raised the sash window a hand's width, aimed the shotgun in their general direction, and fired.

And at the last moment realised his mistake.

Even as he slammed the window on a shout of pain, vesps attacked them from inside the house.

Kelly jabbed with the spear. A creature splashed blood, veered against the wall, came at them again. Huw swung the shotgun and knocked the vesp against the far wall. It thrashed on Lynne's bed, tangling in the sheets, and he brought the gun in an arc over his head, stock first. A wet thud and the vesp was still.

Kelly was slashing at two more. She beat off one with the spear and another angled in beneath her reach, struck her above her left breast, thrashing its tendrils and squirming its body as it attempted to burrow into her flesh.

She opened her mouth to scream but bit it back, as

Huw dropped the shotgun and grabbed the squirming animal. It was surprisingly smooth in his grasp, almost velvety, and as he squeezed and felt his fingers sinking into its soft skin, meeting wetness, crushing bone, three more entered the room.

Huw heaved the squirming vesp at the doorway. It was a lucky throw, the creature striking the bare landing outside and drumming on the boards in its death throes. He scooped up the shotgun and heaved it back over his shoulder, but then Kelly wrapped her arms around him from the side. She grabbed the barrel and held it there. Unmoving. Silent.

The three vesps circling the room heard the sound of their dying cousin, and a moment of brutal cannibalism followed.

"Still... quiet..." she breathed into his ear. She had gasped into his ear less than an hour ago as they came together, and he felt a moment of utter peace and confidence, bottomless love. *We're going to survive this.*

She reached to close the door but Huw held her back, shook his head. He pointed downstairs. *We left our kids down there!*

They eased past the feasting vesps. Kelly held the spear by her side, ready to swing it up and slice into any creature that came for them. Walking slowly, as lightly as possible, Huw could not help but watch them consuming their dead. It was in pieces now, dark blood and innards splashed across the floor, and the other three animals were quickly consuming those spilled parts, leaving very little behind.

Maybe it's good that they eat each other, Huw thought, always filing information. But there were many millions of vesps out there. Cannibalism would not be the end of them.

As Kelly stood at the head of the stairs, and Huw ducked into the bedroom for the packed holdall containing the spare shotgun shells, they heard a scream from below. They locked eyes. Kelly started down two at a time, spear held ahead of her, and Huw wanted to shout, *Be careful!*

The three vesps, bloodied from their meal and now hearing signs of another, arrowed down the stairs after Kelly.

"Another shotgun bang," Jude signed.

We were huddled under the big kitchen table, Lynne with a carving knife in each hand. Jude held a knife too, though I had tried to dissuade him. He'd looked hurt, and I realised that he was trying to protect us. Playing the man.

In my right hand I held a roasting fork, twin prongs sharp and thick. I couldn't bear to imagine thrusting it at someone.

Hiding under the table had seemed too passive. But then I realised that if the Reverend and his people did smash down the back door, there was a good chance we would not be seen. Not immediately, at least.

And still, silent, any vesp that got in would also hopefully miss us.

Lynne and Jude both looked up, heads cocked.

"What?" I asked.

"Something banged," Jude signed.

"The phones?"

"Some are still ringing," he said. "I can't tell where they're coming from. Maybe—" He broke off, startled, and turned to the back door. "Someone's trying to get in."

I crawled to the other side of the table and looked up at the back door. I could see the handle jiggling slightly, but not depressing all the way because it was locked.

Someone grabbed my foot and pulled, urging me back beneath the table, but I drew my leg forward and stood. I went to the window close to the door, pulled the curtain aside, looked out.

In the light leaking from the kitchen window I saw the Reverend standing a little back from the house, watching. He saw me and nodded, pointing a finger. A vesp drifted past his head. He did not even flinch.

I saw movement from the corner of my eye and dropped the curtain, turning around, expecting to see Mum and Dad coming back into the kitchen. But it was someone else. A very tall man, black, slightly built yet powerful, and his jaw hung open, the bloody root of his tongue glistening, seeping.

He came across the kitchen for me.

I saw a flicker of movement beneath the table. Light caught metal, flashed. Lynne's arms swept forward then back again. The knives slashed into the back of the man's ankles.

He opened that bloody mouth wider and screamed.

Falling saved Kelly's life.

As her feet pounded the stairs, the three vesps zeroed in on the sounds and attacked her legs. She tripped and rolled, dropping the spear and tucking her head beneath her arms to protect it. Huw saw her impact halfway down the staircase and roll the rest of the way, crushing one vesp beneath her. The other two spiralled up and then dropped down again as she struck the wall at the bottom.

He was already grabbing up the spear in his spare hand and leaping down the stairs as they attacked. He speared one with a blade and knocked the other aside, stepping over Kelly and trapping it beneath his bare foot. It was smooth beneath his heel, flexing, twisting, and when he put all his weight on that foot he felt things cracking and crushing inside.

Kelly was crawling towards the open kitchen door.

Two more vesps flew along the hallway from the back of the house, and Huw crouched with the spear at the ready, breath held. But they were going for whoever had screamed.

He was sure it had been a man. Not Jude, Ally or Lynne. But he could not be positive.

As the vesps flitted through the open door, Kelly held onto the jamb and stood, swinging herself into the kitchen. She shouted, "No!"

Huw was immediately by her side, spear coming up to tackle the creatures that would fly at her scream... only to see that a knife had fallen from one end. He threw it aside. He hadn't had time to reload the shotgun, and the shells were in the holdall he'd slung onto his back.

A flurry of movement. A vesp fell, Lynne stabbing it again and again. Another struck the wall beside Kelly's head, then turned and snapped past her head as she dropped to her knees.

Beyond, Ally was struggling with a tall man by the

back door. The door stood open, the man's left hand holding it wide, his right arm clutched around Huw's daughter and clasping her tight. She struck at his face, shoulders, neck, but he seemed immune to her blows. But he was not standing quite right. One foot was held from the floor, and as he hopped towards the door he lost balance. They fell by the open doorway.

Jude scrambled from beneath the table and grasped something from the floor, standing above the fallen pair with a roasting fork held in both hands above his head.

The second vesp was persistent, twisting back to search for the source of the sound. It came lower this time, striking Kelly's shoulder and then biting in, hard. She groaned but did not cry out.

Huw and Lynne shared a glance that spoke volumes. She nodded towards the door and Huw went, stepping around his struggling wife, his bloodied mother-in-law, and going for his children. He had to skirt around the table, and for those few seconds he was thinking, *Do it, Jude! Do it, Jude!*

But Jude was too hesitant, too slow.

The man stood and lashed out, striking Jude across the face and sending the boy staggering back against the table. He dropped the fork and fell, hands clutching his nose.

Huw was filled with rage. The bastard had his daughter clasped by the jacket, and with his other hand he'd hit his son. *Punched* him, a ten-year-old boy, in the face. Every instinct, every scrap of what made Huw a father, blazed red as he lunged around the table towards the back door. He dropped the shotgun, stepped past Jude and launched himself.

The man threw Ally outside, past the door and into the cool darkness beyond. And though Huw thought himself ready, he was watching for danger from the wrong direction. In the instant before Huw reached him, the man jumped through the doorway, foot curled around the door's leading edge to pull it closed behind him.

Huw's face connected with the door's edge. Pain roared into his nose and behind his eyes, and the last thing he saw as he slumped to his knees, head back, was the whole mad world spinning.

He dragged me across the garden. No matter how much I struggled, kicked, punched, tried to trip him and kick at where Lynne had slashed with the knife, the man hauled me behind him across the grass. The cold night kissed my skin, and the illuminated house suddenly felt like the only safe place as it receded behind.

I had never felt so helpless. Even with the vesps coming and the world changing so much, I had struggled to maintain an element of control—compiling information, recording details, telling stories and trying to see patterns of truth amongst the chaos.

But now I could do nothing. I was being swept along by the madness of things, and my attempts to swim against the flow were hopeless.

He had me by the back of my pullover, hauling the neckline tight against my throat as he dragged me backwards, my bare heels useless as I tried to dig them into the ground, slow myself down. My arms were raised by the tension in the material. I rolled, turning so that my knees were scraping across the ground, and the half-twist wound the material tighter around my throat. I was finding it hard to breathe. I punched at his calves and ankles, forgetting which one Lynne had slashed, but to no avail. I tried digging my feet in and shoving, hoping to topple him forwards and land on his back, turn his arm, break it. But though tall and thin the man was also solid, and it was like shouldering a tree.

Past him I could see the garden wall, and standing on the other side, two shapes. One of them was the Reverend; I could make out his dog collar glowing faintly in the light spilling from the house. I wondered where the others were, and hoped that Dad had killed some of them. The idea was shocking, but I didn't feel bad thinking it.

I tried to stand but slipped on the wet grass, turning as I went so that the man was dragging me backwards again. And that was how I saw Lynne.

I could not remember the last time I had seen my grandmother running. She'd probably think it was unseemly, and I wasn't sure I'd *ever* seen her moving quicker than a fast walk. But now she was sprinting across the lawn, her twiglike silhouette somehow awful and inspiring at the same time. Threatening and courageous. I would have cried out in delight if I hadn't known what that would bring.

Someone must have warned my abductor. He dropped me and I splayed on my back on the wet grass, banging my head, quickly sitting again as Lynne ran towards me. My mother's mother offered a small, sad smile as she ran past, and I rolled to my left and knelt. I was on my knees in time to see Lynne dive at the tall man, sending him staggering back against the boundary wall, her arms around his chest, head against his neck, feet scrabbling and driving them both over and out of sight.

The Reverend and the other Hushed went to help. I saw the Reverend suddenly trip and disappear with them behind the wall, and the shock was the first real expression other than madness I'd seen on his face.

That was when Lynne must have screamed. Afterwards, Jude would tell me that the scream sounded like a high-pitched cry of delight rather than a screech of fear or pain, and that went some small way to making the memory of what happened next easier. Some very small way.

The shapes came from all around. Some whisked past me from the direction of the house, others dropped from the dark skies, yet more emerged from the trees and shadowed countryside, streaking through the night towards the sudden, loud noise. They converged on Lynne and the men still on the ground beyond the wall, and I never saw my grandmother again. But I remembered that small, sad smile as she'd run past, and my surprise at seeing my old, sick grandmother running so fast. I don't think I'd ever seen her so alive.

Hands closed on my shoulders and I spun around, but it was only Jude, wide-eyed and terrified but still out there to bring me back home. He pressed his finger to his lips in a completely unnecessary gesture, but I nodded as I stood, and we held hands as we went back towards the house.

Guilt sliced in with every step. *I should be helping Lynne! We should all be there, fighting them off and pulling her free, killing those beasts that are killing her.*

But there were at least twenty vesps there, and many

more converging at every moment.

Lynne didn't want our help.

By the time we reached the door my vision was blurred, tears of fear and terror and grief burning away the touch of cool night air on my skin. Dad was sitting just inside the door, head in his hands and blood pooling between his legs. Mum was standing beside him with a stained knife in one hand, roasting fork in the other, and her shirt was slashed and speckled with blood, her shoulder gored, eyes wide.

Her gaze flickered back and forth between us as we reached the safety of the house, and the chaos beyond the wall. The place where her own mother was dying. I wondered why she wasn't running. Later, Jude told me that the last thing Lynne ever said was to our mum: "Stay here, my darling girl."

Jude and I tripped over the door sill and fell into the house, and I turned to see my mother hesitate for only a second before closing the door. She clicked the lock, turned to lean against the door, and slid slowly down until she too was sitting.

In her eyes I saw the ice-cold loss of hope.

PART THREE

GREY

22

An early snowstorm in parts of western Germany has resulted in tens of thousands of vesps becoming slow, lethargic, disorientated, and easy to hunt and kill. Dozens of groups of citizens—some containing police or army members, many more simply well-meaning civilians—have been stalking the silent city of Frankfurt killing vesps with knives and hastily fashioned spears, gardening implements, and bows and arrows. The corpses are gathered into bags and then thrown into the Rhine. There is no accurate count being kept. Communications are difficult. But in this unseasonably cold snap, the fightback has begun.

Reuters, Tuesday, 6 December 2016

There are 1,233 people safe in Antarctica.

Angus MacReady, Halley Antarctic Research Station,
Tuesday, 6 December 2016

They had to leave the house.

It was Jude who marshalled them, brought them together, and thought of everything. He busied himself around the kitchen, pausing every now and then to listen at the door leading into the rest of the house. The phones had stopped ringing. There was no sign of the Hushed. Huw watched his son with pride, but every time he closed his eyes it felt like his skull had been cracked in two, his eyes pulped in their sockets.

He'd smacked into the heavy door's edge face-first, hard enough to break his nose, chip two teeth, and put a three-inch gash in his forehead. The bleeding probably made it seem worse. He was dizzy and felt sick, and suspected he might have a mild concussion. Every time he stood the world swayed, and he remained leaning against the table.

Kelly was also injured and she stood close to him. But her incapacity was of a different kind. She had just seen her mother die—not witnessed it first-hand, but close enough so that the distinction didn't matter. She was shivering, pressed close to Huw's side. He did his best to examine the wounds on her shoulder, chest and hands. They were swollen and bleeding, and quite possibly infected. There was no saying what exotic, unknown diseases those bastard things carried.

Ally seemed okay. She followed Jude, taller and bigger than him yet at that moment doing as he said. Huw watched his daughter, looking for signs of trauma or injuries, but he guessed anything serious was on the inside. That would have more of an impact on her later, but right now it meant that she was still strong and capable.

We're all going to be fucked in the head, he thought. *Maybe the same, maybe in different ways.* He blinked slowly and behind his eyelids everything was red.

They had to bathe, clean and dress their wounds, but proper treatment would have to wait. *Everything* would have to wait. Because they had to get away.

Jude and Ally gathered together everything they could use. The broom handle, now a one-ended spear, the knife stained dark with vesp blood. The holdall he'd brought down from the bedroom, packed with warm clothing and a couple of boxes of shotgun shells. He'd tried loading the weapon but Ally had gently taken it from him, placing it on the table.

Every few seconds Jude went to the window and looked out. He scanned left and right, shading his eyes against the glass to block out the kitchen's weak light.

Huw knew that they might come at any moment. He didn't really know how many of the Hushed there were, and although some might have been injured or killed, there were probably more who had escaped. He might have hit two or three with the shotgun blasts. He felt cool about that, calm, and even if regrets came later, he was glad there was nothing now. The tall man who had grabbed Ally was almost certainly dead, along with Lynne. Maybe the Reverend, as well.

Hopefully the Reverend.

They might attack again. They could be fleeing into the countryside. It could be that the few survivors were huddled down under trees or against walls, adrift now that their leader was vesp fodder.

Huw didn't care. As long as they stayed away, he didn't give a shit about what might happen to those poor, wretched people. That felt harsh, but it also felt right. Every single thing he loved and cared about was in this room.

Jude and Ally stood by the table, Jude frowning and looking around as if to assess what he had gathered. He glanced at his parents and away again, not wanting to look at them for too long. Huw had noticed this, and hardly blamed his son. Huw's face was a bloody mess and he swayed where he stood, and Kelly seemed lost.

Huw squeezed his wife's good shoulder, trying to bring her back to them. She let out a heavy gasp and looked around the kitchen, gaze resting on Huw. She assessed his face, seeing his wounds and his blood, then stared into his eyes.

Huw tried to smile. It hurt his broken nose and split lip, and he could feel tooth shards on his tongue.

Kelly pulled away and went to her children. She buried her face in Ally's hair, then dipped her head and did the same to Jude, and Huw realised that she was smelling them.

Tears blurred his already fluid vision. When he wiped them away Kelly was in front of him again, checking his wounds with a calmer eye.

"You walk?" she whispered.

"Yeah." He touched her face. "You okay?"

She laughed once, softly, then rested her hand on his cheek. "Yeah. Dandy. We need to go."

"I know. Jude and Ally…"

"They've got all they can. But there's one more thing Ally needs."

Huw frowned, confused.

"Her iPad."

"It's upstairs?"

Kelly nodded. "I'll go with her."

"No, I—" Huw moved away from the table and the world swam, and his wife's gentle hands eased him back again.

"I'll go with her," she said again. She lifted the shotgun

from the table, broke it open and reloaded. "Jude, stay with your dad and keep watch. Hold the knife. If you see anyone coming…" She trailed off, unable to suggest a signal that might be safe. There were vesps in the house now, and broken windows, and any noise might bring down the chaos again.

"Kel," Huw said, "get the old woman's medicine bag." They'd seen it in her room, a carrier bag filled with dozens of bottles, foil packets and sachets of medicines they mostly didn't know.

Kelly nodded. She looked across the room at the range cooker, seemingly lost again, eyes distant. Seeing her mother die.

Ally touched her arm, and the two of them went to the hall doorway.

"Won't be long," Ally signed to Huw, and he nodded and smiled, ignoring the pain, loving her more than ever.

Mum went first, taking each stair slowly, shotgun held out in front of her. If she had to use it she'd doom us all, but somehow I still felt safer knowing that she was armed. Maybe I'd watched too much TV, too many horror films.

I carried a knife and the roasting fork. I was shaking, but confident and determined. We went to my room first and I snapped up the iPad from beneath the bed. I took shoes and a jacket too, and in Jude's room we gathered more of his clothes.

There was a vesp roosting in my parents' room. It sat on a dressing table just inside the smashed window, moving gently from side to side as if trying to hypnotise the open space. I thought about crossing the carpeted room and stabbing the thing, but the thought of such sudden violence scared me. It might squeal, thrash, knock things around and bring more of them. So I stood ready with my weapons as Mum walked slowly, so slowly, across the room, gathering up the bag of medicines from beside the bed, bending and picking up Dad's boots, backing out slowly. Each footfall might creak a floorboard. Every movement could shush clothing, click a knee joint, nudge a piece of furniture.

I noticed the smear of blood around the creature's mouth and across its strange, arrow-shaped head. Maybe it was satiated, and slight, subtle noises no longer interested it. It was a possibility I should consider, and when I had the chance I'd write it down. I tried not to imagine what or who it had been eating.

It was another fact that might help us fight them. And now we all had first-hand experience.

We left the house ten minutes later. Dad and Mum held each other up, my mum carrying the shotgun. Jude hefted the holdall of clothes and food, and I carried two hessian shopping bags tied across my back.

Heading for the lane meant that we had to cross the garden. Dawn was breathing across the hilltops to the east, and I could make out three shapes lying on the ground, one of them a little girl. There was no need to go closer because I knew what they were. I wondered what Dad thought. One or two of those he had shot, the others had probably died when the screams of the wounded attracted the vesps. I was sure he noticed the bodies, but he did not even slow his pace.

I was glad. He shouldn't feel guilty. He'd been

protecting us, and right then he was the best, bravest father in the world.

When we reached the gate, Jude went ahead and examined the catch. He turned and shook his head, signing, "I think it'll make too much noise." So we climbed, Jude and me first, then Mum, and finally we all helped Dad over the gate. I was pleased to see that he looked better. He seemed stronger in the weak light, his wounded face no longer bleeding so much.

Mum paused and looked to the right. Over there, around a curve in the wall, lay her dead mother. I remembered again that smile as she'd run past, and I wondered what had been going through her mind. She'd known that she was about to die, and in great pain. But she was also doing her best to protect the family she loved so much.

I couldn't bear thinking about it for too long. It was painful and confusing, and it also felt so hopeless. No one else would know about her sacrifice. No one would care.

Lynne had been a true believer. She and I had often talked about God, and sometimes I saw her unhappiness at my disbelief. But she also respected my opinion, and my insistence that I could not simply change my mind to please her. She'd never tried to force ideas upon me. I hoped her faith had helped her in those final awful moments.

I touched Mum's arm and gestured along the road. She looked at me blankly, then shook her head. She walked along the wall to where Lynne must have been lying. We saw her standing there and looking down for a while. She didn't bend to get any closer. She just looked.

Then she came back, and the only thing she signed was, "No Reverend."

We started walking. Only a couple of minutes later Jude looked back and paused, pointing.

The lights in the house had gone off.

"The Grey?" Jude signed.

I nodded. It made sense. Just when things were so bad, they got worse.

He was waiting for us on a small footbridge spanning a stream a hundred metres from the road. Jude saw him first, and when Mum spotted him she lifted the shotgun and aimed it. For a loaded moment I thought she was going to shoot, but Mum was not so foolish, though her rage radiated from her in fearsome waves.

The Reverend came to us. He was on his own. He was limping properly now, right arm held awkwardly across his chest, his white collar speckled with blood. Perhaps he'd been hit by a few shotgun pellets, and I hoped they hurt. I was sure that later I'd think of him as a wretched, pathetic victim, but right now he was a monster.

I had no idea how he'd escaped the storm of vesps that had taken the tall man and my grandmother. But I would never give him the satisfaction of asking.

There was a ditch beside the road and he stood on the other side, squinting at me. He'd lost his glasses. He didn't even seem to notice the rest of my family. I looked around frantically, suspecting a trap or an ambush of some sort, but there was no one else there. Maybe the other Hushed were all dead, or perhaps they'd abandoned their Reverend after he had failed to get them what he'd promised.

Mum was still aiming the shotgun at him. She was

shaking, and I could see that she was breathing rapidly, but the barrel held steady and true. The Reverend did not even seem to notice the weapon. The longer he stared at me, the more I wished Mum would shoot. If we ran fast enough, perhaps we could get away before his screams doomed him.

But of course we would not escape the vesps that would zero in on us. Not out here in the open. I could see several of them now, in the trees and bushes, and a few flying past close enough to reach us in a matter of seconds.

We're under siege, I thought. It had only become obvious after we'd left the cottage. We were prisoners of the vesps, even out here in the wild and beneath the widest, deepest skies I had ever seen.

Jude stepped close to the edge of the ditch and gave the Reverend the finger. It wasn't funny, not really. But it broke some of the tension that had been building, and it also seemed to break his gaze. He looked at Jude, then at our parents. There was very little communication, even with his eyes. He simply looked us over and turned away, limping back the way he had come. He did not stop at the bridge but kept going, soon consumed by the evergreen forest's shadows as the sun finally broke above the hillsides behind us.

"We need to walk," Dad signed. "Get as far as we can as quickly as possible. Then we'll pause at noon, find somewhere to rest and sort ourselves out." I knew that we should be treating the wounds now—his broken nose and slashed forehead and lip, and especially my mother's vesp bites. But I also knew that he was right. We needed to get away from this place.

Walking as quickly as we could with the injuries we

carried was our way of running.

Jude and I took turns helping Dad. He seemed much better, but still sometimes had to pause to gather himself, shaking his head softly as if to clear it. Mum's injuries didn't seem to bother her too much. But even though we had to walk in silence, she seemed further away than all of us.

I tried not to imagine what the night would bring, now that we had all fallen into the Grey.

We walked for several hours, pausing often so that Dad could try to shake his dizziness away. I was worried that he was hurt worse than he was letting on, but he refused to let anyone examine him closely. He signed that his nose was too sore, so painful that it hurt to breathe, and even breathing through his mouth hurt his damaged lips and broken teeth. Maybe it was that. Perhaps he was simply breathless because it hurt to breathe.

We followed bridleways north along the valley, then down towards the shores of the lake. Windermere, perhaps, or maybe one of the smaller ones. I wasn't sure and it didn't seem to matter. The winter sun beat away the cold, and I was relieved that the rain had finally cleared away. The cool blue sky was a welcome sight.

Vesps flew around, a few higher up, most skimming only metres above the ground. They used their sonar to avoid trees, following the landscape and occasionally skipping around us. I could smell them everywhere, even during those rare moments when there were none in sight. It was as if they were making the world their own by spreading their rank odour.

Several times during that morning's walk, Mum

back-tracked the way we'd come. She was worried that the Reverend was following, and while the rest of us slowed down, she would hide a few hundred metres back to wait. It was always tense, me and Jude glancing nervously at each other while we waited, Dad taking the time to close his eyes and rest. Several times he rooted through the bag of medicines, but none of them were labelled. He told me that he had a pounding headache, but I worried it was more than that.

Mum always came back within twenty minutes. She never saw any sign of pursuit. But I could not shake the idea that the Reverend was still following us. I remembered his staring, mad eyes, and the way he'd wanted me, ignoring everyone else. He had removed his own ability to communicate and craved another, and perhaps in his skewed view of the world I might have been the Hushed's salvation. But he had corrupted everything supposedly good about himself.

It was terrifying how quickly everything had gone bad. I'd heard the saying about how if you take away three square meals you end up with anarchy, but I'd always had more faith in society, had thought people were mostly good. I'd thought that it was a minority that caused trouble. But it now seemed that we had always existed on a knife-edge, and the vesps had pushed it home.

Close to the lake we saw the first group of people. There were maybe fifteen adults and children, walking along a narrow lane that headed down between beached sailing boats to the water's edge. Our two groups saw each other at the same time. We all paused. Tentative waves were offered. I saw a couple of guns resting on shoulders, and several long-handled gardening tools. One man carried a toddler on his shoulders. An old man used a walking stick. They were refugees.

"We need to stay alone," Dad signed, and I nodded in agreement.

Two people approached us, a fat man and a short, attractive woman. He wore a suit and coat, completely ill-prepared. She wore running tights and a waterproof top. They seemed familiar with each other, and their uncertain smiles put me at ease.

"No signing," Dad mouthed at me, and I nodded. I understood.

It was Jude and Mum who went across the field to meet them. Mum left the shotgun behind. When they met they shook hands and started jotting messages on writing pads, the fat man and Jude keeping a watch out for vesps, the two women talking. They conversed for some time, then parted company with another handshake. I was surprised and moved to see the woman draw my mother into a hug.

As Jude and Mum returned, she was writing on the pad, still eager not to reveal our signing abilities to the other group.

We agreed to stay apart. More people, more risk of noise. They're heading for the west coast, Whitehaven. Most of them come from this side of the Pennines. They've gone through it, too.

I raised an eyebrow and pointed at this. Mum mouthed her response.

"Not the Reverend. Other stuff. All bad. There were eight more of them four days ago."

You told them about the Reverend? I jotted on the pad, and Mum nodded.

We watched the people move on along the road, the short woman glancing back several times as she went. As they turned out of sight around a bend in the lane she offered one last wave. I waved back.

We ate a little of the food Jude had gathered, tearing a loaf of bread to share. It was already stale. I knew we'd have to find more food soon, and also shelter. But the idea of approaching houses or settlements worried me.

We continued down to the lake and followed a footpath along the shore. There were more houses, holiday rentals dotting the shoreline and several larger settlements the further north we went. We skirted around these silent, dead places. Vesps sat on rooftops and circled above the villages, and I could only imagine how many bodies they guarded, how many dormant eggs waiting to hatch at the first sign of noise.

Around two in the afternoon we topped a small rise and looked down on what was left of a small town on the lake's edge. There were several hundred buildings arranged around a bay, with a marina, a handful of boats moored, and several larger tourist vessels adrift on the open water.

Some of the town had burned. Blackened buildings pointed charred roof timbers at the sky. Gutted rooms lay exposed to the elements, the remnants of personal belongings blackened and sad. Walls had fallen, and gardens and roads were smeared with charcoal shades of ash and soot. The flames were long gone—I guessed the fire had happened days ago, if not weeks—but the smell was still there. Damp ash, the memory of flame, the waft of rot. It was a sobering sight. I had never seen anything like it, not away from a computer or TV screen, and I hoped I never would again. But I knew that with that hope was a certainty that there were more terrible sights in my future than in my past.

The stillness was disconcerting.

Jude pointed past the town then turned to us, his young face grim. *He should be smiling more,* I thought. *He should be laughing and playing and making things up, not wishing things away.*

"I think we should check one of those houses," he signed. He'd pointed past the gutted lakeside community at a rise in the land, where several big, isolated houses commanded priceless views out across the lake.

Nobody disagreed.

The house was huge, pristine, abandoned. It didn't look like it had been lived in for a while, and I guessed it was a holiday home. We checked that all the outer doors and windows were secure, then Dad sent us back to the other side of the garden while he forced a side door. He took his time, using a shovel from the shed and easing the lock slowly, gently, so as not to make too much noise.

Inside we did a full circuit of the house checking for vesps. And once we were sure that it was empty, and as safe as anywhere could be, we sat in the kitchen and relaxed for the first time that day.

Dad was asleep in seconds.

He dreamed of getting there just in time to stop the car crash that had killed his parents and injured his beautiful daughter. He ran onto the road with his hands held out and shouted, "Stop now or everything will change!" The car skidded to a halt, bumper mere inches from his knees. But he was not about to move. He knew what would happen if he did—he'd seen it all in a terrible nightmare of hospital beds, recovery, and then silent monsters that sought to finish what this crash would begin—and he was nothing if not a good father. He'd do anything to save his little girl.

His parents sat in the front of the car, looking surprised and angry at his intrusion. They were far older than he had ever known them, perhaps the age they would have lived to if the crash had not shortened their lives. But it was not them he was concerned about. Ally opened the car's rear door and jumped out, smiling when she saw her dad and about to ask what was wrong, why he was here, what he was doing in the middle of the road, and he would hear her just once more, remember those sweet tones and the way her voice dropped deeper when she was being cheeky—

She opened her mouth to talk but no words emerged. All she managed to utter was the sound of cold winds across deserted hillsides, heavy rain pummelling mountaintops in endless, eternal efforts to erode them, echoing booms as chunks of ice fell away into shadowy valleys. Distance and time, both stretched out into mindless, endless infinity. The sounds of desolation.

Huw fell forward onto the car bonnet but hit nothing.

"Dad," Jude said. "Dad. Wake up."

Huw opened his eyes. They hurt. Everything hurt, and it took him a while to come to his senses. Jude was standing beside the sofa on which he had been sleeping in the huge family kitchen, tapping his arm lightly as if scared to hurt him.

"Dad?"

"What is it, mate?"

"Mum said to come and see."

"See what?"

"Don't know. Neither does she. That's why she said to come."

That stirred Huw from his prone position, and he groaned past the pounding headache and pains in his face to stand and follow his son. He only then noticed how much the light had faded.

"How long have I been asleep?"

"A couple of hours. Mum said you needed the sleep and that she's worried you've cracked your skull." Jude looked up and back at him with such a wide, innocent expression that Huw had to laugh.

"Don't worry, Jude. If I'd done that my brains would be leaking."

Jude smiled and ran through to the living room, but Huw followed slowly. He'd been trying to assess the pain in his face and head all day. Skull fractures didn't have to be severe, did they? He could still walk, talk and function, couldn't he?

The living room was even larger than the kitchen. At its centre was a U-shaped sofa, big enough for twenty people, which faced out towards a decked veranda with metal and glass balustrading. The first thing he saw were the three vesps hunkered down at the base of the balustrade, sheltered from the weather and motionless. The next was the fire.

It was way across the lake, miles away on the facing hillside, and it was big. It pulsed and reduced; flames seemed to shrink and grow again as if the distance between the house and fire was constantly changing. Huw knew that air conditions could alter the way something so distant appeared.

"Huw," Kelly whispered. She was propped with Ally on one end of the leather sofa, not too close to the window, not too exposed. As she turned to him the reflected fire barely touched her face.

"What time is it?" he signed.

"Gone five. Wanted to let you rest, but then we saw that."

He walked to her side, touched her shoulder, and they watched together.

"What do you think it is?" Jude signed.

"Someone setting fires," Ally said. She'd been watching them, not the distant flames, eager to be involved in the conversation.

"Why would they do that?" Jude asked.

"Trying to kill vesps?" Ally asked.

"Or maybe just because they can," Huw said. Since they'd met the Reverend, he'd been thinking about how this sudden change in society might affect some people. Most would simply be doing their best to survive, like him and his family. But even he had changed, moving on from that strange, stressful, ostensibly civilised society he had inhabited only weeks ago. He had killed people last night, he was sure of it. At least one with the shotgun, maybe more, and if he hadn't killed them outright then his shooting of them had led to the vesps finishing the job. But he had barely thought of them since. They were shapes in the shadows that had threatened his family. They were dangers, they meant nothing to him and he had put them down. Perhaps they would revisit him in nightmares, their tongueless mouths weeping and sad. But he thought not.

He remembered Lynne leaving the kitchen. He'd seen her through a haze of blood and pain, rushing out into the darkness, and he'd already had an inkling of her intention. That death was not meaningless. Her death he would remember.

"There's something else," Ally said. She moved across to the wall and flicked a light switch. Nothing happened.

"The Grey," Huw said, and his daughter nodded. Part of him had hoped it was just the house they had left behind that had lost its electricity. Now it seemed that it was the whole region.

"I want to go," Jude said. "I don't like the fires. I want to get away from here."

"Not by night," Huw said. "We'll stay here, all in this room. Two of us sleep, two of us stay awake and keep watch. How about that, mate? You and me keep watch together?"

Jude looked sad but he nodded.

"I'll bet there are candles somewhere," Kelly said.

"I don't think we should light them."

They found some tinned food in the kitchen and ate a meal of cold beans in curry sauce, followed by fruit cocktail in syrup. The food of the gods. Then they sat silent in the darkness, watching the fire across the lake pulse like a giant, blinking eye.

23

The power is going off. The machinery of automated power plants is under constant attack from vesps, and faults and malfunctions remain untended. Manned power stations have been abandoned. Distribution networks are falling. You should prepare for long periods without electricity, but all government organisations and departments—the police, military and all emergency committees—are working hard to ensure the safety of all residents of the United Kingdom.

Official announcement on all radio, TV and Internet channels, Wednesday, 7 December 2016

They've left us all to die.

@F****Truth, Twitter, Wednesday, 7 December 2016**

The fire was still raging. As we left the house, Jude said he could hear the rhythmic blaring of a distant siren, and at last I had some idea what was happening.

It was like the sound ships, except on land. They were drawing in vesps to burn them. Maybe it was the military, or perhaps some civilian group doing its best to fight back. They were too far away to make out the exact methods. Flamethrowers, perhaps. Fuel cans lobbed in afresh when more vesps came. A column of greasy black smoke pointed an accusing finger at the sky, and it remained in sight for most of that morning.

I remembered the hour Dad and I had spent together the previous evening, talking about what was happening and surfing the Internet.

There was little good news. A lot of the country had gone Grey, and communication was failing rapidly. Phones still worked, but once their charges ran out they went silent. The world was growing larger.

"We're going back to the Dark Ages," Dad said, and he'd smiled, dismissing it like it was a throwaway remark. But it had held a heavy truth that we'd both come to acknowledge as our talk continued. The more we saw online, the darker things seemed.

That first stab of terror had bitten at me as I considered my iPad running out of charge. It contained everything I had collected and written about the vesps, from the first moment they had emerged from that cave. All the evidence, the facts, the rumours and tall tales, all were gathered together in my electronic scrapbook, and when the battery finally died it would all fade away. The analogy to my dead grandmother was striking, and at first I shied away from making it. But it had felt the same as Lynne. Dying out, winding down, I had known that the time would come when she would be gone for ever. Turn off her life and she becomes a mass of flesh, bone and blood set to rot. Turn off the electricity and the iPad is nothing.

"Dark Ages," Dad had said. We had both come to the silent realisation that he was more right than he could have imagined.

Now we walked again, and in our future there would be much more walking. The maps we'd looked at online said it was almost one hundred and thirty miles to Red Rock, Dad's parents' old home. It was a remote house close to Galloway Forest Park. A long way, with so many unknowns in between. But there was hope in Dad's eyes now, and we felt it too. It had become the place we had to be to ride out the storm. It was almost sure to snow, Dad said, for weeks every winter. None of us had really allowed ourselves to doubt that it would be another home. Only once did I think about the Reverend and how there might be others like him, just as mad or madder. Then I had shoved the idea aside because I still needed hope.

"Mum says you never wanted to go there again," I had said, and Dad laughed, then fell quiet for a while. Tapping the table with his finger. Looking into the shadows, face lit only by the soft glow of the iPad screen on standby. Then he told me why.

"It's so stupid. Dad and I had a fight there. A proper fight, if you can imagine that. The year you were born. I can barely even remember what it was all about now, but it marred our relationship for years to come. It hurt us both right up until he died, actually, and that's something I've never been able to forget. It's… complicated. I blamed him for it, and I still do, but I also want to believe he blamed me. Is that weird? I don't want to think he died feeling guilty. And that makes me feel guilty, that he might have, so although the fight was all his fault, I'm the one carrying the guilt about it all. Twisted, eh? Believe me sweetie, don't ever become an adult, it'll fuck you up."

I had smiled at his bad language, but he barely noticed.

"That all seemed so important until recently," he said, shaking his head slowly. He winced. We all knew he was still in pain, though he had mostly stopped complaining. His eyes were bruising, his nose swollen and caked with dried blood, the gash on his forehead raw. But he'd denied that anything was really wrong. *It can't be,* he'd said. *It just can't be wrong, because I have to look after you all. So it isn't. It's all fine.*

I had also talked to him about Mum, how she was, and how I was afraid that she was slowly losing herself.

"She saw something terrible," he said. "And the thing is… you're supposed to see your parents get ill and die before you. Take to their sick bed, wither away, all their family around them. Either that or you go to visit them one day and they're dead on the floor. The end of their story should be ordered, predictable. Full of love, if possible. Not like that. Not like Lynne went. And I know a bit about what she's feeling because of how my own mum and dad died." He looked aside, as if embarrassed to bring up the accident.

Now in the cold light of day, the journey before us seemed greater than ever. Dad hoped that we'd make at least ten miles a day, and we all agreed that we had to be there by Christmas. It was a notional date, one that meant nothing really. But it gave us a marker. We had a little under three weeks.

A car would make the journey in three or four hours.

We considered bikes, but squealing brakes and noisy falls were too great a risk. Besides, Jude had never really taken to bike riding in a big way. Even if we could find something suitable for him, we might only make a few miles before he grew tired or fell off. Jude, bless him, mentioned electric cars, and for a moment Dad's eyes lit up. But the trouble was finding one. They needed recharging frequently. And they still weren't completely silent.

So we were walking. Sometimes we cut across the countryside, following public footpaths and trying to avoid areas turned marshy in the heavy winter rains. Other times we stuck to country lanes if we could, although Dad reckoned we might eventually be able to try a main road, just to see how dangerous it was.

The sun was low, but already at its highest point. It was almost midday. Soon it would be the shortest day of the year.

Huw wasn't sure just how badly he had been hurt. His nose was clotted with dried blood, and if he tried to pick it away it caused waves of agony. Even touching his nose or the area around it brought intense discomfort. So he breathed through his mouth. That drew cool air over his chipped teeth, and he became painfully aware that one of them was badly damaged, the nerve exposed and singing with every breath. He grimaced and accepted it. It was only pain. It wasn't actually damaging him, it was alerting him to damage already done. He would forget what it felt like. It didn't matter. It was only pain.

But the agony of broken teeth, smashed nose, split lip and gashed forehead were only the aperitifs to what might be the real damage. His whole head felt odd, as if someone had jumped on it, jumbled up the bits, and then glued them clumsily back into place. His eyes no longer felt level. He saw better out of his left eye than his right. It could have been his reaction to the pain, he knew, a blurring of vision and skewing of awareness. And the headache that pounded in again and again and refused to shift was hardly a surprise. He'd hit the edge of the door at full pelt, and it was like being hit in the face with a sledgehammer.

But perhaps it was worse than that. He knew that Kelly was aware, and the kids also looked at him strangely now and then, as if expecting him to do something weird. He'd have to keep a watch on it himself.

Ally and Kelly shared taking the lead, and he was happy to follow. This strange new world quickly became smothering in its silence and stillness, and he noticed how Jude was very keen to hold hands with him or Kelly.

The only sound they heard was an occasional breeze breathing across the landscape, rustling trees and bushes. They passed the lake and headed up a steep lane towards a low ridge. There were abandoned vehicles in several places, some neatly parked, some left in a hurry.

They also saw people. Small groups, normally, spotted on distant hillsides or across fields. Sometimes they would wave, more often not. Huw was aware of these other groups' caution reflecting their own, and he never made any suggestion that they should join up with anyone. The larger the group, the more chance of noise. He felt sad at that, and wondered how such caution might develop over the coming weeks and months. Perhaps caution would mutate into mistrust, and a time would come when strangers were the enemy.

He hoped not. But these were new times, and the future was difficult to predict.

Close to sunset, over the ridge and heading down into a wide valley with a much larger lake a few miles distant, they witnessed a horrifying demonstration of the true risks they still faced.

There were maybe fifteen people in the group, and right from the beginning Huw thought it was too many. It was Jude who saw them, pointing left to where two roads joined in a T-junction. The group were following the road, and at the junction they paused and seemed to take stock. They were maybe a mile distant, partly hidden behind rubble walls and dwarfed by the landscape. If it weren't for their bright clothing they probably would not have been visible at all.

Huw and his family soon wished they had not laid eyes on them.

They didn't hear the sound that gave the group away. But vesps rose from all around, drifted down the hillside from above, dropped from the darkening sky, and soon the screams came, the running figures, the waving hands and fleeing shapes as the group split. Under attack they spread over the walls and into the fields, some trying to outrun the vesps, others hunkering down in the hope that they would be passed by.

There must have been a hundred vesps, drawn by the screams. There were several gunshots, muffled by distance and echoing across the hillside. But the chaos did not last for long.

Everyone fell. Vesps rose, circled and came down again, and more streamed in from the surrounding countryside. Huw watched horrified as a small figure ran alone down the hill, climbing over several walls as it went. He could not tell whether it was a boy or girl, but they ran with the familiar gait of a toddler—legs moving fast, arms waving.

He was about to tell his family they had to do something when the shape tripped and fell.

Maybe they cried out in pain or terror. Or perhaps they had been unlucky enough to trip over a roosting vesp. Whatever the reason, they never rose again.

Jude and Ally watched wide-eyed. Kelly had long since buried her face against Huw's neck, desperate not to see.

And then Huw had to nudge her, because there was one survivor.

He stood upright amongst the chaos. Vesps still circled, but the man stood alone beside the road and turned a full circle, so slowly, witnessing what had become of his group. Family or friends, perhaps both, perhaps only people he'd hooked up with in an effort to survive, the sight of their torn bodies was too much for him.

Even from this far away, the silent landscape meant that they heard him begin to shout.

I was shaking. I could feel a pressure building around us, a need for rest, a desire to be close together and talking, communicating. Jude looked strongest out of us all, but Mum's attention seemed to be drifting, and Dad was in pain. I could see it in every step he took. He was holding it in and being brave, but he stumbled a couple of times, kicking at the ground.

Jude froze both times, and I knew that we were making too much noise.

I spotted a hotel from some way off. It looked deserted; no lights on, no sign of movement, and I hoped we would be the only ones there. We'd only need one room, and access to the kitchens for food and drink. It wasn't much to ask.

I led the way, Jude brought up the rear, and just as it was becoming too dark to move safely we climbed the steep slope into the hotel car park.

The front door stood open, yet inside we were alone. The hotel seemed to have been used recently—muddy boot prints had dried on the reception carpets, and a few pieces of hiking equipment were scattered around. It was an old place, characterful without being scruffy, the small lobby's walls lined with local artwork and a couple of comfortable leather sofas. One alcove held a couple of shelves of books on the area, and a big fish tank. The fish were floating, dead. I went closer and saw what might have been fighting scars on some of them. I didn't know if tropical fish would eat each other if there was no alternative source of food. I didn't really *want* to know.

There was still a board of room keys behind the reception. I was pleased they hadn't gone the way of electronic door locks.

There was a vesp squatting motionless on the reception desk. I might have been able to creep past it and lift a key from a hook, but this close it would only have taken one scrape of metal against metal, one nudge of my boot against wood. We stared at each other, none of us able to come up with a plan. *Maybe we can break into a room,* I thought. *Or we could find a couple of rooms open and barricade the door when we're inside, or—*

Jude moved quickly but calmly, in complete control. He hefted the broom handle with the knife he'd been carrying since the cottage, stepped forward, and impaled the creature with one hard stab. He lifted it from the desk and pressed it into the junction between desk and floor, leaning forward with one hard jarring motion. The creature's head almost parted from its body. Blood flowed. It stank.

I looked around at my family in a panic, ready to run or fight if the vesp had let out a call to its brethren. But Mum closed her eyes and nodded at me, and Dad only looked proud.

I turned to Jude and gave him a gentle fist-bump. He pretended to flex his biceps.

Still moving carefully, I stepped behind the desk and lifted a key from its hook. My family followed me through swing doors into one of the downstairs corridors. All the doors were closed. I tried a light switch, but, as I'd expected, nothing happened, so we used a torch to light the way to our room. I tried the door first, just to make sure that it had not been left open and let in a vesp. Then I turned the key and we went inside.

The room was a double, big enough for us all to sit down and take the weight from our legs. We must have covered ten miles that day, maybe more, and I was pleased at the sense of progress.

As I sat on the bed and opened the iPad, the others huddled around behind me. I liked the sense of closeness, the faint scent of sweat emanating from Dad, my brother's constant fidgeting. We had survived one more day together, and that was a good thing.

"Seventeen per cent," I whispered as I opened the folding screen. "Not long left."

We looked at what was happening to the world, and none of it was good.

Dad wanted to go and find the kitchens, but I insisted that he stay. There was still running water in the little en suite, and he needed to try and clean up his bloodied nose. It had been too painful to attempt in the big holiday home the previous night, and we had been too upset.

"You help Dad," I whispered to Jude, taking him aside, "and keep an eye on him." I wasn't trying to make Jude feel responsible. It was genuine. I thought that Dad looked ready to drop, and my little brother was in charge.

Mum brought the shotgun.

The sun had set, and it was a strange, spooky experience walking along the hotel corridor by torchlight. So many doors. So many shadows.

We found the small dining room and moved through towards the kitchens, and that was when we saw the people. Three of them, frozen like statues beside the breakfast buffet counters, one carrying what might have been a hunting rifle. I caught my breath, torch aimed slightly down so as not to dazzle them.

One of them, a woman, raised her hand in greeting, and I responded. Then the woman nodded towards one of the kitchen doors, and Mum and I started walking again.

There were vesps in the dining room. I could only see two but that probably meant there were more hidden away. We could not risk trying to communicate with anyone.

When we were through the doors and in the kitchen,

I saw two more people. They were not together; they moved cautiously around each other almost as if the other were not there. They both looked up and nodded, glancing at Mum's shotgun and looking away again. They were gathering food. Ours was not the only occupied room in the hotel that night.

It was a surreal few minutes. No one moved too close to anyone else, and we all took polite turns visiting the well-stocked larders. Mum went, leaving me leaning against a large oven and trying not to catch the strangers' eyes. It would be too awkward. They could not talk, and the chance of any of them being able to sign was remote.

I wondered what it would be like if this situation was repeated in a few weeks or months, when food was short and the world had moved on, deeper into the Grey and further away from civilisation. I hoped that it would go the same way, but I doubted it. I really doubted it.

Mum returned with a canvas bag of food and we left the kitchen. A woman on her own moved aside to let us through, and I thought for a crazy moment of asking her to join us. But she might be one of a group, and there was no way of telling how many others were with her. I'd seen what happened to larger groups. I caught her eye and she glanced away until we had passed.

The dining room felt so alien, with white tablecloths and places set for dinner, flowers wilted in vases, butter hardened and mouldy in small dishes, drinks glasses gathering dust. Signs of recent times now long gone.

We met no one on the way back to our room, and I felt sad as I closed the door and eased the lock across. Even so close to other people there was a growing distance between us all.

***

"Fourteen per cent," I whispered, and Dad and I stared at the screen. There was nothing either of us wanted to say, and looking further afield at what everyone else was suffering was too painful. So I turned the iPad off and closed the lid, and we settled down to sleep.

Next morning we left the hotel on our own; there was no sign of the other people we'd seen the previous night. The lobby was silent, dining room as still and haunting in daylight as it had been the night before. For a while I wondered whether we had actually met other people at all.

Dad seemed a little better, brighter, his face less etched with constant pain, and he smiled at me when I asked how he was feeling. There was something about the way he answered that made me feel strange. It was like a child responding to a parent. I led us away from the hotel, and Dad seemed happy to follow.

Within ten minutes of leaving we passed a group of corpses beside the road. They had been dead for a while, the rot had set in, but I could still make out the sparkle of moist vesp eggs nestled in gaping wounds, and a dozen of the creatures sat watch on and around the bodies. A little further along the road were several cars that had been abandoned. One of them had flat tyres. *Settling into its final resting place*, I thought, and it was a disturbing idea. That car might be there for ever.

At lunchtime we stopped at a small caravan park and sat in the park shop for an hour, using the toilet, eating some of the food we'd brought along. The shop had been cleared out at some point, and there wasn't much left. But whoever had done it had been careful not to damage the place too much, and there was a pile of ten-pound notes on the counter weighed down with a cricket bat.

I looked at my iPad. There was more talk of vesp-free zones in several places in Europe; cold, high places where snow had already fallen and vesps had become lethargic, easy to kill. There were pictures of piles of vesps being thrown into lakes, and victorious hunters wearing cloth gags over their mouths and waving spiked weapons of many kinds. *Cold Kills Them* the headline proclaimed, and that phrase had become a trending hashtag all across Twitter, spread through Facebook and the other social media sites.

News sites seemed to confirm the images as genuine.

It gave me something like hope.

Huw was handling his pain better. It was still there, a headache unlike any he had ever experienced, but he was trying to live with it. It was pain management, and he knew that in the future he would have to confront its cause. But there were no hospitals open, no experts with X-rays and MRI machines, and he was on his own. That scared him. But having his family around him lessened the fear.

He lived in hope. Red Rock called. They had a hundred miles to go, and there were other groups moving in the same direction, buoyed by some of the news being flashed across the Internet. *Cold Kills Them*.

He was sure that around the world there were people

working on a solution to the vesps. People in bunkers, as there always were during times of national crisis. Scientists and experts, as well as all those who considered themselves important enough to save. As far as Huw was concerned, the most important people in the world were with him now. Jude held his hand, but mostly just to make sure his dad was all right. Kelly walked close to him, grim-faced yet offering him an occasional smile. With the weight of such danger heavy between them, they were closer than they had been in years.

And Ally led the way. His brave girl, who had already been through and confronted so much, was adapting to these new conditions faster than any of them. Theirs had become the silent world that she had already lived in for so long.

His wife came close and touched his hand. He stroked the back of her neck. They smiled at each other and, voiceless, their smiles spoke volumes.

That afternoon, with seven per cent charge left on my iPad, the mobile signal disappeared. I waited a while before checking again, moved around a little, but already knew what it meant. The others watched. Jude seemed unconcerned, but my parents understood. One more layer of isolation, one more step back. The Grey had grown several shades darker.

One per cent… and then that's it. I'll probably still carry the iPad with me, just in case we find somewhere to charge it. Maybe the power will come back on one day, and perhaps the mobile network masts will fire up again. But there's a cold winter to get through first, and when we come out on the other side—and we will, I have no doubt of that—it will be into a whole new world. But that's the future.

For now, all is silence.

About the Author

TIM LEBBON is a *New York Times*-bestselling writer with almost thirty novels published to date, as well as dozens of novellas and hundreds of short stories. Recent releases include *Coldbrook, Alien: Out of the Shadows, Into the Void: Dawn of the Jedi* (Star Wars), *Reaper's Legacy*, and *The Sea Wolves* (with Christopher Golden). He has won four British Fantasy Awards, a Bram Stoker Award, and a Scribe Award.

Fox 2000 acquired film rights to his *The Secret Journeys of Jack London* series, and his *Toxic City* trilogy is in development with ABC Studios. Several other novels and screenplays are also at varying stages of development.

Find out more about Tim at his website
www.timlebbon.net